The Psychic Cafe Mysteries

APRIL FERNSBY

ISBN: 1987447581

ISBN-13: 978-1987447583

CONTENTS

A DEADLY DELIVERY

Chapter 1

"Are you going in or are you going to stand there like a stuffed lemon?"

"Pardon?" I focused on the red-faced man who had just shouted at me.

He gave me an irritated look, jabbed his thumb at the café door and snapped, "In or out? If you're not going in, then shift out of my way. I'm already running late this morning, and I don't need any further delays. Well? In or out?"

"Out." I removed my hand from the café door and stood to one side to let the impatient man enter Erin's Café.

He treated me to another annoyed look before pushing the door open and stepping through.

As the door slowly closed behind him, I caught a glimpse of a young woman inside. Erin, my sister. She was fifteen years younger than me and had been a surprise addition to our family. Mum had been the most surprised.

There she was; standing behind the counter of her café and giving that rude man the most patient of looks as she smiled at him. I hadn't seen her in two years. Two full years without seeing my little sister. We'd spoken on the phone a few times, but those had been stilted conversations.

Well, I couldn't face her, not after what I'd done to her. I was a fool to come here and think I could apologise. I couldn't expect her to forgive me. I couldn't even forgive myself.

I drank in the sight of her beautiful, elfin-like face as the door finally closed. My heart missed a beat as she looked my way at the last second before the door shut in my face. She looked tired, really tired. There was something else too. In that fraction of a second, I could sense it.

I pushed the door open and rushed into the café. Erin noticed me and her hand shook as she handed over a cardboard cup to the rude man. I was aware of him moaning about something or other, but I didn't pay him any further attention. Now that I was closer to Erin, I could see the small lines around her eyes. Her skin was pale and the pale-purple circles under her eyes indicated she hadn't had a good night's sleep for a long time.

I gave her a small smile. I hoped she wouldn't shout at me and demand that I leave. I wouldn't blame her if she did.

The rude man snatched the cup from Erin and said loudly, "This better not be cold. It was distinctly on the tepid side yesterday. I had to stick it in the microwave when I got to work. I should charge you for the electricity I used."

Erin took her attention off me and said to the man, "I'm very sorry about that. That coffee is piping hot."

"It had better be," the man warned.

His rudeness was annoying me now. I turned my head and glowered at him. Couldn't he see there was something going on here? Couldn't he sense the atmosphere between Erin and me? Didn't he realise he was in the way and should clear off?

The man jumped as he caught my hard look. He pulled his cup towards him in a protective manner, turned around and scuttled out of the café without another word.

Erin burst into laughter and said, "I'd forgotten your angry look! What was it Mum used to say? You'd scare the butter right off the toast with that angry look of yours."

I relaxed my features and smiled at Erin. "I don't have an angry look."

"Yeah, you do. It's like this." She scrunched her face up and attempted to glower at me. Her face was too beautiful to look angry. And the happy twinkle in her eyes only made her look cuter.

A huge wave of love washed over me and tears sprang to my eyes. I blurted out, "I'm sorry! So very sorry. I'm an idiot. An out and out idiot. I have no excuses. I don't expect you to forgive me. I just wanted to say I'm sorry."

Erin swiftly came out from behind the counter and moved over to me. She pulled me into a tight hug and said, "There's nothing to be sorry about. I've told you that over and over again. But, yes, you are an idiot. I knew that from the second I saw you. Even though I was a newborn, I knew you were an idiot. A nitwit. A ninny. A pudding-head."

I could hear the laughter in her voice. I stayed in her embrace and said, "You smell of cake."

She laughed and released me. "I always smell of cake. I made a Victoria sponge this morning. Take a seat at the counter and I'll cut you a generous slice. How about a cup of tea? Or would you prefer a coffee?" The twinkle in her eyes intensified. "It might be on the tepid side, but that's the chance you've got to take in my café."

She put her hand on my arm and took me closer to the counter. She pulled a stool out and pushed me gently onto it. As she moved back behind the counter, I had a quick look around the café. I was surprised to see only a few tables were occupied. This used to be the busiest time of the day. Something was definitely wrong here.

Erin placed a steaming cup of tea in front of me along with a huge slice of cake. She leant her elbows on the counter and studied me.

"What?" I said. "Why are you looking at me like that?"

"Because I love you. And it's wonderful to see you again. I can't believe it's been so long. We've got a lot to catch up on." She frowned. "You look lighter. You look different. That worry in your eyes has gone. What's happened to you?"

I felt my mouth twitching and was worried I was going to break into a full grin. Trying to keep serious, I said, "It's over."

A glimmer of hope came into Erin's eyes. "Over? Do you mean…?"

I gave her a nod. "Yes, my marriage is over. Or it will be soon."

Erin raised her hands in the air and pumped them with joy. She let out a holler of delight and then twirled around on the spot. One of her customers let out a quiet tut.

Erin grabbed my hands. "Tell me that again. Slowly. I want all the details. Who left who? Was it you? It must have been. When did you finally come to your senses? Oh! I don't care! I'm just glad you did."

I grinned at her. "It was a few weeks ago. You're right about me coming to my senses. It hit me one day when I was cleaning his shirts. I stood there and looked at the lipstick on his collar. Yes, I know. What a cliché. Lipstick on his collar. And there was perfume on his shirt too. I stared at his dirty washing and thought what a fool I was. To ignore his cheating for years was one thing, but to do his washing after he'd been with his girlfriend was a step too far." My grin died and I swallowed. "Erin, how could I allow him to treat me like that?"

She squeezed my hands. "That's a mystery to us all. You deserve a medal for staying married to Gavin Booth for so long." She looked over my shoulder as someone came into the café. "We are going to have a long and detailed talk about this soon. I want to know everything. I'm here for you. I won't allow you to go through a painful divorce on your own."

My chin wobbled. "Thank you. I didn't just come here to tell you about Gavin, I wanted to apologise for what I did. And I want to know how you are and what's been going on with you. Erin, you look tired. Are you well?"

Erin released my hands and gave me a bright smile. "I'm in tip-top health. My bread delivery is here. Let me sort this out and we'll talk again in a minute or two. Eat your cake!"

Erin smiled at someone behind me. I turned around in my seat and observed the young woman who was walking towards us carrying a stack of baskets filled with bread.

A dizzy feeling attacked me and I grabbed the counter for support. It was happening again.

Chapter 2

Ever since I could remember, I'd had psychic abilities. It was a blessing or a curse depending on what I experienced. It was a blessing when I saw something wonderful in a friend's future, especially when they were going through a difficult time. It was a curse when I saw a close relative reaching the end of their days like I experienced with my wonderful grandma. I didn't just get the visions of what could happen in the future; sometimes I got the smells and tastes to go with them. As if that wasn't confusing enough, I sometimes got images of the past.

With one thing and another over the years, I'd ignored my psychic abilities, and my visions had slowed down. I hadn't had one for a while.

But I was having one now. I had no doubts about that.

I looked closer at the young woman who was carrying the bread baskets. There were two shadows behind her. One belonged to her, but the other one didn't belong to anyone. The second shadow followed her across the café floor with its hands held out. It was hard to say if it was male or female. The shadow suddenly thrust its hands towards the young woman's shadow and pushed her on the back. The woman's shadow tumbled forward and I saw her mouth open in a scream.

I felt someone tapping my shoulder. I looked that way and saw Erin giving me a confused look. She said, "Karis, are you alright? You've gone a funny colour."

A quick glance back at the floor showed me the spooky shadow had now vanished. I cleared my throat and said, "Yes! Course I am. Sorry. I just drifted off there for a moment."

Erin gave me a long look before saying, "Karis, this is Carmel. She works for Nithercott's Bread."

The young woman put the bread baskets on a nearby table and turned her friendly face towards me. She said, "Hi. Erin's mentioned you a few times, but we've never met. Would you like a free sample of bread? We've got some new sesame seed rolls that we've been working on. They're low in salt and we've even got the gluten-free variety." She reached into a basket and handed me a package of four rolls. She took a card from her jeans and gave me that too. "I'd love it if you could give some feedback on our website. If that's not too much trouble?"

I took the card and mumbled, "Thank you. I'll do that." I was finding it hard to meet Carmel's eyes. The vision of someone attacking her was playing over and over in my mind like a horror movie on repeat.

Carmel turned to Erin and continued, "How's the new bread recipe going down with your customers?"

Erin gave me another look before turning to Carmel. "They love it. I didn't tell them it was a new recipe until they'd tasted it. You know what people are like! Your classic loaf is loved by many, and if I'd have told my customers beforehand it had been changed, they would have made their minds up instantly that they wouldn't like it."

Carmel nodded. "Tell me about it. You'd think Mr Nithercott had made a deal with the devil instead of improving his classic loaf. You wouldn't believe the complaints we've had. Even death threats!"

"Really?" I said sharply. "What kind of death threats? Have you been attacked?" I was hoping the vision I'd seen was a remnant of the past.

Carmel gave me a puzzled look. "No, I haven't been attacked. It's Mr Nithercott who's received the death threats. The improved recipe is healthier, but some people don't care about that. They've taken it as a personal insult." She smiled at Erin. "I'm pleased your customers like it. Can I count on your continued orders?"

Erin's smile seemed slightly forced as she replied, "As long as I've got a café, then you're my supplier. Have you got time for a cuppa? Perhaps some cake?"

Carmel patted her stomach. "I'd better not. Mr Nithercott has got me sampling all the new products we're rolling out. I'll be needing some new jeans at this rate. Erin, I've got some new products in the basket. Could I be cheeky and ask you to sample them, please? I trust your judgement."

Erin looked towards the baskets. "I'd love to. What have you got in there?"

"The usual stuff, but with improvements." She waggled her eyebrows. "We've got some exotic products too. Don't be too scandalized, but we've got rolls with cinnamon in them."

Erin let out a mock cry of outrage. "Cinnamon! In bread! Carmel Johnson, this is Yorkshire, not New York! Whatever is going on in that bread factory? You've all gone mad."

Carmel laughed. "It's my fault. I keep coming up with these new things. You'll like the cinnamon ones. They're lovely with a strong coffee or a hot chocolate. We've even got small loaves with seeds in them and we've added protein to them too. It's what people want these days."

Erin shook her head. "Mad. That's what you are. Leave my café immediately before I call the bread police."

Carmel moved towards the baskets. "I'll take these through to the back and let myself out through the back door. Thanks again for your support, Erin. You don't know how much it means to me. I wish all my customers were like you." She picked the baskets up, flashed me a goodbye smile and went through to the kitchen area.

Once she'd gone, Erin gave me a sharp look. "What did you see?"

"Pardon?" I tried to look away.

Erin tapped me sharply on the shoulder. "You saw something when Carmel came in. I could see it on your face. You had one of your vision things, didn't you? Tell me what you saw."

I sighed. There was no point arguing with Erin. Unlike many people, she completely understood about my psychic abilities. I told her about the second shadow.

Erin frowned. "What does that mean? Did you pick up on anything else? Did you smell anything?"

I shook my head. "It could be nothing. I don't know whether it was from the future or the past. For all I know, a disgruntled customer could have shoved her a few weeks ago."

Erin's lips pressed together and she folded her arms. I could tell what she was thinking. She said, "Your visions are not to be taken lightly. They always mean something."

I said, "You're right. You should tell her what I saw. I don't care if she thinks I'm crazy. This could be a warning for her to watch out for angry customers."

Erin nodded and tilted her head towards the kitchen. "That's the back door closing. She must have left. I've got her number. I'll try her on that in a minute or two." She unfolded her arms and pointed to my untouched cake. "What's wrong with that? You haven't had one bite."

"I'm sorry. The vision thing made me lose my appetite." I looked at the clock on the wall behind Erin. "Oh heck! Is that the time? I'm meeting my solicitor in ten minutes to discuss the divorce settlement. I don't want to miss that."

"I don't want you to miss it either. The sooner you get officially divorced, the better. I'll keep this cake for you. You can collect it when you come over for dinner tonight." She held her hand up to ward off my objections. "We've got a lot of things to talk about. I will see you at eight o'clock."

I hesitated a second. "Will Robbie be there?"

She gave me a gentle smile. "He's my husband. Of course he'll be there. He'll be delighted to see you. And he'll be overjoyed about your divorce news."

"Even after…" I couldn't complete my sentence as fresh shame came over me.

Erin shook her head slowly. "Robbie loves you as much as I do. Come over tonight and we'll sort this confusion out. He doesn't blame you for any of it, and neither do I." She laughed. "In fact, he's been round to your house many times over these last two years to try and sort things out between us."

"Has he? I never saw him."

She gave me a pointed look. "That's because you never answered the door to him. Your fool of a husband did." She broke into a huge smile. "I must correct myself. Your ex-husband. Karis, hasn't that got a lovely ring to it? Gavin Booth is going to be your ex-husband. It's giving me a warm glow to think that."

I couldn't help but smile at her dreamy expression. I stood up and said, "You're weird."

"So are you." She flapped her hands at me. "Go. Meet that solicitor. Get divorced. I want all the juicy details later."

I rushed around to her and gave her a hug. "I'm so glad I came into your café. So very glad. I've missed you so much."

"Me too." She patted my back. "We'll have a good catch-up later."

I took my arms away and said, "You will phone Carmel, won't you? As soon as possible?"

Erin produced her phone from her pocket. "I'll do it right now."

I said goodbye and left the café feeling a million times better than when I entered. Well, perhaps not that much. Erin looked tired and her café was almost empty. That wasn't right. I'd get the truth from her later about what was going on there. And the business about Carmel's possible attack was niggling at my mind. Hopefully, Erin would get through to Carmel in time to prevent anything terrible happening.

I nodded to myself. Yes, that's what would happen. Carmel would be alright. I needed to clear my head of all thoughts for now. I needed to be level-headed when I met my solicitor. Gavin Booth was going to be my ex-husband. A smile alighted on my lips. Yes, it did have a good ring to it.

Chapter 3

Later that night, Robbie welcomed me with open arms into the home he shared with Erin. He'd opened the front door as I'd parked in the driveway, and as soon as I was close enough, he had wrapped his big arms around me and gave me the longest hug. It was like being embraced by a friendly bear. Robbie was one of my favourite people in the whole world. There was something so capable and confident about him. He knew a lot of information about a lot of things. He would lend a hand to anyone at any time. If you had a problem, Robbie was your man.

Problems with your washing machine? Robbie would fix it in no time.

Issues with your car? Leave it to Robbie.

Concerns over your roof? Robbie would have his ladder out and be on the roof in a minute.

An apocalypse? Yep. I'm sure Robbie would be able to deal with that too in his no-nonsense and sensible way.

Robbie was a good man. Which is why I felt so incredibly guilty about what I'd done to him.

When he finally let me go, he looked down at me with his kind eyes and said, "It's so good to have you here, Karis. I can't tell you how happy I am to see you again. I'm over the moon to see you've made up with Erin. Not that there was anything to make up. No, it's all been a misunderstanding." He wagged a finger at me in a jovial manner. "And that's what we're going to get sorted out right now. Come in! Come in! We're having pre-dinner drinks tonight in the living room. We've gone all fancy and posh. We don't do this for just anyone, you know."

He took my coat and handbag and hung them on the end of the bannister. As he walked down the hallway, I winced when I noticed how pronounced his limp was. Fresh guilt settled in my stomach and killed my appetite. I wouldn't be able to eat a thing tonight.

Robbie led me into the living room where Erin was waiting with a glass of wine for me. She was wearing make-up and looked more awake than she had earlier in the café.

She handed me the wine and said, "It's non-alcoholic before you start going on about driving. I'm having the same."

I took the glass. "Non-alcoholic? You? Why?"

She shrugged. "It wouldn't be fair on you if I got drunk. I'm being thoughtful and kind. Make the most of it. Sit down. Let's get this elephant out of the room before we have anything to eat."

Robbie let out a loud guffaw and patted his round stomach. "Are you calling me an elephant? I know I've put on a few pounds, but that's no way to talk about your loving husband." He took my elbow and led me over to the sofa. "Sit next to me, Karis, and let me have a good look at you."

I sat down and Robbie turned his attention to me.

Erin sat in the armchair opposite us and said, "It's like I told you earlier, Robbie, she looks lighter, doesn't she? Like a huge, useless weight has been lifted from her shoulders." She gave a sniff of disapproval. "That's exactly what has happened. A useless weight called Gavin Booth has been lifted from her shoulders. Karis, you are still going ahead with the divorce, aren't you? Course you are. You look happy. You can tell me what the solicitor said later. Let's get this other issue out of the way first. Robbie, it's over to you."

I put my glass down on the table in front of me and declared, "Let me talk. I have to say sorry. No, sorry isn't good enough. I regret what happened every day."

Robbie held a hand up to hush me. He said, "No, listen to me, Karis, it wasn't your fault. Let's clear this up once and for all."

I shook my head vehemently. "I'm the one who had the vision. I'm the one who saw you going into that post office. I saw the date on the wall. I saw the face of the man who shot you. I knew enough to warn you!" My voice rose with each sentence.

Robbie said, "There are always risks with my job. I knew that when I joined the police force. You had nothing to do with that man who shot me. No one could have stopped him." He gave me a smile and rested his hand on his leg. "He only clipped my leg. It could have been worse."

"But I saw it before it happened! I could have stopped it." I clasped my hands together in agitation. "You can't patrol the streets anymore. You loved doing that. You're stuck behind a desk now. It's all my fault."

Erin cried out, "Enough! Karis, you did what you could. Have you forgotten how poorly you were when you had that vision? You'd just had your hysterectomy. You couldn't get out of bed. You told Gavin about your vision. He promised he'd tell Robbie, but the lying piece of scum didn't tell him."

I lowered my head and said quietly, "When I found out about the shooting, Gavin said he didn't tell Robbie about my vision because he was too embarrassed to do so. He said I was probably having hallucinations because of the painkillers I was taking." I lifted my head. "I should have phoned you to make sure Gavin had warned you, but Gavin had taken my phone away because he didn't want anyone to disturb me. And I let him. But I should have insisted. I should have done more."

Robbie placed his bear-like hand over my clasped ones and said, "You did all that you could. Gavin made his decision based on what he thought was right. I was shot. I wasn't killed. I've got a limp which gives me an air of mystery. And I now have a desk job which means I don't have to go out in the cold. The worse thing that came out of this was you losing touch with us."

"I couldn't face you," I replied. "I felt so bad and wished I'd tried harder to let you know what was going to happen."

I recalled Gavin's face when we found out what had happened to Robbie. He'd merely shrugged and said that was the risk you took when you were a copper. He didn't feel the slightest shred of guilt over not telling Robbie about my vision. I didn't tell Erin and Robbie any of this now.

Erin said softly, "We never blamed you for Robbie's injuries. Never. We don't want you to blame yourself either. Can we put it in the past now? Forever?"

I looked at her kind face and said, "I would love that."

She grinned at me. "Good. That's settled. Tell me about your meeting with the solicitor. How much are you going to get in the settlement? Has Gavin got millions stashed away somewhere? I bet he has. You hear what dodgy things financial brokers get up to all the time. I'm surprised he never ended up in prison. I bet—"

"Erin," Robbie interrupted her. "I'm sure Gavin doesn't partake in illegal business dealings."

"Erm. He sort of does," I began. "He'd put many investments in my name over the years. At the time, he told me it was because of tax issues and that he'd transfer them over to his name when the time was right. It seems he forgot to do that and I now have lucrative stocks and shares in my name."

"How lucrative?" Erin leaned forwards.

I smiled at her. "Quite a lot. It's going to annoy Gavin. He's going to be furious when he finds out."

Erin nodded. "Good. Great. I hope he cries."

"Erin," Robbie gave her a warning look.

"Don't you look at me like that, Robbie Terris. You're a policeman. You know what these financial types get up to. Well, some of them. That's probably why Gavin didn't come round here often. He couldn't face you and those probing eyes of yours. You're like a human lie detector. One look into those lovely eyes, and the truth comes spilling out." She smiled at him. "Or is that just the effect you have on me?"

Robbie chuckled. "It's the amazing power I have on you, my love. Can we have something to eat now? We don't normally eat this late. My stomach is confused." He looked at me. "Are you ready to eat? Please say yes."

I nodded. "I am. I'm glad we cleared the air." I still felt guilty, but I would deal with that in my own time. "Erin, did you get in touch with Carmel?"

"I did. I told her it was me who'd experienced the vision. As expected, she laughed. But she did say she'd take good care of herself and keep away from anyone who looked like they'd cause her harm." Erin stood up. "Come on, Karis, there's nothing else you can do about Carmel. She's going to be fine."

Chapter 4

"Carmel Johnson is dead."

"What? Erin, say that again." I lowered the sheet of paper I was looking at and gripped my phone tightly.

Erin's voice broke as she repeated the words, "Carmel Johnson is dead. I've just found out."

I put the legal papers to one side and stood up. "Are you at the café now? Are you on your own?"

I heard a couple of sniffs before Erin replied, "Yes, I'm on my own at the café. Karis, you were right to be worried about Carmel. She fell down some stairs at the bread factory. It happened yesterday." She stopped speaking and I could hear her sobs.

"Don't say another word," I told her. "I'm at home but I'm coming over right now."

"Thank you," Erin said quietly.

I made it to the café in fifteen minutes. As soon as I entered, I dashed over to Erin and put my arms around her. She looked as pale as a bleached sheet and she was shaking.

She said, "It's such a shock. I'd only known her for a few months, but she was such a lovely woman. I never got the chance to tell her how much I loved those cinnamon rolls she left for me yesterday." She began to cry.

I stroked her back and took the opportunity to look around the café. It was empty. It should have been full of customers wanting a hot, cooked breakfast.

I said to Erin, "I'm going to close the café. You should go home."

Erin moved away from me. "I can't close the café! I never close the café. Not at this time of the day."

I waved my hand at the empty tables. "There's no one here. You can close it for a short while. At least long enough for me to make you a cup of tea."

"I suppose ten minutes won't hurt," Erin relented. She moved over to the door and locked it. She turned the sign to Closed.

By the time she came back to the counter, I'd poured her a cup of tea. I made one for myself too. I took Erin over to the nearest table and sat her down. I was going to put the cup in her hands, but they were trembling too much at the moment. I placed our cups on the table and moved my chair closer to Erin's.

I said gently, "Tell me what happened. How did you find out about Carmel?"

"Travis told me. He used to deliver my bread months ago before Carmel took over his round." Her mouth twisted slightly in disgust. "I've never liked Travis. He was never on time and he often gave me loaves which had been squashed. And he complained about everything. It was like the world was out to get him. I was glad when Carmel started to deliver my bread instead. I'm going to miss seeing her cheerful face." She looked down at the table.

"What did Travis tell you?"

She looked back at me. "He said there'd been an accident at the factory yesterday. It was late afternoon. Carmel had fallen down some stairs and broken her neck. It was Travis who'd found her. Karis, your vision was right. I should have been more forceful with Carmel when I spoke to her. I should have told her to avoid going anywhere dangerous. I should have told her to go home, get into bed and stay there."

I rested my hand on Erin's arm. "And what do you think Carmel would have said to that? I've tried to warn many people about the things I've seen in my visions. Most of them ignore me. Many mock me. Well, you know what I've been through. It's never easy trying to explain these things. You did what you could."

She shook her head. "It wasn't enough. Karis, I think Carmel must have been pushed down those stairs. She must have. It's too much of a coincidence."

"Did Travis give you any more information? Did he tell you where those stairs were or if anyone saw Carmel falling?"

She turned tear-filled eyes to me. "I was in shock when he told me. I couldn't think straight. He was complaining about something, but I've no idea what. I didn't even check the products he delivered. Karis, what are we going to do about this?"

I removed my hand from her arm and reached for my tea. "What can we do?"

"I don't know, but we have to do something. You saw Carmel being pushed. And now she's dead. It wasn't an accident. We've got to prove that."

"I can't walk into the police station and tell them about my vision. They'll lock me up." I sipped my tea and tried to avoid Erin's gaze.

She tapped her hand on the table. "Luckily for us, we know a handsome officer of the law who believes in your visions. He won't lock you up."

I put my cup down. "I don't know, Erin. I don't want to put Robbie in a difficult position. What will his colleagues think?"

The front door opened and Robbie walked in. He gave us a grim smile and said, "I thought you might have closed the café." He held up a key. "I always have my universal key with me. You never know when it might come in useful. I've just heard about Carmel Johnson."

Erin let out a fresh sob.

Robbie jogged over to her side and pulled a chair up next to her. He put his arm around her shoulders and looked at me. "Erin's already told me about your vision concerning Carmel. Tell me exactly what you saw."

I did so and imitated the actions of the second shadow.

Robbie nodded. "From your vision, it seems Carmel could have been pushed to her death. The initial reports show it to be an accident, but there are no witnesses apart from a chap called Travis. He's the one who found her."

Erin wiped her tears away. "She was pushed. Someone killed her. Robbie, you have to treat this as murder."

He brushed a lock of hair off her face. "I have every faith in Karis' visions just like you do, my love. I'm not dealing with this case, but I'll have a word with the investigating officer."

My heart sank. "They'll think I'm mad."

"Don't be so hard on the police force," Robbie said. "We rely a lot on our hunches and gut feelings. We're all psychic to some degree, though not many would admit it. You leave it with me, Karis. I'll give the investigating officer your details and tell him to speak to you."

Erin asked, "Do you know who'll be dealing with it?"

"I don't. It's a new chap who's come up from London. I haven't met him yet." He gave her a smile. "I'll phone him in a minute. I've taken the rest of the day off so that I can look after you."

"But the café?" Erin protested. "I can't leave it closed all day."

Robbie gave Erin a look which I couldn't decipher. Being psychic was all well and good when it worked, but there were times when I couldn't pick up on anything.

Robbie said softly, "A day away from the café won't matter, not in the general scheme of things. I'll have a quick tidy up and then we'll go home. Let me take care of you. That's what husbands do for their wives."

Erin leaned her head against Robbie's chest.

I felt a stab of jealousy. Gavin had never shown me such concern. Never. Now that I was getting a divorce from him, all his faults which I'd ignored were jumping out at me constantly. It was one bad memory after the other.

Erin said to me, "Karis, why don't you come home with us? I'll make us something to eat while we wait for Robbie's colleague to get in touch with you."

"As tempting as that is, I'd better get home. I need to go through some papers the solicitor gave me. I want to get this divorce finalised as soon as possible." I stood up and added, "I'll phone you later."

Robbie gave me a reassuring smile. "I'll take care of Erin. Phone us if there's anything you need."

I returned his smile before leaving the café. What I needed was a whole new set of memories concerning my soon-to-be ex-husband. The ones I had of him were too painful.

As I drove home, I forced my thoughts to focus on Carmel. It couldn't be a coincidence that she'd died after my vision. Had she been pushed to her death? It was too horrible to think about. But if she had been murdered, I knew I'd have to do all that I could to help the police. I'd let Robbie down when I could have taken action and I wasn't going to do that to Carmel.

Thoughts of Carmel fled my mind as I pulled into my driveway. Someone was trying to break into my house. I parked up, walked over to the would-be intruder and tapped them on the shoulder.

Chapter 5

Gavin jabbed his key at the lock and yelled at me, "Why won't my key work? What have you done to the door?"

I said calmly, "I've had the locks changed. Can you stop bashing your key against my new locks, please?"

Rage infused Gavin's face. "You've done what?"

"Changed the locks," I repeated.

Gavin thrust his useless key in my face. "You had no right to do that! This is my house and you can't keep me out!"

I pushed the key to one side. "Not according to my solicitor. This house is in my name."

"That's a mistake and you know it!" Gavin was almost snarling at me now. "Just like those investments I put in your name. It was a temporary situation. This house and those investments belong to me!"

I took a step back. "I'm not going to discuss legal matters with you. You should get your solicitor to talk to mine."

Gavin's angry expression changed. His new one was even worse. I'd seen him with that same look on his face when he was attempting to outwit a business rival. It was a sneaky, calculating look.

He lowered the key and gave me a wide smile. His tone was softer as he said, "Karis, why has it come to this? Can't we have a civil conversation without getting our solicitors involved? Let's go inside and you can make me a cup of coffee. We'll get this legal business sorted out in minutes. It's not as complicated as your solicitor is probably making out."

I didn't care for his condescending tone one bit. I stood my ground and replied, "You're not coming into my house. I won't be discussing any legal matters with you. Can you leave my property now?"

Panic flashed into Gavin's eyes and his smile wavered. "Let's not get silly about this. You know it's my money which paid for this house. It was my money behind those investments."

"Then why did you put them in my name?" I gave Gavin a defiant look. My solicitor had informed me of the reasons why Gavin might have done that. He also pointed out Gavin had made a grave mistake in doing so as the house and investments were legally mine and there was nothing Gavin could do about it.

Gavin's smile left his face altogether. "I don't know why you're being so stubborn about this. You know you haven't got a head for business. Let me inside and I'll try to explain the difficult parts for you. You'll soon see it's in your interests to transfer those assets to me."

"No, thanks. Are you leaving or do I have to call the police?"

Gavin sighed and ran a hand through his dyed hair. It was another calculating move which I'd seen him use before.

He gave me a sympathetic smile. "Karis, does it have to be like this? Can't we work things out? We have done before. I don't see what the problem is this time."

"I've overlooked your affairs for too long. I wasn't willing to do that anymore. I've finally found some self-respect. Gavin, I deserve better than you." I had never stood up to him like this before. It felt good.

He shook his head slowly. "Affairs? What are you talking about? I haven't had any affairs. It's just your overactive imagination. You know what you're like."

I gritted my teeth. My patience was trickling away like water down a drain. Keeping my voice controlled, I said, "I know all about your affairs. I know the names of the women involved. I know where you met them." I took a moment to steady my nerves. "And I know what you did with them."

Gavin snorted with derision. "You're mad. I always knew that and now you've confirmed it." He gave me a mocking smile. "Did you see me in those idiotic visions of yours?" He actually made quote marks in the air.

That was too much for me. All the anger I felt for him bubbled up. It was followed by intense feelings of shame at myself for putting up with him.

I said, "I know you don't believe in my visions, but let me try to convince you otherwise. Not only did I get images of who you were with, but I was also treated to certain smells and sounds. It turned my stomach."

Malice glinted in his eyes. He reached into his pocket and produced his phone. He tapped the screen and held it up. "Carry on. I've set my phone to record. Does your solicitor know about your visions? Mine does. She said she'd need proof if we're to use that against you."

"Against me? What do you mean?"

"I'm going to prove you're mentally unstable. My solicitor advised me not to, but she'll change her mind when I provide her with evidence. Carry on. Explain clearly what your visions are. This is going to be interesting."

I clenched my hands at my side. He was not going to treat me like some freak show. I began, "The first woman was Cindy. She wore cheap perfume and too much make-up. You met her in a hotel on the night I went into labour with Lorrie. Do you remember the night our daughter was born? You told me you were on a business meeting. You had a lot of those, didn't you? I saw you in the hotel room when Mum phoned you to let you know about Lorrie. You told Cindy to shush, but she giggled. Do you remember that?"

Gavin's voice was less certain now. "No, I don't remember that. You must have dreamt it."

I continued, "There was Brenda after Cindy. I liked her. She was always friendly when I turned up at your office. She must have felt guilty. She wore Chanel Number Five and she liked the seaside. You took her to Blackpool on weekends and stayed at that hotel where we'd had our honeymoon. I thought that was rather tacky, even for you. You even took Brenda to the same fish and chip place. She had mushy peas with hers. I could smell the vinegar on them."

Gavin lowered his phone a fraction. "You can't prove any of this."

"I don't want to prove anything. I want you to know that my visions are real. Let me go on."

I couldn't stop myself from telling Gavin about all the things I'd witnessed. Every single painful one. I wanted him to know the hurt and betrayal I'd felt with each one. Despite my best efforts, I hadn't been able to stop the visions coming. I'd never told anyone about them. I was too ashamed to.

By this point, Gavin had put his phone away and he looked ever so slightly embarrassed.

But I hadn't finished with him. I needed to get it all out. It was like an uncontrollable purge and I was feeling better by the second.

As I was telling Gavin some of the more graphic elements of my visions, I heard a polite cough behind me.

I stopped in mid-sentence and looked over my shoulder. A red-faced man was standing there. He must have heard my X-rated ramblings. My cheeks flooded with heat and I quickly looked away.

The man cleared his throat and said, "Mrs Booth? I'm DCI Parker. I want to speak to you about an accident involving Carmel Johnson. Is this a good time or have I interrupted something private?"

My head snapped back to the man. DCI Parker? No. It couldn't be. Of all the police officers in the world, not him!

Chapter 6

In that moment, DCI Sebastian Parker recognised me too. A friendly look came into his eyes. It swiftly vanished and was replaced with a cold one. I knew that look of old.

He said, "I didn't realise it was you, Karis. I didn't know you were married."

Gavin said, "She won't be, not for much longer." He gave me a pointed look and added, "I'll be in touch." He headed for his car, jumped in and zoomed away sending up a shower of gravel as he did so.

Sebastian Parker said, "Was I interrupting some sort of marital role play? I can come back another time."

"Role play? Of course it wasn't role play." I said brusquely. "I'm sorry you had to hear that language coming from me. I never talk like that. I didn't realise I knew so many rude words. I haven't seen you in a long time, Seb. How are you?"

"It's DCI Parker. Detective Chief Inspector Parker. I was told you have some information about Carmel. Before we continue, does that information have anything to do with your…" He stopped talking and raised his eyebrows.

"My psychic abilities? It's alright. You can say those words." I tried to keep the anger out of my voice. It was bad enough having Gavin feel this way about me, but to have a blast from the past joining in was too much for me today.

DCI Parker lifted his chin. "There's no need to take that tone with me, Mrs Booth. I'm here on official business. Answer my question."

I'd had enough of being spoken to in a condescending manner. I inserted my key into the lock and opened the door. I pushed it open and said, "I'll tell you everything inside. I'd rather not talk on the doorstep. You can come in and listen to me or you can clear off back to the police station."

I'd only walked a short way down the hallway before I heard footsteps behind me and then the sound of the door closing. I headed for the kitchen and switched the coffee maker on.

DCI Parker let out a low whistle and said, "You've done well for yourself, Karis. This kitchen is massive. How many bedrooms have you got?" He moved over to the window and gazed out. "Is that a swimming pool out there? Is it a heated one? It must be if it's outside."

I was surprised at his change in attitude, but I didn't say anything. I much preferred this version of him. He reminded me of the boy he used to be.

I added ground coffee to the maker and pressed a button. "Coffee?" I asked. "I'm having one. And, by the way, this house has six bedrooms. Oh, and it's got an indoor pool too."

DCI Parker whistled again and looked at me. "Wow. You have done well. Or is it your husband who's done well?"

"Why would it be my husband?" I asked. "That's a big assumption to make." He was right to a certain degree, but I wasn't going to correct him.

DCI Parker looked embarrassed and muttered, "Sorry. You're right; that was an assumption. No to coffee, thank you. I can't stay long." He moved away from the window and continued, "Tell me what you know about Carmel Johnson. Did you ever meet her?"

I quickly made myself a cup of coffee and then sat at the kitchen table. DCI Parker remained standing.

I told him everything. From meeting Carmel and the shadows behind her to the limited information her colleague, Travis, had given to Erin earlier today.

As expected, there was a look of disbelief on his face. I'd seen that look many times. People didn't believe a word I told them when it came to my visions. The disbelieving look was usually replaced by a sympathetic one. I knew what most people thought about me. They thought I was crazy and needed medical help. But I was past caring what anyone thought today.

I concluded with, "You can think what you like about my psychic abilities, but I trust them. I know Carmel was pushed. Her death wasn't an accident."

DCI Parker regarded me coolly. "Did you see her being pushed down a set of stairs?"

"No, but—"

"Did you see any signs of the building she was in?"

"No, but—"

He held his hand up. "You saw a shadow pushing Carmel Johnson. Is that right?"

"Yes, but—"

He said, "She could have been pushed at any time during the day. Whatever you think you saw could have had nothing to do with her death. Is that a reasonable assumption?"

I looked down at my coffee. "I suppose so. But I did get the feeling the second shadow was malicious in nature."

"A malicious shadow? Hmm. It's not much to go on, is it?"

I looked up sharply. "Not when you put it like that. Are you treating Carmel's death as an accident?"

"I'm not at liberty to say," he added loftily. "I'll see myself out. Goodbye, Mrs Booth."

I seethed as I cupped my hands around my coffee. I didn't know what had got into me lately, but the meek, feeble woman who'd put up with anything was gone. I didn't recognise this new version of myself, but it felt good. It was like I'd given myself permission to be who I was supposed to be. I liked it.

I said to the empty kitchen, "I'll prove it wasn't an accident. I'll prove Carmel Johnson was murdered."

How I was going to do that wasn't clear to me yet. I was hoping inspiration would dawn on me soon.

And it did. Before I'd finished my coffee, I knew what I had to do.

Chapter 7

I went straight over to Erin's house and told her about my visit from DCI Parker. She was sitting on the sofa with a blanket over her legs. Robbie was at her side and they were holding hands. It soothed my jaded heart to know some marriages survived. I sat in the chair opposite them as I told them about my conversation.

Erin said, "Sebastian Parker? From our street? The one you went to school with?"

I nodded. "The very same."

"And he's a DCI now?" Erin went on. She looked at Robbie. "Why didn't you tell us the investigating officer was Sebastian Parker? You should have warned Karis."

"I wasn't aware you both knew him," Robbie replied. "I've never heard you mention him."

Erin gave him a knowing look. "That's because we never talk about him. Not after the way he treated Karis."

"Oh?" Robbie's eyebrows rose. He shot an enquiring glance my way.

I said, "Let's not drag up the past."

Erin said, "Is he still handsome? I bet he is, the crafty thing. It'll be just like him to keep his looks."

I shrugged. "I didn't notice." I shrugged again. "I suppose he's aged well. He's got all his hair."

Erin gave me a small smile. "Do his brown eyes still twinkle with mischief when he talks? Does his mouth twitch as if he's going to break into a smile?"

"He didn't do any twinkling at me," I informed her. "And I don't recall him smiling. He frowned a lot and gave me dismissive looks."

"Maybe he was trying to hide his true feelings from you." Erin turned to Robbie. "Karis and Seb were a couple in their youth. He was mad about her."

"Oh?" Robbie turned his enquiring look to his wife now.

She flapped her hand at him. "Let's not rake up the past. We don't like Seb Parker, and we haven't for years. Not since the incident. Robbie, can't you talk to him and make him see sense about Karis' vision?"

Robbie shook his head. "I can't interfere in someone else's investigation."

"You don't have to interfere. Just tell him he's wrong and that Karis is right." Erin gave Robbie a bright smile as if that would convince him.

His smile was affectionate in return. "I can't do that, my sugar plum. Not even for you."

"Pah! Some husband you are." Erin shook her head and then winked at him.

"I've got a plan," I announced to them. "Robbie, I know Carmel fell down stairs at the factory. Do you know where those stairs are?" I paused. "You don't have to tell me if you're not legally able to."

"I can tell you. It's already been revealed online by the local press. It's the stairs that lead from the reception area and up to the offices. Before you ask, I don't know why Carmel was there or who she was visiting in the offices. I don't even know who works in those offices. You'd have to talk to DCI Parker about that."

Erin tutted. "Let's not mention his name again. Karis, why do you need to know that?"

"I thought I might visit the area where Carmel died and see if I can pick up on anything."

"Ooo. Interesting," Erin said. "What do you think you'll pick up on? Some image of the person who pushed her?"

"I don't know. I've never been involved in anything like this before. I've just got a feeling I should try to get some more information."

Erin nodded. "You should trust those feelings. You should go over there right now."

"I'm going to, but I need your help with something. I hope this isn't an awful thing to ask, but could you write a condolence card for Mr Nithercott at the factory? That would give me the perfect excuse to go there."

Erin smiled and looked at Robbie. "I told you it was a good idea to write that card, didn't I?"

"You did. I was going to post it later. I'll get it for you." Robbie stood up and headed towards the kitchen.

"I was going to send a card anyway," Erin explained. "But I had a feeling I should write it sooner rather than later. I must have known you'd need it. Perhaps I've got some psychic abilities too." She waggled her eyebrows at me and grinned.

I glanced towards the kitchen door and could hear Robbie singing to himself. I took the opportunity to say what was on my mind. "Erin, is everything alright with you?"

Erin blanched. "What do you mean? Of course everything is alright."

"I know it's my fault that I haven't been to the café for a while, but it was always busy when I went. It isn't like that anymore. Why?"

"Oh, you know what businesses are like. Busy one day and then quiet the next." Her smile didn't reach her eyes.

"Are you having problems with the café? Is there something I can do to help?"

"Things have been quiet lately, but I'm sure they'll pick up. Would you like a cup of tea?" She pulled the cover off her legs.

"What about your staff?"

"What staff?"

"Exactly. I haven't seen any at the café. You used to employ people. Where are they?"

Erin tried again to reassure me. "It's hard to get reliable staff these days. Would you like a biscuit to go with your tea?" She made a move to stand up.

Robbie came back into the room. "Stay right where you are, Mrs Terris. And put that blanket back over you. You're going nowhere, not after the shock you've had."

My senses picked up. I gave Robbie a sharp look. "What's wrong with Erin? What aren't you telling me?" I narrowed my eyes at him and mentally willed him to tell me the truth.

"You can stop squinting at me like that," Robbie said. "There's nothing wrong with your sister apart from her working too hard. She needs to take it easy for a while." He handed me an envelope. "Here's the card of condolence. Now, listen to me carefully. Don't interfere with this police enquiry. If you have a vision while you're at the factory, let DCI Parker know."

Erin said loudly, "We're not talking to him."

Robbie went on, "Or you could tell me. Let me walk you to the door."

I gave Erin a quick hug before I left. I had a lot of hugs to catch up on.

Robbie walked me to my car and as I opened it, he glanced back at the house before saying quietly, "Karis, see what you can do about this Carmel thing. It's upset Erin greatly and I don't like to see her like this." He looked as if he were going to say a lot more, but then he stopped.

"Robbie, is Erin okay? You would let me know if she's not, wouldn't you?"

"Of course. She's fine." He held the car door open for me. "You take care now. If you sense any danger at all in that factory, get the hell out of there and come back here. Understand?"

"I do." I gave him a searching look in the hope of picking up on whatever was bothering him.

He laughed and said, "You'll give yourself wrinkles if you keep squinting like that." He closed the car door and walked back to the house.

I stared at the house for a while. Those two were keeping something from me. Why couldn't I switch my psychic powers on when I needed them?

I shook my head at myself. Maybe it was something I didn't need to know right now. I started the car and set off in the direction of the Nithercott factory. I knew in the pit of my stomach that something was going to happen to me there.

Chapter 8

Luck wasn't on my side as I pulled into the factory car park a short while later. DCI Parker was standing next to a black car and facing the car park entrance. He kept his eyes on me as I manoeuvred my car into the last remaining space. Unfortunately, that space was right where he was standing and I had to give him a polite hand gesture to get him to move. He did so reluctantly and then waited for me to get out of my car.

"Mrs Booth," he began in that cold tone of his, "what are you doing here?"

I held up Erin's card. "I'm here to deliver this condolence card on behalf of my sister. She's been doing business with Mr Nithercott for years. Is that against the law?"

His eyes narrowed. "Why didn't she post it?"

"Because she's not well."

The suspicion on his face lifted. "Isn't she? I'm sorry to hear that. I haven't seen Erin for years. How is she?"

"Fine." I gave him a suspicious look. "Can you stop going hot and cold on me? It's confusing."

"Hot and cold? I don't understand your meaning, Mrs Booth."

I wagged the envelope at him. "One minute you're acting like we're old friends, and the next you're treating me like a common criminal who's got something to hide."

"Have you? Something to hide? What's in that envelope? Did your sister really write it? Or is it a coded letter to Mr Nithercott telling him about your vision?"

I gave him a blank look. "I never thought of doing that. Erin did write it. She knew Carmel and liked her a lot. She's upset over Carmel's death and the least I can do is hand over this condolence card on her behalf. I don't see any problem with that."

He held his hand out. "I can take it for you. I'm going to talk to Mr Nithercott now."

I pulled the envelope out of his reach. "Erin wants me to deliver it. It wouldn't be the same coming from you."

"You can't talk to him at the moment. I've made an appointment to speak to him."

"What about?"

"None of your business, Mrs Booth. I suggest you go home and come back another time."

I leaned as casually as I could against my car. "I'm not going anywhere. I'll wait here all day until Mr Nithercott comes out if I have to." The smell of baking bread caught on a breeze and wafted towards me. My stomach growled in appreciation.

DCI Parker's mouth twitched at one corner. He raised his finger in my direction. "You're dribbling. It's not a good look."

I used the back of my hand to wipe my mouth. "I can't help it! It's the smell of fresh bread."

He let out the smallest of chuckles and looked away.

"Oh, shut up," I mumbled under my breath.

He looked back at me. "That's no way to talk to an officer of the law." He studied me for a moment which made me feel uneasy. What was his problem?

He clicked his fingers and said, "You're up to something. I can see it on your face. You want to talk to Mr Nithercott on your own. You want to find out more about Carmel Johnson. Aha! I know your game, Karis. Erm, Mrs Booth."

I truthfully said, "I wasn't planning on doing that at all."

"You can't fool me. You can go and see Mr Nithercott now, but I'm coming with you. Try anything funny and you'll regret it. I'm dealing with an investigation and I won't have you messing things up."

I pushed my luck and said, "A murder investigation?"

"None of your business." He moved to one side. "After you, Mrs Booth."

I shot him a filthy look but it was wasted as he wasn't even looking at me. He was right behind me as I walked into the factory and over to the reception desk. He didn't even give me the chance to speak to the kind-faced man sitting behind the reception desk.

DCI said to the man, "DCI Parker. Here to see Mr Nithercott. I have an appointment."

The man checked a book in front of him, smiled up at DCI Parker and said, "Yes, Mr Nithercott is expecting you. Up the stairs and it's the first door on the left. Would you like a complimentary box of mini loaves?" He pushed a large basket of delectable looking gift boxes towards the chief inspector.

"No." DCI turned on his heel and walked towards the stairs.

I gave the man an apologetic smile and said, "I'm Karis. Your company supplies bread to my sister's café. We've heard about Carmel's untimely death. We're so sorry. I only met her once, but she seemed lovely."

The man gave me a wobbly smile and nodded. "She was. We're all devastated. The place won't be the same without her. She'd only been here a few months, but she was so energetic and full of life. She had so many wonderful ideas for the company too."

I could feel the sadness coming from him in waves. I said, "And how are you coping?"

"As well as I can. I have to keep going for Mr Nithercott's sake. Would you like a box of mini loaves?"

"I would love some. Thank you. That's very kind." I took one of the boxes and put it in my handbag. I pulled out a fresh pack of tissues and handed them to the man. "Just in case you need them."

He gave me a grateful smile.

I nearly jumped out of my skin as DCI Parker barked, "Mrs Booth! This way. Please."

He was standing on the third step up and waiting for me.

I refrained from rolling my eyes at the impatient police officer and walked towards him. The stairs were wide enough for two people to walk side by side, so that's what DCI Parker did. He matched my every step up with his own. It was like he was frightened I'd make a run for it and race into Mr Nithercott's office before him.

We entered Mr Nithercott's office together and found him sitting behind a large, wooden desk. He was an elderly man and his suit was what my late grandma would describe as "dapper." His tie and pocket square complimented the dark blue of his suit. His eyes were red-rimmed and there was a box of tissues in front of him. I could almost touch the grief which surrounded him.

Before DCI Parker could stop me, I walked towards Mr Nithercott and placed my hand on his arm. "Hello, I'm Karis. You supply goods to my sister, Erin Terris. We're so sorry for your loss."

He patted my hand. "I know Erin. She's been one of my clients for years. Carmel said Erin liked the new recipes. Is that right? Did she? I'm not one for change, but Carmel was all for it. She was a forward-thinker. Such ideas. Such ambition." His gaze dropped. "All gone."

DCI Parker said, "Mrs Booth has brought you a condolence card." He gave me a pointed look.

I placed the card on the desk.

Mr Nithercott looked at me and said, "That's kind of you. I believe Travis will be taking over Carmel's delivery route now." There was a fraction of a pause. "Let me know if Erin has any problems with him."

"I will do. Please let us know when the funeral is. We'd like to be there."

DCI Parker opened the office door wide. "Mrs Booth, you may go now."

I shot him a dark look which he caught this time and his eyes widened. There was no need for him to be so rude.

I left the office and headed for the stairs. I stopped and looked around to make sure no one was there. Then I concentrated on what I'd felt on the way up the stairs. I knew I was going to receive a vision of Carmel's recent past. I steadied myself against the wall and waited.

Chapter 9

The vision began.

I could hear something; the sound of someone breathing. I put my hand on the handrail and felt it vibrating. I let my focus soften.

There she was. Carmel Johnson. Standing on the top step inches away from me. She had her back to me but I could hear her heavy breathing. She was furious about something. Some injustice. I felt it strongly. My eyes smarted as I tried not to cry. I saw Carmel move her hand to her face and wipe something away. Tears?

What was that smell? It was something familiar. Smoke of some sort, but not cigarette smoke. It was sweeter.

A voice called out Carmel's name. It sounded like it was underwater and I couldn't say if it was a man or a woman's voice.

Carmel looked over her shoulder. I saw the bitterness on her face as she recognised the person who'd called her name. Her right hand was resting on her lower abdomen and I felt a flicker of something in my stomach. It felt like butterflies.

Carmel shook her head vehemently at the unknown person and turned her head back. She took a step downwards.

That's when it happened. Hands shot out and pushed Carmel with a determined force. Carmel yelped with shock.

Then she fell. I could hear every sickening thump as her body rolled down the steps.

I instinctively reached out to stop her and cried, "No!"

She landed at the bottom of the stairs with her face looking upwards. I saw her eyes flutter before they closed forever. I whipped my head around to see if her killer was there.

DCI Sebastian Parker was standing there. His face was solemn and his eyes bore into mine. His voice was husky as he said, "Karis, what just happened? You're crying. What did you see?"

I dashed my tears away. "I saw everything. I saw Carmel fall to her death. I know you don't believe in my visions, but I saw her." My voice cracked and I took a second to compose myself. I placed my hand on my lower abdomen just as Carmel had done. "She was pregnant. I felt it here."

DCI Parker gave me an incredulous look. "That's impossible. How could you feel that?"

"I don't know, I just do!" My voice rose. "I've just witnessed a murder. I don't care whether you believe me or not. I saw someone push her. Someone was standing right where you were."

"Did you see who it was?"

"No. I turned around to have a look and saw you instead." I looked back at the bottom of the stairs. "She was all crumpled up like a rag doll. That poor girl. And her poor baby."

DCI Parker said, "Karis, I don't know what to do with this information. I'd like to believe you, but…" his voice trailed off.

I gave him a small smile. "But your sensible mind won't let you. I understand. But you can find out if she was pregnant, can't you? That could be relevant to her death. Don't you think?"

He gave me a long look before saying, "Yes, it could be. I'll see what I can do. Go home and get some rest. If what you say is true, then you've had a tremendous shock."

I was too distraught to argue with him over the truth of my vision. I kept my hand on the handrail as I walked down the steps. Instinctively, I gave the area where Carmel had landed a wide berth. I could feel DCI Parker looking at me, but I didn't give him a backward glance as I left the factory.

I got into my car and looked at the building. Someone killed Carmel Johnson in there. Those visions about her were coming to me for some reason. The guilt over Robbie's shooting came back to me. I should have done a lot more to help him and to prevent that incident. I couldn't change the past, but I was going to make sure I did everything I could to help Carmel.

Chapter 10

I went straight back to Erin's house as I wanted to share my psychic experience with her. I could always rely on my sister to take my visions seriously.

Erin answered the door to me, took one look at my face and said, "You need a strong cup of tea. Come in. Robbie's nipped out to the supermarket."

Once we were settled with a cup of tea in the living room, I told Erin everything.

She shook her head sadly. "That's awful. Just awful. Poor you having to see that. Can you remember anything else about the person who pushed her? Did they have a young voice or an old one?"

"I couldn't make it out. I've been going over and over it. You don't think it was Mr Nithercott, do you? He's got an office near the stairs."

"Why would he do that?"

I gave her a look. "Perhaps he's the father of her child."

"But he's two hundred years old!" Erin exclaimed. She gave me a cheeky grin. "Although, if there's still lead in the pencil..."

I shuddered. "Don't complete that sentence. How well did you know Carmel?"

"Not very well. We only managed to exchange a few words each time she delivered the bread. But she was one of those people who you warm to immediately. She was so genuine. She cared what my customers thought about Nithercott's products. She cared what I thought too. I know she was behind a lot of the new recipes. She had a knack for knowing about changing trends. From the small things she let slip, I don't think everyone was happy with her new recipes."

I settled back in the sofa with my cup snuggled in my hands. "Tell me more."

"It's that man she worked with — Travis. Like I told you earlier, he used to deliver my bread. The miserable so-and-so. From what I gathered, he wasn't happy about Carmel taking over his route."

"Why not?"

"I think it had something to do with all the customers on my route being close together. It didn't take long to deliver bread to us all. Travis' new route takes him longer as his customers are more spread out. I know he didn't like the new recipes and told his customers they had nothing to do with him. He encouraged them to make complaints. And that's what they did. Mr Nithercott got many complaints from people on Travis' route."

"Did Carmel tell you this?"

Erin nodded. "She was upset one day which was unusual, so I insisted she tell me what was wrong. She told me how Travis had got his customers to complain about the bread. He'd also bad-mouthed her at the factory and said she was after Mr Nithercott's job. He'd really upset her with his malicious rumours." Erin's eyes narrowed. "I can just imagine Travis doing something like that."

"When did Carmel tell you this?"

"A few weeks ago. She was back to her usual happy self the day after and didn't mention Travis again." She gave me a considered look. "Do you think it was Travis who pushed her down the stairs?"

"I don't know. What do you think?"

Erin said, "I think he'd do something like that. He's nasty enough. He's the one who found her at the bottom of the stairs, so that puts him at the crime scene."

"What's all this talk about a crime scene?" Robbie came into the room. "I've only been gone for thirty minutes and you're trying to take over my job. Hello, Karis. Are you staying for lunch? I'm going to put the shopping away and then make something for my crime-fighting wife."

A call of hello came from the kitchen.

"Ah," Robbie said as he ran his hand across the back of his neck. "Guess who I saw at the supermarket?"

An elderly woman in a tartan coat ambled into the living room. She beamed at us and declared, "It's only me. Robbie said you were here Karis, and I thought I'd pop in and say hello. "

"Peggy!" I put my cup down, got to my feet and went over to the woman. She was smaller than me by a foot so I had to lean down to hug her. As always, she smelled of roses.

I'd known Peggy Marshall all my life. She'd been Mum's next door neighbour for years. They'd moved into their houses within a week of each other and had become firm friends immediately. Peggy was like a second mum to Erin and me. She was kind-hearted and looked on the bright side of life. She was one of those people who lifted your spirits every time you met her.

She was also the nosiest person in the world. She knew everything about everyone.

Once I'd released Peggy, she looked me up and down and announced, "Karis Booth, you look better than you have in years. It's not my place to say this, but I'm glad you're getting a divorce. That Gavin Booth is one of the worst humans I've ever met. He sucked the life and ambition right out of you. He's like one of those emotional vampires. I saw a programme on the telly about them and I thought to myself that they're just like Gavin Booth."

"How did you know about my divorce?" I asked. The second the words were out of my mouth, I knew it was a silly question.

"I saw Henry at the butcher's. His granddaughter works at the sandwich shop near the solicitors in town. She saw you going in there and mentioned it to Carol who she works with and she said—"

I held my hand up. "I shouldn't have asked you that. I know you have friends all over this town. Nothing gets past you."

Erin noted, "Peggy, you're like the human equivalent of Google."

Peggy gave her a grin. "Erin, how are you? You look peaky."

Erin flashed her a bright smile. "I'm fine. Really fine."

Peggy gave her a look which said she didn't believe her. She went on, "I won't keep you. I hope you don't mind me saying this, Erin, but your mum's garden needs some attention. The weeds are running riot. And her windows are becoming a disgrace. Would you like me to sort it out? I don't mind. I've got a spare key."

Erin replied, "No, thank you. I'm sorry Mum's house is like that. I haven't managed to get round there recently. I've been too busy with work."

I looked at Erin. "I didn't know you were looking after Mum's house. How long have you been doing that? Why didn't you let me know? I could have helped."

Erin looked away from my gaze.

Peggy said, "She's been doing it since your mum went into the care home. She couldn't tell you on account of you two not talking to each other." She looked at Robbie. "But they've got that sorted out now, haven't they?"

Robbie nodded. "They have. At last."

Peggy continued, "Aye, but I'll bet you my last packet of bath salts that Karis still feels bad about you getting shot." She turned her knowing eyes on me. "You do, don't you? There's no point feeling bad. It wasn't your fault. It was that emotional vampire, Gavin Booth. He never supported you and your gifts. Never." She put her hand on my arm. "He couldn't see how special you were. He never appreciated your gift. You're still getting those pictures in your head. You had a vision of that poor lass at the bread factory."

"How do you know that?"

Robbie blurted out, "I told her. I couldn't help it! She wheedled the truth out of me. She should work for MI6."

Peggy chuckled. "I wouldn't be cut out for that sort of work. I like my home comforts too much. Speaking of which, Robbie, would you mind giving me a lift to the bus stop? There's a bus due in five minutes and I'm not sure my legs will make it with all the shopping I've got."

"Course I will," Robbie replied. "When I've dropped you off, I'll call into Lorena's house and give it a good going-over."

I made a decision and said, "No, you won't. I'll do it. It's about time I did my fair share concerning Mum's house. Peggy, I'll give you a lift home. Where are your shopping bags?"

"I've left them in the kitchen. Thank you, Karis. We can have a good natter in the car."

That's exactly what I was counting on. I said goodbye to Erin and Robbie and promised I'd phone them later.

I took Peggy's bags to my car and put them in the boot. Peggy settled herself in the passenger seat with her handbag on her lap.

As soon as we drove away, she said to me, "Right, what do you want to talk about first? The murder of that lass? Or the secrets Erin and Robbie are keeping from you?"

Chapter 11

"Let's start with Erin and Robbie," I said. "What's going on with them?"

"I was hoping you'd tell me that with you being psychic and all. Have you had any visions about them? Any premonitions? Overheard any secret conversations?"

I shot Peggy a quick glance. "No, I haven't. I can't switch my abilities on and off. I wish I could."

"You should go to one of those spiritual churches. I've seen them advertised in the paper. They do psychic development classes. I've clipped the advert out and kept it in my kitchen drawer. I thought it might come in useful for you one day."

"Perhaps. All I've picked up on from those two is that they're keeping something from me. I think it's something to do with Erin's health."

Peggy said, "Aye, that explains it. She hasn't been working full-time at the café. She keeps taking time off. And she's laid her staff off. I thought her and Robbie were having money problems and had decided to cut down on staff. But if there's something wrong with her health, then she would want to cut her hours down." She paused for a few seconds. "What do you think is wrong with her?"

Unease settled in my stomach. "I don't know. I hope it's nothing serious. Like…" I stopped. I was not going to finish that sentence.

Peggy reached over and patted my hand. "Let's not worry about things that aren't there. Erin could simply be cutting down on her hours and doing something else. That café of hers isn't as busy as it used to be. I expect it's the competition. There are two new cafés in town

now and they do all sorts of fancy food. They're not to
my liking, but some people like it. Why don't you sit her
down for a serious talk and get to the bottom of it? I'd
like to know what's wrong with her too."

I caught the worry in her voice and said, "I will do."

Peggy didn't have children of her own. Erin and I were
the closest to a family she had.

We arrived at the semi-detached houses which Mum
and Peggy owned. Even as I pulled up to Mum's house,
I could see the dust on the windows and the foot-high
weeds in the garden. Mum's house was a stark contrast
to Peggy's next door. Her house positively gleamed with
cleanliness.

I sighed as I switched the car engine off. "I'm sorry
about Mum's house. I'll get it cleaned up."

"I know you will. You don't have to do it this very
second. Help me in with my shopping and I'll make you
a ham and cheese sandwich. As usual, I've bought too
much. I know my Jeff's been gone three years now, but I
keep shopping for two. That's the problem with losing
someone so close to you; you keep forgetting they're
gone."

I insisted on carrying Peggy's shopping bags into her
kitchen. Like the rest of the house, it was spotless. It had
a wonderfully welcoming feel to it. It was like the house
was opening its arms and giving me a hug.

I put Peggy's shopping away while she made us some
lunch.

As soon as we sat at the kitchen table, Peggy said, "Let
me tell you what I know about that bakery lass, Carmel.
I never met her, but I know plenty who did. Lovely girl
she was by all accounts. Always inventing new bread
with fancy bits in them. I know about that shifty man
who worked with her. Travis, he's called. He hated
Carmel from the minute she started working for Mr
Nithercott. Eat up, Karis."

I picked my sandwich up. "I will. Why did Travis hate Carmel?"

"Because she was a conscientious worker. She turned up early to work and stayed late. She did her deliveries on time and talked to each of her customers to make sure they were happy with the deliveries. Not like Travis. He couldn't care less about his customers or the bread. He got up a petition, you know. He didn't like that new loaf that Carmel had worked on. He got his customers to sign a petition to get rid of the new recipe, and to get rid of Carmel."

I lowered my sandwich, "Did he? What was his reason?"

"He claimed Carmel was messing with a tried and tested recipe. Some people liked the original Nithercott classic loaf. They didn't want change. But I know the majority loved the new recipe and they wouldn't sign his petition. It wouldn't surprise me if Travis forged their signatures."

"What was he going to do with his petition?"

"He was going to take it to Mr Nithercott. Perhaps he was hoping Mr Nithercott would fire Carmel."

I gave her a slow nod. "What if Travis did that yesterday? And what if Mr Nithercott refused to fire Carmel? Travis could have seen her on the stairs and pushed her in a fit of rage." I put my half-eaten sandwich down. "But that doesn't explain her feelings. She felt angry at someone before she fell. She wanted to get justice."

Peggy frowned. "How do you know that? Oh, you had another vision. Robbie told me you were going to the bread factory. Tell me everything."

I did so.

Peggy nodded. "Carmel could have been annoyed with Travis. Let's say he took his petition to Mr Nithercott. Then Mr Nithercott spoke to Carmel later and showed her the petition. That would have been enough to rattle her."

"Yes, but why would Travis then push her down the steps?"

Peggy shrugged. "Because he's a nasty, little rat of a man. You should talk to him. See what you can pick up. I don't mean to be rude, Karis, but can you hurry up, please? I'm going to see your mum soon and the bus to the care home only runs once an hour. I don't want to miss it."

I picked my sandwich up. "I'll drive you there. I'll spend some time with Mum too."

"But it's not the second Sunday of the month," Peggy said. "You only see her on the second Sunday."

My glanced dropped downwards. "That was Gavin's suggestion. He said it was a waste of time going more often as Mum never recognised me. He said it so many times that I was convinced it was true." I looked at Peggy. "I've been such an idiot about him. I've been an utter and complete fool."

"You're not the only woman to say that about a man. Forget about Gavin Booth. He's out of your life for good. The nincompoop. Let's see your mum, and after that, we'll track down that Travis fella. We'll get the truth out of him."

"Shouldn't we leave this to the police?" I suggested.

"Do you mean that old friend of yours, Seb Parker? He's changed since he went to London. He's gone all hard-faced. Robbie told me what Seb had said to you earlier when he went to your house. No, we won't leave this to that cold-hearted Seb Parker. We're going to find out who killed Carmel ourselves. Eat up."

Chapter 12

Mum had been at Wood Crescent Care Home for the last two years. Everything had fallen apart two years ago. Robbie had been shot and Dad had died shortly afterwards. Mum couldn't cope with the grief and she fell to pieces. Having lost her own husband the previous year, Peggy helped Mum through the grieving process, but it was soon clear that Mum wasn't just grieving. I remember the phone calls from Peggy telling me she'd found Mum wandering around the supermarket in her nightdress. Peggy had also discovered Mum doing gardening in the middle of the night and singing loudly to herself. I'd witnessed one of Mum's turns, and knew it was nothing to do with losing Dad. After difficult conversations with Erin and Robbie, we decided this care home would be the best place for her.

Wood Crescent Care Home had glowing reviews, and the staff genuinely cared for the patients. Even though it had broken my heart to do so, I was content as I could be at leaving Mum here. Her prospects of returning home were slim, but there was never any question of selling Mum's house. Even though we'd never voiced our opinions to each other, Erin and I considered Mum's stay here to be a temporary one. The thought of her not returning home, and back to her former self, was too hard for us to contemplate. So we didn't. I knew deep down that we were fooling ourselves.

The woman on the reception desk gave us a cheery wave as we entered. A delicious smell of fish and chips wafted towards us.

Peggy explained, "They always have fish and chips on a Tuesday. Every week without fail. These old folk like their routines. Why don't you talk to Lorena first? I've got some other people to talk to here. I'll catch up with you in a bit."

She wandered off down the corridor raising her hand in greeting to many people.

I headed towards the Sun Room where Mum spent most of her time. Huge windows overlooked the beautiful gardens and Mum loved to stare out at the trees.

She wasn't the only quiet one who stared out of the windows. I spotted three other residents gazing out while their loved ones sat opposite them with overly bright smiles on their faces as they tried to make conversation.

I walked over to Mum and sat in the chair opposite her. I said gently, "Mum, it's me, Karis."

Mum turned her attention away from the window and gave me a quizzical look. Then she gave me a polite smile, the kind you'd give to a stranger. Even though I was used to it, it still hurt. Mum turned her head back to the view outside.

I persevered, "Mum, I know this isn't my usual day for visiting, but Peggy was coming so I thought I'd tag along with her. Lorrie is doing well in her new job. You remember Lorrie, don't you? Your granddaughter. I told you last time she'd started working for that online protection company." I let out a laugh. "She's not allowed to talk about her job and even had to sign some official papers about confidentiality and all that. When I ask her about her job, she looks as if she's fit to burst with all the information she's come across. You know how bad she is at keeping secrets! I'm not entirely sure it's the best career choice for her, but she loves it."

Mum's attention went to a robin on the grass outside the window. The corner of her mouth lifted slightly as she watched the bird's antics.

I carried on, "I've got a bit of news too, Mum. I've decided to get a divorce. I thought it was about time I came to my senses." I couldn't help but give a hollow laugh. "About time too, you're thinking. I know you never liked Gavin."

Mum turned her head back to me. She gave me such a sharp look that it took my breath away.

Her voice was hoarse as she said, "Gavin? Gone? For good?"

Had she actually understood me?

I nodded. "Yes, Gavin's gone for good."

She lifted a thin hand and held it out to me. She croaked, "Good. I'm happy."

I reached out for her hand. As soon as I did so, an image flashed into my head of Mum and me playing in the garden. It was so real. I could hear our laughter and feel the sun on my bare shoulders. I must have been about nine or ten.

I looked into Mum's eyes and smiled.

She smiled back and said, "Garden. I remember. I can hear you laughing."

"Me too, Mum."

We continued to hold hands and the image of us in the garden intensified. I could even taste the strawberry ice cream which Mum bought for me from the ice cream van.

Tears of happiness rolled down my cheeks as the image continued. It was like being inside a TV show. The colours were so bright and the noises so clear. Unlike a TV show, I could experience the smells too. It was wonderful, even magical.

Mum squeezed my hand and said, "A good day, Karis, a good day. I remember it well. Gavin's gone? For good?"

I nodded, unable to speak. Mum hadn't said this many words since she'd moved into the care home.

Mum gave my hand a final squeeze and said, "Good. I'm glad. He's a nincompoop. I'm tired." She took her hand back and rested it on her lap. Her eyes closed and the smallest of smiles alighted on her lips.

I wiped my tears away.

Peggy appeared at my side. "Karis? Why are you crying? Is she dead? Is Lorena dead? Don't tell me she's passed on!"

I stood up and told Peggy what had happened. I concluded, "It was only a few minutes, but I felt as if I had her back with me. I think she felt it too."

Peggy smiled. "You're a lucky girl to experience that. It must be your psychic powers coming out more now that you're away from that joy-sucking vampire. Mind you, your mum had her psychic moments too. Whatever it was that you just experienced, I'm pleased for you."

We both looked at Mum who was now asleep. She looked peaceful.

I ventured, "Do you think the mum I know is still in there? In her head?"

"She could be. There's no harm in thinking that. I would say don't get your hopes up, but why shouldn't you? That's what hopes are for. Raise them as high as you can. Why don't you have a walk outside in the gardens? It's lovely out there. I'll keep an eye on your mum."

I was about to say no, but then a familiar smell came towards me. It was the scent of that smoke I'd inhaled during my visit to the bread factory. Where was it coming from?

An elderly man in a tweed jacket walked past me and the smell increased. I could see a pipe sticking out from his top pocket.

I whispered to Peggy, "Who's that? I've seen him here before, but I don't know his name."

"That's Cyril. Cyril Simpson. He comes here to see his wife, Maggie. Why do you want to know who he is?

Have you just had a funny feeling about him? Is he going to kick the bucket soon?"

"No. I think he was at the bread factory earlier. That smoky smell is coming from him. Now I know why it was so familiar. I've smelled it before when I've been to visit Mum. It must linger on his clothes."

Peggy looked at Cyril as he left the room. "What was he doing at the bread factory? Don't just stand there, Karis, get after him!"

Chapter 13

I followed Cyril out of the building and into the garden. He walked to the nearest bench, sat down and put his head in his hands. I hated to intrude on such a private moment, but I had to.

"Erm. Excuse me. Sorry for bothering you. I'm Karis Booth."

Cyril looked up at me and my heart twisted at the grief on his lined face. "Yes? What do you want? Have I left something behind? I'm always doing that lately." He squinted. "I've seen you before. Aren't you Lorena's oldest? I didn't know you worked here."

"I don't." I took a seat. I looked at him for a moment. How was I supposed to explain that I'd smelled him in a vision? It sounded weird even to me.

Cyril straightened up and sat back on the bench. He said, "It's so sad, isn't it? To see my Maggie and your mum like that. They're the people we've known and loved for so long, but they're not really there. I wonder what they think about? Do you suppose they still have memories?"

I gave him a slow nod. "I suppose they might. Even if they're only small memories."

"I hope they do. I hope Maggie remembers something about her life however small." He blinked rapidly. "Anyway, enough about me. Did you want to talk to me about something?"

"I did. This is going to sound really strange, but have you been to the Nithercott bread factory recently?"

Cyril gave me a wide-eyed stare. "It's those CCTV cameras! They follow your every movement. It's like living in a fishbowl! Is that where you work? Did old Mr Nithercott send you here to tell me not to go back? Well, you can tell him from me that I won't be going back! And not one morsel of his disgusting bread will pass over my lips again. Never!"

I wasn't expecting such an outburst. "I don't work for Mr Nithercott."

"I don't blame you. He's a disgrace to the bread profession. Changing his recipe like that! No respect for his loyal customers. Why are companies so keen to improve everything these days? Why can't they leave stuff alone? I loved Nithercott bread. The old one, not the new one. That's why I went there. To let him know how I felt. I'm sure I'm not the only one."

"What did you say to Mr Nithercott?"

"I told him how I felt. He was very nice about it and offered me some free loaves as compensation. But it was something with sunflower seeds in it. Seeds in a loaf? Can you believe that? What's the world coming to? I told him he wasn't being fair to his loyal customers and he should continue to bake the old bread. He said he couldn't and that he had to move along with the times. He said the old bread had too much salt in it and young people don't like that now." He shook his head sorrowfully.

An image came to me while he was talking. I saw a young couple inside a café. The man had a striking resemblance to Cyril, and he even had a pipe sticking out of his top pocket. From the clothes and surroundings, I could tell the image was from a long time ago.

I said gently, "Did your Maggie like the old recipe too?"

Cyril's wrinkly face broke into a smile. "She did. Nithercott's bread has a special place in our hearts." He waved his hand at me. "You don't want to hear about that. You've probably got something important to do."

"I haven't. I would love to hear more about you and Maggie."

"Okay. You asked for it." Cyril took his pipe out, looked at it and then put it back in his pocket. "Maggie used to work at a top-end department store in Harrogate. I fell for her the second I saw her. I was desperate to talk to her, but she worked in the perfume department and I didn't have an excuse to go over to her. I admired her from afar. She caught me staring at her one day and waved at me. She beckoned me over and asked if I had a woman in my life. I said yes, I had my mum. Maggie gave me a free sample of lilac perfume to give to my mum. She said I had to promise to return the following week and to let her know what Mum thought."

"That's a good chat-up line," I said with a smile.

Cyril grinned. "She was a bit of a minx was Maggie. Anyway, I went back time and time again. Maggie couldn't keep giving me free samples, so I paid for the cheapest items I could. I wasn't making much money then, but I was happy to spend it all at Maggie's counter. Mum loved our courtship days because she ended up with lots of perfumed products.

"I finally gathered my courage and invited Maggie out. To my amazement, she said yes. I took her to a posh café where they had tablecloths and waitresses." He tapped his pocket where his pipe was. "I even bought this so that I'd look grown-up and refined. That café was so posh that our sandwiches had their crusts removed! I don't know why they did that; the crust is the best bit. I kept my mouth shut, though. If that's how posh people eat their bread, who was I to argue?"

"Indeed," I said.

"The bread they served us was Nithercott's, the classic loaf. It had only just come out then and it was hard to find it in the local shops. Maggie loved it. And I loved it because she did. It became our thing. We stayed loyal to Nithercott's bread throughout our lives. We even had those posh sandwiches at our wedding!"

I gave him a nod. "I can understand why you're so upset about the new bread."

"It's not just the past memories of the bread," Cyril explained. "Ever since Maggie's been in here, her memory has got worse and worse. The only thing that got any reaction from her were the sandwiches I brought her. I made them specially with the crusts cut off. When she took a bite, I'd see a spark in her eyes like she was remembering something. It was my old Maggie. I know it was." He sighed heavily. "I took her some of the new bread yesterday. She didn't even touch it. She gave it one look and then stared out of the window. I lived for that spark in her eyes, and now it's gone. It's all Mr Nithercott's fault."

"I'm so sorry about that. Is there anything I could do to help?"

He gave me a wry smile. "You could convince Mr Nithercott to make the old bread again."

"I might just do that. When you were at the factory, did you see a young woman?" I described Carmel to him.

"Yes, I did. I was coming out of Mr Nithercott's office and heading for the stairs. I saw her coming up. She caught my eye as she had a look of Maggie about her. She gave me a lovely smile and bounded up the steps." Faint spots of colour came to his cheeks. "I did turn around and watch her as she walked away. Don't tell Maggie that."

"I won't. Where did the woman go?"

"She carried on down the corridor towards some doors. She went inside one of them and I heard—" He stopped abruptly. "No, I shouldn't say."

I said, "You can tell me."

"I heard a man shouting at her. Then I heard a woman shouting back. It must have been the young woman."

"Did you hear what they were saying?"

"He was saying something about her going too far, and then something about her ruining his plans. She yelled back that he needed to grow up. She sounded furious. I don't like people shouting at each other, so I quickly left." He pulled his pipe out and gave it a quizzical look. "I keep forgetting I've run out of tobacco. My local shop has stopped selling it. First, it's my bread, and now it's my tobacco. This world is getting too hard for me to deal with."

I picked up on his despair. I couldn't leave him like this. I said, "Have you looked online for the tobacco?"

"Online? You mean that internet thing? No, I haven't. I don't trust that internet."

I took my phone out. "Do you know the name of it?"

"Course I do. I've been buying it for years." He gave me the name and I tapped it into my phone.

I held my phone towards him. "Look, you can get it from this online shop. They'll deliver it to you."

"Will they?" His eyebrows shot up so much that they almost left his forehead.

I nodded. "I can order it for you. I've already got an account with this retailer. If you give me your address, I can make sure it goes there."

"Really? You will? How kind. How will I pay for it?"

"You won't. I will. It's my treat. And when you run out, you can phone me and I'll sort some more out for you. I'll give you my number."

Cyril's eyes welled up. "That's so very kind. I don't know what to say." He gave me his address. "Just order a small packet. Thank you."

I ordered him two of the larger packets. I wrote down my number for him and then we chatted for a few more minutes.

At one point, Cyril frowned and said, "Why did you ask me about going to the bread factory? You never did explain that."

I was saved from answering that question as Peggy came over to us. She said, "Karis, your mum is still asleep. I think we should go now. Hi, Cyril. How are you?"

"Hello, Peggy. I'm keeping well. You?"

"I can't complain, Cyril, I can't complain. See you later."

We walked back to the car, and when we got in, Peggy looked at me eagerly and said, "I know where we can find Travis. Let's go and interrogate him."

Chapter 14

A short while later I said to Peggy, "I've never been to a pub at this time of the afternoon before. Are you sure Travis will be here?"

Peggy nodded. "According to my sources, this is where he goes when he's finished his deliveries for the day. Once he's finished, he takes the van back to the factory, catches the number twenty-two bus and comes straight here. He only does this on Tuesdays, Wednesdays, and Thursdays." She frowned. "I'm not sure where he goes on Mondays and Fridays. I'll ask my sources about that. It might be relevant to our investigation."

I shook my head at her. "You really are a mine of information."

Peggy's eyes twinkled. "You'd be a mine of information too if you spoke to as many people as I do."

We went into the pub and over to the bar. I got myself an orange juice, and Peggy said she could manage a small gin and tonic. As neither Peggy nor I knew what Travis looked like, we asked the woman behind the bar if he was in.

She seemed surprised at our request and pointed to a corner of the pub. "Are you his friends? I didn't know he had any friends. There he is, sitting in his usual spot. There's something a bit different about him today. He's barely uttered a word since he came in. He normally complains non-stop the second he enters. Woe betide anyone who gets within hearing distance of his complaints. Travis is a man who thrives on complaining about anything and everything." She passed our drinks over to me and I paid her.

I said to the woman, "What does he complain about the most?"

"His workplace, of course. The big question is if he hates it so much, why does he still work there? That's what I've asked him when I've been unlucky enough to be near when he complains. He told me the shifts fit in with his lifestyle." She cast a sorrowful look in Travis' direction and added, "It's not much of a lifestyle. He goes to the factory, does his shift and then comes here for most of the evening. Still, you can't tell some people what's best for them, can you?"

Peggy replied, "Indeed not."

As we walked away from the bar, Peggy said to me quietly, "If we're going to get some information from Travis, let me try reverse psychology on him. I saw a programme on the telly about that. I know what to say and do. Follow my lead. If you pick up on any psychic visions or whatnot, let me know afterwards."

Peggy set off at a determined walk towards Travis. As I got closer, I got a better view of him. If my grandma were still alive, she would say he looked as if he needed a good wash. His hair was greasy and slicked back from his plump face. He was wearing a T-shirt with the Nithercott logo on it. I noticed it was coming apart at the shoulder seams. His trousers had stains on them which I didn't want to examine too closely.

Peggy plonked herself down on the chair opposite Travis and gave him a wide smile. Travis blinked in surprise and pulled his pint glass closer to him. I noticed it was half full and there was already an empty pint glass on the table.

Peggy said brightly, "Are you Travis? Do you work at that bread factory? I'm Peggy, and this is Karis." She indicated for me to sit down. I sat at her side and gave the confused Travis a small smile.

Travis shot Peggy a defensive look and said, "What's it got to do with you who I am? I don't know why you're bothering me. There are other tables to sit at. Can't a man sit alone and enjoy his pint at the end of a working day?"

"Of course you can, lad," Peggy said, still smiling. "Are you Travis or not?"

He gave her a sharp nod and took a swig from his beer.

Peggy continued, "Then I've got the right person. I know you deliver bread to the corner shop on Alfred Street. I want to know what's happened to it? I've been buying my bread there for years and years and what happened when I went there last week? I'll tell you what happened, Travis. I ended up with something that tasted nothing like the bread I know and love. What happened to it? Did I get a dodgy batch?"

Travis shook his head. He pushed his glass to one side and rested his hands on the table as if settling in for a talk. "It's the new stuff Mr Nithercott has authorised. You're not the only one to complain about it. I can't stand the stuff myself. I don't know what was wrong with the old one. Everyone loved the old one. I've told Mr Nithercott that over and over again, but will he listen? No, he won't. I'm just a delivery driver and what do I know, eh?"

Peggy cast him a sympathetic smile. "I would have thought you would know exactly what the customers wanted. With you being on the front line, so to speak. Mr Nithercott should know that. He should respect your opinion."

Travis lifted his chin slightly. "Yeah, that's right. I am on the front line. I'm not stuck in some office wearing an expensive suit. Mr Nithercott should listen to me. I know what people want. I'm an expert in these matters."

"I'm sure you are," Peggy said. "How long have you worked at the bread factory?"

"About fifteen years now."

Peggy probed, "Have you always been a delivery driver?"

Travis lifted his chin a little more and said proudly, "No, I started off sweeping up on the factory floor. I worked my way up to be a delivery driver. And that's good enough for me. I know my place. Not like some."

"Oh? What do you mean by that?" Peggy asked.

A bitter look came into Travis' eyes. "Let's just say that some people who work at the factory have ideas above their station. They think they're better than anyone else. They think they can make things better when there's nothing wrong with things to begin with." He moved his head a bit closer. "That new bread you got last week, I know the person who's behind that. She was one of those ambitious sorts who never knows when to stop. She used her good looks on old Mr Nithercott to make sure he used a new recipe. What's that word? Beguiled. That's it. She beguiled him with her womanly ways. And now I've been left to sort out the aftermath of her mistake. People don't like new things. They like the old stuff. I can't be doing with too much ambition in a person. It's not right. Anyway, she's gone now."

Peggy suddenly gasped and a hand flew to her chest. "I've just remembered something! One of my friends told me about someone dying at the bread factory. It hasn't been on the news, so I told my friend she must be wrong. Is it true? Has somebody died at the factory?"

Travis gave her a knowing nod. "It's not public knowledge yet, but that ambitious woman I was telling you about just now, it was her. I found her. She was called Carmel."

Peggy leaned forward, her eyes wide. "You found her? How awful for you. You poor thing. If you don't mind me asking, what did you see and where did you find her?"

"I found her at the bottom of some stairs near the offices and the staffroom. It was quite a shock, I can tell you. I'd been in the staffroom having my toast and tea and when I came out, I walked along the corridor outside. As soon as I got to the top of the stairs, I could see Carmel at the bottom. Her legs were at a funny angle so I knew something was wrong." He stopped talking and swallowed. I was surprised to see his eyes shining with tears. He continued, "I thought she'd just fallen at first. But she hadn't. I can't believe she's gone. She was annoying, but she did smile a lot. Even at me."

Peggy shook her head and said, "What a waste of a life. How did she fall? Did you hear her scream or yell?"

Travis shook his head.

"I have my music on when I'm in the staffroom. I don't like talking to other people in there. They talk nonsense and it gets on my nerves. I still had my earphones in when I came out of the room. If Carmel screamed, I didn't hear her."

Peggy tutted. "You poor lad. Did you notice anyone else hanging around the stairs?"

"No, it was just me." He blinked rapidly and swiftly got to his feet. "I have to go. I've got things to do." He abruptly walked away.

Peggy turned to me and said, "He didn't even finish his pint. Was it something I said?"

I said, "He was in love with Carmel. Despite what he said about her, I could clearly feel the love he had for her, and still has. Did you notice that he said Carmel used to smile at him? I think she might have been the only one to do that. Perhaps he was using that petition to get her attention."

Peggy nodded. "I got the impression he was fond of her too. But that puts us in a quandary, doesn't it? What if Travis met Carmel at the top of the stairs and decided to ask her out? What if she laughed in his face, and in a rage, he pushed her down the steps?"

I sighed. "We're no closer to finding out who pushed Carmel."

Peggy downed her gin and tonic in one, smacked her lips together and said, "Let's not give up so easily. You just need to use your psychic powers a bit more. We'll get to the bottom of this. You'll see."

Chapter 15

I drove us back to Peggy's house. On the way, she said, "Are you going to do something about your mum's garden now? No, I suppose you won't, not at this time of the day. It's getting a bit dark, isn't it? You could make a start on the inside. What about giving those windows a quick going-over? I could help you with that if you like? Perhaps a quick blitz in the living room too. I know where Lorena keeps her dusters. No one is living in the house, but the dust still settles. I don't know where it comes from, I just don't."

I pulled up outside Peggy's house, checked the time and said, "I should be getting home. I've got a lot of legal papers to go through and I want to get them sorted out as quick as possible."

Peggy nodded vigorously. "Of course you do. You've got other things to do. Your mum's house can wait a bit longer. You're a busy woman. You get yourself home and sort yourself out." She released her seat belt, grabbed her handbag and gave me a big smile. "It's been smashing to see you again, Karis. Keep in touch, won't you? Let me know how this murder thing goes with Carmel. And if you find out what's wrong with Erin, will you let me know, please? I do worry about you both."

"Yes, of course, I will. Do you want me to walk you to your door?"

Peggy let out a little chuckle. "No, I can find it on my own. You take care now, Karis. Bye for now." She hesitated a few more seconds before getting out of the car.

She gave me three goodbye waves as she walked up the garden path and towards her front door. As she went inside she gave me another wave before closing the front door.

I was about to drive away when a funny feeling came over me. I was getting another vision. I took my hands off the steering wheel and closed my eyes. Was it going to be something involving Carmel again?

It wasn't about Carmel this time. It was about Peggy. I saw her sitting in her living room and talking to a photograph of her late husband. She said, "Jeff, why did you have to leave me so soon? I feel lost without you. I don't know what to do with myself. I try to keep busy, but it's not the same without you. I do miss you."

She sighed heavily, placed a kiss on the frame and then put the photograph back down on the table next to her. She said, "I'll catch up on my telly programmes. I've got plenty to watch. I've been learning such a lot from those documentaries. You would have loved them, Jeff."

My vision progressed and I saw Peggy turning to the television, switching it on and I saw a long list of recorded programmes on the screen. Then, like a photograph album which was being flicked through, I saw Peggy sitting in the same chair watching her TV but wearing different outfits each time. It was like I was fast-forwarding through the next few years of her life, or was I seeing something from the past? Either way, it was obvious Peggy was a lonely woman. I could understand loneliness.

I quickly reversed my car into Mum's driveway and then marched round to Peggy's house. I rapped on the door and when she answered I noticed she was carrying the framed photo of Jeff.

Peggy said, "What is it? Has something happened?"

I said to her, "I can't face going back to an empty house. I'd prefer to stay at Mum's house. Peggy, will you come into Mum's house with me? I haven't been inside since she went into the care home, and I'm worried I'm going to be overcome with memories. I could do with a friend at my side."

"I don't want to intrude on your private time. I'm sure you'd rather be alone, wouldn't you?"

I shook my head. "I don't want to be alone at all. You could help me with a bit of housework. Your house is immaculate and I'd love to get Mum's looking something like that. You'd be doing me a great favour by helping me. We could also have a good gossip about what's been going on in your life. I haven't been in touch with you like I should have. We could make an evening of it. I'll even get us a takeaway."

"A takeaway? On a Tuesday? Karis Booth, you've gone mad." Peggy gave me a smile. "If you really want my company?"

"I do. If that's alright with you?"

Peggy gave me a nod. "I'll pop Jeff back on the table. Come in a minute."

I followed Peggy into her living room and noticed a neat pile of boxes next to one of her chairs. I pointed to them and said, "What's going on here? Have you started a postal delivery service?"

She chuckled. "No, those are my craft supplies. I've been learning all sorts of new crafts on that YouTube. Things I've wanted to know how to do for years but I've never got around to it. I've always enjoyed knitting, but I never got the hang of crocheting. I followed this lovely girl on YouTube who showed me how to do it. I'm going to have a go at cross-stitch too. And jewellery making. And quilting. Those videos are ever so helpful. I like to keep myself busy on a night. You can have a look at some of the craft kits I've ordered. I'll show you what to do. I'm becoming quite an expert at all sorts of things."

Peggy collected her handbag and locked the house up. We completed the short walk to Mum's house and I braced myself for the flood of memories. The memories came, but they were all happy ones. As I walked around the house with Peggy at my side, I told her what I was experiencing. The birthday parties. Christmas mornings. Easter egg hunts around the house and garden. Peggy and Jeff were in most of my memories, and at her insistence, I described what she was wearing and what Jeff was saying. We shed more than a few happy tears as we completed our tour of the house.

"Well," I declared, "that was very therapeutic. It's made me very hungry. What kind of takeaway would you like? Pizza? Chinese? Indian? Thai?"

Peggy replied, "That's too much choice! Can we just go for a pizza, please? Can we have some of that garlic bread too? I do love it. I know it makes me stink to high heaven the following day, but I can't get enough of it."

I placed our order and then had a good look in Mum's kitchen and discovered a couple of bottles of wine. I held them up to Peggy and said, "Shall we?"

Peggy grinned. "One bottle for you, and one for me? Stick a straw in the end and we're good to go." She laughed when she caught my startled expression. "Only kidding. One glass will be enough for me. Perhaps two. At a push, three."

Before I opened the wine, Peggy insisted on having a quick dust around in the living room. While she did that, I phoned Erin. She didn't answer, so I left a message for her.

Twenty minutes later, Peggy and I were settled in the living room with glasses of wine at our sides and pizza on our laps.

I found a box set of murder mysteries and said to Peggy, "Perhaps we should watch something like this and get our little grey cells working."

"Excellent idea, Sherlock. Or should I say, Miss Marple? Hang on, should I be Miss Marple and you can be Hercule Poirot? What about that Jessica Fletcher from Murder, She Wrote? If we're going to be investigating a murder, we really should decide who we're going to be." She reached for a big slice of garlic bread.

"I think we should just be ourselves. We're good enough as we are."

With her cheeks bulging with garlic bread, Peggy nodded and said, "I always knew I was perfect and now you've confirmed it. My Jeff said I was perfect in every way. The silly old fool." She smiled at the memory.

We both managed to get on to our third glass of wine by the time the murder mystery had ended. We were feeling pleasantly smug with ourselves as we'd both worked out who the murderer was before the sleuth did.

I said to Peggy, "I'm having a lovely time. Thanks for being with me."

Peggy was just about to reply when a thunderous knock sounded out on the front door.

Peggy exclaimed, "Who the heck is calling at this time of the night? Karis, it's the murderer! They've found out we're looking into Carmel's death! They've tracked us down! Quick, find a weapon." She grabbed the nearest empty pizza box and got to her feet.

Luckily, I had a now-empty wine bottle at my side, so I grabbed that and slowly followed Peggy to the front door. In my slightly drunken state, I was convinced that Carmel's murderer was standing there too.

I raised my empty bottle and quickly pulled back the front door.

Peggy rushed forward and bashed the man standing there with her empty pizza box. She declared, "You don't scare us! We know what you did and we will seek justice! Take that!"

DCI Parker warded off the pizza box attack and cried out, "Whoa! Stop that immediately! It's against the law to attack a police officer. Peggy, you nearly had my eye out with the corner of that box then."

Peggy lowered her box, and I lowered the wine bottle.

"Well, well, well," Peggy said. "It's the London boy. Have you solved Carmel's murder yet? No? I didn't think you had. Karis and me have been making excellent progress on the case, and we'll have the murderer locked up before the end of tomorrow."

His expression hardened. "I only came here to check on your mum's house, Karis. Mum told me no one is living here, so I was suspicious when I saw the lights on. What's this about your murder investigation?" His nose wrinkled. "Have you been eating garlic? Are you both drunk?"

"Yes, we are!" Peggy declared happily. She reached out, grabbed the detective chief inspector's sleeve and pulled him into the house. "We'd better talk about this murder investigation right away," she said. "You're making a pig's ear out of it. Thinking it was an accident? Pah! Let us put you right."

Chapter 16

Peggy dragged DCI Parker into the living room and pushed him onto the sofa. She sat at his side, patted his knee and said, "Would you like a drink of wine? We can spare you a glass."

He said rather testily, "No, thanks. I think there's been enough drinking going on in here."

"Please yourself," Peggy said as she reached for her half-full glass. She took a sip, smacked her lips together in appreciation and put her glass back down. "Now then, Seb, let's have a bit of a chat before we get down to business."

"It's DCI Parker," came his curt reply.

Peggy patted his knee again playfully and said, "Not at this time of the night, lad. You're not on duty, are you?"

He shook his head.

"Well then," Peggy declared, "you are going to be Seb to us tonight. If you don't like it, you can leave."

"You can call me Seb for now," he relented.

"Right then, Seb, tell us what you've been up to. I know you went down to London and picked up some funny ways, but what brought you back to Leeds? Have you come back to keep an eye on your mum and dad? Or did you come back for a promotion? I heard from your mum you were a detective inspector down in London, but now you're a detective chief inspector. Does that mean you moved back here for a promotion? Or was it to return to your roots? Or to look after your mum and dad? Or maybe it was a mixture of all?"

Her questions were making me feel dizzy and I couldn't remember her first one.

Seb looked like a rabbit caught in the headlights, and for a moment I was tempted to ask Peggy to stop her interrogation. But I wanted to know why he'd come back too, so I cradled my glass of wine, settled back in the chair and watched the show unfold.

With my defences down, I noticed Seb looked quite handsome in his casual wear of jeans and a dark jumper. Hmm. He'd been working out too. The sober side of my mind tried to tell me to stop having such observations, but I ignored it.

Seb began, "As usual, Peggy, you're right about all of those reasons. I did get the promotion based on me returning to Leeds. Not that I minded as I have missed this place. And you're right about me wanting to keep an eye on Mum and Dad. They've both had health issues, and I want to be around in case they need me."

Peggy gave him a nod. "Yes, I know about their health issues. They're only at the end of the street, after all. We all stick together around here, and you can rest assured that if anything happened to them, we'd look after them."

He flashed her a brief smile. "I know you would, but I still want to be near. I've just been over to their house now which is why I noticed the lights on in Lorena's house." He looked my way and added, "I wasn't expecting to find you here. I thought you'd be back at your own house having a dip in one of your swimming pools."

I frowned at him. Was there a hint of amusement in his voice? Was he making fun of my lovely swimming pools? The cheek of him.

Peggy tapped him on the shoulder and he turned his head back to her. She said, "How far have you got with your investigation? Karis told me what you said to her earlier about her visions. That's very rude of you, Seb. You know her visions are real. Or at least, you used to." Her face creased in concern. "Now that I come to think of it, I never did find out why you two fell out when you were young. Why was it? You were such good friends. You did everything together. It all changed when you went to high school. Seb, it was probably your fault. What did you do to upset Karis so much?"

Seb pulled at the neck of his jumper and said, "It's all in the past. I don't want to talk about it."

The wine had given me a strength which I didn't know I had. I'd already shouted at my soon-to-be ex-husband today, so I reasoned another shouting match wouldn't go amiss.

I aimed my wine glass in Seb's direction and said loudly, "I'll tell you why, Peggy. Oh yes, I'll tell you why."

Seb shot me a pleading look. "There's no need to go over the past, Karis."

Peggy said, "Let her get it out. She's having a good day for releasing her past emotions and it's not your place to tell her to stop doing so. Don't be so selfish, Sebastian Parker, think about Karis. She's obviously carrying a great hurt from her past which you're at the centre of. Let her vent. Be a man about it."

Seb gave me a resigned look and said, "Go on then, you might as well tell me how you feel."

I took a fortifying drink of wine, set my glass down and shuffled to the end of my seat. "Peggy, you're right about us being best friends in our youth. I thought we always would be. Seb knew about my psychic abilities right from when we were little. He loved it when I experienced something and he encouraged me to do it more and more. I told him about my visions before I even told Mum or Dad. He believed me every time when I told him about an image I'd seen in my head."

Seb looked down at his knees and didn't say a word.

I was getting into the flow now. "Things changed when we went to high school. I made the mistake of telling my school friends about some of my visions. I thought they'd be as understanding as Seb. I was mistaken. They made fun of me and started to call me Krazy Karis. Yes, crazy with a K. They even scrolled it across my books and on my desk. There were nasty things written about me in the girls' bathroom. I confided in Seb and he was so supportive. At first. But then things changed. One day I overheard him laughing and joking with some people, and he called me Krazy Karis too."

I stopped talking as those hurtful memories whooshed into my brain and exploded like a firework. Every insult, every jeer, every smirk from my school days came back to me one after the other. My voice was thick with emotion but I carried on, "I asked Seb why he would say such things, and he said it was time I grew out of my visions, and they were making me look like an idiot. He refused to talk to me after that. We were a couple at that stage, but he just left my life like I meant nothing to him."

Peggy let out a loud gasp of outrage. She turned her full force on Seb and shouted, "How could you? How could you do that to Karis? Everyone on this street knows about her special gift, and we all support her. Even your mum and dad support her! What sort of a man are you? You lily-livered coward! You namby-pamby, yellow-belly excuse of a man!"

Seb gave her a slow nod. "I admit it. I was a coward. I wasn't strong enough to stand up for Karis. She was much stronger than me and gave people a mouthful when they made fun of her. But I gave in to peer pressure. I wanted to fit in with the majority rather than be with someone who others were making fun of. I was weak. I'm so ashamed of my behaviour." He looked at me and said, "I did come round here and tried to apologise to you. But Erin answered the door and insulted me every time. She even threw a bucket of water over me once. She said I didn't deserve to be on the same planet as you. I agreed with her. No apology would ever make up for how I treated you."

I gave him a small smile. "I didn't know about you coming round here to apologise."

He gave me a smile in return. "I don't expect you to forgive me. I can't even forgive myself."

I thought about how I felt over Robbie's shooting and said, "I can sympathise with that feeling."

Peggy said, "Seb, you should have made more of an effort to apologise. Well, we can't change the past, but you can make amends for it now. When Karis told you about her vision concerning Carmel, why didn't you believe her?"

"Because I'm a level-headed police officer who's been trained to deal with facts only. Truth be told, I did believe her. But I could hardly admit to that, could I? I'm too stubborn to do so. One of my many faults, so I've been told. Can we talk about something else now? Talking about how I treated Karis makes me feel worse than any criminal I've dealt with. Peggy, I want to know what you meant by your earlier comments. What's this about your murder investigation? Karis, Have you picked up on anything else concerning Carmel? Have you had any more visions or feelings? You can tell me about them."

He gave me a big smile and he looked very much like the friend from my youth. However, those memories from high school were still fresh in my mind, and I was wary of how he would take the information I was about to give him. No matter how much he smiled at me, he wasn't going to get back in my good books that quickly. However, I did want Carmel's murderer to be found, so I put my feelings to one side.

Between Peggy and myself, we told Seb what we'd found out about Carmel and her relationship with Travis.

Seb listened quietly and then said, "I've already questioned Travis about his whereabouts at the time of the incident. There's a CCTV camera along the corridor leading to the staffroom. It points at the door, and the footage shows Travis walking along with his earphones in."

"CCTV?" I said. "Why didn't you tell us about this earlier? Have you checked the footage that looks over the stairs?"

He shook his head. "For some reason, the camera doesn't cover the stairs. You were right about Carmel being pregnant, though. She was in the early stages of her pregnancy."

Peggy shook her head. "The poor girl. What are you going to do next, Seb? How can we help you?"

He replied, "You can help me by staying out of this investigation. If Karis is right, it means there's a murderer out there. I don't want either of you putting yourselves in danger." He hesitated and then added, "But thank you for letting me know what you've found out. This could be very useful. I'll let myself out." He got to his feet and looked down at me. "I know this is long overdue, Karis, but I truly am sorry for how I acted during my foolish youth. I have no excuses."

I gave him a half shrug. I would have loved to say I'd forgiven him, but I wasn't at that stage yet.

As soon as he'd left the house, Peggy rubbed her hands together and said eagerly, "Let's see who can solve this murder investigation first — us or the London boy." She yawned and looked at the clock. "Is that the time? Karis Booth, you're a bad influence on me. I never stay up so late. I'd better get myself back into my own house and into bed before the neighbours start talking."

She stood up, finished the rest of her wine and walked unsteadily towards the front door.

I helped her out of the house, along the path and into her house. Because I was more steady on my feet than Peggy, I helped her upstairs and into her nightwear. She hummed and sang to herself as I did so. It was like looking after a child. I tucked her into bed, gave her a kiss goodnight on the forehead and then left her house making sure the door was locked.

Five minutes later, I settled down in my childhood bed and smiled at the posters which Mum had kept on the wall. Having had three glasses of wine, I expected to fall asleep straight away. But that didn't happen. Something was niggling at the back of my brain. Somebody had said something today which was bothering me. I couldn't quite put my finger on what it was, but still, the feeling persisted.

I eventually drifted off to sleep and had dreams which involved Peggy and me racing after faceless murderers.

As soon as I woke up, I knew what had been bothering me the night before.

Chapter 17

"I can't believe how stupid I've been!" Peggy exclaimed.

I was in Peggy's kitchen the following morning, and she looked surprisingly bright and awake considering she'd had a late night and three glasses of wine.

I said, "It came to me this morning. I knew something was bothering me at the back of my mind last night, but I couldn't work out what it was. As soon as I woke up, it became clear. Both Travis and Cyril referred to Mr Nithercott as old Mr Nithercott which made me wonder if there was a young Mr Nithercott." I took a drink of the tea that Peggy had insisted on making me. It was extra strong and gave me the caffeine boost that I needed this morning.

Peggy said, "I heard Travis say that too, but it didn't register with me at the time either. Of course, there's a young Mr Nithercott too. I knew that." She shook her head at herself. "I don't know why I didn't point this out to you. I must be getting old or something. We haven't taken young Mr Nithercott into account in our investigation. I must admit that I don't know much about him. I don't even know his first name."

I said, "I've been online this morning to find out more about him. He's called Flynn, and he's worked in the family business for years. He's Mr Nithercott's grandson. Flynn's father died a few years ago."

Peggy nodded. "I think I remember something in the papers about that. How old is he?"

"He's thirty-three. He's single, and from the photographs I've seen online, he's quite handsome but in a way that's too obvious, if you know what I mean?

Everything about him is perfect and he doesn't have any physical flaws."

Peggy's eyes narrowed. "Never trust a man who is too handsome. Do you think he's the father of Carmel's baby?"

"I don't know. We should talk to him, but I can't think of a reason as to why we should. We can't just turn up at the factory for a chat. I suppose DCI Parker has spoken to him about Carmel's death."

Peggy shook her head in disgust. "Don't refer to Seb by his official title. He doesn't deserve it. I still can't get over what he did to you at school."

I gave her a shrug in the hope of convincing her I wasn't bothered.

My phone rang at that point. I looked at it but I didn't recognise the number. I answered it and listened to the woman on the other end. Once she'd given me her message, I said I'd be there right away.

I ended the call and said to Peggy, "That was a nurse from the hospital."

"Who's dead now?"

"No one. But Cyril Simpson has been injured. He's broken his leg. He had my number and insisted the nurse phone me this morning. He wants to talk to me."

Peggy's eyebrows rose. "Cyril? Cyril from the care home? You barely know each other. Why does he want to talk to you?"

"I don't know, but that's what I'm going to find out. Do you want to come with me?"

Peggy took a long drink of her tea, put the cup down and said, "Of course I do! It could be something to do with our murder investigation. Let me pop to the toilet before we set off. That tea always goes straight through me."

Cyril looked very pale when we saw him in his hospital bed later. His right leg was in plaster and had been raised above the bedcovers. The nurse told us he'd been in an agitated state since they brought him in yesterday and kept calling my name. They'd had to sedate him to enable him to have a good night's sleep. As soon as he'd woken up, Cyril had badgered the nurse to get in touch with me. I was as confused as Peggy as to why he should want to talk to me.

Peggy sat on a chair at one side of Cyril's bed. and I sat at the other.

Cyril gave me a tired smile and said, "Thank you for coming to see me. You were so kind to me yesterday, and I didn't know who else to call. I had a feeling you'd appreciate what I'm about to tell you. It's funny how we were talking about Nithercott bread yesterday, and now here I am as a result of that company."

I felt my stomach clench in apprehension. "What do you mean by that? What happened yesterday?"

Cyril indicated his head towards his broken leg. "That's what happened to me yesterday. The doctor said I'm lucky to be alive. He said I could have broken my neck in that fall down the stairs."

Peggy spoke up, "Fall down the stairs? What do you mean by that? Come on, Cyril, get on with your tale."

Cyril gave her an impatient look. "That's what I'm trying to do, Peggy, if you give me a minute."

I was concerned about how pale Cyril's face was and said, "You take your time. We're not in any rush."

"After our conversation yesterday, Karis, you got me thinking about that new Nithercott bread again. I thought if old Mr Nithercott didn't want to listen to me, then young Mr Nithercott might. I went to see him after I left the care home. I went into his office and politely explained my predicament. I told him all about Maggie and what the bread meant to us." He pressed his lips together and took a moment to compose himself. "It was a mistake to go there. Young Mr Nithercott barely listened to what I was saying. He kept tapping away on his phone and when he did look at me, it was like I was a nuisance."

Peggy tutted in disgust.

Cyril carried on, "He didn't even care when I said Maggie was in a care home and the memory of Nithercott bread was the only thing that brought a spark to her eyes. When I'd finished talking, he said he couldn't care less about the old bread and it was people like me who were causing delays in his plans. He said he had a ten-year plan and he was sick to death of people interfering in that. He went on to say it was one obstacle after another. He muttered about having just got rid of one obstacle, and he was prepared to do it again."

Peggy interrupted him, "What did he mean by obstacles? Did you ask him?"

Cyril said, "I didn't. He just went ranting on and on, and he started shouting at me. I told Karis yesterday that I don't like people shouting, and I made to leave the office. That young Mr Nithercott was very rude and he swore at me and told me to get out of the factory and never return. I went as quick as my legs would carry me out of the office and along the corridor. I was halfway down the stairs when I could have sworn I felt someone push me. I toppled all the way down and I must've banged my head or something because everything went black. When I came round, young Mr Nithercott was kneeling next to me. He told me I'd slipped and fallen down the stairs by accident. He said he'd called an ambulance and they would be here soon."

I shared a shocked look with Peggy and then said to Cyril, "Do you think young Mr Nithercott pushed you down the stairs?"

Cyril gave me a slow nod. "I think that's exactly what happened. He was in a foul mood when I left his office. He had a look in his eyes as if he'd lost control of his senses. He tried to convince me it was an accident, but I definitely felt hands on my back before I fell. I can't tell the police as they wouldn't believe me. They'd believe Mr Nithercott, wouldn't they?" He looked towards his elevated leg. "I could have died. Who would visit Maggie then?"

Peggy had a face like thunder. She said to Cyril, "We've got contacts in the police force. We'll get in touch with them. Then we'll go and see that nasty Mr Nithercott."

Cyril said, "I don't want to cause any trouble."

I reached over and gently patted his pale hand. I said, "You're not the one who's going to cause trouble; it's going to be me. I'll contact the police. I'll tell them everything. You get as much rest as you can, Cyril. After I've spoken to the police, I'll go and sit with Maggie. I was going to see Mum later anyway."

Peggy piped up, "I'll sit with her too. I'll get some of my friends to do the same."

Tears flooded Cyril's old eyes. He gave me a gentle smile and said, "I don't know how you managed to come into my life yesterday, Karis, but I'm so glad you did. Will you really contact the police about this?"

I gave him a firm nod. "I'm going to speak to Mr Nithercott too. He doesn't scare me."

Cyril shot me a warning glance. "Be careful around Mr Nithercott. He's a bad one. I felt that as soon as I entered his office. Be very careful around him."

Chapter 18

When we left the hospital I said to Peggy, "I'm going to the police station now. I'm going to tell Robbie about this latest incident. He'll take care of everything."

Peggy gave me a pained look. "As much as I want to see Flynn Nithercott brought to justice for Cyril's accident, I've got some commitments this morning, and I can't come with you."

"What commitments?"

"I've got some old friends who are housebound. I call on them on a regular basis and do things for them around the house. I don't like to let them down as I'm often the only company they have all week. Would you mind going to the police station without me? You can let me know how you get on later."

"Where do these friends of yours live?"

"Joyce lives twenty minutes away and there'll be a bus soon. If I speed up, I can make it to the bus stop in time."

"Peggy, I can give you a lift there. You don't need to worry about getting the bus. I'm happy to give you a lift."

Peggy shook her head. "But you need to get to the police station as soon as possible."

"I insist on giving you a lift first. Don't argue."

I dropped Peggy off at her friend's house and then headed over to the police station. I asked for Robbie at the reception area and he came out to see me.

My first question to him was, "How's Erin? I left a message for her on the phone last night, but she hasn't got back to me. I've tried her again this morning and she's still not answering. Is everything alright with her?"

Robbie gave me one of his kind smiles and said, "She is absolutely fine. She's back at work this morning after having a good night's sleep. Now then, have you come here to check up on Erin or is there something else you want to talk to me about? I understand from my new friend, Sebastian Parker, that you've been interfering in his investigation. I told him he must have the wrong Karis Booth as the one I know would never do anything like that." He gave me a little chuckle and took me over to the side of the reception area.

I quickly told him about my visit to Cyril at the hospital. All joviality left Robbie's face.

He said, "This is a serious turn of events. It doesn't put Flynn Nithercott in a good light. I can't do anything with this information as I'm not dealing with the case. You'll have to speak to Seb about it immediately. Come on, I'll take you over to his office."

"Can't you tell him for me? He'll only think I'm interfering again."

"But you are interfering again. However, Cyril got in contact with you and volunteered this information. You did the right thing by coming here and letting us know. At least you weren't reckless enough to go zooming around to Flynn Nithercott's office to confront him face-to-face. That would have been a silly thing to do." He gave me a long look and continued, "You were going to go over there and confront him, weren't you? I can see it on your face."

I looked away from his accusing eyes and said, "I did consider it for a minute. Perhaps two minutes. But like a good citizen, I came here instead."

I followed Robbie through a set of doors and he pointed me in the direction of Seb's office. As I walked over there, I noticed there was a younger man in the office with Seb and the door was ajar. I couldn't help but overhear their conversation.

The younger man said, "Seeing as you grew up around here, you'll know your way around town. I was in the year below you at school. You won't remember me, but I remember you. You used to hang around with that weird girl." He clicked his fingers in the air. "She had a nickname. What was it now?"

Seb had his back to me and didn't see me standing at the door. He said, "Krazy Karis. That was her nickname."

The other man burst out laughing and said, "That's it! Krazy Karis. Didn't she think she was a psychic and could see into the future? What a freak!"

I took a sharp intake of breath. Seb turned his head and looked my way. Panic filled his face and he shot to his feet.

I turned around and walked quickly away, my eyes stinging. Hearing that awful nickname said with such derision brought a host of unwelcome memories crashing down on me.

I was outside and heading towards my car when I felt a hand on my shoulder. I turned around to find Seb standing there.

He held his hands out and said, "Karis, I'm so sorry about that. I wasn't making fun of you. Honest. I realise it didn't look that way to you. I keep putting my foot in it, don't I?"

I tried to smile, but my mouth refused to cooperate. I said tightly, "You were only answering a question. It's not your fault."

Seb ran a hand through his hair. "I shouldn't have told him the name. I should have said I didn't remember it. I'm a prize idiot. If I find out he uses that stupid nickname anywhere in my vicinity, I'll arrest him. I'll lock him away and put some gaffer tape over his mouth so he can never speak again. The same goes for anyone else who uses it."

I managed a small smile. "And what would you arrest people for exactly?"

"I don't know, I'd think of something. Karis, what are you doing here?"

"Before I tell you that, let me make it clear that I didn't go out seeking this new information. Cyril phoned me."

"Cyril? Who are you talking about?"

I quickly told him about Cyril and his so-called accident.

Seb's nostrils flared and he said, "This puts a different slant on the whole Carmel incident. I didn't know about Cyril's accident. I should have been told about it immediately. Accident or not, anything involving the Nithercott factory needs to be reported to me." He put his hands on my shoulders, looked me directly in the eyes and said, "I've no right to ask you this, not after what you've just overheard, but I'd like you to come with me to the factory when I confront Flynn Nithercott."

"Why?"

"Because I want to know if you experience anything while I'm interviewing him. Any psychic visions or premonitions. Any emotions you get from him. You were always good with this when we were little. You were great at working out when my mum was in the perfect mood for me to ask her for ice cream. Do you remember that?" He gave me a gentle smile. "Since we spoke last night, I've done nothing but recall all the good times we had together. You were such a good friend to me, and I was the worst friend in the world to you." He took his hands off my shoulders.

"Yes, you were the worst friend in the world. Possibly the universe. But I will come with you to speak to Flynn Nithercott. I'm sure he'll like to know how Cyril is getting on following his accident at the factory."

"Good," Seb said. "We'll go in my car."

He made to walk away.

I put my hands on my hips. "Don't you give me orders, Detective Chief Inspector Parker. I'm capable of driving to the factory on my own. And that's what I'm going to do."

Seb said, "Stop being so stubborn. I'm only offering you a lift."

"I'll meet you there," I said stubbornly.

I didn't give him another look as I got into my car and drove away. It gave me a small amount of pleasure to see Seb's confused look in my rear-view mirror. Serves him right. Trying to give me orders! The nerve of him. A couple of apologies doesn't make us best friends again.

Chapter 19

I took an instant dislike to Flynn Nithercott. It wasn't just because he'd pushed Cyril down the stairs: there was something inherently nasty about him. I could feel it the second we entered his office.

His office was located in between old Mr Nithercott's office and the staffroom. As we walked up the stairs towards his office, Seb told me the CCTV camera hadn't been aimed at Flynn's door on the day of Carmel's accident. That was convenient, I thought to myself.

Flynn Nithercott invited us to sit down. There was an impatient tone in his voice and a hardness in his eyes. He sat on the leather chair behind his desk, clasped his hands together and rested them on the desk. I noticed his knuckles were white. He looked like a wild animal who was getting ready to attack.

Flynn said, "What can I help you with, Detective Chief Inspector? I thought you had all the information you needed about Carmel's accident."

Seb hadn't introduced me when we'd entered, and Flynn didn't ask who I was. He'd given me a dismissive glance and then acted as if I wasn't there.

Seb began, "We're still making enquiries about Carmel Johnson's death."

"Why?" Flynn snapped. "It was an accident."

"That's for us to decide," Seb continued. "Mr Nithercott, how well did you know Carmel Johnson?"

A muscle twitched in Flynn's jaw. "What do you mean by that?"

"How was she as an employee?"

"She was okay. Reliable. Punctual. Got on well with the other members of staff. Why are you asking me this?"

Seb's tone was polite as he continued, "It's routine. How did you get on with her?"

Flynn glanced at some drawers underneath the desk. It was only a quick glance, but I noticed it.

Flynn said, "I didn't have much to do with her. She spent time with Grandad, though. He liked her for some reason. She bothered him constantly about her new ideas for our bread. He's such a soft touch that he actually put some of her ideas into practice." He gave a half shrug. "Some of the things she came up were decent enough. Sales have increased somewhat." He flashed a glance at the drawer again. "Is there anything else? I've got a lot of work on today."

Seb opened his palm in my direction. "This is Mrs Booth. She was contacted by a friend of hers earlier, Mr Cyril Simpson. Do you know Mr Simpson?"

"No. Should I?"

I had to press my lips tightly together to stop myself shouting at Flynn Nithercott. Seb had warned me to stay quiet throughout the interview and I was finding it a challenge to do so.

Seb said, "Mr Simpson came to see you yesterday. I checked with the young man on reception just now who's confirmed that. Mr Simpson is an elderly man and he spoke to you about your bread. He wasn't happy with the new recipe."

Flynn had the nerve to smirk. "That old fool. Yeah, I remember him now. Turned up and then gave me an earful of his complaints. I can't do with moaning customers. If they don't like our bread, they should stop buying it."

It was taking all my willpower not to say anything.

Seb's tone was now icy cold as he said, "Mr Simpson suffered an accident here yesterday, as you well know. He fell down the stairs. Apparently."

Flynn said, "Apparently? What are you getting at? I don't like the tone in your voice."

"Two similar accidents in a short period of time is more than a coincidence, Mr Nithercott. I've checked the stairs and there's nothing sticking up which would cause a person to trip. The carpet is of the anti-slip material, so that isn't at fault either."

"Now just a minute!" Flynn exploded.

As he did so, a vision came to me. Flynn's cry of outrage faded and I was oblivious to my surroundings as the image became clearer.

Carmel was in here. Her face was red with rage. She flung something at Flynn and stormed out of the office. Flynn picked the item up, opened a drawer at his side and flung the item in. He slammed the drawer shut.

The vision faded.

There was something important in that drawer at Flynn's side. I had to look inside. My vision showed me it wasn't locked, but I could hardly lean over and open it.

Flynn continued to shout at Seb, and Seb continued to remain professional.

Think! Think! What could I do?

My attention went to a jug of water on the table behind Flynn. There were some empty glasses next to the jug. There was an obvious move I could make, but would it work? It was a ridiculous move and Flynn would see right through it. But I had to do something.

Doing an impression of a gentle Victorian lady, I wafted my hand over my face and declared loudly, "My goodness! Isn't it hot in here? I feel all flushed. Would you mind if I had a glass of water?" I wafted my hand even more.

Flynn was too busy shouting at Seb to hear my request.

Nonetheless, I went on, "I am going to pass out with this heat. I need water!"

Seb shot me a worried look. "I'll get it for you."

I was on my feet in a flash. "No need. I'll get it!"

I went over to the jug and poured a full glass of water. My hands were shaking and a fair amount of water splashed onto the carpet. Keeping up my maiden-in-distress act, I moved closer to Flynn and announced, "I feel so weak and feeble. I can't hold on to this heavy glass."

Then, in the most melodramatic fashion, I threw the water over Flynn Nithercott.

He jumped to his feet, turned to me, and let out a very rude curse.

I put the glass down and said, "I'm so sorry! It was an accident. Let me dry you. Have you got any tissues? You must have. Let me look for them."

"Get out! Just get out!" Flynn shouted.

I ignored him, shoved him to one side and opened the desk at his side. There it was. That was what Carmel had thrown at Flynn.

I picked the item up and said, "Oh, this is a baby scan photo. Are you going to be a father, Mr Nithercott? How wonderful."

Flynn made a lunge for the photo, but I nimbly moved to one side and said, "This has got the mother's name on it. Carmel Johnson. I didn't know you were a couple."

There was a stunned silence.

Seb came over to my side and took the photo from me. He treated me to a long look which said, "I'll be talking to you later about your little performance, Mrs Booth."

Flynn held his hands up, "I can explain."

Seb said, "The facts are speaking for themselves. You've lied to me about your relationship with Carmel Johnson. What else have you been lying about, Mr Nithercott?"

A mask of rage came over Flynn's face. "Alright! We did have a fling, but I never wanted to be a father. I told Carmel that. It was her responsibility to make sure that never happened. She stormed in here and told me she was going to have our baby. I couldn't have that! I have a ten-year plan, and it doesn't involve babies. I told her the child was her problem and she should deal with it. She threatened to tell Grandad. I knew he'd force me to take responsibility." He paused and his shoulders dropped. "I didn't mean to kill her. I thought a fall down the steps would get rid of the baby."

I looked away from Flynn's face. I couldn't bear to look at him.

Seb started saying something about arresting Flynn Nithercott. I wasn't paying attention. All I could think about was Carmel and the bright future which had been taken away from her.

Chapter 20

After receiving a dressing-down from Seb, I left the factory and went over to Erin's Café. I found my sister behind the counter. A lone customer sat at a table in the corner.

Erin's face lit up as I entered. "Hey there! I've been trying to call you. Sorry I didn't return your messages from last night and this morning. Have you got time for a cuppa and a slice of chocolate fudge cake? I've made it fresh this morning."

"I'll say yes to both." I pulled a stool out in front of the counter and sat down. Erin came to sit at my side bringing tea and cake for us both.

The lone customer stood up, waved to Erin and left the café. I heard Erin's soft sigh.

I said to her, "What's going on with the café? Why is it so quiet?"

"Never mind about the café. It's just one of those seasonal things. I want to know what's happened this morning. I got through to Peggy and she told me about Cyril and his fall down the stairs. She said you were going to call in at the police station. I phoned Robbie and he told me you left the station with Sebastian Parker." She pulled a look of disgust. "I don't know how you can bear to be anywhere near that treacherous man."

I pulled my tea towards me. "He's not so bad."

Erin pinched my arm. "Who are you? Where's my sister gone? Are you a robot?"

I laughed. "Don't be silly. Did Peggy tell you about our visit last night from Seb?"

Erin shook her head. "No, she didn't." She pulled my slice of cake towards her. "You are not having a bite of this delectable cake until you tell me everything. And I mean everything. Don't leave one single detail out."

I proceeded to tell Erin every little detail. She made the occasional comment in between shovelling cake into her mouth. I was worried she was going to start on my cake soon.

When I'd finished, she shook her head and said, "I can't believe it. How could Flynn Nithercott do that? You hear about these things, but you don't expect them to happen so close to home. Poor Carmel. I don't understand why Flynn Nithercott pushed Cyril down the stairs, though. What had Cyril done to annoy him?"

"I think he was just in the wrong place at the wrong time. Flynn probably pushed him for the fun of it. That Flynn Nithercott is a nasty piece of work. I'm glad he's going to be locked up."

Erin looked at me for a moment before saying, "Are you glad you got involved? Are you glad you solved Carmel's murder?"

I flashed her a swift smile. "I'm glad I acted on my visions. I wouldn't say I solved her murder. I only wish I could have prevented it."

"You didn't know she was going to die. Don't be too hard on yourself. I bet DCI Sebastian Parker is glad you helped him. He wouldn't have got a confession from Flynn if you hadn't opened that drawer. He should be thankful to you."

"I think he was, in a grudgingly roundabout sort of way. He did tell me off, but it was a toned-down telling-off. I think he's truly sorry for what happened at high school. Anyway, I can't dwell on the past. What's done is done."

Erin's eyes narrowed. "I can dwell on the past. And when I see that excuse of a man, I'll tell him how I feel about him." She gave me a nod to confirm her words.

Then she did something which made my heart skip a beat. She rested her hands on her lower abdomen.

I jabbed an accusing figure at her. "You're pregnant!"

Erin smiled. "I am. I'm surprised it's taken you so long to pick up on that. Call yourself a psychic!"

I stared at her stomach which was ever so slightly rounded. I said, "I don't always pick up on things from close family members. Why didn't you tell me straight away?"

Her smile fell. "Robbie and I decided not to say anything until I was further along. Not after the last three times."

"Three times?" I looked into her eyes. "Erin, I know about two miscarriages. When you did you have a third one?"

Tears came to her eyes. "It was after Robbie had been shot. It must have been the shock. Karis, I think it will be different this time. I think this baby will survive. Can you feel anything? Can you look into my future? Please."

I put my hand on her stomach and concentrated. "I'm not picking up on any images. That doesn't mean anything. Like I said, my visions don't always work with close family members. Erin, is this why Robbie has been so protective of you?"

She nodded. "When I lost the third baby two years ago, I couldn't get pregnant again. Robbie used some of our savings so that we could try IVF. We only had enough money for one go. And this is it. I've had to take time off work because of the procedures. I've had to let staff go too because I don't have the money to pay them." She gave me a wobbly smile. "I think I'll have to sell the café. It's not making a profit for me because I can't put in the hours. But the sacrifices will be worth it when I hold my child in my arms."

The café door opened and a couple came in.

Erin stood up and said, "Customers. Great. Will you excuse me while I see to them?"

"Erin, is there anything I can do to help you with your pregnancy or work?"

"No, thank you. Robbie and I will manage. We always do." She walked over to the customers and showed them to a table.

The café around me faded and a vision came to me. It was bright and clear.

Erin was heavily pregnant. She was standing behind the counter and serving a customer. There was pain on her face.

The customer walked away.

Erin clutched her stomach and cried out in pain. Blood trickled down her legs.

The vision changed. I was now looking at a hospital bed.

Erin was in bed, her face as white as the sheets which covered her. Her stomach was smaller now. Robbie was holding her in his arms. They were both crying. There was no baby in sight.

The vision faded. I was back in the café and Erin was walking towards me.

"Karis, what's wrong?" she asked. "Are you crying? Why?"

I gave her the biggest smile I could manage. "These are happy tears. Listen, I've got to go. I've got those divorce papers to sort out. I'll call you later. Take good care of yourself. Why don't you close the café when those customers have gone? You could go home and get into bed. You have to take things easy."

She shook her head. "You're as bad as Robbie. I couldn't possibly stay in bed. I need to be doing something."

I gave her a hug before leaving the café. I knew my vision was an image of what could happen based on the present circumstances. I also knew that if the present circumstances were changed, then the future could change too.

I had an idea of what I could do. Well, more than one idea. There was no way I was going to let Erin and Robbie lose this baby. I would do everything I could to help them.

Chapter 21

It was two days later when I was ready to reveal my plan to Erin and Robbie. I was sitting in their living room with Peggy at my side. I had revealed everything to Peggy including my vision of Erin losing her baby. Peggy had agreed with my plans and had thrown herself into action with a surprising amount of energy.

Erin and Robbie were sitting on the sofa and holding hands. Peggy and I were in armchairs at their side.

Erin looked at me, over at Peggy and then back at me. She said, "You both look as if you're going to burst with some news. Either that or you're constipated. Don't keep us waiting any longer. Karis, you said you had something important to tell us. Come on; out with it."

I began. "I'm going to sell my house and move into Mum's. I've already put my house on the market."

"Really?" Erin asked. "Why have you done that? I thought you liked your house. If I had a house with two swimming pools, I'd never leave it."

Robbie pulled on Erin's hand and said, "I think we'll find out Karis' big plans quicker if you keep quiet. Save your questions for the end."

"Thanks, Robbie," I said. "I'm going to move into Mum's house because I love living there. The neighbours are wonderful."

"That's me," Peggy said cheerfully.

I smiled at her. "The other neighbours are okay too. There are too many awful memories associated with my house. I want a fresh start. The divorce is going through now. Gavin has put aside any claims to those investments. I think that was on the advice of his solicitor. Anyway, with one thing and another, I've got more money than I know what to do with." I shared a smile with Peggy. "That's not strictly true. I know what I am going to do with it. Erin, I'd like to invest in your café. The building next door is up for sale and I think the café should be extended."

"No. You can't do that," Erin argued. "You must spend the money on yourself. You deserve to spoil yourself."

I didn't want to play the guilt card, but I had to. I said, "Erin, I'll never stop feeling guilty over what happened to Robbie. But if you agreed to my plans, I know my guilt will be lessened. Don't you want me to feel better?"

Peggy joined in, "Yes, Erin, don't you want your sister to feel better? Stop being so selfish and let her help you."

Erin said, "You devious pair. You've got this all worked out, haven't you? May I ask what your plans are for my café once you've extended it?"

"First of all, I'm going to employ staff. Lots of staff. Erin, you can do the baking. No one else makes cakes like you do. But you won't be running around after customers. And you won't be on your feet all day. You can do your baking in the morning, and then that's it. You'll rest. You can stay at the café and talk to people, but no more being on your feet all day."

Robbie said, "I like the sound of that. Karis, you look as if you've got other plans for the café. Tell us."

"I thought we could run classes there. Perhaps during the day or after the café had closed. We'd have to get proper licences and insurance, but we can work those details out later."

"What sort of classes?" Erin asked.

Peggy said, "Anything and everything. We could start with craft classes. I know a lot about things like that. I don't like to blow my own trumpet, but I am good with my hands. I would love to teach others about crafts and things like that. I know the best places to get the cheapest materials. Erin, you could run some bakery classes too. I know I'd love that."

Erin gave her a slow nod. "Yes, I could do that."

I went on, "With the extended premises, we could cater to more people. You could have a quiet area with bookshelves so that people can read in peace. That area could be used for a book club too. And there could be a section for parents and toddlers. We could give the children a soft play area and the parents, or whoever is looking after the children, could have a cup of tea, a sit-down and a natter."

Erin nodded again. "I do like the sound of that. What else have you got up your sleeves?"

I reached into my handbag and produced a folder. I handed it to her. "As well as activities and clubs in the café, I thought Peggy and I could take our craft classes to those people who are housebound. We could take them some of your cake too. Free, of course."

"It would mean a lot to them," Peggy said. She paused for a few moments. "Loneliness is a terrible thing. People suffer in silence. If there's something we can do to help them, then we should."

Erin shared a look with Robbie. He gave her a gentle smile and a nod.

Erin declared, "Let's do this!"

I went over to her side and put my arm around her shoulder. "Thank you. There's one more thing. I want you to take it easy. You leave all the planning to me. I don't want you getting stressed. I mean it. You're carrying precious cargo."

"Okay, bossy boots. I can take it easy," Erin relented.

"Hallelujah!" Robbie cried out. "I've been telling her that for months."

"I'll put the kettle on," I said. "We've got lots to discuss."

I stood up and Peggy took my place on the sofa and began to give Erin more details about our plans.

I hadn't had any new visions about Erin yet. I hoped she'd take things easy now and give that baby the best chance of surviving that she could.

I had experienced other visions as I'd made my plans these last few days. They'd all involved Seb Parker. In each vision, he'd warned me to stay out of his murder investigation. The background changed in each vision. How many murder investigations was I going to get involved in? Would I be able to stop any of the murders?

I sighed as I filled the kettle. My psychic gift was a blessing and a curse, but if I could use it to help murder victims, then that's what I would do.

THE END

A FATAL WEDDING

Chapter 1

"It's no good, I have to go again," Erin said as she danced from foot to foot.

"But you've just been to the toilet," I said.

"I know. I can't help it. I'm nervous." She glanced towards the café door. "Are you sure this is a good idea? You've got better things to spend your divorce settlement on than me and this old café."

I smiled at her. "I want to spend my money on this old café. This is a good investment opportunity. I'm not doing this because I love you or anything silly like that." My smile increased. "In fact, I can barely bear to be in the same room with you most times. I rue the day Mum gave birth to you. I was having a great time being an only child until you turned up and ruined everything."

Erin gave me a mock glower. "It's a good job, I know you're joking, Karis." She winced and continued to move from side to side.

I gently turned her around and aimed her towards the ladies'. "Go on, before you have an accident. I've cleaned the floor once today, and I don't want to do it again."

"But what if our first clients arrive?"

"I'll deal with them." I pushed her gently again.

"But I want to be here to greet them. This is our very first craft event and I want to make sure it goes smoothly. I don't want them to leave us any bad reviews on that website you set up. Or on that Facebook page of ours."

I said, "If you don't go to the toilet, the first review could include you making a mess on the floor like an untrained puppy. Go!"

The café door opened and Erin spun around. She hissed, "They're here!"

A man in his early forties came in. His eyes twinkled and his face was full of warmth.

Erin sighed. "It's only Robbie." She turned away and rushed to the ladies'.

Robbie called after her, "That's a fine way to talk about your husband!" He chuckled and walked over to me. "Is she going to the lavvy again? She spends so much time in there that she might as well live there."

"I think part of it is due to nerves. It's not all down to her pregnancy." I hesitated. "Robbie, how's Erin's health? I've tried to get her to take it easy, but it's like talking to a brick wall. She just won't listen."

Worry flickered in Robbie's eyes. "I know she won't. But since you've put money into her café and employed staff to help her, she has taken it a fraction easier. Has she been bothering you again about seeing into the future? I keep telling her to leave you alone. I told her you can't switch your psychic ability on and off like a tap."

"She's been too nervous about tonight's event to ask me about that today." I saw the hope alight in his eyes and I knew he was hoping I'd had a vision about their much-wanted baby too. I gave him a gentle smile and said, "I haven't had any visions about the baby. None at all. Sorry."

That was a lie. I'd had a vision a few weeks ago when I'd been in the café with Erin. She'd had three miscarriages in the past, and her present pregnancy was as a result of a course of IVF. She and Robbie had used all their savings to pay for the treatment and couldn't afford another one if this pregnancy went wrong. My vision had shown Erin losing her baby. Despite the horrific vision, I knew it wasn't set in stone. I'd had enough visions in my life to know that future events could be changed if steps were taken in the present. And that's what I was doing. I was taking every step I could to prevent Erin from losing her baby. I'd invested in her café, employed more staff to help her, and I nagged her constantly to sit down. I didn't know what else I could do.

I realised Robbie was talking to me and tuned back into the present.

He said, "Yes, so I've checked the adjoining wall and there won't be any problems once it comes down. I've got a good idea of what it will cost. I know some building contractors who won't rip us off. Seeing as you're the owner of the building next door, do you want me to contact them on your behalf?"

It took me a moment to work out what he was talking about. I'd bought the empty building next to Erin's Café with the purpose of extending the café premises. Robbie was a man of many talents and he'd insisted on checking the property out to give him an idea of how much work needed doing. As well as being a police officer, Robbie was a dab hand at DIY.

I said to him, "That would be great, if you don't mind?

I don't want to burden you with it."

He gave me a gleeful smile. "I'm looking forward to it. I'm going to do as much work as I can on the building too. I love getting my hands dirty."

Erin chose that moment to return. "Robbie Terris! Stop talking dirty to my sister. I've only been gone two minutes."

He rushed over to Erin and put his arm around her waist. "I've only got dirty talk for you, my love. What are you doing on your feet? I brought that comfy chair from home and put it here for a reason. It's not an ornament."

Erin rolled her eyes. "I've been sitting down for most of the day. Karis has insisted on it. You know how bossy she is."

I was going to argue with her, but then I realised she was right. I was going to force her to rest until that baby was born. I lifted my chin and replied haughtily, "Indeed, I am very bossy. It's one of the perks of being your older sister. So, sit down and be quiet."

Erin sucked her breath in and placed a hand on her lower abdomen.

Immediately, Robbie and I asked, "Are you alright?"

She gave us a tight smile. "It's trapped wind if you must know. I don't see why I have to share every aspect of my pregnancy with you two nosy parkers." She looked towards the café door again. "Is everything ready? Do you think they'll enjoy it? Should we ask them for a review or leave it up to them? Robbie, are you still okay to take photos for the website? Don't take any if everything goes wrong. Karis, have you—"

Robbie softly placed one hand over Erin's mouth.

"Stop worrying. Everything is under control. Tonight is going to be an amazing success. They will love it. They will tell everyone they meet about the wonderful time they've had. There won't be one single problem. Nothing will go wrong."

She lowered his hand from her mouth and gave him a worried look. "You've cursed us now. Everything is going to go wrong." She looked at me. "Concentrate. Have one of your visions about tonight and what's going to happen. Force one out. Come on. You must be able to do that."

I shook my head at her. "I'm not having this conversation again. You know it doesn't work like that. Anyway, we don't need to worry about anything. We've got a secret weapon."

The café door opened and a group of chattering women entered. At the back of the group stood our secret weapon.

Chapter 2

Our secret weapon was an elderly woman called Peggy
Marshall. Peggy had been Mum's next door neighbour
ever since they'd moved into their homes as newly-
weds. Peggy didn't have children of her own and was
like a second mum to Erin and me.

Peggy bustled forward through the group of women
and began to unbutton her tartan coat. She cast a smile
our way and declared, "We're here! Sorry we're a bit
late. It's all Christine's fault. She hasn't left the house in
months and I think she'd forgotten where her door is!"
She followed this comment with a laugh.

A woman older than Peggy joined in with her laughter.
"You might be right about that, Peggy. I'm glad you
forced me to come tonight. I haven't been out past seven
o'clock at night for decades."

Peggy took her coat off and then reached out for
Christine's. "You'll have a smashing time tonight. Pass
me your coat and I'll hang it up. Then I'll show you
around the café. You lot are our guinea pigs tonight."

Erin gasped and dashed over to the group. "Peggy,
don't call them that. They're not guinea pigs. They are
our valued customers." She smiled at the group. "I'm
Erin Terris. Welcome to our first, official craft evening.
You can hang your coats up over there. They will be
perfectly safe. A craft table has been set out to the right,
as you can see." She opened her arm to the right.
"Customer facilities are to the left if you need them."
Her other arm moved in that direction. "Refreshments

will be provided shortly. Peggy has already informed us of any allergies. Free Wi-Fi is available if needed. If you have any questions at all, please don't hesitate to ask me."

"By heck!" Peggy declared. "There's no need to sound so formal, Erin. These aren't members of the royal family. It's only Christine and her family. You know them, and they know you."

Erin's smile wavered. "I know that. I'm trying to be professional."

A young woman stepped forward and said, "Thanks so much for doing this, Erin. You've saved my life! When Peggy told Auntie Christine about your craft evenings, it was me who asked about wedding favours. My supplier let me down at the last minute and I was dreading having to make them all myself. I haven't got a crafty bone in my body." She stopped talking and her hand flew to her mouth. "Oh! I didn't mean it in that way. I meant I'm not very good at crafts."

Erin laughed. "I know what you mean. Other than baking, I'm useless at crafty stuff too. That's why we've got Peggy. She's going to show you how to make those wedding favours." She looked over her shoulder at me. "Karis, come over here and introduce yourself. Robbie, put the kettle on and bring those sandwiches over."

Robbie clicked his heels together and saluted. "Yes, my love!"

Erin tutted and turned back to the group. "Ignore my husband. To be honest, we're all a bit nervous tonight. We were hoping to have the café extended and refurbished before we had our first official evening. But when Peggy told me about your wedding favour problem, Bryony, it seemed the ideal opportunity to have a craft event."

I came to Erin's side and gave the group a small smile.

Erin put her arm around my shoulder and continued, "It's all thanks to my lovely sister, Karis, that we're so organised tonight. And Peggy, of course. They've organised everything."

Peggy chuckled. "It's thanks to Karis that I'm not stuck at home in front of the telly. She's got me out of the house and feeling useful again. Karis, you know Christine, don't you? We used to go to bingo together years ago. Christine doesn't get out as often as she should on account of her dodgy knees."

Christine nodded in my direction. "Hello, Karis. Peggy's told me all about your recent news. You're looking well."

Peggy went on, "Karis, you know Bryony's mum, Alison. She's the proud mother of the bride."

Alison gave me a kind smile which matched her daughter's. She said, "I haven't seen you for years. I thought you'd moved away from town."

Peggy said, "She might as well have. Alison, I told you about Karis and that cheating husband of hers. She's just gone through a divorce, thank the Lord. That's why she's got money to invest in Erin's business. Didn't Christine tell you? I've told her everything."

Christine nodded. "I did tell her, Peggy. Every sordid detail."

I shook my head at Peggy. As much as I loved her, she did test my patience sometimes.

Peggy must have seen how annoyed I was because she said, "Karis, there's no need to look at me like that. I don't tell all and sundry your news, just close friends. Christine's known you and your family for years. She cares about you." A mischievous twinkle came into her eyes. "And when Christine's gone home, I'll tell you a tale or two about her and the wicked things she did in her youth."

Christine chuckled. "Oh, Peggy, you are a cheeky one."

Bryony gave me a kind smile and said, "I'm sorry to hear about your divorce, Mrs Booth. I hope you're not too upset."

I heard Peggy muttering something about me being ecstatic about getting rid of Gavin Booth, but I ignored her. I said to Bryony, "These things happen. Some people are not meant to be together. When are you getting married?"

"The day after tomorrow," she replied. She put a hand on her stomach. "I get butterflies every time I think about it. I can't wait to be married to Harry."

"Yeah, and I can't wait to have your bedroom." A woman younger than Bryony stepped out from behind Christine. I hadn't even noticed her come in with the group. She gave her surroundings a bored look, looked down at her phone and went on, "I don't know why I have to be here. Why are you bothering with wedding favours anyway? Who needs them?"

Bryony gave her a tight smile. "I do, Leila. And you're here because I need all the help I can get." She looked back at me. "Sorry about my sister. She doesn't want to be here."

Leila snapped, "There's no need to apologise for me. It's not my fault that silly cow destroyed—"

Christine interrupted her, "Leila! There won't be any cross words tonight. Your sister has been through enough. We're here tonight to support her. We're going to make the best wedding favours we can. And don't even think about going on that phone of yours. Do you understand me?"

Leila's gaze dropped. She put her phone in her pocket and mumbled, "Yes, Auntie Christine."

There was an uncomfortable silence and no one knew where to look.

Robbie came trundling over with a trolley. He said brightly, "Who wants a cup of tea?"

Peggy replied, "Everyone. Come on, let's have a sit-down. I've got the materials that we'll need set out on the table over there."

She took Christine gently by the elbow and steered her towards the long table at the side of the room. The other women followed her.

Erin moved over to Robbie and helped him with the hot drinks.

I couldn't move. A vision concerning Bryony was manifesting in my mind.

Chapter 3

In my vision, I saw Bryony's hands on the side of her face and tears streaming down her cheeks.

"Stop it!" she cried out. "You're ruining them! Stop it!"

She was standing in a bedroom and I could see stripy green wallpaper behind her and a single bed.

The view in my vision changed and I witnessed a hand ripping apart something made of pale-pink lace. Small items dropped to the wooden floor. I recognised them as sugared almonds just before a heel ground them into dust.

While this destruction was going on, Bryony pleaded, "Please, don't do this. Please!"

The vision vanished and I came back to the present moment. I didn't know whether I'd witnessed Bryony's past or if it was something that could happen in the near future. That was the problem with having psychic visions; they didn't come with instructions.

No one had noticed my trance-like state, not even the eagle-eyed Peggy. Bryony's group were busy settling themselves at the craft table, and Robbie and Erin were handing out hot drinks and delicate sandwiches.

I walked over to the table and said, "Erin, let me help with those sandwiches. I think Peggy's got a job for you."

After I'd seen that awful vision of Erin losing her baby, I'd confided in Peggy about it and she'd been as horrified as me. We agreed to do all we could to ensure

Erin took it easy. Of course, Erin didn't know about that vision, and I was never going to tell her about it.

Erin now gave me a suspicious look. "What does Peggy need my help with? It looks to me as if she's got everything under control."

Peggy picked up at the mention of her name and called over, "Erin, you need to sit next to me. I've got a special assignment for you." She pulled the chair out at her side. "Sit here. Hurry up. We need to get on."

Erin shot me another suspicious glance before handing the tray of sandwiches to me. She went over to Peggy and sat down.

Peggy pushed a pile of cut-out cardboard pieces towards her and said, "I'll tell you what to do with these in a minute." She clasped her hands together and looked around the table. "Right, are we ready to begin? Have you all got something to eat and drink?"

There were nods from the seated women. Robbie took his phone out and began to take photos.

Peggy continued, "As you know, Bryony's wedding is coming up and we need to make her wedding favours as a matter of urgency. Bryony, do you still need fifty of them?"

Bryony nodded. "Yes, please."

Her sister, Leila muttered, "I don't see the point of wedding favours. Why don't you give people something useful instead? Like a bottle of wine or something."

Christine shot Leila a warning glance and Leila slunk down in her chair.

Peggy raised a finger at Leila and said, "I've been reading up on wedding favours. Weddings are full of traditions and the favours are part of it. They're a thank-you gift from the bride and groom to their guests. The ones we're going to make tonight will include five wishes."

Leila butted in, "Five wishes? What do you mean? Do we have to give them five more gifts? I've already put twenty pounds in a card for them."

Peggy treated Leila to one of her hard looks and Leila sank further down in her seat. I was worried she was going to slither to the floor in a minute.

"We're going to put five wishes in the favours," Peggy continued. "The five wishes are represented by five sugared almonds. And what are those five wishes, you might ask?" She tilted her head as if expecting someone to ask that very question.

There was silence.

Then Robbie shouted, "Peggy Marshall, what are those five wishes? You must tell us immediately." He grinned at me.

Peggy tutted. "There's no need for sarcasm, Robbie. Those five wishes for the bride and groom are health, wealth, happiness, fertility and longevity." She smiled at Bryony. "I think that's a great start to your married life."

Bryony blushed and gave her a shy smile.

Peggy held up a bag of pastel-coloured objects. "These are the sugared almonds. Fresh almonds have a bittersweet taste and they are covered in sugar to make them sweeter for the happy couple. All marriages have their bittersweet moments, but these almonds are given in the hope of the marriage having more sweeter moments than bitter ones." She suddenly looked my way. "Karis, did you have sugared almonds at your wedding? I can't remember."

All eyes looked my way.

I shook my head. "Gavin didn't want them." I glanced at the floor.

"Aye," Peggy said. "That explains it. I remember throwing rice when you two came out of the town hall. Gavin gave me such a look when I did that. I think a grain of rice got lodged in his ear."

Erin grinned and said, "You should have thrown the whole packet at him. Or one of those boil-in-the-bag ones!"

I pursed my lips as an unnecessary amount of laughter came forth from Peggy and Erin.

Peggy put the bag of almonds down and picked up a circle of pale-pink lace. I stiffened. It looked like the same lace I'd seen in my vision.

"This is the colour we're going to use. I love this shade, Bryony," Peggy said with a smile. "I've got some pink silk to complement it. I've also managed to get some small flowers to make into a posy for the top of the favours."

"Thank you," Bryony said. "You've gone to so much trouble."

"It's been no trouble at all," Peggy told her. "I've enjoyed every minute. Here is a completed favour I made earlier." She held up a beautiful wedding favour and everyone aahed in delight.

I knew Peggy was good with her hands, but the delicate favour topped with tiny flowers and ribbons was exquisite and looked very professional.

"Wow, Peggy," Erin said. "I didn't know you were so talented."

"Hush," Peggy said with a small smile. "It's easy when

you know how. And that's what I'm going to show you now. Karis, help me pass the materials around."

I went over to Peggy and collected the items she passed to me. She whispered, "I want a word with you soon. You've had one of your vision things, haven't you?"

I raised my eyebrows in question.

"Don't look so surprised. I saw you gazing into the distance earlier. Is it something to do with our present company?"

I nodded.

She continued in a whisper, "We'll speak about it soon."

I handed the materials out and then watched in amazement as Peggy took over. She was clear in her instructions and showed the group what to do every step of the way. There were some mishaps, but Peggy soon sorted them out. I noticed more than one person sneaking a sugared almond into their mouths – Peggy included.

Erin was given the task of writing a thank-you message on the cardboard pieces. She had extremely neat handwriting and it was the perfect job for her. She was soon absorbed in her task.

As ordered by Erin, Robbie continued to take photos of the event.

Once everyone had got the hang of what they were doing, Peggy took me to one side and I told her about my vision.

I concluded, "The wedding favours I saw didn't look like the ones you've just made. They didn't have those flowers on the top. That vision came to me for a reason, but I don't know why."

Peggy nodded. "Leave it to me. I'll find out more. Bryony told me she'd been let down by her supplier, but it seems that wasn't the case." She looked towards the table which now looked like a production line. Everyone was chatting happily, and Robbie had joined in with the making of the wedding favours.

I said to Peggy, "I don't want to ruin the happy atmosphere."

"Me neither. I'll pick the right moment before I raise the subject. I think we've nearly finished making them all now." Her brow puckered. "How did I do? Was I clear enough? Could I have done anything differently? I've been practising for days making those favours. Do they look okay?"

"They're perfect, as are you. Shall we give our customers some cake now? Erin's been busy all afternoon and she's made far too much."

"That's an excellent idea."

Peggy walked over to the table and examined the finished products. Like a teacher talking to a child, she lavished praise on everyone. Even the surly Leila preened when Peggy told her what a marvellous job she'd done.

Peggy and I collected the finished items and carefully placed them in prepared boxes at the back of the café. Robbie and Erin brought out plates piled with a variety of cakes. I tried to help Erin but she gently pushed me out of the way and told me she could manage. So instead, I brought out the sparkling wine which had been chilling in the fridge.

Our customers were soon tucking into the cake and

enjoying the wine. Talk soon turned to weddings. Christine and Alison shared stories of their happy days. They'd worn the same wedding dress and it was going to be Bryony's turn to wear it next. Erin and Robbie added their story. My eyes filled with happy tears as I recalled that wonderful day. I didn't talk about my wedding, and thankfully, no one asked me to.

Peggy didn't need to raise the subject of Bryony's previous wedding favours because Leila did it for her. It was clear from Leila's slurred speech that she'd had more than her fair share of the wine.

Leila raised her glass and declared, "This is for you, Peggy. I've had a great night. I thought it was going to be rubbish, but it's been alright. I'm glad we've got the wedding favours sorted out. Bryony was doing my head in about them. It's all that Fay's fault. She's the one who destroyed those other wedding favours. She's crazy, that one."

Christine tried to shush Leila.

Leila wasn't having any of it. "That Fay should be locked up after what she did to you, Bryony. She's crazy. She's got that mad look in her eyes. The kind that killers have. You see it all the time on the telly. That crazy, mad look! Stay away from her, Bryony, before she finally snaps and kills you."

Christine whipped the glass from Leila's hand and snapped, "That's enough! We agreed not to talk about Fay."

"I'm just saying," Leila argued. "Bryony needs to be careful around Fay. She's dangerous."

I shared a concerned look with Peggy. I'd had a strong vision a few weeks ago about a young woman. She had been murdered soon after that vision. Was it going to happen again? Was there going to be another murder soon?

Chapter 4

Despite Leila's outburst, Christine managed to get the topic of conversation back to Bryony's wedding. But her voice seemed too cheerful, and Leila's words hung in the air like a bad smell.

Erin offered more cake, but no one took her up on her offer.

After another ten minutes of strained conversation, Christine stood up and announced, "I've had a wonderful evening, but I'm ready for my bed. Is anyone else ready to leave?"

People began to mutter about it being late and they got to their feet.

Peggy said, "Thank you all for coming. Bryony, the wedding favours are packed up and ready to go."

Erin added, "I'll put the leftover cake in boxes, too. There's no point in it going to waste."

Bryony came over to Peggy and gave her a smile. There was a worried look in her eyes which hadn't been there before. She said, "Thank you so much for organising this at such short notice. Not only have you helped us make the most beautiful wedding favours, you managed to get Auntie Christine out of her house. At last! I was getting concerned about her and the hours she spends in her house. I think this short outing has given her enough confidence to go to my wedding now. She wasn't sure she'd be brave enough to leave her house, but I think she'll be okay now."

Peggy replied, "The pleasure is all mine. I wish you

joy and happiness on your special day. If Christine plays silly beggars and refuses to leave her house on your wedding day, let me know and I'll sort her out."

Bryony laughed. "I might just do that. Thank you again."

We helped Bryony and her family take the boxes of wedding favours and cakes to their car which was parked outside the café. There were many calls of thanks as they got in and drove away.

Erin locked the café door and declared, "I don't know whether that was a success or a failure."

"Definitely a success," Robbie said. "The wedding favours were made, people were fed and everyone had a good chat. Someone got drunk and said the wrong thing. Sounds like the perfect night to me."

Erin shook her head at him. "You are strange. Help me clear up."

"No," I said too loudly. "I'm going to do the clearing up."

"And I'm going to help," Peggy announced. "Erin, you look exhausted. Go home and leave everything to Karis and me."

"But I—" Erin began to argue.

Robbie already had Erin's coat in his hands. He slipped it over her shoulders and said, "You've known Peggy long enough to know you shouldn't argue with her. I want some alone time with my beautiful wife. Come on, my sugared almond."

Erin opened her mouth to protest, but Robbie proceeded to steer her towards the back door. He called out, "Bye you two! Karis, I'll send you those photos for the website. Goodnight and sweet dreams!"

I could hear Erin grumbling as she was manoeuvred out of the building.

When she'd gone, Peggy said, "I wish your sister would take to her bed and rest. I can't stop worrying about her."

"Me neither. I keep hoping I'll have another vision about her. I've been hugging her in the hope of triggering one, but with no luck."

"You can't force it." She gave me a studied look. "Are you telling me the truth? Have you had another horrible vision which you haven't told me about?"

I shook my head. "I would have told you if I had."

"Make sure you do. I don't want you keeping things like that to yourself. Right, let's clear this mess up. I want this café looking spic and span."

We put some music on and got to work. We chatted as we cleared up, and Peggy gave me some ideas for other craft evenings we could have. Our talk turned to the one we'd just had and we tried to work out who this Fay person was.

Peggy said, "I recall Christine talking about her once, but it wasn't anything important. I think she's one of Bryony's friends. I can remember how annoyed Christine looked when she mentioned Fay's name. I wonder if it was Fay in your vision? She could have destroyed the other wedding favours. It certainly sounds that way. I'll call on Christine tomorrow and get to the bottom of this. If Fay is behind the destruction of those other favours, we don't want her getting her hands on the new ones."

I nodded and then took the empty wine glasses into the kitchen. As I was filling the sink with hot water, I had my second vision of the evening.

An awful picture came into my head, and I stared at the wall in front of me.

Peggy tapped me on the shoulder and said, "What have you seen now?"

I turned around. "I saw the wedding favours again. It was the ones we've just made. They were set out on tables. Someone was picking one up and carefully opening it. They sprayed something onto the almonds." My nose wrinkled. "I could smell something sour yet sweet. I don't know what it was. The person then tied the favour back up and moved on to the next one."

Peggy's eyebrows shot up. "Someone was tampering with my favours?"

I nodded. "I think they could have been poisoning them. We have to do something."

"We will do. We'll visit Christine first thing tomorrow. I won't let anyone spoil Bryony's day." She tapped her chin. "I think we should make some spare favours just in case. Erin's already written more cards than we need, so we've got plenty of those. Let's finish up here and go back to my house. I've got enough material to make fifty more favours. For all we know, the ones we've just made could have already been poisoned. It's not worth taking a chance with them."

We worked as quickly as we could and then headed over to Peggy's house. She lived in a semi-detached house down a quiet street. Mum's house was attached to Peggy's and I'd recently moved in there. Unfortunately, Mum was staying at the Wood Crest Care Home. She hadn't been herself since Dad died two years ago and the care home was the best place for her. Saying that, I'd give anything to have her back home.

As soon as we entered Peggy's house, she said, "I'll put the kettle on. It's going to be a long night."

I took in her tired face. "Peggy, I can make the favours. I saw how you made them. You've had a long day. Go to bed. I'll take everything round to Mum's and make them there."

"Nonsense! You'll only make a mess of it. I could do these with my eyes shut." She smiled. "I am a bit tired, but I can do this. I'll make a start and you make us a cuppa." She took herself over to the sofa, sat down and pulled a bag of supplies out from beneath the sofa. She looked back at me and added, "Get us some biscuits while you're in the kitchen. The chocolate ones. We need the energy."

I did as I was told. As I finished making the tea, I heard a knock at the front door. Peggy opened it and I made out the mumble of voices talking.

A minute later, Peggy came into the kitchen and said, "Karis, the police are here."

Chapter 5

"The police?" I repeated. "What's happened? Has there been a murder?"

"A murder? No. It's only your police friend, Seb. He's in the living room. I think you should tell him about your latest visions. Come on. Bring the tea and biscuits with you." She turned around and left the kitchen.

My police friend – Seb. Or to give him his full title: Detective Chief Inspector Sebastian Parker. He wasn't my friend. He had been when we were young. He'd been my best friend. He'd completely understood about my psychic abilities and had supported me. Until we went to high school, and then he'd given in to peer pressure and made fun of me, just like everyone else had done in that awful place. He'd returned to Leeds recently and our paths had crossed. He'd apologised sincerely for his past behaviour. I believed his apology was sincere, but for some reason, I was finding it hard to forgive him.

I put the cups and plate of biscuits on a tray and went into the living room. If Seb Parker thought I was going to offer him a drink, he could think again. I held my head high as I entered the living room and placed the tray on the table in front of Peggy. I sat at her side and gave a curt nod to the man who was perched on the end of the armchair. He was in casual attire and not his business suit.

Seb smiled warmly at me. The nerve of him, acting as if we were still friends. "Hi, Karis. How are you?"

"Fine," I answered stiffly.

"Good. Good." He clasped his hands together, then unclasped them and rested them on his knees. "Good."

Peggy said, "Seb's here with a bottle of his mum's elderberry wine for me. She makes a great wine. We can have a glass after our tea."

Seb said, "I've got a bottle for you too, Karis. Mum insisted on it. She said to let you know you can call in to see her anytime. She's pleased you've moved back into your mum's house."

Seb's parents lived at the end of the street and I'd always got along with them.

"Tell her thank you. I'll call in to see her soon," I replied. Good manners got the better of me. "Would you like a cup of tea or coffee? The kettle's just boiled."

"No, thanks. I've had three cups with Mum. You know what she's like for drinking tea." That smile again, as if we should be sharing memories.

Peggy looked at me and then at Seb. She said, "Karis has had some of her visions again. I think you need to know about them."

"Oh? Have you witnessed another accident?" Seb asked. "You know you can tell me about it."

I looked down at my knees. Why was I suddenly finding it hard to look at him?

Peggy continued, "It's obvious Karis hasn't forgiven you yet for your past behaviour. I don't blame her. I'm finding it hard to be civil to you, Sebastian Parker."

Seb sighed heavily and I looked at him. There was genuine remorse on his face. He held his hands out. "Look, Karis, I am sorry for what I did and said at high school. I can't apologise enough. And I'm sorry I didn't believe you immediately when you told me about that accident you'd foreseen. I should have known better."

Peggy sniffed in disapproval. "You mean the murder? Karis helped you solve that case. So did I. You would still be treating it as an accident if we hadn't helped you."

Seb smiled. "I appreciated your assistance; you know I did. Can we put my past behaviour in the past, please? Karis, tell me about your latest visions. What did you see?"

I managed to return his smile this time. I told him about our evening and he listened without taking his eyes off me.

He said, "Can you tell me more about the smell you experienced? Did it smell like arsenic? Cyanide? Bleach?"

I frowned. "I know what bleach smells like, but not the others. I don't make it a habit to go around sniffing dangerous things."

"Of course not." His eyes twinkled at me. "That was a silly question. If I brought some simulated smells to your house, would you have a sniff of them? It would help to narrow down whatever was sprayed on the almonds."

I was touched he was taking my visions so seriously. "Yes, I could do that."

Peggy said, "What do you mean by simulated smells? Do you have scratch and sniff books you use for training?"

He laughed. "Sort of." His gaze went to the pink circles of fabric on Peggy's lap. "Is that what you made the wedding favours out of?"

"It is," Peggy replied. "We're making some more in case they're needed." She sighed. "It's going to take us a while to make them."

"Would you like some help?" Seb offered. "I have surprisingly nimble fingers, so I've been told."

Peggy let out a snort of a laugh. "Who told you that? And what were you doing at the time? No, don't answer that. I don't want to know. Yes, I could do with some help. Move a bit closer and I'll show you how to make them. Karis, you move closer too. I might need you to make some."

Seb sat next to Peggy and watched intently as she showed him how to make a wedding favour. To his credit, he picked up the process straight away and soon produced a favour which was almost as good as Peggy's.

Peggy picked one of his hands up and examined it. "Hmm. Manly hands, yet nimble fingers. Unusual in a man. Karis, look at his hands."

I was looking, and Seb could feel me looking. I cleared my throat and passed Peggy my attempt at a wedding favour.

Peggy examined it and gave me a benevolent smile. "Not a bad attempt. Try again."

Seb let out a sound which sounded like a snigger. He said, "If Peggy was giving out gold stars, I'd get one, Karis. You wouldn't."

I smiled at his childish words. "Yeah? You'd get a gold star for being an idiot, Seb Parker. And one for being a know-it-all."

He sniggered again. "You're just jealous. Peggy, pass me some more material. This next favour will be even better."

He looked like the young boy who'd tried to beat me at the egg and spoon race on sports day. The competitive side of me was too tired to take any action and so I picked my cup of tea up, settled back on the sofa and let him get on with it.

Seb was so intent on his work that he didn't notice Peggy falling asleep. I did. I reached over and tapped one of his manly hands. I pointed at the snoozing pensioner.

Seb smiled, put his work down and whispered, "I'll carry her upstairs."

He gently lifted her and headed for the stairs. I heard Peggy mutter, "Watch where you put your hands, Detective Chief Inspector, or I'll put in a formal complaint."

Seb rolled his eyes at me and took Peggy upstairs. He returned a minute later and said, "I've put her on the bed and pulled a cover over her. How many more favours do we need to make?"

I made a quick calculation. "Forty-two. You don't have to do them all. I'll have a go."

"I don't mind. Anyway, you'll only make a pig's ear out of them." He gave me a mock smug look. "Not all of us are worthy of a gold star."

I shook my head at him. "Teacher's pet."

He laughed and sat next to me. "I wouldn't mind a cup of tea if the offer still stands."

"Of course. Help yourself to a biscuit. There's no point putting them back in the packet now."

"I'll wait till I've finished these. I'd hate to get chocolate on them." He turned his attention back to the pink material.

I made myself another drink as well as one for Seb. I took them through and placed them on the table. Seb had already completed another two favours.

In an effort to be more friendly, I said to him, "Tell me more about your life in London. How long did you work there? Where did you live?"

He proceeded to tell me about his life as a police officer in London. I'd forgotten how entertaining he could be when telling a tale, and how good he was at mimicking people. He had me laughing more than once.

All too soon, he'd finished all the wedding favours. He helped me to tidy up Peggy's room before we left. I locked Peggy's front door using the spare key I had.

I said to Seb as we walked down the path, "Thanks for making those favours."

"That's okay. I'll call around tomorrow with those simulated odours. Let me walk you home."

"It's only next door."

"I know it is, but it's late. You never know who's hiding in the shadows."

He suddenly shrieked and leapt to one side as a fox darted out from a bush and ran across our path.

"Some bodyguard you are!" I said with a smile. "Would you like me to walk you home now?"

"Don't be silly. I'm a big, strong man." He puffed his chest out. "With surprisingly nimble fingers. Goodnight, Karis. I'll see you tomorrow. Phone me if you have any more visions I should know about."

I could see his interest was genuine. I nodded. "I will do. Seb?"

"Yes?"

"Thanks for taking me seriously."

"You are more than welcome." He winked. "Let Peggy know I'll pick up my gold star tomorrow." He ambled away down the street.

I watched him for a while. Was I ready to fully forgive him yet? I honestly didn't know.

Chapter 6

I didn't have time to think about Seb because I fell into an exhausted sleep as soon as my head hit the pillow. The second I woke up the following morning, I had a horrific vision which made me break out into a sweat.

Once the vision had ended, I forced myself out of bed and stumbled to the bathroom. I jumped when I saw my pale face in the mirror. I would need an extra dollop of make-up today. I didn't have time for that now. I needed to tell Peggy what I'd seen as soon as possible. With trembling hands, I pulled yesterday's clothes on and stumbled out of the house.

Peggy opened her door to me before I reached it. She cried out, "Karis! What's happened? I saw you leaving your house. You look as white as a sheet." She reached out for my arm. "Your blouse is buttoned up wrong. Come inside and let me sort you out."

Peggy took me inside and into her neat, cosy kitchen. She sat me down and presented me with a hot cup of tea. She said, "Have my tea. You're shaking. Do you want me to sort your buttons out, or can you do it yourself?"

I gave her a small smile. "I'll do it myself." I took a sip of the hot liquid and immediately felt its reviving effects.

I opened my mouth to speak, but Peggy shook her head and said, "Take a few more sips. Do you want anything to eat? I'm just about to make some toast."

I shook my head, cradled the cup and drank some more. I could feel myself calming down.

Peggy sat next to me and looked at me with concern.

"Are you ready to talk?"

I put my cup down and nodded. "Peggy, as soon as I woke up, I had a vision about Bryony. She was in her wedding dress. There was blood on it." I paused and took a moment to steady my voice. "There was a lot of blood on it."

"Was she dead?"

"No. She was holding a knife."

Peggy nodded. "Okay. Give me all the details. Where was Bryony standing?"

"It looked like a hotel room. A big, fancy room. There was a suitcase on the bed behind her, but the clothes were strewn about the bed. I think I saw a passport on the bed too, but it was damaged. I saw Bryony standing there with a long knife in her hands. It was like I was in the room and standing a few feet away from her. She wasn't the only one in the room."

"Who else did you see?"

"I saw her Auntie Christine. Her face was pale. Her eyes were wide with horror and she was staring at Bryony. Christine said, "Bryony, what have you done?" Then she looked down at something on the carpet. Or rather, someone on the carpet."

Peggy gasped. "Who was it?"

"I couldn't make it out. It looked like a pile of clothes, but there was a pool of blood beneath the clothes. It must have been a person. I couldn't see anything else clearly." I lowered my head. "The blood was so red. There was so much of it. I could feel the horror in the room as if I was there."

Peggy patted my hand. "You poor love. Do you remember anything else? Anything at all?"

I shook my head. "I couldn't take my eyes off the blood. It was such a stark contrast to the white of Bryony's dress. Peggy, I think this means Bryony is going to kill someone. And on her wedding day too."

She patted my arm again. "It does look that way. As painful as it was, you had this vision for a good reason. We'll have to somehow stop this event from taking place. Bryony is getting married tomorrow, so we've got time to do something." She frowned. "This possible murder could be related to the other visions you've had. Maybe the person who destroyed the original favours is the murder victim. I'm assuming it's the same person who was going to poison the newer favours. Perhaps Bryony killed whoever it is in self-defence."

"That is possible. I think I should phone Seb and let him know."

"Oh?"

"He asked me to keep him informed of any other visions I might experience."

"Oh?" Peggy said again. "Seb and not Robbie? Are you sure about that? From the icy looks you were giving Seb last night, I thought he'd be the last one you'd phone."

I gave her a half-shrug. "We had a good chat when you went to bed. And he did believe everything I told him about my visions."

"Hmm. Just be careful with him, Karis. You can be too trusting sometimes. Look at how long you put up with that useless husband of yours. If Seb so much as passes a snide comment or a sly look about your psychic abilities, you let me know. I won't have him hurting your feelings again. I just won't." She cast a dark look at the wall in front of her as if picturing Seb Parker there. Her dark look cleared. "He did make a good job of those wedding favours, though."

"He did. Nimble fingers." I smiled as I remembered his last comments before he walked away. "I haven't brought my phone with me. I'll ring him when I go home. I'm not sure what he'll be able to do."

Peggy stood up. "Let's have some toast and then we'll make a plan of action."

"I don't think I can manage anything to eat."

"You can, and you will. I insist. I'll make us another cuppa. We'll have to keep our strength up if we're going to prevent a murder."

She turned away from me and began to busy herself with the toast and tea. I offered to help but she turned me down. As I watched her preparing our food and humming to herself, a light feeling of peace settled on me. It was nice to be taken care of once in a while.

Once our food was ready, Peggy refused to speak until we'd eaten the buttery toast. She said, "I can't think on an empty stomach, and I can't listen very well on one too."

When we'd finished eating, I said, "We should visit Christine first and find out more about Fay. It's obvious something has gone on with her and Bryony. Well, you heard what was said last night when her name came up."

"Or more importantly, what wasn't said. Yes, we'll call on Christine first. I've got some books for her anyway. She loves historical romances and I saw some on offer at the market. I've got some spare wool for her too. She likes to do a bit of crocheting. It helps her arthritis to keep her fingers moving."

I studied Peggy for a moment. "You do a lot to help other people. You've always been like that. You're an amazing woman, Peggy Marshall."

She flapped a hand at me. "It's too early for soppy comments like that. I do what I can. Why wouldn't I? We're all here to help each other. Anyway, since my Jeff passed away, I like to keep busy." She broke into a smile. "Since you escaped from your loveless marriage and came back to the land of the living, I've been busier than ever. With this new craft business at the café and these murder investigations, I'm busier than ever."

"I don't want to burden you. Let me know if things get too much for you."

Peggy lifted her arm and attempted to flex a muscle. "I'm made of stern stuff." She lowered her arm. "Right, it's time for action. Go home, phone that policeman, and then have a shower. Karis, do you know you're wearing yesterday's clothes?"

I nodded. "I was in a rush to get here."

"Fair enough. But put something fresh on. We need to look our best if we're going to have a day of trying to find a possible murder victim." She put her head to one side. "A bit of make-up wouldn't go amiss either. Off you go, then. I'll see you back here in thirty minutes."

I stood up and almost felt like saluting her. I was glad to have Peggy in my life. If I could clone her, I'd make sure everyone could have a Peggy in their lives too.

Just as I had that lovely thought, Peggy said to me, "Give your hair a good wash, Karis. And don't forget to use deodorant. You're a bit ripe this morning."

Chapter 7

Peggy gave me an approving look as she let herself into my car thirty minutes later. She sniffed and said, "I like that perfume you're wearing. Your mum used to wear that too. Did you speak to the policeman?"

"He didn't answer, so I left him a message. I asked him to phone me as soon as possible. I didn't want to go into details about my vision over the phone. I've spoken to Erin this morning too. She told me Bryony's posted a lovely review on our new website. Robbie sent me some photos of the event last night, but I haven't had time to put them on the website yet." I sighed.

"You can't do everything all at once," Peggy said. "How's Erin feeling this morning?"

"She sounded cheerful. She complained again about the new staff and how they won't let her stay on her feet for too long."

"Good. I'm glad they're doing that." Peggy patted the fabric bag on her knee. "I've got that wool and those books for Christine. I've phoned her to let her know we're coming over. She's wary about answering the door to anyone. She likes to know when visitors are calling. Karis, she knows about your psychic stuff. She understands. We could mention the damaged wedding favours, but I think we should keep the possible murder to ourselves. We don't want to upset her."

"I agree."

Peggy gave me Christine's address and we headed in that direction. On the way, Peggy asked me what Bryony had written in her review. I repeated it and smiled to myself when I saw Peggy's head lift with pride.

"She said that about me?" Peggy asked. "She said I was an expert? And professional? And a great teacher? She wrote that on the website for the whole world to see?"

"She did. And she was right about you. We'll have to start planning the next craft evening soon. I know we planned to wait until the café had been extended, but if we keep the numbers small, we could manage with the café as it is."

Peggy nodded. "I'll put my thinking cap on. Turn left here. Park in front of her house so she can see us."

I parked outside the bungalow and saw a net curtain being pulled back. A face peered out at us.

Peggy shouted, "Christine! It's us! Karis and Peggy! We're getting out of the car now!"

"She can't hear you." I rubbed my ear. "On second thoughts, the whole street might have heard you just then."

Christine had the door open for us as we walked down the concrete driveway. She beamed. "Two visitors in one day. Come in, come in! I've put the kettle on."

We entered the house and I was immediately struck by the amount of memorabilia everywhere. I was standing in the hallway and could see into the living room at our side. Ornaments lined every surface. Framed photos were on all the walls with barely a gap between them. A cat wound its tail around my legs and another cat walked over to the gas fire and settled down in front of it.

Christine laughed at my expression. "I know I've got too many items in here, but I like to have my memories where I can see them. I don't know if Peggy's told you, but I was never blessed with children. Alison's like a daughter to me, and Bryony and Leila are the closest I've got to grandchildren."

I frowned. "Bryony called you Auntie last night. I thought you were Alison's sister."

Christine chuckled. "I'm flattered that you think I look so young. No, I'm the sister of Alison's mum, Winnie. Winnie died when Alison was young, so I took her in and brought her up. Officially, I'm a great-aunt or something to Bryony and Leila, but I prefer the simpler version. Would you like a tea?"

Peggy said, "I'll make it. Christine, take Karis into the living room and show her your photos. I've got some more books for you, and some wool. I'll put them in your kitchen cupboard."

Christine clasped her hands together. "You are thoughtful, Peggy. How much do I owe you?"

"Nothing. Tea for you too?"

Christine nodded. Peggy strode down the hallway, and Christine led me into the living room.

She picked a ginger cat off the sofa and said, "Take a seat. You might have a feline visitor in a minute. I hope you don't mind cats."

I sat down. "I don't mind them at all." I looked at the photos on the wall.

Christine took a seat in the chair at my side and put the cat on her knee. "I love my photos. So many treasured moments. Look at my girls. So beautiful. I sit here and think about how lucky I am to have them in my life. You must feel the same about your daughter. It's Lorrie, isn't it? How old is she now?"

"She's twenty-three. Yes, I have many photos of her. I've got some on my phone." I took my phone out and showed an image of my beautiful daughter to Christine.

Christine smiled, stroked the ginger cat and looked at her framed photos again. "Aren't these phones wonderful? You can take all your photos with you wherever you go. I don't need to do that, though. I don't leave the house often. Not anymore. I feel safe here. I've got my memories. And my family comes to see me all the time." She turned her face to me. "I so enjoyed last night. I wasn't sure I was going to make it. I don't like leaving my home, certainly not at night. But Peggy insisted. She said Bryony would love me to be there. I had a wonderful time. I'm ready now for the wedding. It's going to be a marvellous day."

The image of Bryony and Christine came into my mind. I couldn't let that happen to this lovely woman.

Peggy came bustling into the room and placed a tray on the table at the side. She passed a cup of tea to me and one to Christine.

"Thank you," Christine said. "I was just telling Karis how much I loved last night. You were right to make me go, Peggy. I can't wait for the wedding day now. It's going to be a day to remember. I've already got my camera in my bag."

Peggy shared a quick look with me and then sat at my side. Her tone was very casual as she said, "What did you do with those wedding favours we made? Has Bryony got them?"

"No, they're in my spare room. I said I'd keep them here and we can take them to the hotel tomorrow."

Peggy went on, "Don't be alarmed, but Karis had a

vision about them getting damaged." She hesitated. "Someone dropped them. It wasn't anyone she recognised. Would you mind keeping an extra careful eye on them? Just in case?"

"Oh, yes, of course. I won't let anyone else touch them. Thanks for letting me know. It must be wonderful to have premonitions, Karis."

I managed to smile. "Most of the time. I don't want those favours to be ruined. Will you make sure they're safe, please?"

"I will. I'll make sure I'm right next to them when they go to the hotel. Peggy, did I tell you Bryony's getting married at The Oak Tree Hotel? They've booked the honeymoon suite too. Bryony showed me some photos of it on her phone. It's a lovely room."

I looked down at my cup. I suspected I'd already seen the room in my vision.

Peggy said, "Yes, you did tell me where the wedding was taking place. How many people are going?"

"Not that many. I think Bryony was getting the final numbers today as a few people can't make it now. Oh! I've got the wedding dress hung up in my spare room. Would you like to see it? It was Winnie's wedding dress, then mine, and then Alison's."

I stiffened. Peggy must have picked up on my body language because she said, "Maybe later. Let's have our tea first. Christine, I hope you don't mind me bringing this up, but what was all that commotion about Fay last night? I know you've talked about her before, but I can't recall what you said."

Christine pulled a look of disgust. "Fay Spencer. She was at school with Bryony. I never liked her. There's something devious about her. It's like she's always calculating her next move. She was practically a leech on our Bryony at school. The other children didn't like Fay because she was always telling tales on them. Not only that, she used to steal from them too. I don't know why she did that because she never went short of anything. That didn't stop her from pinching money and food out of bags. Whenever someone discovered what she'd done, Fay would blame someone else. Our Bryony was the only one who showed her any kindness. Fay latched onto her and would barely let her out of her sight. She spent more time at Bryony's house than her own. Every time Bryony had something new in her life, be it clothes, jewellery, a new hairstyle, Fay would want it too." She took a sip of her tea and I could see how upset she was.

Peggy noticed too but carried on. "Did they remain friends after school?"

Christine nodded. "Bryony couldn't get rid of her. Fay followed her to high school and university. You know Bryony works at the local school? She teaches the younger ones. Fay tried to get a job there, but she wasn't successful. She does volunteer work instead. The teachers don't like her. I know the children don't. But they can't turn volunteers away."

"Did Fay have anything to do with the original batch of wedding favours?" Peggy asked. "Bryony said she'd been let down by her supplier. Was Fay involved somehow?"

Christine gave her a small smile. "You hit the nail on the head there. Fay did make a batch of wedding favours. She insisted. From what Alison's told me, Fay

147

wasn't happy about Bryony getting married. She didn't want Bryony spending less time with her. They had arguments about it. Bryony put her foot down and told Fay she was getting married to Harry no matter what Fay said. From all accounts, Fay relented and said she'd make the wedding favours as her way of saying sorry. But a few days ago, Bryony came here in tears and said Fay destroyed the batch she'd made."

Peggy asked, "Did she say why?"

Christine shook her head. "I didn't press her. She was too upset. She said she'd told Fay she was no longer invited to the wedding. Good riddance is what I say."

Peggy nodded. "Fay Spencer? Is she Linda Spencer's daughter? Linda who works at the big library on Tuesdays, Wednesdays and Thursdays?"

"That's her. They still live on Mortimer Street. Have done for years. Why are you asking?"

"No reason," Peggy said. She was a convincing liar.

Chapter 8

A short while later, we parked outside the terraced house where Fay Spencer lived.

I looked at the house and said, "Are you sure this is a good idea? Fay might not be in."

"But her mum might. She works shorter hours on a Tuesday since she started having problems with her back. That's what John at the post office told me a few weeks ago. Linda doesn't go into work until after lunch."

I shook my head at Peggy. "Not much gets past you, does it? If Fay's mum is in, what are we going to say to her?"

Peggy tapped the side of her nose. "Leave that to me. I'll suss out her daughter's frame of mind in a discreet manner. We'll find out if Fay's the type to poison wedding favours with no regard for the people she might hurt. I'm not sure how I'm going to work that into a conversation, but I'll think of something."

Peggy didn't need to do any sussing out. It was Fay who answered the door. We soon worked out her identity when Peggy asked, "I'm looking for Linda. You must be Fay. Is that right?"

Fay gave her a suspicious look as she hung on to the half-opened door. "Yeah, I'm Fay. What do you want with Mum? She's out shopping."

Peggy smiled at her. "I'll catch up with her later. I've just heard about Bryony's wedding. It's tomorrow, isn't it? You must be excited. Haven't you been best friends for years? That's what her Auntie Christine told me. She said you two are as thick as thieves."

The side of Fay's mouth moved upwards. "Yeah, that's us. Best friends forever. We do everything together. No one knows Bryony like I do. But I won't be there at the wedding."

"Oh?" Peggy's hands flew to her chest. "Really? That is a surprise. Why not?"

Fay opened the door wider. "It's complicated."

"Do you want to talk about it?" Peggy offered as she lowered her hands. "Your loyal friendship with Bryony fascinates me. According to Christine, Bryony has been your friend for years and years. You must have something special together."

Fay's face lit up. "We have. You can come in and wait for Mum. She might be a while. Come in and I'll tell you why I'm not going to the wedding."

We followed Fay into the living room and sat down. I noticed the framed photos of a young Fay lined up on the mantelpiece. She was scowling in each image.

Fay turned her full attention on us, and I was momentarily taken aback by how bright and wide her eyes were. As she began to talk, her smile seemed too wide and eager.

She said, "I'm not going to the wedding because I know Bryony doesn't love Harry. She's only pretending to love him because she feels sorry for him. He kept pestering her to get engaged. I told her to say yes so that we could have a wedding. We like going to weddings. I said she could get a divorce afterwards. I told her I'd help her organise the wedding. I told her where to get her dress and which one to buy." She rolled her eyes.

"But Bryony's mum said she had to wear that old wedding dress which she'd worn. What a stupid idea! Her mum doesn't understand her, not like I do." She gave us a manic smile. "I know what's best for Bryony. I always have done."

Peggy gave her an understanding nod. "When did you decide you weren't going to the wedding?"

"A few days ago. I couldn't lie to myself anymore. I know I should support Bryony, but I told her I couldn't pretend this wedding was real a minute longer. She's stupid. She said she loves Harry now, but she doesn't. I know she doesn't. She'll soon realise she's made a mistake by marrying Harry, and she'll come running back to me. It'll take me a while to forgive her. But she is my best friend, so I will forgive her one day."

"That's very kind of you," Peggy said. "Did you make some wedding favours for Bryony?"

Fay's eyes glittered with something that looked like malice. "I did. She forced me to. Then she destroyed them. She was mad at me for not going to her wedding and said she couldn't bear to look at them. She tore them to pieces right in the middle of my bedroom. It took me weeks to make them."

I knew she was lying. Apart from it being written on her face, I knew it hadn't been Bryony who'd destroyed those favours. In the hope of picking up on my earlier vision again, I said, "Could I use your bathroom, please?"

"Yeah. It's upstairs on the left."

I shot Peggy a look as I left. I needed her to keep Fay engaged in conversation down here.

Peggy said to Fay, "Tell me more about your

friendship with Bryony. It sounds like you've had the patience of a saint in putting up with her."

I didn't hear Fay's response as I headed up the steps. I soon located her bedroom. I recognised it from the stripy green wallpaper and the wooden floor which I'd seen in my vision. There was a single bed in the room along with a wardrobe and a set of drawers. Photographs of Bryony and Fay were stuck on the walls. Bryony's smile looked forced.

I closed my eyes and recalled my past vision. It didn't come to me, but a new one did. I saw Bryony standing in this spot. Fay was facing her.

Bryony's cheeks were wet with tears. She pleaded, "Stop telling lies about Harry. You know he hasn't been messing around with anyone. You know that."

Fay said, "He might not have messed you around yet, but he will. I can tell. I've seen how he looks at me. He fancies me. Your marriage won't last. You'll see I'm right. He doesn't love you."

"He does love me. And I love him. You have to accept that I'm going to marry him. Please."

"I won't accept it!" Fay suddenly yelled. "Why did he have to come along and spoil everything? You've never got time for me now! Never! It's not fair. I was your friend before he was. Don't marry him! He's not right for you. No one is right for you! We don't need anyone else. We've got each other."

Tears rolled down Bryony's cheeks. "I don't want to talk about this again. You won't see sense, Fay. Those rumours you're spreading have upset Harry. You know he hasn't been unfaithful. Those rumours have upset me too. This can't go on. Things have to change."

"Nothing needs to change! Nothing! I won't let you marry him. I won't let you marry anyone!" Fay's hands curled into fists at her side.

Bryony wiped her tears away. "You can't stop me. The wedding is going ahead. I think it's best if you didn't come. I don't want any trouble."

Fay snarled and advanced on Bryony. "I have to be there. I'm your best friend."

Bryony gave a small shake of her head. "You haven't been a good friend to me for years. It's taken me a while to see that. You're too controlling. We need some time apart while I think about things. I'm asking you to keep away from the wedding."

Fay let out a howl of anger and turned towards the bed behind her. She picked up an item which I recognised as a wedding favour. She began to rip it apart.

Just like in my earlier vision, Bryony cried out, "Stop it! You're ruining them! Stop it!"

"I made them, and I can ruin them," Fay hissed. She dropped it on the floor and then ground her heel into the almonds which had tumbled out. "I'm going to ruin your wedding too. I won't let you marry that stupid man. You'll thank me for it one day. You'll see I'm right and you'll come running back to me begging to be my friend again."

The vision faded. I collapsed onto the bed, reeling from the hate in Fay's voice. She was going to poison those new wedding favours. I knew that for certain now. Was she intending to kill Harry? Or everyone at the wedding? I wasn't sure how this new information linked up with the image of Bryony in her blood-spattered wedding dress, but I had to do something to stop Fay getting near those favours.

Chapter 9

"Unhinged," Peggy announced as we drove away from Fay's house. "That's the word I'd use to describe Fay Spencer. Unhinged. She looks normal enough at first sight, but as soon as you start talking to her, it's clear she's got an unnatural view of the world. Did you hear how she was talking about Bryony? As if she owned her! She wants to control every aspect of Bryony's life. I wouldn't want someone like Fay at my wedding, that's for sure."

I nodded. "I had another vision in Fay's bedroom." I gave Peggy the details.

When I'd finished, Peggy tutted and said, "Poor Bryony. How nasty of Fay to say those things to her, and then to destroy those wedding favours. Fay is an evil individual. I wonder if she's planning on turning up to the wedding? It sounds more and more like she's going to be the one to sabotage those new favours. We should let Christine know about this." She paused. "But that would only upset her. We could tell Alison instead. But she'd be upset too. I wouldn't want them to be on edge throughout Bryony's special day. No, we'll leave Christine with that white lie about the favours being damaged by someone dropping them."

"You know my visions don't always come true. They're just a possibility of what might occur based on the present circumstances. Our visit might have caused Fay to rethink her plans of going to the wedding."

"Or we could have just added fuel to the fire of her

hate and made her more determined to go." We pulled up outside Peggy's house and she craned her neck. "Who's that parked on your mum's drive? Are you expecting anyone?"

"No." I peered closer at the dark car. "Oh, I think that car belongs to Seb."

"The cheek of him parking in the drive! He should park on the road like everyone else. He's got a nerve." Peggy got out of my car and bustled over to Seb's car. I saw her rapping on the driver's window.

When I went over to Seb, I saw spots of colour on his cheeks. Peggy must have given him a huge piece of her mind.

He muttered, "I'm sorry. I just thought I'd wait here for Karis." He looked my way and relief washed over his face. "Ah! There you are. I got your message and thought I'd come straight round. I've been here ten minutes. I left you a message to say I was here. Do you want to park here? Am I in your way? I'll move."

I shook my head. "It's fine. I think Peggy and I will be going out again soon."

"Oh? Has it got anything to do with Bryony's wedding and your visions?"

"None of your business," Peggy snapped. She winced. "I need to pay a visit to the little girls' room. Stay right where you are, Sebastian Parker. I haven't finished with you yet." Her voice softened. "Thank you for making those favours. You've done a marvellous job." She scurried away and towards her house.

Seb shook his head. "She always makes me feel like a naughty young boy. I've worked in London for years. I've dealt with hardened criminals. But one hard look from Peggy and I turn into a quivering wreck."

I smiled. "She has that effect on many people. Are you here in an official capacity?"

"I am." Seb opened the car door and got out. He was wearing a smart suit and looked very professional. He leant against his car and said, "Have you had another vision? Is that why you phoned me?"

I nodded. "I've had a couple since I spoke to you last." I told him about the first one concerning Bryony in her wedding dress. Then I informed him of the latest one at Fay's house.

Seb shook his head slowly. "I'm not sure what to do with this information."

"Me neither," I admitted. "Peggy thinks we should warn Bryony's family about the possible poisoning. But the last thing you need on your wedding day is to be on the lookout for something like that. We might have to sneak into the function room at the hotel and replace the favours with the ones you made. But I'm not sure how we'd do that. I don't like the idea of sneaking about."

Peggy came rushing up the driveway. "There's no need to do any sneaking about! Christine has just left me a message on my answerphone. There are some spare places at the wedding and she'd like us to go. We can keep an eye on things. If Fay turns up, we can throw her straight back out. And we'll guard those wedding favours with our lives."

I let out a sigh of relief. "That would solve one problem. But what about Bryony and the knife? Can we prevent that from happening?"

Peggy said, "We could do with some extra help. Christine said we could each bring a guest if we wanted to." She gave Seb a pointed look. "How about you?"

Seb straightened up and ran his hand down his tie. He smiled at me and said, "I'd be delighted to be your guest."

Peggy whacked him on the arm. "I didn't mean for you to be Karis' guest! I meant for you to be mine. Karis doesn't want you hanging around her all day. She'll be too busy looking out for Fay and getting ready for any more visions she might have. No, I need you at my side. If we see Fay, you can tackle her and bring her down. I'd do it but I don't want to hurt myself."

"Oh. Right. Yes. Of course." Seb cleared his throat. "I can do that. Be your guest, I mean. Not tackle Fay to the ground. If she turns up to the wedding, I can question her and perhaps escort her from the premises if that's what the family wants."

Peggy shook her head at him. "That'll have to do. Did you bring those smelly things for Karis to sniff? You said you were going to sort something out."

"Yes, I've got them in the car." He moved towards the door.

"She doesn't need to sniff them now," Peggy pointed out. "You can do that tomorrow at the wedding. If there's anything dodgy on those almonds, I'd rather you were affected and not Karis."

"Oh. Right. Yes. Of course." Seb repeated his earlier words. I felt a twinge of sympathy for him.

Peggy clasped her hands together. "Seb, the wedding starts at ten. It's at The Oak Tree Hotel. Dress smartly. Pick us up at nine. That gives us plenty of time to snoop around the hotel. We'll inspect the favours and then look out for Fay." She nodded as if the matter was solved.

She turned to me. "I'll need a wedding outfit. And some shoes. I've got a dress which would be suitable, but it's seen better days. Will you come to Leeds with me and help me choose something, please? I could do with a second opinion. Jeff used to do that with me. He had good taste when it came to clothes."

I smiled. "Of course. I might get something for myself too. We'll have to get Bryony and Harry a wedding present too."

Peggy nodded. "I've got some vouchers in the house. I'll go and get them." She looked back at Seb. "You can look into the background of Fay Spencer. She lives on Mortimer Street with her mum, Linda. Find out if she's got a criminal background. Don't be late picking us up tomorrow." She gave him a sharp nod and then headed back to her house.

Seb's face was a picture of bewilderment. He said, "What just happened?"

"You've been Peggyied. That's my official word for the effect Peggy has on people. Seb, you don't have to go to the wedding. I'll think of an excuse for you."

He looked into my eyes for a second too long. "I'd like to be there. Between us, we might prevent Bryony from doing whatever it is you saw in your vision."

"Do you believe my visions are real? Or are you trying to make up for the past?"

"I do believe in them. I always have." Again, his look lingered.

I felt my cheeks growing warm and looked away from him. Too loudly, I said, "Okay then! See you tomorrow! Bye for now! Cheerio!" I turned around and began to walk away. I groaned inwardly. I'd never said cheerio in my life before.

There was laughter in Seb's voice as he called out, "Toodle-pip!"

Chapter 10

Despite having a busy day shopping with Peggy, I didn't sleep well that night. I couldn't get the image of Bryony in her ruined wedding dress out of my mind. Peggy and I were certain that if anyone would try to ruin Bryony's wedding day, it would be Fay. We hadn't considered anyone else. What if we'd been wasting our time on Fay when we should have been talking to other people in Bryony's circle of friends? My vision had shown a body lying on the floor of the hotel room, but who was it? And could Peggy and I prevent it from happening?

I gave up on sleep at six o'clock and decided to get up. As I had time to spare, I checked on the website that I'd set up for the café. Erin had sent me a message the previous night to say she'd uploaded the photos of our first craft evening to the site. I looked at them now and smiled as I read the funny captions Erin had placed beneath each image. I checked the visitor stats and was delighted to see we'd had over a hundred visits to the site. Most of them were from local areas. I was even more delighted when I checked our list of subscribers and found a list of twenty people who wanted to know about upcoming events.

Despite it being so early in the day, I sent a message to Erin to notify her of my findings concerning the website. I knew she'd be as pleased as me. I had considered telling her about my latest visions, but decided she didn't need to know. She would only get upset, and that's the last thing I wanted for her. I was aware I was trying to wrap her in cotton wool, but I had to until the baby was born.

I busied myself over the next few hours and by the time eight o'clock came around, I decided to check on Peggy to see if she was up.

Of course she was. I should have known she would be. Peggy greeted each day in the early hours with an impressive amount of energy.

When I entered her kitchen via the back door, I said, "You look lovely, Peggy. That dress looks even better on you today. And you've done your make-up. I didn't think you'd be ready so early."

Peggy performed a slow twirl and the skirt of her dress fluttered gently outwards. She came to a stop. "You know I like to get up early. As soon as I wake up, I check I'm not dead, then I leap out of bed and get ready for the day. Well, not leap. I think my leaping days are over, but you know what I mean. I barely slept a wink last night! I've already had three cups of tea this morning to wake me up. I'm just about to have another. Would you like one?"

"Yes, please." I sat down at the kitchen table. "I didn't sleep either. I'm so worried about Bryony. Who does she hate enough to stab?"

"We haven't got the full facts. For all we know, she could be acting in self-defence. I don't suppose you've had any more visions, have you?"

I shook my head. "I tried. I wish I could control them more. Perhaps if we'd have gone to Bryony's house, I could have picked up on something there."

"And what excuse would we give her for turning up?

We could hardly say, 'Excuse us a moment while we try to stop you slaying someone on the happiest day of your life.' That wouldn't have gone down well." Peggy busied herself making cups of tea.

I put my hand on my stomach and tried to soothe the ache inside. Worrying always affected my stomach. I jumped as there was a sharp knock at the front door.

"I'll get it," Peggy said.

She left the kitchen and came back with Seb. She jerked her thumb at him and said to me, "Look who it is. Bright and early. He scrubs up quite well, doesn't he? He looks quite handsome in that fancy suit."

Seb smiled, "You do know I can hear you?"

Peggy chuckled. "Would you like a tea?"

"I would. Thank you."

She pushed him towards the table. "Sit down. You're making the place look untidy."

He sat opposite me and gave me a bright smile. "Morning, Karis. You look nice today." His eyes widened. "That's not to say you don't look nice every other day, but you look extra nice today. That's a nice dress."

I returned his smile. "You look nice too." My smile increased. "We should think of a better word to use than nice. Do you remember that English teacher at school who would roar with rage if anyone used the word nice in their writing? He hated anyone using it."

Seb laughed. "Mr Shingle? Yeah, I remember him. I gave him a Christmas card with Baby Jesus on the front and I wrote 'Have a nice Christmas' in huge letters inside."

I waved my hand at him. "Yes! I remember that! His

face went purple and I thought he was going to explode. He tore the card into pieces and Ella Jenkins started crying because—"

"Because she thought he'd hurt Baby Jesus!" Seb finished for me. "She wouldn't stop crying until Mr Shingle apologised."

"You never did tell me if you'd written that message on purpose or if it was unintentional," I said.

His eyes twinkled with the mischief of a young boy. "Who can say? Maybe I did. Maybe I didn't."

Peggy put a cup of tea in front of him and said, "You most likely did it on purpose, you little scamp. Don't forget you're my date today, Seb Parker. I want you to compliment me at regular intervals and pay full attention to me. Except when you're looking out for a possible murder victim." She put a cup in front of me and then sat down.

Seb said, "I've made some enquiries about Fay Spencer. As soon as I mentioned her down at the station, everyone started throwing comments at me. It seems they all know about Fay Spencer. Some of my colleagues have had regular run-ins with her."

"Tell us more," Peggy said eagerly.

"Fay Spencer is known for causing arguments wherever she goes. In the past, she's argued with shopkeepers and claimed they shortchanged her. She's had a go at the local postwoman and said she was opening Fay's letters and reading them. She stands outside local pubs and verbally abuses people who come out. Why she does that, I don't know. She often phones the police station and complains about her neighbours being too noisy. She's even been involved in a couple of physical fights with her neighbours."

Peggy let out a low whistle. "Unhinged. That's what she is. Has she ever been arrested?"

"No, but she's been cautioned a few times. She always claims she's innocent and the other party is to blame."

I said, "That's her view of her friendship with Bryony. I really hope she doesn't turn up to the wedding and spoil things."

"If she does, we'll be ready for her," Seb said. "Peggy, I'll put those spare wedding favours in my car in case we need them. I've printed out some images of Fay and I'll distribute them amongst the hotel staff if needed."

"Are you allowed to do that?" I asked. "She hasn't done anything wrong yet."

"But she has a reputation for being a troublemaker," Seb advised me. "That's enough for me to take precautions." He took a drink of his tea. "Peggy, this is a smashing cup of tea."

Peggy lifted her chin. "Thank you. I know how to make a decent cup of tea. I've had years of practise." She patted her hair and gave Seb a pointed look. "Well?"

"Well what?" Seb asked.

"How do I look? You told Karis she looks nice. How about me? I am your date after all."

He grinned. "You look beautiful. As pretty as a picture. As radiant as a rose on the first day of Summer. As graceful as a—"

"There's no need to go overboard," Peggy interrupted him. "Nice would have done. Hurry up and drink your tea."

Seb shook his head. "I can't win with you, Peggy."

She gave him a cheeky smile. "You're getting there,

Sebastian Parker. You just have to try a bit harder."

Chapter 11

Peggy sat in the passenger seat on the way to the wedding and quizzed Seb relentlessly. I sat behind her, and being the nosy sort, listened to every word that was said.

"Seb," Peggy began, "your mum told me you're looking at some of those apartments down by the canal. They're a bit pricey, aren't they? But I suppose you can afford it now with your promotion and all. Have you been to look at any yet? Are you looking for one or two bedrooms? Some of those apartments have a swimming pool and a gym, don't they? I wouldn't mind having a look at them. You can take me with you when you go to have a look. Not that I'd want to live somewhere like that. I don't want to be in the centre of Leeds. It's too noisy."

She paused for breath and Seb said, "I've only looked at a couple. I can't stay living at Mum and Dad's for much longer. I'm not sure if I'll take one of those apartments or not."

Peggy said, "Do you want me to go with you for a second viewing? I will do. Your mum said you'd also been looking at those new houses not far from our street. I haven't seen inside them yet. Is it true you can choose your own kitchen and colour of carpets? Isn't that amazing? It's like ordering a house from a catalogue. I'm free on Wednesdays if you want to arrange a viewing then. Karis can come with us." She turned her head to look at me. "Karis, do you want to come with

Seb and me to look at his new house?"

I caught Seb's eyes in the rear-view mirror. I could see the sparkle in them and knew he was trying not to smile at Peggy's bossy ways. I said, "I don't think Seb wants us in his way."

"Nonsense!" Peggy declared. "He'd love to have us there." She turned her head back to Seb. "Are you alright going to this wedding, Seb? I feel I may have forced you to come with us."

"You didn't force me." He paused. "Well, I suppose you did, but I don't mind. I like a good wedding."

Peggy sucked in her breath. "Even after what happened with your marriage? It didn't last long, did it?"

I glanced at Seb's reflection in the mirror again. The sparkle had gone from his eyes.

His voice was strained as he said, "Some marriages are not meant to last."

Peggy nodded. "Aye, I know that. Yours didn't make it past the first year. Your mum said that wife of yours was too flirty. Is that right? Did she mess you about?"

Seb stared straight ahead and I saw a muscle twitch in his jaw. "I'd rather not talk about it, Peggy."

"Sometimes it helps to talk about these things," Peggy persisted. "Take Karis here, she put up with her awful marriage for decades. Poor love. But she's come out of it in one piece. Do you know her ex-husband? Gavin Booth? He's as slimy as a toad. I never took to him, but I couldn't say that in front of Karis." She looked over her shoulder at me and smiled. "I hope you don't mind me talking about you. We're all friends in this car. I'm trying to make Seb feel at ease so he'll tell us about his marriage. Not that I'm prying or anything."

I caught Seb's eye once more and was pleased to see them crinkling up in laughter.

Seb shook his head. "It's a good job I like you so much, Peggy Marshall. I'll tell you about my short-lived marriage. I met her in London at a party. I wasn't one for going to parties, but I was dragged along by my colleagues. I drank too much and I danced too much. My future wife, Lucy, got the impression that I was a party animal."

Peggy laughed. "You? A party animal?"

Seb joined in with her laughter. "I know. Lucy was a party animal, though. That was the problem. I tried to keep up with her wild ways but found it a struggle. Our marriage was a mistake. She continued to party, but I couldn't. I wanted to concentrate on my career." He hesitated, and when he spoke again, his voice was tinged with bitterness. "After we were married, she continued to party – but with someone else. I put up with it for some reason, but then decided I'd had enough."

Peggy reached over and patted his hand. "I'm sorry you had to go through that. You made the right decision by ending it. Some people put up with bad marriages for years. They never find the courage to leave. They think it's better to be married, no matter how painful, than to be on their own. Karis, I'm not having a dig at you."

"I know you're not," I said. "But you are right. Seb, I'm sorry about your marriage."

"It's alright. It's all in the past. I don't mind being on my own."

Peggy turned her face to me. "He's thinking of getting a dog. That's what his mum told me. We could go with him to choose one."

Seb shook his head. "Is there anything about me that you don't know, Peggy?"

Peggy chuckled. "I like to know what's going on. If you want to know anything about my life, just ask. I'm an open book."

Seb turned left and drove through the open gates of The Oak Tree Hotel. A long, gravel drive took us to the impressive stone building.

Peggy said, "By heck! Look at this place. I've never been here before. I've been past it on the bus a few times. Karis, I never told you how Christine has saved up for years to pay for Bryony's wedding. That's how they can afford to have it here. She's got money put by for Leila's wedding too. Whenever that day will be. Seb, park near the door then you don't have to walk too far in case we need those extra wedding favours."

Seb did as he was told. He got out of the car, walked around to Peggy's side and helped her out. I was already out of the car and looking around us. I was searching for Fay.

Peggy looked towards the hotel again. "Considering how much Christine has spent on this event, I hope Bryony's marriage lasts longer than yours or Karis'." She grinned up at him.

Seb let out a loud laugh and looked at me. He said, "I can never tell if she's insulting me or not." His smile faded. "Karis, try not to look so worried. If Fay is here, we'll find her."

Bryony's mum, Alison, came rushing out of the hotel. She came over to us, her hands twisting in agitation. "Peggy! Karis! I'm so glad you're here. Something terrible has happened!" Tears trickled down her cheeks.

Chapter 12

Peggy put a comforting arm around Alison's shoulders and said, "There, there. Calm yourself down, Alison. You're going to ruin your lovely make-up if you keep crying like that. Take a deep breath and tell us what's happened."

Seb surprised me by producing a tissue from his pocket and handing it to Alison.

Alison took it and dabbed at her eyes. She explained, "Peggy, it's the wedding favours. I know what you said to Auntie Christine yesterday about keeping them safe. And that's what we did. Auntie Christine never let them out of her sight until they were placed safely on the tables in the function room. I was on the way to the ladies' when I noticed someone in that room. It wasn't a member of staff, and it was too early for any guests to be in there, so I had a closer look. Peggy, it was Fay Spencer! She shouldn't be here. She was doing something to the wedding favours. I shouted at her. She dropped the wedding favour she was holding and bolted from the room. She shoved me out of the way as she did so. I banged into the door."

Peggy tutted and shook her head. "Are you okay? Are you hurt?"

Alison dabbed her leaking eyes again. "I'm fine. It was just the shock of seeing her here. Bryony doesn't want her here, and neither do I. I've never liked that woman. She's got an unhealthy obsession with Bryony."

"Unhinged. That's what she is," Peggy advised. "Did

you see what she was doing with the favours?"

Alison shook her head. "I didn't." Her eyes widened. "You don't think she was doing anything to them, do you? You don't think she's crazy enough to poison them or anything ridiculous like that? She wouldn't. Would she?"

Seb said, "I'll have a look at them. Did you see which way Fay Spencer went?"

Alison shook her head again. "I didn't. Peggy, what are we going to do about those favours? Should we get rid of them all? Bryony will be so upset if we do that."

Peggy advised, "We took the precaution of making more of them. They're in Seb's car."

Relief washed over Alison's face. "You have? Oh, Peggy, thank you. Karis, thank you too. That is such a relief. I haven't told Bryony about them or about seeing Fay. I don't want to upset her. She's in the honeymoon suite getting ready. Auntie Christine is with her."

The image of Bryony and Christine in that room suddenly appeared in my head. With horror, I realised I hadn't noticed a wedding ring on Bryony's finger in my vision. It could have been there; I just hadn't been looking for one. I wasn't sure if the possible murder was going to happen before or after Bryony's wedding service. It could be happening right now.

Peggy gave me a concerned look. "Karis, are you alright?"

I forced a brightness to my voice. "I thought I might call on Bryony and Christine and say hello. They're in the honeymoon suite. Both of them."

Peggy immediately picked up on my meaning. She turned to Alison and said, "Seb and Karis will sort out the wedding favours. I'm sure Seb can speak to the hotel manager about Fay too. If she's still here, someone will find her. Why don't I take you up to your room? Christine said she'd booked rooms for the family, so I presume you have one. You could do with touching up your make-up. While you're doing that, I'll pop into the honeymoon suite and say hello to the blushing bride."

I proclaimed, "I'll come with you!"

Peggy shook her head at me. "No, you stay here and help Seb. If I need you, I'll let you know." She put her hand on Alison's elbow and swiftly led her away and into the hotel.

I turned to Seb. "Peggy can't go into that room alone! She might find—" I stopped speaking and raised my eyebrows at him. "She might come across a crime scene."

Seb gave me a sharp nod. "I'll follow her. You stay here and don't move. If you see Fay Spencer, don't do anything stupid." He jogged towards the entrance.

I swallowed my rising panic and looked around at the woodland which surrounded the hotel. I would have appreciated the beautiful trees more if I wasn't so worried. Cars began arriving and parking at the side of the hotel. People dressed in their best clothes got out of the cars and ambled towards the hotel, most of them bearing gifts wrapped in wedding-themed paper. Everyone looked so happy and at ease just as you would expect them to look at a wedding.

I recognised a few of the guests and returned their friendly greetings as they walked past me. I somehow managed to keep my voice calm.

While I was taking in the scene, I kept looking out for

Fay Spencer. I know Seb told me not to do anything stupid. But what did that entail anyway? Would locking her in the boot of Seb's car constitute doing something stupid? If I was keeping her out of the way for a few hours, wouldn't that be classed as helpful?

I casually walked to the rear of Seb's car and tried to open the boot. It was locked. That was thoughtless of him. The boot on my car often jammed and it opened after a good whack from me. I whacked Seb's boot. Nothing happened. I whacked it again.

"Hey! What are you doing to my car?" Seb walked towards me. "Are you trying to break in?"

"No." I looked away from his accusing glance.

"Were you trying to get it open for some reason, Karis Booth? Did you have the ridiculous thought of putting Fay Spencer in there?"

I still didn't look at him. I concentrated on the nearest tree. "No." I heard him laughing and looked back at him. "Is Bryony okay? And Christine?"

He nodded. "Yes. I put my ear next to the door of the honeymoon suite and had a good listen. Peggy can talk the hind legs off a donkey. Let's go and inspect those wedding favours." He gave me a studied look. "If you see Fay Spencer, let me know. Don't approach her on your own. She's known for being violent. Okay?"

"Okay. I can handle myself, though."

"I know you can. You've always been able to take care of yourself."

We walked into the hotel and over to the reception area. Seb asked to speak to the manager. An older woman in a suit appeared and introduced herself as the manager. Seb explained Alison's concerns about the favours and Fay Spencer. The manager was visibly shaken and took us to the function room.

When we got there, Seb said to her, "Thank you. We'll take it from here."

The manager nodded. "Let me know if you need anything else from us. We want this wedding day to be a happy day for the couple. Nothing is too much trouble." She walked away.

I said to Seb, "Thank you for including me on this. You didn't have to. Don't you want help from one of your police colleagues?"

"Not yet. It might come to that soon, though." He took a pair of latex gloves from his pocket and put them on. He caught my startled expression. "I never leave home without them. These and a packet of tissues. You never know when rubber gloves and tissues will come in handy." He grimaced. "That didn't come out right."

I smiled. "I know what you meant."

"Karis, don't touch anything. I'll do the touching." He grimaced again. "That didn't sound right either."

He picked up the nearest wedding favour and carefully pulled on the ribbon. I felt a flicker of sadness as I thought about the joyful evening when these had been made. I half hoped Fay hadn't done anything other than examine them. It would take a mean mind to want to destroy such items.

Seb opened the favour and carefully inhaled.

"What can you smell?" I asked him.

"Almonds. Not surprisingly." He sniffed again. "There is something else too. Some poisons have a similar scent to almonds. You probably know that from your days of reading Agatha Christie stories." He put the favour down and reached into his jacket pocket. "I've brought something from the station to undertake a preliminary test."

I shook my head in amazement. "What else are you hiding in your clothes?"

He flashed me a small grin. "Wouldn't you like to know?" He opened the small, plastic tube which he'd taken from his jacket and retrieved a cotton wool bud from another pocket.

I watched in astonishment as he performed a minor chemical experiment which involved him producing more items from his pockets, He was like a magical chemist.

When he'd finished his examination, he gave me a serious look and announced, "There is poison on these almonds. Enough to cause severe illness or even death. This is more than an act of revenge by a resentful friend; this is a case of attempted murder." He looked around the room at the other wedding favours. "Possible multiple murders. I'm calling for backup. No one is going to be allowed into this room."

"But what about Bryony's wedding? What will she do? She's going to be devastated when she finds out what Fay has done."

He gave me a gentle smile. "I'll deal with everything. Trust me. You find Peggy and tell her what's happened. Leave everything else to me."

I looked into Seb's eyes. The eyes I'd known from childhood. I nodded and said, "I'll leave everything to you. Thank you, Seb."

"For what?"

"For believing in me and my visions."

"I've always believed in you. Now, clear off before you inhale any poison and expire on me. I don't have time to be dealing with a deceased body."

Chapter 13

I left Seb and headed for the stairs. I met Peggy halfway up and quietly told her what Seb had discovered.

Peggy wavered on her feet, and I put my hand out to steady her. She said, "That wicked woman! How could she do that? She's evil, pure evil. What's Seb going to do?"

"I don't know. He told me to trust him. And do you know what? I do trust him. I can't honestly say I've forgiven him for what he did to me, but I think that day will come sooner rather than later."

She gave me a small smile. "I know it will. I haven't quite forgiven him yet either. I'll keep giving him a hard time until you tell me otherwise. I'm always on your side, Karis. You know that." She aimed a worried look towards the area above us. "You should see how happy Bryony looks. Christine too. I know your vision about the poisoned almonds has come true, but I hope your other one won't."

"Me too. Maybe someone will find Fay and take her away from the hotel before Bryony's any the wiser." I pressed my lips together.

Peggy gave me a sharp look. "What? What are you keeping to yourself?"

"In my vision, I couldn't work out the identity of the body on the carpet. We've been presuming it was Fay, but it could be someone else."

Peggy nodded. "I've been thinking that too. We'll just

have to keep a close eye on Bryony today. If she wanders off, one of us should follow her, especially if she goes upstairs to her room."

"Peggy, there you are," Alison said from the stairs above us. She descended towards us. "Did your police friend have a look at those favours? Did he find anything suspicious? I hope he didn't. Now that I've had time to think, I'm sure Fay was only having a look at those favours. She wouldn't have done anything silly to them."

I was momentarily lost for words. I looked at Peggy and could see she was too. Neither of us could think of a suitable lie.

Our knight in a suit and tie bounded up the steps to us. It was Seb and he said, "Hello, I was just about to come looking for you, Mrs Hughes. I did have a look at those wedding favours. When I was in the room, I detected the smell of gas. It was only a slight whiff, but it's better to be safe than sorry in the circumstances. I've advised the manager of the situation and we've decided to move your wedding party to a different room. It's one at the back of the hotel."

"Oh!" Alison's hands flew to her chest. "But the seating arrangement? And the flowers? And the table settings? Bryony and Auntie Christine have been working on those details for months."

Seb cast her a reassuring look. "The manager is taking care of everything. Just as a precaution, we will substitute those wedding favours with the newer ones. I'd be happy to explain the situation to your daughter and aunt." He smiled. "The manager has assured me the other room is much bigger and has a conservatory which looks out onto the woodlands."

Alison gave him a slow nod. "A conservatory? A view of the woods? Yes. That does sound nice. I'll let Bryony and Auntie Christine know. Thank you." She turned away and headed back up the stairs.

Once she'd gone, Seb said to us, "I've given the manager a photo of Fay Spencer. She's taken copies and will distribute them amongst her staff. She's going to check the CCTV coverage, and one of my officers will be with her when she does that. There are going to be undercover police here soon, and they've already been briefed about the situation. I've explained they need to keep a low profile while looking for Fay Spencer. No one will disrupt Bryony's wedding, not Fay Spencer and not my officers. Bryony won't know anything until the wedding is over. We don't know where Fay is at the moment, but an officer has been sent to keep an eye on Fay's home in case she turns up there."

Peggy suddenly grabbed Seb's arm and pulled him towards her. She planted a big kiss on his cheek. She released him and said, "Thank you, Seb. You've thought of everything. What will you do when you find Fay? Lock her up, I should think."

"Once we have enough evidence, we'll take the appropriate action." He looked down towards the bottom of the steps. "Some of my colleagues are here. I have to speak to them. I'll catch up with you two later."

I said, "You might want to wipe Peggy's lipstick off your cheek before you talk to your colleagues." I touched my left cheek.

Seb pulled out a tissue and held it up. "See? You never know when you need a tissue."

He rubbed at his cheek and missed Peggy's lipstick

entirely. Before he knew what was happening, Peggy grabbed the tissue, spat on it and then rubbed Seb's lipsticked cheek as if she were polishing a piece of silver.

I smiled at Seb's horrified expression as he tried to pull away from Peggy.

Peggy thrust the tissue back into his hands and said, "You can go now."

Seb dashed down the steps as if in fear of being attacked by Peggy again.

We didn't get the chance to discuss what Seb had organised as Alison came down the steps again. She smiled and said, "Bryony and Auntie Christine are delighted with the change of room. Auntie Christine said it's the room they originally wanted, but she couldn't afford it. We need to make our way to the chapel now. The ceremony is about to start." She clasped her hands in glee. "I am so excited! This is going to be a day to remember. Follow me and I'll show you where the chapel is."

She walked down the steps with a happy smile on her face.

Peggy and I followed. With each step I took, the fear in my stomach grew. I had the strongest feeling that my premonition about Bryony in her bloodstained dress was going to come true, and there was nothing I could do to stop it. I knew this was going to be a day to remember – but for the wrong reasons.

Chapter 14

The ceremony began.

The groom looked nervous and excited.

The bride looked radiant as she walked down the aisle with her Auntie Christine.

The wedding guests oohed and aahed as they watched her join her husband-to-be at the front. He grinned at her and they gazed into each other's eyes as if no one else existed.

I pressed my hands on my knees to stop my legs shaking. Seeing as my hands were trembling too, my legs shook even more. My stomach felt like a washing machine on a turbo spin as it whirled with nerves. I pressed my lips tightly together to stop myself from screaming at Bryony and telling her to make a run for it.

Peggy leant herself against me and whispered, "You need to get a grip on yourself, love. People are beginning to stare at you."

I glanced left and right and noticed a few guests giving me concerned looks. I attempted to smile at them but failed.

Peggy prised one of my clenched hands from my knee and held it in hers. She whispered, "Everything is going to be alright. You'll see."

I tried a smile in her direction and failed again. How could I explain to her how agitated I was feeling? It was like being in the middle of a horror movie. I knew what was going to happen because the scene had already been filmed, and there was nothing I could do to stop it unfolding. I looked closer at Bryony. I could kidnap her and drive away with her. I'd have to borrow Seb's car. Where was he anyway?

As if reading my thoughts, he slid into the seat at my side. He noticed my nervous state and took my other hand. His hand was big and warm. I felt a fraction of comfort.

He moved his head closer to mine until we were touching. I felt his breath on my ear as he whispered, "Fay Spencer isn't here. The CCTV shows her leaving the hotel. Another camera shows her boarding a bus on the main road."

I gave him a nod. That should have given me comfort, but it didn't. It now looked like Bryony was going to kill someone other than Fay.

My trembling subsided as I concentrated on the wedding ceremony. I cast careful glances at the people in the room. Did any of them look angry? Resentful? Murderous? No. They all looked extremely happy. But a smile can hide many an emotion.

I continued to scrutinise the guests and before I knew it, Bryony and Harry were married. They kissed and a cheer went up.

Peggy and Seb released my hands as they joined everyone else in applause for the new couple. Bryony and Harry walked arm in arm down the aisle, smiling at everyone. They looked like the happiest people alive.

They went through to a room to complete the legal paperwork, and everyone began to chat.

Peggy said to Seb, "I heard what you said about Fay getting the bus. Which number bus was it? Have you checked to see where she got off? Has someone followed

184

her home? When are you going to arrest her?"

Seb said, "We're taking all the necessary action." He looked at me. "You look as if you could do with a drink. I'll go to the bar and get one for you. What would you like?"

I shook my head. "Nothing for me. Unless they do coffee. I would love a strong coffee."

Peggy said, "I'll have a gin and tonic. Make it a large one. Thanks."

Seb gave us a nod and left the chapel.

Peggy said to me, "Have you had any more visions?"

I shook my head. "No, but I feel sick to my stomach with apprehension. Where's Bryony now? Has she come out of that room yet? Did you notice anyone giving her funny looks?"

"What sort of funny looks?"

"As if they have a grievance against her. As if they're going to have an argument with her."

"No. Everyone looks happy." Peggy got to her feet. "Come on; let's begin our covert surveillance of Bryony. Wherever she goes, we'll be close behind. Remain discreet at all times."

I stood up. "I will."

We left the chapel and hovered discreetly around the room where Bryony and Harry were. Seb brought our drinks over and we filled him in on what we were doing.

He didn't seem at all surprised. "Fair enough. I'll have a word with my colleagues and see how they're doing with the CCTV footage. Some of the favours have been taken away for examination. We should have the results soon." He walked away.

Bryony and Harry came out of the room. They didn't

notice us standing there as they only had eyes for each other.

We followed them through the hotel and towards the function room at the back. Their guests who were milling around followed them too. Peggy and I blended right in as we all trailed behind the happy couple.

Peggy and I stopped at the entrance to the room and Peggy said, "Wow, this is a spectacular room. Look at that conservatory. I always wanted a conservatory. And look at that view." She squinted. "Is that a rabbit outside that glass door or are my eyes playing tricks on me?"

"It's a rabbit." I looked around the room. "This is good. It's open-plan with lots of light. We'll be able to keep an eye on Bryony."

And that's what we did. We moved around the room and chatted to people while all the time watching Bryony. If she noticed us staring, she didn't say anything. Thankfully, we weren't the only ones staring at her. She was so beautiful and radiant, it was hard not to look at her.

Peggy was on her second gin and tonic by the time we took a seat at one of the tables. The wedding favours which Seb had made looked magnificent on the tables. I noticed many people picking them up and giving them looks of appreciation. Some men were opening the favours and popping the almonds into their mouths. They must have been hungry. Their wives were giving them the blackest of looks.

Peggy said quietly, "Thank goodness you had that vision about the poisoned almonds. Otherwise, we'd have dead bodies all over the place. Trust the men to gobble the almonds up. These favours are a keepsake, not a snack."

When everyone was seated, the speeches began. Thankfully, they were all short. Christine brought a tear to everyone's eyes as she gave a heartfelt talk about how Bryony was like a granddaughter to her. Seb appeared at that moment, took one look at Peggy and me, and passed us each a clean tissue.

The speeches were over and the food was served. Seb reassured us his colleagues were still on the case concerning Fay Spencer, and she'd been spotted going into her house on Mortimer Street.

He said, "We should have some details back from the lab soon about the poison. We can't approach Fay Spencer until we have a written statement from Alison Hughes to say she saw her touching the favours. The hotel's CCTV shows Fay going into the room, but there aren't any cameras inside the room. Because of Fay's colourful past, we have her fingerprints on file. That function room is being dusted for prints as we speak."

Peggy shook her head at him. "Can't you speed things up? I don't feel right knowing that Fay is free to walk about."

Seb looked Alison Hughes' way. She was sitting next to Bryony and smiling at whatever her daughter was saying to her. Seb said, "I can't interrupt her. Not yet. If Fay leaves the house, she'll be followed by my officers. How are you two getting on with your surveillance?"

Peggy gave him a sharp look. "I do hope that wasn't a mocking tone in your voice, Sebastian Parker."

"I wouldn't dare mock you," Seb declared.

"I should think not. Our surveillance is going very well. Between us, we've followed Bryony everywhere.

Even to the toilet."

I pointed out to Peggy, "We should keep an eye on Christine too. She was with Bryony when I had my vision."

Peggy nodded. "Good point. Here comes our food. At last."

The food which was placed on our tables looked delicious. I know Bryony would have taken a long time to decide on what to serve her guests, but I wasn't hungry. I forced myself to eat a bit of chicken and a few roast potatoes, but I couldn't manage any more than that.

Seb wolfed down his food and then looked at mine. He waved his fork at me. "Aren't you eating that?"

I shook my head and pushed my plate towards him. "Would you like it?"

He grinned. "Of course." He swapped his empty plate for my half-full one and was soon wolfing that down too. I'd forgotten he had such a healthy appetite.

Peggy did well with her food too. When the desserts were served, I took one look at the strawberry trifle and knew I wouldn't be able to eat it. Peggy and Seb had an argument about who should have it. In the end, I scooped half into each of their dishes.

"It's like dealing with children," I told them.

When the food was finished and the plates cleared away, the dancing began. Everyone beamed with delight as Bryony and Harry took their first dance as a married couple. Once their dance was over, other couples joined them on the floor.

Peggy stood up and grabbed Seb's sleeve. "Come on, young man. You know you want to dance with me. Let me know if you can't keep up."

"It looks like I don't have a choice," Seb muttered to me as he was dragged away.

I smiled as I watched Peggy and Seb dancing together. Seb was much taller than Peggy, and he had to bend quite a bit to hold her in his arms. I looked around at the other couples and noticed how they were smiling with pure happiness and how their eyes were bright with joy.

Seb was suddenly at my side with his hand outstretched towards me. "Quick, Karis! Dance with me before Peggy comes back. She's gone to the ladies'. I'm having to bend myself in two to get to her height. My back's killing me."

"I'm not sure. I'm not in the mood for dancing."

"Neither was I." He pulled me into his arms and led me on to the dance floor. Before I could protest, he said, "Tell me about your Lorrie. I don't know much about her. How often do you see each other?"

"Not as much as I'd like to." Thoughts of my beautiful daughter came to my mind. I could talk about her non-stop. And I proceeded to do so. Seb smiled at me constantly as I told him about Lorrie's many achievements.

I was so lost in my thoughts about Lorrie that I didn't notice a man standing patiently behind Seb until he reached out and tapped Seb on the shoulder.

Seb looked at the man and raised his eyebrows in question.

In a low voice, the man said, "Sorry to disturb you, sir, but I wanted to give you an update." His glance went to me.

Seb said, "It's okay. You can talk in front of Karis."

The man continued, "The suspect is still at home. One

person did leave the property. An older woman. Must be the suspect's mother."

I froze. I stared at the man, found my voice and said, "What was she wearing?"

"She was in a light-blue suit. With a hat. She must have been going to some sort of function."

"But it's Wednesday," I said quietly. "Linda Spencer works at the library all day on Wednesdays." Panic gripped me as an image of someone's face flashed into my mind. I grabbed Seb's lapels. "She's here! Fay is here! I saw someone on the dance floor with the same wide eyes and big smile that Fay has. It's only just registered with me. She was wearing a light-blue suit and a hat. It must be her!"

Seb gently pulled my hands from his lapels and said, "Is she still here?"

I quickly scanned the room. "No. No! She isn't." My heart missed more than one beat when I noticed something else. "Bryony and Christine aren't here either."

Chapter 15

Peggy came rushing across the dance floor to us. She waved her hands in the air, "They've gone! I've lost track of them. I only popped to the toilet for a minute. Those gin and tonics are going right through me. Karis, where are Bryony and Christine?" She lowered her hands and stared at me. "Why are you looking so pale? What's happened?"

"Oh, Peggy, I think Fay is here," I said. "I think I saw her in this room dressed as her mum."

"The sneaky snake." Peggy's eyes narrowed. "Where is she now? I'm going to throw her out."

Seb held his hand up. "No one is doing anything except me." He spoke quietly to the police officer at his side. The officer nodded and then walked swiftly away. Seb looked back at us and continued, "My officers will scour this hotel. They'll also check the CCTV immediately. The officer who's parked outside Fay's house will see if Fay is still inside."

Peggy blurted out, "But she isn't! If Karis saw her here, that means Fay Spencer is definitely here." Her head swivelled left and right. "Where did Bryony and Christine go? Can you see them?"

My glance went towards the ceiling. Fear made my voice tremble as I said, "They might have gone to the honeymoon suite."

Peggy grabbed my arm. "We have no time to lose. Come on!"

Seb blocked her way. "You two are going nowhere.

Stay right here. That's an order."

"But we need to check on Bryony," Peggy argued as she tried to push Seb out of the way. He didn't budge an inch.

He calmly said, "I will check on Bryony and her aunt. You two remain here." He gave Peggy a stern look before walking away.

As soon as he'd left the room, Peggy hissed, "No one gives me orders. Come on. Let's find Bryony ourselves."

I didn't argue with her. I didn't have the strength to. My feet felt full of lead as Peggy dragged me out of the room and up the steps towards the honeymoon suite. We saw Seb standing outside the door. The door was ajar and Seb called out a hello. There was a mumbled reply, and then Seb pushed the door open and strode in.

Peggy said, "Someone is in there." She swallowed nervously. "I've suddenly got a very bad feeling about this."

I nodded. "Me too."

Peggy held my hand as we fearfully walked along the carpeted landing. With my heart thudding in my ears, we stopped at the open door.

And there it was. The exact scene from my vision.

Bryony had a knife in her hand. Blood was on her beautiful dress. She was as still as a statue as she stared at the carpet.

Auntie Christine was sobbing and saying, "Bryony, what have you done?"

Unlike my vision, I could now look closer at the prone body on the carpet. It was a woman dressed in a light-blue suit. Blood pooled beneath her and spread across the carpet. The grey wig she'd been wearing was askew and we could see her face. It was Fay Spencer.

Peggy's hand flew to her mouth, but not before she let out a strangled cry.

The noise alerted Seb and he looked our way. In three strides, he was over at our side. I expected him to be furious at our disregard for his orders. Instead, he gave us a sympathetic smile and said quietly, "I'm sorry you had to see this. Please leave. I don't want you to contaminate the scene. Have a stiff drink in the bar. Don't speak to anyone. I'll deal with Bryony's mum and the guests. I'll talk to you later. Okay?" He reached into his pocket. "If you can't face sitting in the bar, take my car and go home. I'll pick it up later." He gave his car keys to me.

We could only nod in response. We both dipped our heads and walked away. We didn't want to look at the terrible scene a moment longer.

Peggy began to sob as we walked down the stairs. I put my arm around her as we descended.

As we reached the bottom step, we could hear the happy laughter and loud, cheerful music coming from the function room. The celebration was in full swing.

Peggy said to me, "Can we go home? I can't bear to see Harry's happy face. Or anyone else's."

"Of course. Our handbags are still in the function room. I'll get them." I gave her the car keys. "Let yourself into Seb's car. I'll be as quick as I can."

Peggy walked away with her head low.

I lifted my chin, put a smile on my face and walked into the function room. My smile wavered when I saw Harry and Alison dancing together. Their cheeks were flushed and their eyes bright with merriment. I quickly looked away. Their worlds were going to come crashing down on them very soon. My heart went out to them. I quickly collected our handbags and rushed out of the room.

Peggy's cheeks were wet with tears when I got into the car.

I looked at her and said, "This is my fault. I should have done more to prevent it. I should have told Bryony and Christine about my vision."

Peggy shook her head vehemently. "This isn't your fault. Not in any way. Fay was determined to get to Bryony somehow. If it wasn't today, it would have been another day."

I argued, "I should have known it was her in that suit. I should have told Seb she was here. I could have prevented this."

Peggy continued to shake her head. "You only met Fay once. How were you supposed to recognise her when she was in disguise? Bryony and her family have known her for years. They didn't recognise her. Perhaps the police officer outside Fay's house should have been more vigilant, but there's no point going over that now."

I looked down at my knees. "I know that, but I still feel guilty. I should have done more."

Peggy reached out and put her hand under my chin. She lifted it and turned my head so that I was looking at her. She said, "Karis, you did all that you could. You made sure those poisoned almonds were removed. You saved lives. I know you can't make sense of your visions, but don't you think that some of them will come true no matter what you do to prevent them?"

I shrugged. "I don't know. This is too sad. Poor

Bryony. On her wedding day. Why did she kill Fay? What happened in that room?"

Peggy released my chin. "Seb will let us know soon enough. Let's go back to my house. I could do with a strong cup of tea. Are you okay to drive? We could get a taxi if you're not up to it."

I gave her a small smile. "I'll drive. I've never driven an unmarked police car before. I hope I don't put the siren on by accident."

"In any other circumstances, I'd insist that you did do that and have some fun with it." She looked towards the glove box. "And if things were different, I'd have a look through this glove box and see what Seb's got in there. Isn't it funny how it's still called a glove box? No one puts their gloves in there anymore. I think I'll have a look anyway." She pressed the button and the glove box opened. A packet of latex gloves fell out followed by two packets of tissues. Peggy shook her head. "Trust Sebastian Parker to have gloves in here. He's such a nerd. Is that the right word? Let's see what else he's got in here."

I left Peggy to her snooping and concentrated on getting us home. No matter what Peggy said, I still felt incredibly guilty about Bryony. There must have been something I could have done to prevent this devastating situation. Was there anything I could do to help Bryony now?

Chapter 16

I picked Peggy up early the next morning and we headed over to Erin's Café. I parked around the back and we used the rear door to enter the café. The smell of cooked bacon and sausages wafted towards us.

Peggy said, "I wish I had more of an appetite this morning. Your Erin does a lovely cooked breakfast, but I couldn't face one at the moment. I didn't even manage my toast earlier. That's not like me at all."

Erin was busy by the oven when we entered the kitchen. I was glad to see two members of staff assisting her.

"Hello," I called out to her.

Erin looked our way and her blotchy face told us she'd been crying. She gave the spatula she was holding to the young woman at her side, wiped her hands on her apron and came over to us. She put her arms around me and hugged me tightly.

It took me a moment to find my voice. "Erin, what is it? What's happened? Are you okay? Is the baby alright?"

She pulled herself free and gave me a nod. "It's Bryony. Robbie told me what had happened at the wedding last night when he came home. I can't stop thinking about her. It's so sad. For that to happen on her wedding day too. I can't get her smiling face out of my head."

The young woman who'd been given the spatula came over to us and said, "Erin, you sit down and talk to Karis and Peggy. We've got everything under control here. I'll bring you out a pot of tea."

Erin gave her a small smile. "Thanks, Jen. I could do with a sit-down. Are you sure you can manage?"

Jen nodded. "We can."

Erin, Peggy and I walked through to the main area of the café and took a seat at the table nearest the counter. The café was half-full, and there was a low murmur of conversation going on as customers ate a variety of breakfast food.

Erin placed her hand on mine and said, "Robbie spoke to Seb about Bryony. Seb told him about your vision with Bryony and the knife. Karis, why didn't you tell me about that? You shouldn't have to experience something like that on your own."

My glance went to her rounded stomach and then back to Erin's face. "I didn't want to upset you. Besides, I've got Peggy to talk to about my visions. You've got enough going on in your life without me bothering you."

Erin squeezed my hand. "You never bother me. I'm concerned about you. I know how visions upset you sometimes, and this one must have been horrific."

I nodded. "It was. Seeing the real thing was even worse. Peggy's lost her appetite."

Peggy gave a nod of agreement. "I have. Poor Bryony. That Fay Spencer must have done something to make Bryony do what she did." She shook her head sadly. "We'll never know what that was. According to Seb, Bryony won't talk about what happened. She's admitted she killed Fay, but she won't say why."

"Oh?" Erin said. "I didn't know about that. When did Seb give you that information?"

I said, "He called at Peggy's house briefly last night to collect his car. He'd let us borrow it after the incident in the honeymoon suite."

"Did he?" Erin's eyes narrowed. She hadn't forgiven Seb for what he'd done to me at high school. She'd seen how upset I'd been over it, and had even thrown a bucket of cold water over Seb when he'd called at our home.

"He did," I confirmed. "He couldn't stay long last night as he wanted to get on with the investigation. Bryony admitted to killing Fay as soon as Seb walked into the honeymoon suite. Then she went quiet and wouldn't say anything until she was taken to the police station. When giving a statement, she just repeated the same thing. Once Bryony was taken away, Christine had a panic attack and was taken to hospital."

"No! Is she alright?" Erin asked.

Peggy answered, "She is. I phoned Alison this morning. Christine insisted on going back to her own house. She said she feels safe there. I doubt she'll leave her house ever again. I'll call on her later and see how she is."

Jen came over to the table with a large pot of tea and three mugs. She placed them on the table and then brought over milk and sugar. "Is there anything else you'd like?" She asked. "Can I get anyone something to eat?"

We all shook our heads and Jen walked away.

Erin said, "Robbie told me about the poisoned almonds. Have the police been inside Fay's house yet? Have they found any poison? I can't believe she would do that to those lovely wedding favours."

"She wasn't a nice person. She was a wicked, evil woman," Peggy said. "May she rest in peace. Seb told us they were still making enquiries when I asked him the same questions. I think that's his polite way of saying it's none of my business. The cheek of him. If it wasn't for Karis and her visions, the police could have been dealing with many murders at that wedding party instead of one. He owes us the truth."

We looked towards the main café door as it opened. A group of six young men bustled noisily into the café.

Erin's face lit up. "Great. More customers. It's been too quiet this morning. Let me see to them." She made to rise but Jen beat her to it and dashed over to the customers with a welcoming smile.

Goosebumps broke out on my arms and I was instantly wary. Something wasn't right here. I looked closer at the group of men. A couple of them were on their phones. They looked up from their phones, pointed to the side of the café and nodded.

"What's going on with them?" Peggy asked. "Why aren't they sitting down?"

The group moved over to the side of the café and began to take photos using their phones. Jen was saying something, but she couldn't be heard above the chattering group.

I stiffened when I heard one of them say, "That's where she was sitting. Right there. You can see it here on the website photos. Bryony Hughes. Sitting right there with murder on her mind."

Erin leaned towards me and said, "What did he just say?"

The man who had spoken laughed and pulled on the

sleeve of one of his friends. "Here, Nick. Go and sit down there. Pick up a knife and pretend to stab someone. Look like you're going to murder someone. This is going to look awesome on Facebook."

Erin gasped. "Karis! Did you hear what he said? Why is he saying that? I don't like it."

I didn't like it either. I pushed back my chair, stood up and marched over to the group. I said to Jen who was hovering at their side, "These are not customers. You can leave them to me."

Jen gave me a worried smile before walking away.

The young man called Nick was already sitting in the area where Bryony had sat. He'd managed to find a knife and was waving it madly in the air in a stabbing motion. His friends were laughing and taking photos.

I tapped the nearest one on the shoulder and he turned to look at me.

With barely controlled anger, I said, "What do you think you're doing?"

"Taking photos. What does it look like?" He gave me a disgusted look before turning his head back to Nick.

I tapped him more roughly now. He looked back at me and I said, "Stop that right now."

He snapped, "You can't stop me. Everyone knows about the wedding day murder. It's all over the news. I found your website and I saw the evil bride. I want some photos for my blog. It's not often we have a murder around here. People like to know about these things." His eyes narrowed. "Hey, you're on the website too. You were here when that murdering bride was here." He had the nerve to raise his phone at me ready to take a photo.

I snatched the phone from him and held it aloft. "You don't have my permission to take photos."

He tried to grab the phone back, but I moved it out of his way. He yelled, "I can take photos wherever I want to. Give that back!"

I gave him a cool look. "No, you can't. You're obviously not customers, so you must be trespassers. That's against the law. You're taking photos without the owners' permission. That's also against the law." I had no idea if any of this was true, but the man suddenly turned pale. I continued, "I have contacts at the police station who could be here within minutes. You could all be arrested and issued with fines. You are causing emotional stress to me and my customers. I can make a civil claim against you for that. I hope you have plenty of money."

The group fell silent. They lowered their phones.

Nick put the knife down, stood up and said, "Come on, lads. I don't want to have a visit from the police. Not again. This isn't worth it." He walked towards the door. His friends began to follow him.

"One more thing," I gave the phone back to the man in front of me and took my own phone out. I quickly took a photo of the bewildered-looking group. "I now have photos of you all. If I see one image of this café online which has been posted by you, I'll have my legal team after you quicker than you can say "Google." Nick, I assume from your comments that you're known to the police?"

He nodded sadly.

"Then I'm sure you don't want to have any meetings with them again soon. In which case, you should delete those photos on your phone immediately."

He gave me another nod before tapping on the screen of his phone. "Done." He looked at his friends. "You'd better do what she says. Mum's going to throw me out if I get into trouble again."

I moved to the door and blocked the groups' exit until they'd all deleted their recently taken photos. They were subdued as they left the café. I leant against the door. They'd probably realise I was making it all up soon. I'd have to deal with that later.

When I went back to Erin, I saw she had her phone out. Tears were rolling down her cheeks and she was shaking.

I sat next to her. "What's wrong?"

She held her phone up. "Our website. Look at those awful comments. Read what people are saying about our café. They think we had something to do with the murder. It's all over our Facebook page too."

Peggy tutted. "They're ogres. That's what they are. I saw a programme on the telly about it. Internet ogres. Nasty bunch with no lives of their own."

I took the phone from Erin and said, "You mean trolls, Peggy. I'll deal with this." I quickly scanned the comments and the viciousness of them took my breath away.

Erin placed her hands on her stomach. She was still shaking. "What are we going to do? We can't carry on with our business. Not now. People won't want to come here for food; they'll come here to gawp like ghouls."

I closed down the pages on Erin's phone and handed it back to her. "That isn't going to happen. I'll take care of everything. I can temporarily close our website down and block people from commenting. I can do the same with our Facebook page too."

"But the café? We should close it. I don't want anyone else coming in and taking photos." Erin's tears were falling more quickly now.

"We will not close our café because of vultures." I stood up and helped her to her feet. "I'm going to stay here and look after the café. I'll deal with any vultures, ghouls, trolls and even ogres. You are going home. You're in no state to drive, so I'll order a taxi." I looked at Peggy. "Will you go with her, please? And stay with her?"

Peggy nodded. "I certainly will. I won't let her go on the internet either."

Erin tried to argue with me, but I was adamant about her going home. I wasn't going to let anyone upset my sister.

Ten minutes later, I waved goodbye to Erin and Peggy as they got into a taxi. Then I walked behind the counter and rested my hands on it.

Jen came to my side and said, "What should we do if any more horrible people come in?"

I gave her a determined look. "You leave them to me."

Chapter 17

Jen did leave any unwanted visitors to me, and we had a few of them. I'm ashamed to say I took my anger over Bryony's situation out on them. I shouted at those who came in to stare at the area where Bryony had been sitting, and I went to the window and made slightly obscene hand gestures at the people who gawped in. Not only was I annoyed because I hadn't helped Bryony, I was furious that Erin had been upset by the resulting actions of thoughtless people.

I can't say whether it was my actions or not, but by the time three o'clock came around, the café was empty. Jen was the only member of staff left at this point, and I told her to go home.

She gave me a worried look. "I don't mind staying. I've already cleaned the kitchen and I'd like to clean the café area. I don't want Erin to come back to a filthy floor."

"It's kind of you to offer, but I'll do it. It doesn't look that bad. We haven't had that many customers to sully the floor." I smiled. "It might help me to calm down if I give myself something physical to do. You might have noticed that I've been in a bad mood."

"I don't blame you." She shook her head. "Some people have no decency. Have you heard from Erin? Is she okay?"

"I didn't want to pester her with constant messages, so I pestered Peggy instead. Erin's fine. Peggy has looked after her all day. In fact, Erin's having a nap now.

Peggy's going to stay there until Robbie comes home. Thanks for your help today. I'll make sure you get paid till the end of the day. Off you go."

"Thanks, Karis." Jen smiled at me before collecting her coat and leaving the café.

I turned the sign on the café door to closed and locked it. I couldn't face any more customers today. I was too annoyed to be friendly. I'd had a nagging feeling all day that something wasn't right with Bryony. It was like someone kept tapping me on my shoulder to tell me something important, but when I turned around, no one was there. Only it wasn't someone tapping my shoulder, it was some invisible force niggling at my brain. If I was going to have a vision, I wished it would hurry up and show itself.

I filled the mop bucket with hot, soapy water and took it into the main café area along with the mop. I placed the chairs upside down on the tables and then set to work. The motion of swirling the mop in the bucket and then moving it back and forth across the floor began to soothe me. Perhaps if I felt calmer, a new vision would come to me.

Back and forth the mop went. In and out my breaths went, getting deeper by the second.

Then some idiot banged on the café door. I turned my back on whoever it was and continued mopping.

The nitwit knocked again.

"We're closed!" I yelled without turning around.

Once again, the knocking sounded out.

I growled with rage. I spun around, marched over to the door, unlocked it and flung it open. I waved my wet mop at the twit who was standing there and cried out,

"We're closed! Clear off!"

The wet mop connected with DCI Sebastian Parker's face. I watched in slow motion as he opened his mouth in horror and strands of the mop fell in.

He spluttered and shoved the mop out of the way. "What the hell are you doing?"

I lowered the mop and put it behind my back as if that would make it invisible. "I'm so sorry. I didn't know it was you. Would you like a towel? There's been one idiot after another showing up here today, so I had to close the café."

He took a tissue from his pocket and wiped his face. He said, "I know about those so-called idiots because they've been down to the police station to make complaints about the madwoman at Erin's Café. Why have you been insulting your customers?"

My shoulders dropped. "They weren't customers. They only came here to gawp because Bryony had been here recently. Some of them were taking photos." I moved the mop in front of me and rested my weight on it. I suddenly felt very tired.

Seb came into the café and took the mop from me. He closed the door and locked it. "You need to rest. I didn't realise those complaints had come from those sorts of people. We get them all the time at the station. Gruesome lot." He guided me over to Erin's comfy chair which was behind the counter. He quickly made me a cup of coffee and placed it in my hands.

I tried to argue and said, "But the floor! I have to clean it."

"I'll do that." He grabbed the mop. "Don't be ogling me while I move about. I'm not one of those stripping acts."

Despite my weariness, I couldn't help but smile.

Seb got to work on the floor and soon had it clean. I didn't ogle him, but I did stare a bit too long at him. It took my mind off other matters – or so I told myself. Mopping had calmed me down; watching someone else do it was even more calming.

Once the floor was clean, Seb came over to me and leaned against the counter. He said, "I was going to call on you later, but when we got those complaints about the madwoman at Erin's Café, I told the desk officer I'd deal with it. Do you want to give me the full details?"

I did so. Seb was shocked at the people who'd been to the café. He was outraged when I told him about the comments online. And he was incensed when he heard how upset Erin had been.

His hands clenched into fists and he said, "I've got to know Robbie well over the last few weeks, and he's told me about Erin's pregnancies. How dare anyone upset her? Would you like me to arrest anyone? I can, you know."

I shook my head. "It's okay. We can handle it. I hope. Peggy's looking after Erin at the moment. How's the investigation going?"

His hands relaxed and a sadness came into his face. "This has been an awful day. I've had many terrible days before, but not here in my hometown. I had to tell Linda Spencer that her daughter had been killed. That was bad enough, but then I had to search Fay's room. We found the same poison which had been used on the almonds. If I could have spared Linda Spencer that information, I would have done. But she had to be told." He shook his head sadly. "I don't think she'll ever get over what Fay tried to do. Linda's gone to stay with a relative for now."

"So it was Fay who poisoned the almonds?"

He nodded. "It was. We found her fingerprints in that function room and on the wedding favours. All of them."

I shook my head. "But why did she go back to the hotel later? Wasn't poisoning the almonds enough?"

"We don't know. Bryony must have had a conversation with Fay before she killed her, but she won't give us that information. She's staying silent. She wouldn't speak to her mum or sister when they went to visit her." He gave me a long look. "How are you doing?"

My eyes stung and I looked away. "I feel dreadful. I keep thinking I could have done something to stop it. I knew it was going to happen."

Seb came to my side and hunkered down in front of me. I looked at him. He said softly, "You did all that you could. Fay would have made sure she confronted Bryony somehow. If you'd have stopped that incident happening in the honeymoon suite, it would have happened somewhere else. You did stop many people being poisoned. You know that, don't you? We could have been dealing with many murders."

I gave him a small nod. "That's what Peggy said."

"She's a wise woman. Don't tell her I said that. Karis, there's something else on your mind. What it is?"

I told him about that niggling feeling I was having about Bryony.

He said, "Would it help if you went back to the honeymoon suite? You might experience another vision there."

"Could I do that? Isn't it a crime scene?"

"It is, but all the evidence has been collected. It's still closed to the public, but not me." He straightened up. "We'll go there now."

Seb helped me tidy up the rest of the café and then we drove over to the hotel. I phoned Peggy on the way to check on Erin. My sister was still fast asleep.

It didn't take us long to reach the hotel. Seb quickly spoke to the manager, and before I knew it, we were standing in the honeymoon suite.

The vision came to me immediately.

Chapter 18

In my vision, I was standing at the end of the bed in the honeymoon suite. An open suitcase was on the bed and I saw clothes neatly folded inside. A couple of passports lay on top of the clothes.

The door to the room opened, and I heard the distant sound of music playing. I recognised the song as it was the first one I'd danced to with Seb. A woman in a blue suit came into the room brandishing a knife. She moved closer to me and I recognised Fay's features. She'd applied a lot of heavy make-up and had drawn wrinkles around her mouth and eyes. She'd made a good job of making herself look older.

Her wide smile turned manic and she began to laugh. She said softly to herself, "Think you can kick me out of your life, Bryony? Think I'll go quietly and never bother you again? You can think again, best friend. I will never leave your life. Never."

She walked slowly around the room muttering to herself. As she came closer, I recognised the knife in her hand. I'd seen it at the side of the wedding cake downstairs. Bryony's mum had bought it for the happy couple. It had been engraved with their names and the date of the wedding. It had gone from being a treasured souvenir to a murder weapon.

Fay moved over to the bed and examined the open suitcase. She picked up a pale-pink jacket and smiled to herself. "I picked this going-away outfit for you, Bryony. Do you remember? You wanted something in purple, but I knew better. I always know what's better for you. Let me make some adjustments to this beautiful jacket."

With her eyes shining with malicious glee, she used the knife to rip through the sleeves of the jacket. When she'd finished, she reached for the matching skirt and ripped that too.

Fear trickled down my spine as Fay laughed uncontrollably at what she'd done. Not content with destroying Bryony's clothes, she started on those belonging to Harry. She sliced through an expensive-looking shirt and ripped apart a pair of tailored trousers.

She cackled to herself. "Looks like you two will have to find something else to wear when you go on that stupid honeymoon of yours. I picked the destination and the hotel. Do you remember, Bryony? You wanted to go somewhere else, but I knew better. I always know better."

She stopped talking and hovered the knife over the passports. A slow, wicked smile spread across her face. "Actually, I don't think you two deserve a honeymoon. Not after how you've treated me."

She put the knife down on the bed and then picked the passports up. She giggled as she tore them apart. "You won't be going anywhere. Not now. Serves you both right."

There was a noise at the door and Fay jumped. She quickly retrieved the knife and turned towards the door which was now opening.

Fay muttered to herself, "I wasn't expecting a visitor. Who could it be? The blushing bride? Or the useless groom? I have a special wedding gift for you." She held the knife aloft and walked towards the door, her smile increasing by the second.

Instinctively, I leapt towards Fay and cried out, "No!"

My vision faded and I landed heavily on the carpet. The fall winded me and I couldn't breathe for a moment. I felt big hands pulling me to my feet and pushing my hair back from my face.

Seb looked at me with concern. "Karis, are you okay? Are you hurt? What did you see? You're shaking."

He led me over to the bed and sat me down. He put his arm around my shoulders and waited for me to speak.

I told him what I'd seen. I said, "Fay was intent on destroying everything. I think she came to the hotel to hurt Bryony."

"Did you see Bryony walking through the door?"

I shook my head. "I should have waited. But I couldn't help myself. I really felt like I was in this room with Fay. I could feel the evil emanating from her."

Seb nodded. "I'm going to speak to Bryony again and find out what happened when she confronted Fay. Bryony could have acted in self-defence. You can come with me and tell her about your vision. I'm sure Bryony will understand."

I shook my head. "Seb, we have to go somewhere else first."

Chapter 19

Seb drove us over to Christine's house. It was Alison who answered the door to us. Her eyes were red-rimmed and her face blotchy.

As soon as she opened the door wide enough, I moved forward and gave her a hug. She hugged me back and I heard a sob coming from her. I released her and said, "Words can't express my sorrow at what's happened. Is there anything I can do to help?"

Alison indicated for us to come inside. She said, "There's nothing anyone can do. Bryony won't even talk to me or Leila. I've been to the police station three times so far, and she refuses to see us. I just want to know why she did it. I can't make sense of it. What was Fay doing in that room? Why was the wedding cake knife there? Fay must have provoked Bryony. She must have. I know my daughter. She's not a killer." She looked at Seb with pleading eyes. "Can't you do something? Can't you make Bryony talk? Can't you force her somehow?"

Seb shook his head. "I'm sorry. We can't do that."

I put my hand on Alison's arm. "How's Christine doing?"

Alison's eyes welled up. "She's in shock. She hasn't spoken since we brought her home from the hospital. She hasn't slept and she hasn't eaten anything. I managed to force a cup of tea on her, but that's all. She's in the living room staring out of the window. I'm so worried about her."

"Could I speak to her?" I asked. "I don't know her

very well, but I could try to get her to talk."

"Anything is worth a try. Thank you. I'll come with you."

I'd explained my reasons for this visit to Seb on the way here. He'd been surprised, but he understood. I told him why I needed to speak to Christine alone.

He now said to Alison, "Could I have a drink of water, please? If that's no trouble."

"Oh, of course. Where are my manners? I should have offered you a cup of tea. Karis, would you like one?"

"That would be lovely, thank you."

Seb said to Alison, "I'll help you make it."

They walked down the hallway and into the kitchen.

I went into the living room and looked at the elderly woman who was sitting by the window. She was wearing her dressing gown and slippers. She seemed smaller than when I'd last seen her, almost as if she'd shrunk into herself.

I pulled a padded stool over and placed it directly in front of her. Christine didn't register my presence.

I took her thin hands in mine and said gently, "Christine, it's me, Karis Booth. We've met a few times. You know about my psychic side. I'm going to use my abilities on you now. If you don't want me to do that, please give me a sign."

Christine didn't move and continued to stare out of the window.

I continued, "This might not even work, but we have to try."

I closed my eyes and thought back to the vision I'd had in the honeymoon suite. I focused on Fay's face as she walked towards the opening door with the knife in her hand. It was like trying to get back into a dream once you'd woken up. I tried not to force it and took some deep breaths.

The vision came back to me. I was in the honeymoon suite again. The door opened, and Christine came in.

Her eyes widened when she saw Fay. Christine cried out, "What are you doing here?"

Fay merely grinned and took a step closer to Christine.

Christine's glance went to the bed and the damaged clothes. "What's happened? Did you do that? Why?"

Fay sniggered. "I wanted to give the happy couple an unforgettable wedding day. They'll think about me every year on this day. If they're still married, that is. I don't think their marriage will last. Harry isn't right for Bryony. No one is right for her. She doesn't need a husband. She's got me, her best friend."

"You're mad!" Christine exclaimed.

Fay dashed forward and brandished the knife at Christine. She spat, "Don't call me that! I hate it when people call me that!"

Christine began to tremble and backed up a step. Fay reached out and slammed the door shut.

"You're not going anywhere, Auntie Christine." A calculating look came into Fay's face. "I've destroyed Bryony's clothes and ripped her passport up. She won't be happy about that. But is that enough? What will really hurt her?" She tapped the knife on her chin as she pondered her own question. "Perhaps if I hurt her beloved Auntie Christine she'd finally feel the pain that I'm going through."

Christine gasped. "You're a wicked girl! You don't scare me. Get out of here immediately!" She suddenly lunged forward and grabbed the knife.

Fay yelped in surprise as the knife was whipped from her hands. She rushed at Christine and knocked the elderly woman into a wardrobe.

From where I was standing, I felt the stabbing pain in my back as Christine connected with the ornate handles on the wardrobe. The knife flew from Christine's hand and landed on the carpet near the bed. Christine slithered to the floor and cried out in pain.

Fay rushed towards the knife. She stopped when the door opened and Bryony stepped in.

Bryony took in the scene, marched over to Fay and began to yell at her. Fay yelled back and the two women started to argue. I wasn't paying attention to the arguing women. My eyes were on Christine as she dragged herself across the floor towards the knife. She picked the knife up and got unsteadily to her feet.

Holding the knife at waist height, Christine called out, "Fay, I won't let you ruin Bryony's wedding day! Get out of here immediately!"

Fay spun around and lurched towards Christine. She didn't notice the knife at Christine's side until it was too late.

Bryony's eyes widened in shock as she saw that Fay had been stabbed. She moved forward and took the knife from her shocked aunt. She wiped the knife on her dress. Fay was now lying motionless on the carpet.

Bryony said quietly, "I did it. I stabbed her. It was me. That's what I'll tell the police."

Auntie Christine shook her head, "No! I won't let you. It was my fault."

The door opened and Seb came through.

Bryony declared, "I killed Fay Spencer."

Auntie Christine began to sob and said, "Bryony, what have you done?"

My vision faded. I was back in Christine's room and still holding her hands.

Christine was looking at me with tears streaming down her face. I said to her, "I saw everything. I saw you talking to Fay, and I know what happened. I know it was an accident."

"I tried to stop Bryony taking the blame. But she wouldn't listen. And now she's in trouble. She'll go to prison. It's all my fault. I tried to tell the police, but my words wouldn't come out. They were stuck in my head. Will you help me tell the police? The words might get stuck again. You can tell them for me."

I nodded. "Of course I will. Christine, it was an accident. The police will understand."

"But I killed Fay. It's because of me that she's dead. I have to take Bryony's place in prison. She's got all her life ahead of her. I haven't got many years left. It doesn't matter if I go to prison. Karis, help me explain this to the police. They have to lock me up for what I've done."

Seb and Alison came into the room and caught Christine's words.

Just like an echo of my vision, Alison said, "Auntie Christine, what have you done?"

Chapter 20

A few hours later, I was pacing up and down Erin's living room. I checked my watch for the hundredth time and said, "Why hasn't he phoned me? Why? Why?"

From her reclined position on the sofa, Erin said, "Karis, I don't know. If you wear a hole out in my carpet, you can pay for another one."

Peggy was sitting at the other end of the sofa with Erin's feet on her lap. She added, "You'll get that electric static running up your legs if you're not careful. I had a friend who got that. She was going on a blind date one night, and she spent over an hour pacing up and down her carpet, just like you are now. When she met up with her blind date later, she shook his hand and the poor fella got a tremendous electric shock. He wet himself. He ran off in embarrassment and my friend never saw him again." She shook her head. "She's still single. She replaced that carpet with pine floorboards."

I stared at Peggy, not sure what to say.

Robbie, who was sitting in an armchair at the side of the sofa said, "Peggy Marshall, are you making that up?"

Peggy gave him an indignant look. "I certainly am not. Robbie, can't you make yourself useful and get in touch with Seb? Find out what's going on at the station. He must have questioned Christine by now. What's the hold-up?"

Robbie shook his head. "I can't interrupt him." He looked at me. "Seb did say he'll let you know what happens. He's a decent sort, and you can trust his word."

Erin made a huffing noise and looked at her husband. "What do you know about Sebastian Parker? Were you there when he upset Karis? No, you weren't. Did you see his smug smile when his friends called her Krazy Karis? No, you didn't. I did. I saw every mean thing he did. Just because he's helped Karis and Peggy with their investigation, it doesn't mean he's a decent sort."

Peggy nodded in agreement. "That's true. Although, I think he has changed as he's got older. Karis thinks so too. She was dancing with him at the wedding. They were smiling at each other."

Erin let out the loudest cry of outrage I'd ever heard. "Dancing? Smiling? Karis, were you drunk?"

"No," I attempted to defend myself. "I can't keep holding on to feelings of resentment about Seb. It's not good for my health. Anyway, Bryony's situation is more pressing to me right now."

Erin gave me a dark look. "We'll talk about your dancing and smiling habits later." There was a knock at the front door. Erin said, "Karis, seeing as you're already up, get that."

I had a feeling I knew who was at the front door and I rushed towards it. I closed the living room door on the way out.

Just as I thought, it was Seb at the door. He looked exhausted and his tie was slightly askew.

"Sorry to bother you so late," he began, "I didn't want to give you the news over the phone."

"What news? Why do you look so worried?"

A voice boomed out behind me, "Seb, don't stand on the doorstep. Come in."

"Thanks, Robbie. I won't keep you long." Seb came

inside and followed Robbie into the living room.

I could have sworn I heard Erin hiss as he entered. She looked at him as if he were the devil. I'd have to speak to her later and explain how supportive Seb had been recently. I wasn't sure I'd entirely forgiven him, but I was definitely getting there.

Robbie motioned for Seb to take a seat. Seb sat down and kept his gaze averted from Erin's hard look.

Robbie said, "Can I get you something to drink? You look all done in."

Seb gave him a tired smile. "No, thanks. I can't stay. Mum is keeping my dinner warm in the oven."

"Well?" Peggy demanded. "What's happened? Have you set Bryony free? Have you locked Christine up? I hope you haven't. It was self-defence. Karis explained everything to you about what happened in that room. If you've locked that poor old woman up, I'm going to set up a protest group! I know a lot of people. We'll march up and down in front of your police station until you let Christine go! That's what we'll do."

Erin nodded. "And I'll join you."

Robbie held his hands out. "Will you let the poor man speak?"

Seb said, "Thanks, Robbie. Peggy, in answer to your questions, Bryony has been released."

"That's great news," I said. "Did Bryony admit the truth?"

Seb gave me a wry smile. "After a while. Christine confirmed what you'd told me. I watched the CCTV which showed Fay going into the honeymoon suite first, and then a short while later, Christine going in. I noticed a hotel maid further down the corridor and I interviewed her to see if she'd heard anything. She had. She'd heard Fay shouting and assumed it was a TV show. The words she'd heard were the same ones you'd told me."

Peggy said, "You should have spoken to that maid straight away."

Seb nodded. "I know that now, but we had no reason to think Bryony was lying to us when she confessed to the murder. I showed Christine's statement to Bryony, but that wasn't enough to get her to admit the truth." He looked my way. "I remembered what you said about Christine falling against those ornate doorknobs on the wardrobe. With her permission, I got a doctor to look at her, and he saw the perfect imprint of those doorknobs on her back. They only have those particular doorknobs in the honeymoon suite. It confirms her story of being attacked by Fay. And with Fay's history and that business with the poisoned almonds, Christine's statement of self-defence is believable."

"How believable?" Peggy asked. "Is Christine going to be charged with manslaughter? Do I need to get a protest group ready or not?"

Seb smiled at her. "I would say not. I'm going to do all I can to make sure Christine isn't charged. We'll collect statements from Fay's neighbours and ex-colleagues. They will show the state of Fay's mind. Christine and Bryony are back at home, and that's where they're going to stay if I have anything to do with it. If anyone higher up than me claims it was manslaughter, I'll start a protest group myself."

Erin said, "Will Karis have to be interviewed? Will she have to explain about her visions?" Her voice hardened. "I don't want her to be ridiculed again."

Seb finally looked at Erin. "Neither do I. No, Karis doesn't need to be interviewed." He turned his attention to me. "But I do want to thank you. If it weren't for you, Bryony would still be in prison and Christine would still be in her shocked state."

He smiled at me and I smiled back.

Erin cleared her throat noisily. "That's enough smiling."

Seb got to his feet and said, "I'd better be going. Erin, congratulations on your pregnancy. You look radiant. How are you?"

"I'm okay," she answered curtly.

"Good. Good." He gave her a smile before walking towards the door. "I'll see myself out. Goodnight."

I went after him and walked with him down the path to his car.

He said to me, "Erin's never going to forgive me, is she?"

"She will do. Peggy is softening towards you."

He looked into my eyes. "And what about you?"

I gave him a half-shrug. "I can now bear to be in your company for more than five minutes, DCI Parker. I no longer want to cause you physical harm." I couldn't keep my smile in. "And I know who to turn to when I need a tissue or a pair of rubber gloves."

He laughed. "So true. Karis, if you have any more visions that I need to know about, don't hesitate to get in touch. I mean it."

"I know you do."

We said goodnight and he drove away.

When I went back inside, Peggy was scuttling back to the sofa. I said to her, "Were you looking out of the window at us?"

Her cheeks coloured. "Of course not. I was just straightening the curtains, wasn't I, Erin?"

Erin didn't reply. Her face was twisted in agony and her hand was on her stomach.

I flew over to her side and placed my hand over hers. "What's wrong?"

"I don't know." She winced.

There was a horrified silence. I kept my hand over Erin's.

We suddenly looked into each other's eyes and burst into tears.

Robbie dropped to his knees at my side. "What is it? Erin! Speak to me!"

Erin got herself under control and continued to look at me. "Did you feel that too?"

"I did." I smiled at her.

"What?" Robbie declared. "What did you feel?"

"Peace," I told him. "Utter peace and joy. It came from the baby. He or she wanted to let us know that everything is going to be okay. I felt it move. Did you, Erin?"

She nodded. Tears rolled down her cheeks. "I've never felt this with any of my other pregnancies. Robbie, the baby said hello to us. I felt it. I think this baby is going to be alright."

Robbie burst into tears and put his head in his hands. He mumbled, "I'm so happy. So very happy."

"Let me have a feel." Peggy came over to us and gently placed her hand on Erin's stomach. "Oh, yes. I can feel a small movement."

Neither Erin or Robbie saw the worried look that

passed between Peggy and me. Erin thought the baby was saying hello, but was it really saying goodbye?

I pushed that awful thought out of my head. That wasn't going to happen. I wouldn't allow it.

Putting as much conviction into my lie as possible, I said, "Erin, I just got a message from the baby. It wants you to stop working immediately and take to your bed. Furthermore, it would like its Auntie Karis to wrap you up in cotton wool and not let you move out of bed until it's born."

"Nice try, sister," Erin said. "I know when you're lying. Right, get your hands off me. I've got things to do." With our help, Erin stood up. "I'm putting the kettle on. I can't lounge around all day." She headed towards the kitchen.

Robbie stood up. "Wait for me, my love." He went after her.

When they'd gone, Peggy whispered, "Is there anything I should know about the baby?"

I shook my head and whispered back, "No, but we still have to make sure Erin takes it easy."

"We can do that." Peggy gave me a measured look. "We'll have to do that in between solving murders. It seems like you've become a magnet for murders. I wonder who's going to bite the dust next?"

THE END

TEA AND MURDER

Chapter 1

"Are you trying to poison me?" I poured the tea into the sink and turned to give my sister, Erin, an accusing look.

"Pardon?" she replied from her sitting position at the kitchen table. She wasn't even looking at me; her attention was on her phone.

I waved my empty cup in the air. "Poison me? That tea tasted disgusting. What did you put in it?"

She looked up from her phone. "What did I put in it? What do you think?" She picked her cup up and took a sip. "Mine tastes fine. In fact, it's a smashing cup of tea even if I do say so myself."

"Your taste buds have probably gone weird because you're pregnant. Have you changed your tea bags?"

"No."

"Your milk?"

"No."

"Is there something wrong with your water?" I gave her tap a suspicious look. "Have you had any letters from the water company saying they were doing maintenance work? Was the water a funny brown colour when you ran it?"

Erin shook her head at me. "If the water was a funny brown colour, do you really think I would have made us a cup of tea from it?" She looked back at her phone. "Why hasn't he replied to me yet? What's taking him so long?"

I hadn't finished with my questions about the tea. I moved over to Erin's fridge and opened it. I took out the carton of milk, opened it and sniffed the contents. I declared, "This isn't off. It must be something else that's wrong with the tea."

Erin wasn't listening. She was glowering at her phone and mumbling, "Text me back, Robbie Terris. Text me back right now."

I left Erin to glower at her phone while I made myself a fresh cup of tea. As I made it, I sniffed various items for any suspicious smells. I had a sniff of the kettle, the water, the tea bags and the cup. I smelled the milk again for good measure. When the tea was made, I took a careful sip.

"Yuck! This one is even worse!" I announced.

Erin's head turned in my direction. "Are you still going on about tea, Karis? What is your problem?"

I lifted my cup. "It's this. It tastes sour. How can I enjoy my morning without a decent cup of tea?"

"I've got more pressing issues than your morning cup of tea." She looked at her phone once more. "Robbie hasn't replied to me. He said he'd let me know this morning. Some husband he is! Leaving me sitting here like a lovesick teenager waiting for his text."

"Robbie's the perfect husband, and you know it." I focused my attention back on my cup. "Could it be the teaspoon? Have you changed your washing-up liquid?"

"Karis! Stop going on about your tea. If you don't like it, make yourself a coffee."

I instantly felt guilty about my behaviour when I saw Erin's face flush. "Sorry, Erin. You're right. I'm being silly. I'll make myself a coffee instead. Is there anything I can get for you? Some toast? A biscuit? A bacon sandwich?"

"Will you stop treating me like an invalid? If I wanted something to eat, then I'd get it myself!" Erin's face flushed even more, and she placed a hand on her stomach. She caught me looking and said, "Don't even think about asking me if the baby is alright. Every time I pull a face or put my hand on my stomach, you nag me about the baby. You're almost as bad as Robbie. Can't a pregnant woman have some peace?"

I pressed my lips together and gave her a smile.

Erin's eyes narrowed. "Karis, you would tell me if you'd had a vision about my baby, wouldn't you?" Her gaze softened and she nodded to herself. "Yes, you would tell me. I know you would."

"Of course I would," I lied convincingly before turning my back on her. I began to make myself a coffee.

I'd experienced a psychic vision concerning Erin a few weeks ago. In it, she'd lost her baby – the baby which Robbie and she so desperately wanted. I hadn't told her about that vision, and I never would. The things I saw were only an indication of what could happen in the future, and I knew events could change. Which was why I was trying to make Erin take it easy. But she was a stubborn individual.

I quickly made a coffee and joined Erin at the table.

She looked at me expectedly as I took a tiny slurp of the coffee. "Well?" she asked. "What does that taste like?"

"It's lovely." I took another drink. "It's perfect."

Erin leaned back in her chair and gave me a studied look. "So, it was just the tea that tasted weird?"

I nodded.

"There could be more going on here than meets the eye, my dear sister," Erin mused.

"What are you going on about?"

She tapped the table. "You, my dear sister, could be experiencing a vision of the sensory persuasion, and not one of your normal visual ones."

"Pardon? Can you stop using such big words and tell me what you're thinking?" I took another drink of coffee. It really was lovely. I'd always considered myself a tea drinker, but my tastes could be changing.

Erin explained, "You could be getting a vision through your taste buds. You know how you've become a magnet for murders recently—"

"I wouldn't call myself a magnet," I interrupted her.

"I would. Anyway, like I was saying. You're a magnet for murders and you might be picking up on something now. You could be psychically linking yourself to a murder victim who's going to die by drinking tea." She pushed her own cup to one side. "I hope it's no one we know."

I scoffed, "Don't be silly! It'll be because of my age and changing tastes. Something like that." I finished the rest of my coffee and smacked my lips together. "I think I'll have another one."

Erin put her hand on my arm and her eyes widened. "Karis, this isn't like you at all. You only have one coffee in a day, and that's only after you've had fifty cups of tea."

"Don't be silly," I repeated. I paused and looked down at my empty cup. I salivated as I thought about my next hit of coffee. I thought about tea, and my stomach clenched in disgust. I looked back at Erin. "There could be a modicum of truth in what you're saying."

Erin's phone beeped and she grabbed it. She smiled as she read the text. "Yay! It's from my wonderful husband. He says we can go there now!"

"Is it safe?" I asked. "Has all the dust gone? I don't want you breathing in a load of dust."

Erin replied, "Yes, it's safe. Robbie's had some of those air purifiers going for days."

"What about the paint? I don't want you breathing in any fumes. Will there be dust sheets on the floor? Are they secured properly? I don't want you tripping over a loose bit."

Erin gave me a look of exasperation. "Stop acting like a mother hen. Robbie has made sure the premises are safe for me. He's even worse than you when it comes to my welfare." She broke into a smile. "Karis, don't you want to see it?"

I returned her smile. "I do. Let's go."

Chapter 2

Robbie met us at the entrance to Erin's Café. He broke into a cheery smile when he saw us rushing towards him.

He said, "By heck! You two got here quickly. Did you fly here?" He gave Erin a quick kiss on her cheek. "You're looking radiant as ever, my love. Have you been taking it easy this morning?"

Erin attempted to push him to one side. "Stop fussing and move out of the way. Let me inside."

Robbie held his ground and didn't budge. His eyes twinkled as he looked at me. "Karis, have you got something to say to me? I can tell what you're thinking. Go ahead, there's no need to be polite."

I blurted out, "What on earth are you wearing?"

Robbie grinned and turned around so we could get the full effect of his outfit. He proudly proclaimed, "These are my working overalls. Every man should have a sturdy pair of denim overalls." His hands rested on the belt which was fastened around his rotund stomach. "This is my tool belt. As you can see, I have a variety of tools." He tapped his left ear. "I have the obligatory pencil behind my ear ready to use at a moment's notice. I haven't used it yet, but it's there for when the occasion should arise." He beamed at us.

Erin sniggered and said to me, "He looks like one of the Waltons, doesn't he?"

Robbie shook his head but continued to smile. "It's a good job I love you so much, Erin. I know how much you fancy me in this outfit. Don't forget my offer still stands."

"What offer?" I asked. "Or is that a private matter?"

Erin's lips pursed in disgust. "He wants to buy me a matching pair of overalls. He thinks I would look cute in them."

"You look cute in anything," Robbie said with a loving smile. "Are you coming in or what? I haven't got all day to chat. I've got work to do." He held his hand out and Erin placed her hand in his.

For once, my sister was lost for words as Robbie led her into the building. I was just as dumbstruck.

We stood in the centre of the room which had been the main part of Erin's Café. This was where the tables and chairs had been. A counter had been at the back of the room with the kitchen behind that. Those things had gone now. All that was left was a huge room.

Erin found her voice and said, "The walls have been plastered. They're all smooth and bump-free. I've never seen them like that before." She continued to take everything in. "Oh! New electric sockets! They're shiny. And there's so many of them. The ceiling! It's white. Where did those water stains go?"

I put my hands on Erin's shoulders and gently turned her to the left. I said to her, "Look at the extended area."

She did so. She gasped. "Karis! Look at all the room we've got. Did you know that building next door was so big when you bought it? It's much bigger than my café. It goes further back."

"I knew it was big, but it looks bigger now. The kitchen can go at the back of this new area. There's plenty of room."

Erin shook her head in disbelief and turned her face to me. Her eyes glittered. "It's too much, Karis. That building must have cost you a fortune."

"I wanted to buy it. I wanted to help you. Anyway, what else was I going to use my divorce settlement on?"

"You should have gone on a cruise instead of investing in my business. No, correct that. It's our business now."

She gave me a watery smile. "I'm so glad you did this. It's going to be so exciting." She looked at Robbie. "When will it be finished? When can we open the café? This building work is taking ages!"

Robbie replied calmly, "It's been one week, as you well know. We've done a huge amount in that week. Follow me, my impatient flower, and I'll show you something amazing."

He took Erin over to the new area and stopped at the furthest wall.

I followed them and said to Robbie, "You didn't have to take time off work to do this. We could have managed. Somehow."

He grinned at me and tugged at the top of his overalls. "And miss the chance to wear this? I'm having a whale of a time. The police station and the criminal world can manage without me for a while." He turned his attention to the drawings which were stuck on the wall. "This is a rough idea of how the café will look when it's finished."

Erin moved closer to the drawings. I did the same. We stared silently at them.

Robbie pointed to each one and explained, "This will be the main area where your normal customers will sit. As you can see, this new counter will show off your delicious cakes much more, Erin. And this area here will be separate to allow children to play safely while their guardians take a welcome break. I've already ordered the toys for the little ones."

Erin and I were still silent.

Robbie continued, "This is the kitchen. We've got everything you could possibly need in there, Erin, but feel free to change it around or add to it."

She gave him a small nod.

"And this will be the area where you can hold your craft evenings," Robbie proclaimed. "There's going to be plenty of storage, so you don't have to worry about that. These sofas and low tables give this area a more relaxed feel, don't you think?" He chuckled. "Excuse my drawing of those women knitting. I'm not very good at drawing people. It's just to give you an idea of what it would look like with customers."

Erin's voice was barely audible as she said, "It's perfect. All of it. Every little detail. Karis, look at it. It's our dream. It's coming alive."

I nodded and looked over at Robbie. "Thank you so much. I didn't know you'd made these sketches."

Robbie gave me a broad smile. "That's what a proper workman does. He prepares the way. This is only a rough idea. You can change things around later." He paused. "Karis, do you want to tell Erin about the other thing now?"

"I do."

"What other thing? Isn't this enough?" Erin asked. She wiped away a tear which had escaped. "This is more than enough."

I took her hands in mine and said, "Now, don't start shouting at me, but I've also bought the property upstairs."

Erin opened her mouth and looked like she was going to shout at me.

I quickly went on, "I negotiated a good deal with the buyer. The area upstairs has been empty for years. I thought we could have a quieter space up there. A place where people could go to catch up on their emails and that sort of thing. We'll have bigger tables and more sockets for people to charge their phones and whatnot. We could also have bookshelves where people can borrow books for free, or just read them while they're here. It would be the perfect place for our book club. We could even start a writers' group. There's a lovely view from the windows. It gives the room a relaxing feel."

Tears flowed freely down Erin's face. "You've done too much. Far too much."

I released her hands and wiped her tears away. "It's not just for you, it's for me too. I need a fresh start. We'll need more staff for upstairs, and I've already got applicants lined up. We can interview them together. There's going to be a lovely staffroom upstairs too. We'll take good care of our staff. And there'll be an area just for you if you need to have a lie-down."

Erin was like a human waterfall as the tears rolled down her cheeks. She couldn't speak. Robbie pulled her into his embrace and kissed the top of her head.

He looked over at me and said, "I think she approves."

The door to the café opened, and a man in a checked shirt and jeans entered. He was carrying a cardboard tray full of cups and he boomed, "The cavalry has arrived! I have brought refreshments from the outer lands! Tea for everyone!"

Robbie laughed. "Thanks, Howie. Come over here and meet my wife and her sister."

Howie walked towards us, still smiling.

The scene in front of me began to fade. My knees felt weak and I leaned against the wall for support. I was having a vision. And it was a strong one.

Chapter 3

In my vision, I saw Howie sitting in a big armchair in a living room. He was wearing a suit and tie and had just accepted a cup from a woman standing in front of him. The woman was wearing a long, flowery dress and had a lot of make-up on her young face. I couldn't read her expression as she stared silently at Howie.

Howie said loudly, "Thank you for the tea. Let's get back to the matter at hand. Who would benefit from his death? Are there any illegitimate children he didn't know about?" He took a swift drink from his cup and turned his head to focus on something in front of him. He went on in the same loud voice, "Maybe his daughter is not his. His wife could have been lying to him for years about him being the father."

His face suddenly drained of colour and he began to cough. The woman in front of him fiddled with the pearl necklace around her neck.

Howie coughed some more. The cup fell from his hand. He clenched his chest and slithered to the carpet.

The woman let out a small scream but then continued to play with her necklace. She glanced at Howie's prone body and her brow puckered. She stared some more. Then she let out a piercing scream and yelled, "Help! Somebody help!"

Someone was shaking my shoulder. I came back to the present and saw Erin's concerned face inches from mine. She whispered, "Have you just had a vision?"

I could only nod. I pushed myself away from the wall and tried not to look at Howie who was standing a short distance away and chatting happily to Robbie.

Erin put her hand on my arm and said, "Let's talk elsewhere. You look like you're about to collapse." She took me over to the area where the counter used to be. She found a couple of chairs from somewhere and forced me into one. She rubbed my hands and said, "Tell me everything."

I glanced over at Robbie who was giving me a concerned look. Howie was still chatting away to him and wasn't looking in our direction.

Keeping my voice low, I told Erin about the vision.

Her eyes widened. "He must have been drinking poisoned tea. This explains why your tea earlier tasted disgusting. This can't be a coincidence. I knew something was going on."

I shook my head. "I don't know what to make of it. I don't know for certain he was drinking tea in my vision."

Erin said, "Let me prove it to you." She stood up and walked away. She went over to Robbie and Howie and talked to them for a few seconds. She took two cups from the cardboard tray Howie was holding and came back to me.

As she sat down, I said, "You didn't tell them about my vision, did you?"

"Course not. I told them we were having a sit-down while we took in our new surroundings. But I will tell Robbie about what you saw later. You know he always believes your visions." She took a drink from one of the cups. "This tastes perfectly okay to me. You have a drink."

I took the cup and had a small drink of the tea. The taste of something sour and disgusting filled my mouth. It took all my good manners not to spit it out.

Erin nodded. "By the look on your face, it was another foul-tasting drink. Karis, this taste sensation must have something to do with your premonition. The tea, or whatever it is that Howie is going to drink, will have been poisoned. Do you agree?"

I placed the cup on the floor. "I think so."

"And that tea is going to kill him. Agreed?"

"I don't know if it's going to kill him. He fell to the carpet, and then my vision faded."

Erin said, "We have to do something about this. We have to prevent Howie from being murdered."

"I don't know if he is going to be murdered," I pointed out.

"Okay. Then we have to stop him having a coughing fit and falling off his chair. If he isn't going to be murdered, he could still be affected by whatever he drinks. Perhaps seriously affected."

I looked over at the men. "Let me think about how I'm going to tell Howie this. It's not something I can just blurt out."

The door to the café opened and a woman came in. I froze. I knew that woman.

Erin frowned at my expression before looking at the new visitor. She said, "She looks familiar. Where have I seen her before?"

My words felt forced as I said, "It's Vanessa Kett. We went to high school together."

Erin's eyebrows rose. "Vanessa Kett? That Vanessa Kett? The evil girl who made your life hell at high school? The one who made fun of your visions? Isn't she the one who came up with that nasty nickname?"

I nodded without taking my eyes off the woman. I said to Erin, "Vanessa scrawled that nickname across the bathroom walls. She wrote it on my books. She even wrote it on the chalk board at the beginning of each lesson."

Erin banged her cup down on the floor and made to rise. "Let me at her. I'm going to punch her right on the end of her skinny nose! Then I'm going to grab her by the scruff of her neck and fling her out of my café!"

I put my hand on Erin's arm and gently pushed her back down. "You'll do no such thing. I can fight my own battles." I looked at Vanessa who was now talking to Robbie and Howie. "She might have changed. People do."

Erin made a humph kind of noise. "She's coming this way. If she says one wrong word, I'm going to tackle her to the ground."

Vanessa walked over to us with a smile on her face. She was wearing an expensive-looking suit and her face was perfectly made up. I caught a whiff of her perfume as she came closer. It smelled expensive. A designer handbag swung casually from her elbow.

She stopped in front of Erin and declared, "Hello! You must be Robbie's wife. I don't think we've met before. I'm Vanessa McGarry. That's my husband, Howie. He's helping your spouse with this business project." She cast a look around her. "It's only a small job. This won't take my Howie long. He's used to dealing with much bigger projects. He runs his own building company, don't you know? I'm surprised he was able to fit your spouse in at such short notice. He's usually run off his feet with work. Of course, I make sure he takes time off for our holidays. We love our holidays. Elaine, have you ever been to Barbados? Or the Seychelles? We love it there."

Erin's mouth had dropped open during Vanessa's speech. She blinked and said, "No, I haven't. And it's Erin, not Elaine."

"Is it?" Vanessa frowned as if it were Erin who had got her name wrong. "Howie said you're going to make this into a little café of sorts. That's nice for you. People always need somewhere cheap and cheerful to go."

I heard a low growl coming from Erin, and I could see she was getting ready to give Vanessa a colourful tongue-lashing.

Then I made the mistake of drawing attention to myself. I stood up and said, "Hi, Vanessa. You probably don't remember me. We went to school together."

Vanessa's mouth dropped open as she looked at me. Her glance travelled slowly up and down me, and a nasty look came into her eyes. It was a nasty look that I knew well. She shrieked, threw her head back and let out a loud cackle. I would say she sounded like a witch, but that would be an insult to witches.

Her cackle caught Robbie and Howie's attention, and they stared our way.

Vanessa finished laughing and yelled, "Krazy Karis! It's Krazy Karis! After all these years! Howie, get over here. It's Krazy Karis!"

Erin leapt to her feet and shouted, "Shut your mouth! Don't you dare call my sister that! You evil creature!"

Vanessa was too busy laughing to pay any attention to Erin. She waved her hand at Howie who was striding towards her. "Howie, it's Krazy Karis! She was at school with me. She was such an idiot! She thought she was psychic. Can you believe that? She thought she could see into the future. What a freak!"

"She's not a freak!" Erin yelled. "She can see into the future! She's just had a vision! Karis saw your husband dying! He was murdered by a cup of tea. What do you think about that?"

Vanessa's laugh died.

Howie stopped in his tracks.

Robbie moved swiftly towards us.

There was steel in Vanessa's voice as she said, "What did you just say about my Howie?"

Chapter 4

Robbie came to our defence and said, "Karis, you don't have to say anything. Erin, don't say another word." He looked at Vanessa and added, "I think it's best if you leave now."

Vanessa glared at me. "I'm not leaving until you tell me what you think you saw. What's wrong? Are you too scared to talk about your so-called psychic visions now? I can't believe you're still claiming you've got special powers. You should have grown out of that by now. You're pathetic."

I saw Erin's face turning red. This confrontation wasn't doing her any good. I lifted my chin, faced Vanessa's hostile stare, and told her what I'd seen.

She did something totally unexpected. She burst into laughter. She put her hands on her hips and doubled over as her laughter increased. Howie looked embarrassed and tried to get her to stop.

Erin's hands were curled into fists now, and her eyes narrowed as she focused them on Vanessa. Robbie noticed Erin's agitated state and put his arm around her shoulders to keep her from jumping on Vanessa.

Vanessa finally stopped laughing. Her look was full of hate as she jeered, "You're more stupid than I remember, Krazy Karis. Are you trying to impress me or something? Did you know I was going to come in here soon? That's it, isn't it? You knew I was coming in, and you thought you'd try to impress me with your fake psychic abilities. You're so pitiful. You should be locked up."

"That's enough!" Robbie called out. I had never heard him raise his voice before. "Leave immediately, Vanessa. You are not welcome here."

Erin shouted out, "What Karis saw is true! She's never wrong. She's just told you your husband is going to die, and you laugh? What sort of a monster are you?"

Vanessa retorted, "I'm not a monster at all. Your stupid sister has deceived you too. She must have seen the play."

"What play?" Erin asked. "What are you talking about?"

Vanessa jerked her thumb at me. "Ask Krazy Karis."

I said, "I don't know what you're talking about."

Vanessa jeered, "Yeah, of course you don't. Let's all play along with your lie."

Howie cleared his throat and said, "I don't think Karis is lying about the play." He looked my way. "I'm in a play called A Murder To Laugh At. It's on at the local church hall. I play a police inspector. At one point, I'm poisoned by tea. And then I—"

"She knows what happens!" Vanessa snapped. "She must have seen the play. Then she made up a story about having a stupid vision. She fooled her sister, and now she's trying to fool us. She's beyond pathetic."

Vanessa McGarry didn't get the chance to say another word. I grabbed her arm and dragged her towards the door. Anger made me strong and she was unable to free herself from my grasp. I opened the door and pushed her outside.

Right into the path of DCI Sebastian Parker.

Vanessa pulled her arm free and yelled, "Get your hands off me, you madwoman!" She took in the sight of the policeman and recognition came into her eyes. "Seb! Seb Parker! I don't believe it. You're back from London, and just in the nick of time. Arrest her!"

Seb said coolly, "Hello, Vanessa. Who would you like me to arrest?"

Vanessa jabbed her finger my way. "Her! Krazy Karis! She's just attacked me! She threw me out of this

241

building. Don't just stand there. You are still a policeman, aren't you? Do something! You were at school with Krazy Karis. You know what she's like."

Seb's expression hardened. "I do know what Karis is like. She's a wonderful person with a caring heart. She isn't crazy now, and she never was. If you continue to insult her with that ridiculous name you made up years ago, I will be forced to speak to you about verbal assault."

"What?" Vanessa stared at him. "Why are you saying that? You used to call her that too."

"I know, and I'm deeply ashamed of that. I was an idiot for doing so. But that was a long time ago, and I've grown up. I hope you have too, Vanessa."

"But she's still crazy! She threw me out of this building!"

Seb gave her a small nod. "That would be the building which Karis co-owns with her sister. She has every right to evict anyone she sees fit to. I'm presuming Karis had a reason to make you leave. Were you causing a disturbance?" He looked at me and I saw the smallest of twinkles in his eyes. "Karis, would you like to file a report against Vanessa and her conduct inside your building? You can include a verbal assault claim too."

Despite being a grown woman, Vanessa stamped her foot on the pavement like a belligerent toddler. "I don't believe it, Seb Parker! What's got into you? She's got you fooled! You should have heard what she said about my Howie!"

Seb gave her a pleasant smile. "I don't care what she said about your Howie. I do care that you're causing a disturbance now. And you're blocking the pavement. Would you move along, please?"

Vanessa let out a couple of curse words before stalking away.

Seb's pleasant smile dropped as he watched her walking around the corner. He looked at me and said, "I hoped I'd never see Vanessa Kett ever again."

"Me too. She's called McGarry now. She's married to the building contractor who's renovating the café. I hope she doesn't come back."

"If she does, you phone me. I won't have anyone talking to you like that. It's bad enough that I called you that awful name at school; I won't have anyone else saying that to you."

I smiled at him. "Thanks. I can handle Vanessa. She doesn't scare me. She used to at school, but not anymore."

"What was she saying about her husband? Did you have a vision about him? You can tell me about it."

"I know I can. Seb, I know you're truly sorry for what you did to me at high school. And I know you have faith in my visions. I appreciate it."

He gave me a hopeful look. "Does this mean you've forgiven me?"

I nodded.

He punched his fists in the air. "Hallelujah! Miracles do happen." He jigged on the spot and waved his arms around.

I laughed. "You idiot. Stop doing that. People are staring."

He lowered his hands. "Let them. I don't care. Tell me about your latest vision."

I did so. I also told him what Vanessa had said about Howie being in a play.

When I'd finished, he said, "You're not going to believe this. I came here to ask you a favour." He pulled something from his pocket. "Mum's given me these tickets. She was supposed to be seeing a play tonight with a friend, but now she can't go. I was going to ask you to come with me." He gave the tickets to me.

I shook my head in disbelief. "These are for Howie's play."

"Talk about a coincidence," he said. "Or maybe this is something which is meant to be. Will you come with me? If we watch the play, we might be able to work out what your vision means."

I nodded. "As long as you check the tea before Howie drinks it. I don't want to take any chances."

Chapter 5

I could tell Seb was going to be trouble as soon as we walked towards the church hall later that evening.

He stopped at the noticeboard and shook his head. "Look at the name of this play. A Murder To Laugh At. What sort of a title is that? Murder is never something to laugh at. What are people thinking of?"

I pulled on his arm and dragged him towards the entrance to St Anne's Church hall. "It's only a title. I'm sure whoever wrote it wasn't insulting anyone. Hurry up, there's a queue at the door."

Seb muttered something under his breath, and then walked along the path with me. He said, "There's no need to rush, we've got allocated seats. There had better not be anyone sitting in our seats. I hate it when that happens. People should respect the reservation system. Have you ever been on a train and someone is sitting in your reserved seat? You stare at them, and then they look away innocently as if they've done nothing wrong." His face was scrunched up in annoyance and he glowered at an elderly woman in front of us.

I swatted his arm. "What's wrong with you, grumpy-face? Why are you in such a bad mood?"

He sighed heavily. "It's that business with Vanessa earlier. It's really got to me. I hated how she treated you at school, but I never stopped her. She scared me. Because I was such a wimp, I lost your friendship. We've wasted so many years of not being friends." There was a wistful look in his eyes. "If we'd have stayed friends, things could have been different between us now."

"We're friends now," I told him. "Although, if you carry on being a misery guts, I'll find someone else to sit with inside."

He gave me a half-smile. "I'll try to cheer up. Tell me again about your vision and what Howie said."

We joined the end of the queue. I kept my voice low as I reminded Seb about my vision.

He said, "I'm going to speak to whoever's in charge and find out who supplies the drink to Howie. I might even stay near the stage and keep an eye on whatever he drinks."

I gave him a nod. "That's a good idea. Thanks."

He reached into his pocket and produced a small paper bag. He gave it to me and said, "Take this now in case I don't join you for a while."

"What is it?"

He shrugged. "Just a pick and mix I put together for you. I know how you like your sweets. I think I've remembered all your favourite ones."

I was speechless for about three seconds. "Thank you. That's so kind." I opened the bag. "Jelly babies. Sherbet pips. Pear drops! Are those pieces of fudge? What flavour are they?"

"I got you a mixture. There's mint, chocolate and banana. Don't eat them all at once."

I moved the open bag towards him and said reluctantly, "Would you like one? Don't take the fudge."

He smiled and patted his pocket. "You can have them all to yourself. I've got my own bag of sweets. I know what you're like when it comes to sharing sweets."

I shot him a smile and put the bag in my handbag. Then I took it out, picked out a cube of fudge, popped it in my mouth and put the bag back.

Once we got inside, Seb gave me the tickets and then went off towards the stage area. I found our seats and put my folded coat on Seb's seat. I didn't want anyone to sit there by mistake, not after what Seb had said about reserved seats earlier.

While I was waiting for the play to start, I helped myself to more sweets. I wasn't the only one tucking into a snack. Many people in the chairs around me were taking treats out. I frowned when I saw a middle-aged man opening a family size packet of crisps. Crisps! At a play? What was he thinking?

The hall was soon full, and there was an air of excited expectation. After a few more minutes, the lights around the hall dimmed and the ones near the curtain-covered stage lit up. The audience began to quieten down.

Seb hadn't joined me at this point, so I presumed he was still on tea patrol.

A man in a tweed jacket came on the stage and some people at the front cheered. Were we all supposed to cheer? Was he a local celebrity?

The man opened his arms wide and cast us a benevolent smile. He boomed, "Welcome! Welcome! Thank you for joining us on this special evening. Many of you have been to our past productions. You know we're only amateurs when it comes to this acting business, but we always give it our best shot. You're in for a real treat tonight. May I politely request that all phones are switched off. Also, recording of this performance is prohibited. Without further ado, may I present," he paused for dramatic effect, "A Murder To Laugh At!" He bowed his head and walked backwards off the stage.

Everyone clapped and the curtains were pulled back. I stopped clapping when I saw the scene on the stage. It was the room I'd seen in my vision.

The play began, but I couldn't focus on what was happening because my stomach was in knots of apprehension. Seb was still absent. I wasn't sure if that was a good thing or not. Had he discovered the poisoned tea? Was he arresting someone right now?

I tried my best to focus on what was happening in the play. There was a character called Lord Gresham. He was played by the man who'd introduced the play. He didn't have many lines because he was murdered ten minutes after he first appeared. A few minutes after that, Howie McGarry came onstage. He was wearing the clothes I'd seen in my vision. My heart was pounding at this stage, and my armpits felt unpleasantly damp.

I heard a commotion at the end of the row I was sitting in. I looked that way and saw Seb making his way towards me, disturbing everyone on the way. He sat at my side and gave me a small smile.

I raised my eyebrows in question. In reply, he gave me a thumbs-up gesture. I had no idea what that meant.

I concentrated on the play. The young woman in pearls appeared. She was the daughter of Lord Gresham. In his role of detective, Howie questioned her about the suspicious death of her father. He hovered near the armchair at the front of the stage as if he were going to sit down soon. The young woman offered him a cup of tea. I leaned forward in my seat. The events I'd seen in my vision were going to happen soon.

Seb muttered something. I turned my head to look at him. He jerked his thumb at the stage and mumbled, "That's not correct police procedure. They've got it all wrong."

I frowned at him and turned my head back to the stage. Howie was sitting down now. The woman had moved over to a tray at the side of the room and was picking up a cup of tea.

CRUNCH!

I jumped as the man with the family packet of crisps munched on his snack.

Really? I shot him an annoyed look, but he didn't register it and dipped his hand back into the open packet.

Onstage, the woman in pearls passed a cup to Howie. Howie said, "Who would benefit from his death?"

CRUNCH!

I gritted my teeth as I gave the crisp-eater a hard look. Howie was drinking the tea now.

Seb muttered something else under his breath. The crisp-eater continued crunching.

All of a sudden, Howie started to cough. His face turned red. He dropped the cup and slithered to the carpet. The young woman gave a half-hearted scream.

I froze. I could hear the loud thudding of my heart in my ears.

Then something weird happened.

Howie abruptly got to his feet and yelled, "Aha! Think you can poison me, eh? I saw you putting poison in my tea, young lady. Luckily for me, I always carry a vial of antidote in my pocket. I took the precaution of taking a small dose while your back was turned. Aha! Now I know for sure it was you who killed Lord Gresham! Aha!"

I looked over at Seb and whispered, "What just happened?"

Seb's face was a picture of disgust. He whispered back, "This is a disgrace. I never saw him taking anything out of his pocket. Do they think we're stupid?"

I didn't know whether to be relieved that Howie was alright, or to be worried that my vision hadn't come true.

The play didn't last much longer. All the loose ends were tied up far too quickly. Seb continued to complain about the lack of proper police procedure, and the man munching on his crisps continued to crunch away.

Once the play was over, Seb and I quickly left the hall and walked towards his car.

I said to him, "It didn't happen. My vision didn't come true."

"Aren't you glad about that?" he asked.

"I am, but what happened to change the events? Was it something you did?"

He shrugged. "It might have been. I spoke to the woman who makes the tea for Howie to drink onstage. She told me Howie likes everything to be authentic during a play, so he makes sure proper tea is used. And it has to be warm too. I kept by her side until the tea was placed at the side of the stage. No one interfered with it."

We stopped at his car and he opened it.

I got in, fastened my seat belt and said, "Perhaps whoever was intending to harm Howie saw you near the tea. They could have changed their minds."

He glanced over at me. "You don't look happy about this. What's wrong?"

"Something doesn't feel right. I couldn't hear what Howie was saying onstage when he was sitting down. I don't know if his words matched the ones in my vision."

Seb gave me a knowing look. "It was that man eating crisps, wasn't it? Noisy thing. Some people have no consideration."

"It was you too. You kept moaning about police procedure."

He held his hand up. "Don't get me started on that. Whoever wrote that play should be arrested for crimes against humanity. As if a police officer would carry an antidote with him at all times! I should make a formal complaint."

I smiled at his annoyed expression. "And will you?"

He grinned. "No. Despite the errors in the play, I enjoyed spending time with you. Have you got to rush home? Or do you have time for fish and chips?"

"Now that I know Howie is still alive, I think I could manage something to eat. You'd better get your own chips, Seb Parker, because I'm not sharing mine."

Seb laughed before driving us away from St Anne's Church.

Despite my words, there was something bothering me about Howie McGarry. I had the strongest feeling that he wasn't out of danger yet.

Chapter 6

My suspicions about Howie's wellbeing were confirmed the next morning when I took a sip of my first tea of the day.

It was vile. I spat it into the sink immediately. The disgusting taste lingered in my mouth, so I dashed upstairs and brushed my teeth for the second time that morning.

I decided to discuss this matter with one of my best friends. She lived next door and I knew she'd be up at this early hour. Despite being in her late seventies, Peggy Marshall had the energy of a person much younger.

I left the house and walked the short distance to the adjoining semi-detached. I knocked on the front door and Peggy yelled at me from inside, "Karis, let yourself in!"

I found her in the kitchen, sitting at the table. She was peering at the computer screen in front of her. She didn't look up as I walked over to her. I said, "How did you know it was me at the door?"

Peggy said, "I recognised your knock. I'm just in the middle of a sentence. I won't be a moment. Put the kettle on."

I looked at the computer screen. "Peggy, you don't have to do a blog post every day. The visitors to our website don't expect fresh content all the time."

She chuckled. "But I like doing it. And our visitors like it too, they've told me so in the comments. It's like writing in a diary, but the whole world can read it. It's very therapeutic. Apparently, I'm very witty and have a way with words." She tapped at the keyboard. "There. That's my words written for the day."

"What have you written about? I read yesterday's post about your visit to the wool stall in the market. Did that woman really say that to you?"

Peggy looked my way. "She certainly did! The nerve of her. She claimed something was wrong with my eyesight. I told her my eyesight was perfect and it was her batch of wool that was wrong. Anyone could see the red colours didn't match in that bag she was trying to sell me. As if I could knit a jumper using that batch of wool!" Peggy tutted. "She had a nerve trying to get one over on me. She'll know better next time. That's what I've been telling my readers today. I told them to always check their wool before buying a batch of it. Check every single ball even if that takes extra time."

Something at the end of the table caught my attention. I said, "Isn't that the batch of wool the woman tried to sell you yesterday? I recognise it from the photo you posted."

Peggy chuckled. "It is. After giving her a piece of my mind, I said I'd take that wool off her for half price. She agreed. I think she just wanted me out of the way."

I frowned. "But what will you use it for? You said the shades of red didn't match."

"Ah, but it'll be perfect for my first knitting lesson." She pointed to the screen. "I did that poll-thing online like you suggested. My readers are very interested in knitting lessons. We could make that our first craft evening in the new place. What do you think?"

"Have we got enough local people interested?"

"Many. Too many, in fact. I might have to get someone to video it for those who live too far away. Is it too early to give my readers a date? Is the new café nearly ready? How's the work coming along?" She held her hand up. "Don't answer any questions until we get a cuppa. Keeping my readers entertained is thirsty work. Let me make the tea. I need to stretch my legs."

She stood up and moved over to the kettle. Once she filled that and switched it on, she opened the tea caddy.

I called over, "No tea for me, thanks. I'll have a coffee."

Peggy spun around. "What? No tea? You want coffee? Karis Booth, what's going on? You always have tea in a morning."

"I've had another vision, and it's affecting how tea tastes. I can't bear the taste of it at the moment."

Peggy's hands flew to her chest. "No tea? You poor love. That's awful, truly awful. I want to know everything about this new vision of yours."

She quickly made drinks for us and then we sat at the kitchen table. I told Peggy about my vision and my subsequent trip to the church hall with Seb. I informed her what Vanessa had said to me in the café, but I didn't tell Peggy how awful she'd been and the names she'd called me. Peggy had the same quick temper as Erin when it came to my welfare.

When I'd finished, Peggy shook her head slowly. "We have to do something. This could be a potential murder we're looking at. We dealt with those other two murders, and now it looks like we've got another one."

"I don't know if Howie is going to be murdered," I pointed out.

"I think he will be. Why else would you have seen him collapsing and that woman screaming? And why else would you be off your tea? Something's wrong. What did you say the name of that play was again?"

"A Murder To Laugh At."

She pursed her lips. "That's a ridiculous title. Murder is never funny."

"That's what Seb said."

She gave me a sharp look. "You're smiling. Why are you smiling? Is it something to do with Seb? Have you finally forgiven him?"

I nodded. "I have. There's no point holding on to anger, is there? Anyway, he bought me a pick and mix. And fish and chips. And he takes my visions seriously."

She smiled. "I'm glad to hear that. I'll take it easier on him when I next see him. But if he does anything to upset you, just let me know and I'll sort him out. Hang on while I make a quick phone call to one of my friends."

She walked into the living room and I heard her talking loudly to someone on the phone.

When she came back, I said, "You've managed to get us tickets for the play. And for tonight too. That's great."

Her eyes narrowed. "How did you know that? Did you have another vision?"

"No, I heard you. You're very loud when you're on the phone."

"I like to make myself clear. I can pick the tickets up later. Do you want to go with me tonight? We can keep a close eye on Howie and see what happens to him."

"Yes, I'd love to go. That would put my mind at ease. Thanks, Peggy."

Peggy returned to her sitting position. "What will we do if he starts dying for real onstage?"

"I don't know."

She patted my hand. "We'll think of something." She looked towards her computer screen. "The comments are already coming in about my latest post. I'd better reply to them. I don't want to be rude. I'll put another post on our Facebook page too. People seem to like those."

"Peggy, is this too much for you? I can deal with the blog posts and all the other online stuff too."

"I love doing this," Peggy declared. "I love being part of this new adventure you and Erin are having. It's making me feel useful again. My body might be showing its age, but my mind is as sharp as ever."

My phone rang. It was Robbie. I listened to what he said and then replied, "Okay Robbie, I'm on my way. See you soon." I ended the call.

Peggy said, "What did Robbie want?"

"It's Erin. She's at the café and getting in everyone's way. She's sweeping up and cleaning everything. Robbie said they can't get on with the heavy work until she's gone, but she refuses to leave. He wants me to take her out for the day. Do you want to come with us?"

"I'll say no. I've got my readers to think about. Being a blogger is a serious business. I have commitments to the World Wide Web. You go. I'll see you tonight when we go to the play. You can tell me how the building work is going then."

I quickly drained my coffee and left Peggy's house. I kept up a cheerful demeanour as I said goodbye to her. As soon as I got in my car, my cheerfulness left me. When Robbie had spoken to me just now, I got the strongest feeling that something was wrong with Erin. It wasn't anything Robbie had said, but as soon as he'd said Erin's name, a cold feeling of dread settled in my stomach like a block of ice.

Chapter 7

Robbie was standing with Erin outside the café when I arrived. He was wearing his overalls again, which made me smile for a moment.

I pulled up outside the café.

Robbie jogged over to the passenger door and opened it. He said, "Don't get out. You're not stopping. Take your sister away for the day. As much as I love her, she's being a nuisance. I think she could do with a nap."

Erin called over from the café door, "I can hear you, Robbie Terris. There's no need to talk about me as if I'm a child."

Robbie ignored her and continued talking to me, "She could be hungry too. Get her something to eat, but nothing too sugary. Phone me if she becomes too much of a handful. Thanks, Karis."

He moved away from the door, and a few seconds later, Erin got in. She put her handbag on her knee and folded her arms. She shot an annoyed look at her husband through the window. Robbie gave her a joyful wave, blew her a kiss and went into the café.

"Have you been naughty?" I asked her.

"Don't you start on me," she said with a hint of stubbornness in her voice. "I was only trying to help. I only wanted to speed things up. But he wouldn't let me. He said I was asking too many questions and that I should leave him and his worker friends to get on with it."

I smiled. "And were you asking too many questions?"

She grinned. "A bit. I'm interested, that's all." She pulled the hair back from her face and pointed to her ear. "I've pinched Robbie's pencil. He'll be looking for it all day." Her grin widened.

I shook my head at her. "Erin, are you feeling okay today?"

"If you ask me how the baby is, I'm going to throw this pencil at you," she warned. "Or better still, I'll tell Robbie it was you who pinched it."

I repeated her earlier words, "I'm interested, that's all."

"I'm fine. The baby is fine. Everything is fine. Okay?"

"Okay. Where do you want to go?"

"Drive around town for five minutes so Robbie thinks we've gone. Then we'll come back and park further down the road. We can spy on Robbie from there."

"We'll do no spying today," I told her. "I know where we can go. How's Howie this morning?"

"Oh! I forgot. You went to see his play last night. He said he saw you in the audience. What happened? Did any part of your vision come true?"

I drove away from the café and began to tell Erin about my evening.

She was of the same opinion as Peggy. "You need to see the play again. Something could happen to Howie during a future performance."

"I'm going with Peggy to see it tonight. You can come with us if you like? I'm sure she can get you a ticket."

She shook her head. "No, thanks. His ignorant wife might be there. I won't be able to keep calm if I see her, not after what she said to you." She looked out of her window. "I know where we are. Are we going to see Mum?"

"We are. I know we saw her a few days ago, but I'd like to see her again." I hesitated. "Do you think she looks any better? Do you think she recognised us last time? I thought I saw a flicker of something in her eyes when we first went in. Did you?"

"I wish I could say yes, but I didn't see anything. Mum hasn't changed since she went into the care home, Karis.

I know we keep hoping she'll get better and come home, but that isn't going to happen. We have to accept that."

"We don't," I argued.

A few minutes later, I drove into the grounds of Wood Crescent Care Home and parked in the visitors' area. We found Mum in her favourite area in the Sun Room, sitting by the window and looking out at the garden.

We sat in chairs in front of her, but she didn't look our way.

I said, "Hello Mum. It's me, Karis. Erin's here too. We thought we'd pay you a surprise visit."

There was no response from Mum, but that didn't put me off. I proceeded to tell her about the work we were having done on the café. Erin joined in and told Mum how Robbie had practically thrown her out of the café this morning.

"I was only trying to help, Mum," Erin said. She rested her hand on her stomach. "I know I'm pregnant, but I'm not an invalid."

Mum's head suddenly turned our way. Her eyes alighted on Erin and a ghost of a smile settled on her lips. The smile died, and Mum's eyes narrowed slightly.

I'd shared a vision with Mum a few weeks back, and I knew her mind still retained memories of her family.

I leaned forward in my chair, took one of Mum's hands in mine and said, "Mum, what's wrong?"

She didn't take her eyes off Erin as she whispered, "The baby. Hospital. Now."

Erin stiffened. "Mum? Say that again. Please."

Mum took her hand from mine, shuffled to the end of her chair and placed her hand over Erin's hand. She said, "Hospital. Now. Go."

I stood up. "Come on, Erin, we have to go to the hospital immediately."

"But I feel fine." Erin looked up at me. "Karis, Mum is talking. I haven't heard her talk for two years. We can't leave her."

Mum took her hand back and said, "Go. Now." She turned her head away and stared out of the window.

I pulled Erin to her feet. "We're going to the hospital now."

"But—"

"No arguments," I said sharply. "We're going and that's that."

I had to force Erin away from Mum and out of the care home. She kept insisting she was fine and wanted to stay with Mum. I ignored her protests.

I put Erin in the car and fastened her seat belt. She'd stopped arguing with me by this point and was silent.

As we drove away from the home, Erin said quietly, "Do you think Mum had a vision about me and the baby? Do you think something terrible is going to happen to the baby?"

"Not if I can help it."

I drove as quickly as I could and we soon arrived at the hospital. I helped Erin out of the car and inside. Her face was white now and beads of sweat dotted her forehead.

In a frightened tone, she said, "Karis, I don't feel well at all. It's come over me all of a sudden. Don't leave me, will you? Whatever happens, I want you by my side."

"I'm not leaving you. Keep quiet now and I'll do all the talking."

And that's what I did. The woman on the reception desk must have seen the worry in my eyes because she summoned a doctor immediately. When the doctor arrived, she took one look at Erin and took her into an examination room. I was allowed in and I held Erin's hand as she was looked over.

When the doctor had finished, she announced, "Everything is okay with you and the baby, Mrs Terris.

But I'm concerned about your blood pressure. It's far too high. Have you been overexerting yourself recently?"

"No," Erin said.

"Yes," I confirmed.

The doctor flipped through Erin's notes. "I can see how important this pregnancy is to you. I think it would be wise for you to stay here tonight. I'd like to keep an eye on you. Is that okay with you?"

"No," Erin said.

"Yes," I confirmed. "Thank you."

The doctor continued, "A private room has just become free. We'll put you in there, Mrs Terris. The nurse will take you there. I'll check on you later." She gave Erin a long look. "You need to rest. Not just for your sake, but for the baby too. Okay?"

Erin said, "Yes. Thank you."

The doctor left and a nurse entered. She brought a wheelchair with her. Erin surprised me by not arguing about the sudden appearance of the wheelchair. She meekly sat in it and bowed her head. She held her hand out for me, and I didn't let go of it until we reached the private room.

The nurse settled Erin into bed. I took the opportunity to phone Robbie.

He was at the hospital in a flash. I told him what the doctor had said and then left him to have some private time with Erin.

I thought it would be better to leave Robbie and Erin alone for the rest of the day. I didn't want to intrude. But Erin had other ideas.

When I attempted to say goodbye to the couple, she said, "Where do you think you're going? You promised you'd stay with me."

"But you've got Robbie," I pointed out.

Robbie was sitting at Erin's side. He nodded. "That's right. I'm not going anywhere."

"I want you to stay with me, Karis," Erin said. Her bottom lip trembled. "You promised. Please."

I wasn't used to seeing her like this, and I could tell how worried she was. I said, "I can stay."

"All day? And all night?" Erin asked.

"If the staff let me," I answered. "Let me tell Peggy where we are. She'll only worry if I don't return home."

I left the room and made a quick call to Peggy. She was upset by the news and told me to stay by Erin's side. She said she'd still go to Howie's play and keep an eye on him. She said she might even start a rumour about the tea being poisoned before the play started in the hope of Howie doing away with the tea altogether.

Peggy said, "I can be very persuasive if needed. Don't you worry about Howie. I'll make sure he doesn't pop his clogs tonight."

Once I'd said goodbye to Peggy, I returned to Erin's room and sat in the chair at her other side. Robbie and I did our best to raise her spirits. We watched hours of TV. Robbie found some board games in a cupboard and we played those. Robbie even ordered a takeaway and had it delivered right to the room. I don't know how he managed that.

The nurses and doctors came by at regular intervals to check on Erin. They were pleased with her progress.

The kind nurses brought in camp beds so that Robbie and I could stay in Erin's room all night.

We didn't get to sleep for hours that night. It wasn't because the camp beds were so uncomfortable, it was because my chatty sister wouldn't stop talking. She talked about everything. Our childhood. Mum and Dad. And our plans for the café. I was pleased to see her so animated, but blimey, could she talk!

After being checked over the next morning, Erin was released. Robbie said he'd take her home and stay with her all day.

I yawned as I said goodbye and got into my car. I was planning on getting into bed as soon as I returned home. I was exhausted.

But that didn't happen.

Someone was waiting for me in the kitchen.

It was Peggy. She'd been crying.

I took one look at her pale face and said, "It's Howie McGarry, isn't it?"

She nodded. "He's dead. He died last night during the play."

Chapter 8

Peggy was inconsolable. She shook her head sadly and said, "I should have done more. I should have prevented this."

I sat at her side and put my hand over hers. "Don't be so hard on yourself. Tell me what happened."

She gave me a weak smile. "When I got to the church hall, I saw some people I knew in the queue. I made up a ridiculous story about seeing another play where an actor had poisoned the drink of a fellow actor because he was jealous of him. I said these things happen all the time in the acting business. I made sure my voice carried throughout the queue. Then someone in front of me told me they knew Howie McGarry. She went on about the tea he drinks during the play. She was worried the same thing could happen to him. Apparently, Howie had a few enemies amongst the acting profession."

My eyebrows rose at that comment, but I didn't say anything.

Peggy continued, "Well, you know what people are like once they hear a rumour. Or a made-up story in this case. I caused quite a commotion. The other people in the queue told this woman she should warn Howie about a possible poisoning. And that's what she did."

"What happened after that?"

"I didn't know if the rumour would work on Howie, so I left a note for him with the woman who took my ticket. I told her it was urgent. I wrote the note before I left home and put it in a sealed envelope."

"What did you write?"

She looked guilty for a second. "It was quite dramatic. At first, I thought I would let him know about an attempted poisoning. But Howie might not have taken that seriously. So I told him I was going to kill him. I said I was going to sneak poison into his tea and make sure he died in the middle of the play." Spots of colour came to her cheeks. "I shouldn't have done that. I know that now."

I stared at her for a moment. Then I found my voice, "So, Howie McGarry died last night. And there's a threatening note from you somewhere? I hope you didn't sign it."

"I'm not that stupid," Peggy said. She sighed. "I take that back. I am that stupid. I shouldn't have written that note. It didn't work anyway. He still drank that tea. It was just how you described it. He fell off his chair and didn't move. That young lass in the pearls started screaming the house down. The curtains closed, and a few minutes later we were asked to leave the hall."

"Has it been on the news yet? I haven't had time to catch up on anything this morning."

She nodded. "There's not much information at the moment. The man on the radio said a local man had died under suspicious circumstances at a church hall." She looked down at her hands and I was surprised to see tears falling onto the table.

"Peggy, you did all that you could to stop this. We've been in this situation before. Sometimes, we can't stop terrible things happening."

She looked up at me. "I know. But I feel responsible."

"You're not responsible. Only the person who killed Howie is. Let me make you a cup of tea." I stood up and walked over to the kettle. I filled it with water and switched it on. "Peggy, have you had anything to eat?"

"I haven't. I couldn't face anything. I am a bit hungry now, though."

"I'll make us some toast. I haven't had anything either. I didn't fancy the food at the hospital." I reached for the toaster.

"Oh! The hospital! Erin! I forgot." Peggy came over to me. "With all this Howie business, I clean forgot about Erin. Is she okay? How about the baby?"

I told Peggy about Erin as I made her some toast and tea. I made some for myself too.

We sat at the kitchen table and discussed how we could help Erin. Then our talk turned to Howie, and we speculated as to who the murderer could be. We didn't know Howie well, and we didn't come up with many suspects.

Peggy suddenly stared at me. "Are you drinking tea?"

I looked in surprise at the cup in my hand. "I am. I was on autopilot when I made it."

"How does it taste?"

"Lovely. Perfect." I frowned at my cup. "I don't know whether to be pleased or not. What does this mean?"

"It means we have to find out who murdered Howie McGarry," Peggy declared. "There's a reason why you have these visions, and why tea tasted funny to you. These are signs telling you to get involved. You might get some more premonitions which will lead us to the killer. We have to get ourselves involved in the investigation."

"We can't do that. We should leave everything to the police."

She shook her head. "You know what happened last time. And the time before that. If you hadn't got involved, those murders wouldn't have been solved. You're on friendly terms with Seb now. Tell him you're going to help. Tell him I'll help too."

I was about to argue, but my phone rang. It was Erin. She said, "Karis, have you heard about Howie?"

"I have."

She tutted. "While I'm extremely sad that Howie has died, part of me wants to tell Vanessa that your vision

266

was right. Would I be an awful person if I phoned her up and told her that?"

"You would be a terrible person if you did that, Erin. Get that thought out of your head right now."

She tutted again.

"Is there a reason for your call?" I asked. "Are you okay?"

"Yeah, course I am. Robbie's gone to the café to talk to the workers. He's going to stop the work for today and send them home as a sign of respect for Howie."

"How is Robbie?"

Erin sighed. "You know what he's like. He puts a cheerful face on. I could see how upset he was when we heard the news. He said he'd only leave me for a short while if I promised to get in touch with you." Her tone turned indignant. "He wants you to look after me like some invalid or child. You don't have to. I can take care of myself."

I looked over at Peggy and saw the sadness in her face as she looked at her plate. I said to Erin, "I'm coming over. Peggy's coming with me." I said goodbye and ended the call.

"Are we going over to Erin's?" Peggy asked. "Is something wrong?"

"No, we're just going to babysit her for a while. We need to keep her occupied. I've got an idea on how we can do that. You can help me. We'll have to collect some things from your house first."

Once we had everything we needed, we headed over to Erin's house.

As soon as we walked in, I announced to Erin, "You're going to learn how to knit. Peggy's going to teach you."

Erin folded her arms. "I don't want to knit. I tried it once, and I didn't like it."

"That's because you didn't have a teacher as wonderful as Peggy," I told her.

Peggy blushed. "I wouldn't say that."

"I would. You taught me to knit when I was young. And now you're going to teach Erin."

Erin argued, "Can't we do something else? Can't we watch the TV?"

"This is for our business," I informed her. "Our first class in the café will be a knitting one. This will be good practice for Peggy. If she can teach someone like you to knit, then she can teach anyone."

"What do you mean by that?" Erin asked.

I ignored her question and said to Peggy, "Could you manage the casting on process with Erin? Or is that too advanced?"

Peggy sized Erin up and declared, "I'll do my best. I'll start off with the basic knitting stitch and we'll see how she does." She ambled over to the sofa with the bag of materials she'd brought with her. She sat down and patted the seat next to her. "Come on, Erin. You're going to love this. We'll have you knitting away in no time."

"I doubt it," Erin mumbled under her breath. She gave me an imploring look. "Do I have to do this?"

"Yes. Go." I pointed to Peggy who now had her knitting needles out.

Erin grumbled a bit more and dragged herself over to the sofa. She looked like a sulky teenager.

I went into the kitchen and took my phone out. It had been vibrating with messages for the last ten minutes. I had a feeling I knew who was texting me.

I was right. It was Seb. He wanted me to meet him at St Anne's Church hall immediately.

As I didn't want to tell Erin and Peggy where I was going, I called out from the kitchen, "I'm just popping out for a while. Bye!"

I heard them both shout back, "Where are you going?"

I ignored them and dashed out of the door.

It didn't take me long to reach the hall. Seb was waiting at the side of the road as I pulled up in my car. He was holding a clear plastic bag. There was a piece of paper in the bag.

When I got out of the car, Seb said, "Did Peggy Marshall kill Howie?"

Chapter 9

I averted my gaze from the plastic bag and feigned innocence. "What makes you say that?"

He flapped the bag in the air. "This is Peggy's writing. I recognised it from a card she sent to Mum last week. And I can see the imprint of an earlier letter on it. I can clearly make out her name and address."

I made a mental note to tell Peggy not to make that mistake again.

Seb lowered the bag. "Don't even think about warning her not to make this mistake again."

"I wasn't thinking that," I replied as indignantly as I could. It's hard to be indignant when you're lying.

He shook his head at me. "You need to work on your poker face. Tell me why Peggy sent this threatening letter to Howie McGarry."

I told him the reasoning behind Peggy's actions. I concluded, "She didn't mean any harm. She was trying to help. Where did you find the letter?"

"At the back of the stage under one of the props. It had been opened and scrunched up."

"Oh? Do you think Howie read it?"

"I don't know. If he did, it didn't have the required effect. He still drank the tea which was given to him onstage."

I said, "Maybe the killer got to the letter before Howie did. Are you going to dust the letter for fingerprints?"

He gave me a serious look. "Are you trying to tell me how to do my job, Mrs Booth?"

I couldn't tell if he was serious or not. Until a twinkle came into his eyes.

He went on, "I will make the necessary investigations. This letter wasn't the reason why I wanted you to meet me here." He glanced towards the church hall. "I could do with your help." He looked back at me.

"Help? In what way?"

"In the psychic ability sort of way." He frowned. "If you know what I mean. The church hall is empty now. Could you come inside and see if you can pick up on anything, please? We're making the normal investigations, but you've helped me a great deal in the past. Would you help me again? You have a unique ability."

I was touched by his words. "Yes. Of course. Yes. Thanks." I wasn't sure what I was saying thanks for.

Seb put the plastic bag in his pocket. He turned towards the church hall. "I can't tell you much about my investigation so far. We're talking to many witnesses and have various lines of enquiries to take."

I couldn't help but smile at how official he sounded. I nodded as I followed him towards the hall.

He continued, "I have spoken to the woman who made the tea. She's mortified about what's happened. She made Howie's tea as normal last night and then left it at the side of the stage. From what I saw when we were at the play the other night, the tea is in plain sight for anyone in that area of the hall. Unfortunately." He shook his head. "Perhaps I should have said something to Howie about the tea the other night. I could have prevented this."

"Feeling guilty doesn't help," I told him. "Peggy's full of remorse. I am too. But some events can't be altered. You saw that when we were growing up. You saw how many times I tried to stop things happening, but they happened anyway."

He stopped at the door and gave me a considered look. He said, "I never realised how difficult this psychic thing is for you. You've had a lot to deal with."

I smiled. "It helps when I have support from my friends. Come on; let's get on with this."

We entered the hall. It was silent and empty. There was a heavy, oppressive atmosphere.

Seb said quietly, "It's different from the last time you were here. Where do you want to go first? The stage? The scenery from the play is all there."

I nodded and then made my way to the stage. My heart missed a beat when I saw the chair where Howie had taken his final breaths. I was half expecting a chalk outline of his body to be on the carpet. Thankfully, there wasn't an outline of any sort.

I moved closer to the chair, took a few deep breaths and closed my eyes. I focused on the vision I'd had previously of Howie.

Nothing happened.

I didn't get any new visions or sensations.

I opened my eyes and gave Seb a shake of my head.

"Keep trying," he said.

I sat in the chair and tried again.

Still nothing.

I tried standing in many areas of the stage.

Still nothing.

"Sorry," I said to Seb with an embarrassed smile. "I'm not getting anything."

"That's okay. I know you can't force it. We can try the dressing rooms now."

I was about to leave the stage, but something caught my eye. I said to Seb, "There! I saw a shimmer of something on that row of chairs." I made a quick count. "The third row back."

"What did you see?"

"It looked like the shape of a man. Hang on, I'll have a closer look."

I went over to the third row and shuffled along until I came to the right chair. The shimmering image had gone by now, but I sat down and closed my eyes.

A vision came to me.

I heard the faint chattering of people around me.

Then silence with only the rustling of packets.

Howie's booming voice. I was looking at him through a small screen.

Then the sound of Howie coughing.

Screams followed.

All the time, I was looking at the stage through a screen.

The image faded. I jumped when I saw Seb sitting in the chair next to me.

He said, "You saw something, didn't you?"

"I did. The man who was sitting here recorded the play on his phone."

Seb frowned. "That's prohibited."

"I know, but that's what he did. There's something important about that footage he recorded. I can feel it. We need to find out who was sitting here."

Seb pulled his phone out. "I'll find out straight away."

"There's no need to do that!" a voice announced. "I know who it was."

Seb looked at the woman who had just spoken. His eyes narrowed, "Well, if it isn't my number one suspect. Hello, Peggy. I'd like to have a word with you about a certain letter."

Peggy did her best to look innocent. "Letter? What letter? You're talking nonsense, Sebastian Parker."

Seb wasn't put off by her act. "The letter you wrote to Howie. I recognised your writing from that get well card you sent to Mum. And there was an impression on the letter from a previous correspondence. I saw your name and address."

Peggy pressed her lips together. She berated herself, "Rookie mistake, Peggy Marshall. Don't make that error again."

Seb's mouth twitched, but he remained solemn as he said, "I have to take this matter seriously, Peggy. If anyone else had found that letter, you could be looking at a prison sentence."

Peggy lowered her head and held her arms out. "I understand. Cuff me. Lock me up. Do what you have to. I'll come willingly." She lifted her head and looked at me. "Karis, I've taken some fish out to defrost. It'll be no good to me if I'm in prison. You have it. It's a nice piece of smoked cod. I've got a tin of mushy peas in the cupboard. The peas will go nice with that fish. Take that too."

Seb stood up. "You're not going to prison, Peggy. Not this time. What's the name of the man who was sitting in this row?"

Peggy put her arms down and walked along the row of chairs behind us. She took a seat. I turned around to look at her.

Peggy explained, "I was sitting here in D6. The annoying man with a phone was right in front of me in C6. I saw him recording the show on his phone. His phone kept getting in my way, so I tapped him on the shoulder and told him to put it away. It was Kyle Graven. Do you know him?" She looked at me and Seb.

We both shook our heads.

Peggy continued, "He's a nice enough lad. Got himself a job at that phone shop down the road. Still lives at home with his mum. Anyway, he said he was recording the play for his mum. She was supposed to come out with him, but she had that flu that's going around. Seb, I think it's the same one your mum had. I couldn't tell Kyle off after he said that. I told him he needed to be more discreet as the director had already told us not to record the play." She paused and looked away. "Perhaps I shouldn't have told him that. He might have broken some laws or something."

Before Seb could reprimand her, I said, "I'm glad you did say that to him. I've just had a vision about Kyle. The footage he took is important."

Peggy looked back at us and gave us a broad smile. "Then I did the right thing. Seb, this good deed rules out that letter-writing mistake. Give the letter to me, and I'll throw it in the bin."

"Nice try, Peggy, but that letter is staying with me. I know which phone shop you mean. I'll speak to Kyle now."

Peggy stood up and announced, "We'll come with you."

"No, you won't," Seb said.

"Why not? We can help you," Peggy argued.

"I don't need your help. I've spoken to many members of the public before. I can manage perfectly well on my own. Besides, I don't want you getting in the way."

Peggy pressed her lips together so tightly that her lips almost disappeared. She gave Seb a hard stare.

In return, he gave her a smile. He said to me, "Thanks for your help. I'll let you know how I get on." He winked at Peggy before swiftly walking away.

As soon as he'd gone, Peggy let out an indignant huffing noise and declared, "Can you believe the cheek of that man!"

I stood up. "He's only doing his job. He didn't mean to offend you. How did you know I was here?"

"Robbie came home and I asked him about Howie's case. He said Seb is dealing with it, and that he was presently at the scene of the crime. It didn't take me long to figure out you'd be here too. Did Seb ask for your help?"

"He did."

"And look at the thanks you get for helping him! Up and off he's gone without a thought for us." She shook her head in disgust.

I gave her a smile. "He'll be in touch with us soon. He's going to need our help with the footage."

Peggy's face lit up. "Is he? Did you have a vision about that? Did he look sheepish when he asked for our help again? I hope he did."

"I didn't see much of Seb's face, just part of the footage as it played on my computer. Let's go back to my house." I paused. "Peggy, we couldn't stop Howie being killed, but with Seb at our side, we can try to find out who murdered him. Will you help me? You don't have to if it's too upsetting for you."

"Of course, I'll help you. We're becoming quite the experts when it comes to murder investigations. And the sooner DCI Sebastian Parker realises that, the better."

Chapter 10

Sure enough, Seb sent me a text a short while later to say he needed my help again. I told him where we were and he soon pulled up outside my house.

I opened the front door to Seb and gave him the coffee I'd made for him. Peggy was right behind me. She told Seb exactly what she thought about him constantly asking for our help. Seb took it in his stride and nodded as if he agreed with Peggy's every word. I think she was expecting him to argue with her and it took the wind right out of her sails when he didn't.

She concluded, "Let that be a lesson to you, Sebastian Parker. Did you speak to Kyle Graven?"

"I did." Seb took a step forward.

"Have you got his phone?" Peggy asked as she blocked his way.

"I have."

"Did you ask him how his mum is?" Peggy continued with her interrogation.

Seb shook his head. "I didn't think that information was necessary to my investigation."

Peggy gave him a look of disgust. "Good manners cost nothing. If Karis and I were dealing with this investigation, I would have asked Kyle about his mum. Don't just stand there letting a draught in. We're in the kitchen." She turned around and walked away.

I shared a smile with Seb and said, "She's supposed to be taking it easy on you. I think she still feels guilty about Howie."

"I can understand that. Thanks for the coffee. Why are you in the kitchen? Are you having an early lunch?"

"No. I've got my computer ready, so you can plug Kyle's phone into it. You want me to look at the footage, don't you? You want to see if Howie's last performance matches my vision. That's why you're here."

Seb opened his mouth to speak. Then closed it again.

We went into the kitchen and found Peggy sitting at the table with a blank notepad in front of her.

Seb quipped, "Is that the same notepad you used for your letter to Howie?"

Peggy lifted her chin. "You're not here to talk about any supposed letters I'd supposedly sent."

Seb took a seat and soon had Kyle's phone linked to my computer. We watched the footage Kyle had taken on the night Howie McGarry died.

Knowing that Howie was dying and not acting, made the footage difficult to watch. I couldn't focus on the first screening because my eyes filled with tears. A quick glance at Peggy showed her eyes were brimming too.

Seb played the footage a few more times.

I noticed something. "Go back to that part where Howie talks about Lord Gresham. Seb, I think Howie has added another line to his speech here. When we went to see the play, I'm sure he didn't say anything about Lord Gresham's daughter not being his own. And he didn't say anything about Lord Gresham's wife lying to him for years."

Seb frowned. "I can't remember exactly what he said when we saw the play. Are you sure he didn't say those words? Didn't he say them in your vision?"

"He did." I pointed to the computer screen. "And he said them on the night he died, just like my vision. But when we saw him, I'm almost certain he didn't say them. It's only come to me now that there is a difference."

"How certain are you?"

I gave him a pointed look. "Not one hundred percent. When we were at the play, someone was muttering to himself during Howie's speech. And that annoying man was eating crisps." I turned back to the screen. "Look at this. When Howie says those extra words, he turns his head towards the audience. It's like he's addressing those words to someone there. Watch it again."

Peggy and Seb did so. Their mouths fell open when they got to the part where Howie looked at the audience.

Peggy said, "You're right. I was too worried at the time to notice he was staring right out at everyone. He's definitely searching for someone. But who?"

Seb looked closer at the screen. "From the angle of his head, it looks like someone sitting near the back. Is it my imagination or does he smile ever so slightly when he says those words?"

We watched the footage again and concluded Howie McGarry did smile as he delivered those words.

I said to Seb, "You should speak to the director about those extra words."

"Telling me how to do my job again?" he asked.

"Somebody has to," Peggy retorted.

"I shall ignore that, Mrs Marshall." Seb took his phone out and scrolled through it. "The name of the director is Toby Dawson. As you know, he played Lord Gresham too."

"Toby Dawson?" Peggy asked. "Wait a moment. Don't move." She stood up and left the kitchen. She returned with a sheet of green paper and put it in front of Seb. "This is a programme from last night. Toby Dawson's daughter was in the play too. She was the young woman in pearls. She's called Amber Dawson."

Seb picked the programme up and read it. "Amber Dawson wrote the play too. I should arrest her for a weak plot and the lack of proper police procedure."

Peggy chuckled. "You should. I'd worked out who the killer was in five minutes. Seb, I've never met Toby Dawson, but I know his wife. She's called Gaynor and she works at the bank I use. I'll speak to her about Howie and find out if he had any enemies."

Seb put his phone away. "Peggy, you won't be speaking to anyone about this investigation."

"But I—"

Seb cut her off. "Thank you for the help you've given me. You too, Karis. I appreciate it. But we're dealing with a murder. Someone must have hated Howie a lot to kill him in front of everyone like that. I don't want either of you putting yourselves in danger." He gave Peggy a smile to soften his words. "I don't want you to get hurt, Peggy. My life wouldn't be worth living if anything happened to you because of me. I would have the whole town out for my blood. You know how much everyone admires you."

Peggy blushed. "I wouldn't say that. Not everyone. Not Lizzy Warburton who I went to school with. We fell out over a boy when we were both ten. She's never forgiven me."

Seb said, "Okay. Everyone except Lizzy Warburton would be after me. I'll let you know how I get on. I'll see myself out." He unplugged Kyle's phone and left the house.

Peggy was silent for a full minute. Then she said, "Oh, Karis. I forgot to tell you that I have to go to the bank. I have to deposit some money urgently."

"Peggy," I began, "you know what Seb said."

She looked away from me and stood up. "You don't have to come with me. I'm going anyway."

I got to my feet. I could almost feel the guilt which was hanging over Peggy. I said, "I'll come with you. But if Seb finds out, I'll tell him it was my idea."

She gave me a grateful smile. "Thank you, Karis. If Seb finds out, I'll tell him it was my idea. I can't stay here staring at the walls, I've got to do something about poor Howie dying."

Chapter 11

Peggy went into her house and collected the money which needed to be deposited urgently into her bank account. The bank was a short walk away so we decided to leave the car behind and stretch our legs.

As we walked along, Peggy gave me some theories about who could have killed Howie. She said, "The spouse is always a suspect. You went to school with Vanessa. What was she like? Is she capable of murder?"

I chose my words carefully. "She wasn't the kindest of people. I'm not sure if she would be capable of murder, though. But there again, who knows what people are capable of? When she came to the café, she seemed proud of Howie and his business success. I can't think why she'd want to kill him and in such a public manner too."

Peggy said, "Perhaps she wanted his money all to herself. Or perhaps he was spending too much time with his acting friends and she thought she'd put an end to it. Is she the jealous kind? Does she hold grudges?"

I took too long in trying to choose my words this time and eventually said, "I don't know her that well."

Peggy stopped walking and put her hand on my arm. "Karis, there's something you're not telling me. Did Vanessa give you a hard time at school?"

I gave her a small nod.

"Was she one of those who called you that cruel name?"

Another nod. "She's the one who gave me that nickname."

Peggy's mouth settled in a grim line. She carried on walking. "When can we talk to the grieving widow? I was going to take it easy on her, but not anymore. She's my prime suspect now. Where does she live?"

"I don't know. I don't want to talk to her. Peggy, let Seb deal with Vanessa. Please."

"Okay. For now. Who else would want Howie dead? We don't know anything about the other people in the play. Or the people behind the scenes. What about the woman who made the tea? What do we know about her?"

"I'm sure Seb is dealing with all of that."

"I suppose he is," Peggy relented. "What about Howie's building firm? How's that doing? Is it successful? Or in trouble?"

"Vanessa said it was successful. She told Erin and me about the exotic holidays they go on. She was wearing expensive clothes when we saw her."

Peggy said, "She could be lying. I know I haven't met her, but I don't like her. What about the staff Howie employed? How did they get on with him? What about his business rivals? Did he have any?"

Peggy stopped walking again and put a hand on her forehead. "I'm giving myself a headache with all these questions. We've got our work cut out for us. I don't think I'll have time to do my blog post today."

"Seb and his officers are dealing with all of this. Let them get on with their job. If I get any visions, then I'll let Seb know. Peggy, you don't have to get yourself involved so much."

She lowered her hand. "I suppose you're right."

We continued walking.

I said, "How did you get on with Erin and her knitting lesson?"

Peggy shook her head. "That sister of yours would test the patience of a saint. She wants everything done immediately. I did get her to do a full line of stitches, but it was a struggle. But like you said, if I can teach Erin, then I can teach anyone."

We continued walking and chatted about how best to organise our knitting classes. We soon arrived at the bank and went inside.

There was only one customer at the counter and we queued behind him.

Peggy looked over her shoulder before reaching for her purse. She whispered to me, "You have to be vigilant in banks when you're carrying a large amount of money. You never know who's hanging around ready to steal your life savings."

I looked behind us. There was no one there.

Peggy opened her purse and took out a ten-pound note. Her glance darted left and right as she put her purse away.

I stared at her. "Ten pounds? Is that it? Is that the money that needed to be deposited urgently?"

She looked away from me. "I'll have you know that this is a large amount to many people." She craned her neck. "That's good. Gaynor Dawson is behind the counter. I thought she might be at this time of the day. Leave the talking to me."

The customer in front of us left, and we took up a position in front of a smiling, middle-aged woman.

Peggy handed over her ten-pound note and gave Gaynor a big smile. "Hello, Gaynor. Just this small deposit today."

Gaynor returned Peggy's smile. "Morning, Peggy. Can I have your bank details, please?"

Peggy moved her head closer to the glass partition, looked left and right, and quietly recited her bank details.

"Thanks," Gaynor said. She tapped away at a screen in front of her and a drawer opened at her side.

Peggy said, "Isn't it awful about Howie McGarry?"

"Who?" Gaynor replied with her eyes still on the screen.

"Howie McGarry. He died last night at St Anne's Church hall. He was in your husband's play."

Gaynor looked at Peggy. "Oh, yes. Of course. It is awful. Toby was in pieces when he came home. What an awful thing to happen."

Peggy nodded. "I was there. I saw everything. It happened right in front of your daughter. How is she coping?"

"Not very well," Gaynor admitted. "She thought Howie was overacting at first. But when he didn't get up after that coughing fit, she knew something was wrong."

Peggy shook her head sadly. "The poor thing. Do the police know what happened yet? Do they think he was hurt on purpose?"

Gaynor's eyes widened. "Murder? Is that what you're saying?"

Peggy looked as if she was going to say more, but a stern-faced older man in a suit walked over to Gaynor and said, "Is there a problem, Mrs Dawson? You appear to be taking a long time over this transaction."

Gaynor gave the man a quick smile. "No problem, Mr Thomas. I've concluded the transaction now." She looked back at Peggy. "Thank you for your custom, Mrs Marshall. Have a lovely day."

Peggy said thank you to Gaynor and then walked away from the counter. I turned to follow Peggy, but something stopped me. I looked back at Gaynor and Mr Thomas and heard them saying something. I listened carefully.

Peggy was waiting for me on the pavement outside. She said, "What took you so long? Were you having another vision?"

"No, I was eavesdropping. I heard Mr Thomas ask Gaynor about overtime. He said she can do some shifts at the weekend. She told him she didn't need the extra money any longer." I looked back at the bank. "I don't know why, but I feel this is important information."

Peggy gave me a slow nod. "Interesting. It was well worth coming here. Let's go back to my house and make a plan of action. Let's see who else we can question."

"As long as we don't interfere in Seb's investigation."

Peggy gave me a haughty look and announced, "I would never interfere in a police investigation." As she walked away, I heard a chuckle coming from her.

Chapter 12

When we returned to Peggy's house, she said, "I'll have to get on with my blog. People will be waiting to hear from me. I can't let them down. What shall I tell them about the knitting evening? Have you got any idea when that will happen?"

"I don't. I'll have to speak to Robbie about it."

A look came into Peggy's eyes as if she was considering something. "Karis, don't think I'm meddling in police business, but why don't we go to the café and see how the building work is coming along? We could talk to some of Howie's employees about him while we're there."

"I'm not sure about that. I've been to the café recently and there's not much to see. Apart from Robbie's plans. He's made a good job of those."

"Hear me out. I don't want to go there just to find out more about Howie." She smiled. "That's a bit of a lie. It wouldn't hurt to have a general chit-chat about him while we're there. But I thought we could take photos of how the building looks now and then post them on our site. It'll give me something to put on my blog too. People like to hear about this sort of thing. You know how popular makeover shows are. Everyone loves the before and after photos. This could generate an online buzz for us. Is that the right expression?"

I thought about her words. "You could be on to something there. We can post regular updates about the work. I'm sure Robbie won't mind us putting his drawings online too. We'll ask him about that. Do you really think people will be interested?"

Peggy nodded. "I'll do an online survey again. I know what I'm doing with those now. I'll do that, and you put the kettle on. Could you rustle us up a sandwich, please? I've got some nice ham in the fridge." She walked away with a determined look on her face. It was lovely to see her looking happy.

Peggy sat at the kitchen table and muttered to herself as she worked on her survey. I made us cups of tea and sandwiches. I felt a twinge of sadness as I made the tea. Could I have done more to help Howie? Perhaps I could have stopped him being killed onstage. But if someone wanted to kill him, they would have found another way to do it.

I froze as a new thought came to me.

"Peggy, do you think Howie was killed by mistake?"

Peggy paused in her typing. "What do you mean?"

"Perhaps the tea was meant for someone else?"

She frowned. "But it was put there just for Howie."

"That's true. But what if the tea wasn't poisoned? There could have been something in it which caused an allergic reaction in Howie."

"Like what? Low-fat milk? Soy milk? Organic tea bags?"

I shook my head. "I don't know. It's just a thought."

"Has Seb told you it was actually the tea that killed Howie?"

I replied, "No, he hasn't. I'm just assuming it's the tea."

Peggy returned to her typing. "Give Seb a call. Ask him about that. He owes you that much information considering all the help we've given him."

As if reading my mind, Seb phoned me. I answered the phone while putting the sandwich in front of Peggy.

"Hi, Seb. I was just thinking about you," I began. I put Peggy's tea next to her sandwich and headed for the living room.

"Were you?" he said. "What were you thinking about? My boyish good looks? How professional and commanding I look in my suit?" He followed this with a laugh. "That's what Mum says anyway."

My cheeks warmed up, and I was glad he wasn't here to witness my embarrassment. He did look handsome in his suit, but I wasn't going to tell him that.

I said, "You never told me what killed Howie."

"Didn't I? I thought I did."

"No, you didn't. Was it the tea?"

"Yes. There was a huge amount of poison in it. It must have tasted disgusting."

Even though Seb couldn't see me, I nodded as I recalled how vile my tea had tasted. "Have you spoken to Toby Dawson yet? Are you able to give me any information on him? I don't want to pry."

Peggy called out from the kitchen, "I do! Speak up, Karis. I can barely hear you in here."

Seb laughed. "I can tell you what Toby said. Then you can tell Peggy. I asked Toby about the extra lines Howie had said during his last play. Toby said he hadn't noticed, but said it was like Howie to adlib during a performance. He was known for it. Toby said he didn't mind too much as long as Howie didn't change the direction of the story."

"But he did change the story by saying those extra words. He added a new reason for someone killing Lord Gresham. Did you point that out to Toby?"

"I did. Again, Toby said he didn't notice." He hesitated a second. "Toby Dawson didn't notice because he was talking to someone at the side of the stage."

"Who?"

"Vanessa McGarry."

I took a sharp intake of breath. "Vanessa? What was she doing there?"

"According to Toby, Vanessa was waiting for Howie to come off the stage. She claimed she had something important to discuss with him. Something that couldn't wait. I'll be speaking to her soon about that."

"Seb, was she standing near Howie's tea while she was waiting?"

"She was. And your next question will be whether or not she had the opportunity to slip something into Howie's tea. Yes, she would have had that opportunity."

We were both silent for a moment.

I spoke first. "What are you going to do now?"

"I'll be speaking to Vanessa."

"Are you allowed to do that? With you knowing her?"

Seb replied, "I knew her a long time ago. We were never friends. Karis, this goes without saying, but I'll say it anyway. Keep away from Vanessa McGarry. She's got a nasty side to her, as you know. If she contacts you for any reason, get in touch with me immediately. Okay?"

"Okay."

"I have to go now. I'll keep in touch. Say hello to Peggy for me. She's probably standing right next to you listening to every word."

I said, "No, she's in the kitchen."

"I'm not. I'm here," Peggy said behind me. I turned around and saw her standing there with a half-eaten sandwich in her hand. She grinned and yelled, "Bye for now, DCI Parker!"

Seb returned her farewell before ending the call.

Peggy pointed her sandwich at me. "That is interesting about Vanessa, isn't it? She sounds like a rotten egg to me. Anyway, I've posted that survey online and I've already got some replies. Yes, my readers would love to see photos of the café renovation."

My phone rang again.

Peggy sighed. "Can't that policeman leave us alone for a minute?"

It wasn't Seb. It was Erin.

"Karis!" she cried out. "Come around here quickly!"

"Erin? What is it?" I clutched the phone tighter.

"It's Vanessa. She's banging on my front door! She's screaming at me. Robbie isn't here. He's out buying paint and he's not answering his phone."

In the background, I heard Vanessa yelling at Erin and demanding that she open the door.

I said to Erin, "Don't let her in. We're on our way. Phone Seb immediately."

We raced out of the house and into my car.

I stared at the road ahead and said, "If Vanessa McGarry hurts my sister, I'm going to kill her."

Peggy said, "You'll have to wait until I've killed her. Drive faster."

Chapter 13

Vanessa was still banging on Erin's front door when we arrived. Erin was peering out of the window, her face drawn and pale. The neighbours on either side were looking out of their windows too. One of them was on his phone.

I jumped out of the car and ran along the path towards Vanessa. I was aware of Peggy calling my name behind me, but I ignored her. My only concern was for Erin's safety.

Vanessa thudded her fists on the door and yelled, "Let me in! I know you're in there, Krazy Karis! You can't hide from me! Come out and face me."

I tapped her on the shoulder and announced, "I'm right here." I was surprised at how calm I sounded. "Stop banging on the door. You're scaring my sister."

Vanessa spun around. The hate in her face startled me, and I took a step back. Her hair was messy and streaks of black mascara decorated her cheeks. She opened her mouth to speak, but she never got the chance to say a word.

Seb appeared out of nowhere and stepped into the space between Vanessa and me. He held his hand up and said quietly, "Enough, Mrs McGarry. There will be no more shouting. I'd like you to accompany me to the station."

"No!" Vanessa screamed. "I'm not going anywhere." She thrust her hands out and pushed Seb to one side. He stumbled to the ground. She turned the full force of her anger on me.

I heard Robbie somewhere in the distance calling out Erin's name.

I faced Vanessa and braced myself. "What do you want to say to me?"

"You! It's all your fault that Howie died!" Vanessa's lips pulled back in a snarl as she advanced on me. "You put the idea of killing Howie into someone's head! You and your stupid visions. How many people did you tell about Howie being killed in his play? How many people did you lie to? This is all your fault. You're crazy. That's what you are. Crazy through and through. And now I've lost my husband because of you."

I noticed Seb was now on his feet, but I didn't pay him any attention. I looked into Vanessa's pain-filled eyes. I could feel the ache in her heart. I took a step forward and wrapped my arms around her. She struggled against me, and I felt her hands raining down on my back as she tried to get free. But I held on to her. She yelled obscenities in my ear. I continued to hold her.

After a while, Vanessa went limp and I could sense a wetness on my shoulder. I felt her body trembling against me. Her sobs were quiet in my ear.

I patted her back and said, "It's okay. You can let it all out. I'm not going anywhere."

We stayed in that position for the next five minutes. I saw Seb giving me a quizzical look. I managed to give him a small smile of reassurance in return.

Robbie walked past us and gave me a quick nod. He went inside the house and I heard him calling to Erin. I heard her reply, and she said she was okay.

Peggy came over and stood next to Seb. They watched us silently.

Vanessa finished crying and moved out of my arms. She cleared her throat and mumbled, "Sorry about that, Karis." She busied herself looking for something in her handbag. "Where is a clean tissue when you need one?"

Seb handed her a fresh packet of tissues.

Vanessa gave him a tight smile in return. "Thank you. You said something about me going to the station? Would you like me to go with you now?"

"Yes. We'll go in my car."

"Very good." Vanessa held her head high and walked away without giving me another look.

Peggy said, "What just happened there? Why did you hug her, Karis? It's the last thing I would have done."

I shrugged. "She needed a hug."

Peggy tutted. "She didn't even say thank you."

"She didn't need to." I turned to Seb. "I could feel how much love she has for Howie. I don't think she killed him."

Peggy pointed out, "She might have. She could be feeling guilty about it now. That's why she cried so much. What do you think, Seb?"

"I'm not making any comments until I have the full facts," Seb answered. "Karis, are you okay? Did Vanessa hurt you?"

"I'm fine, thanks. I'd better check on Erin. Will you let me know how things go with Vanessa?"

"Of course." He gave us a nod of farewell before walking away.

Peggy and I went into Erin's house and found her in the arms of her husband.

Robbie looked at us and said, "I only nipped out for some tins of paint. I didn't even hear my phone ringing. I only saw Erin's messages when I got back in the car. Are you alright, Karis?"

"I'm fine. How's Erin?"

Erin mumbled a reply, "I'm okay. A bit shook up, but I'm okay now." She rested her head against Robbie's chest.

Robbie said to her, "You are not leaving my sight. Ever."

Peggy tapped Robbie on his back and said, "Did you manage to buy that paint?"

"Yes. Why?"

"Is it for the café?"

"Yes, again. Why?"

"Where is it now?" Peggy continued.

"It's in the car. Why are you so interested in paint?"

Peggy answered, "Karis and I are going over to the café. We're going to take some photos for the readers of my blog. I have quite a lot of readers."

"I know," Robbie said. "I'm one of them. Did that woman at the market really insult you?"

Peggy waved her hand at him. "I don't have time to talk about that now, Robbie. If you want to know what happened, read my blog. Where are the keys to your car?"

"In my car."

"In your car? What sort of a policeman are you?" Peggy asked.

Robbie still had his arms wrapped around Erin. He gave Peggy a pointed look and said, "I was in a hurry. Why do you want to know where my keys are? Are you going to steal my car?"

"No, just the paint," Peggy said. "Well, I'm not stealing it. We'll take it to the café for you. Is the café locked? Have you got a spare key? I think I should have a spare key anyway."

Robbie replied, "The café is open. The builders are inside."

"Oh? Are they?" Peggy tried to sound innocent, but she wasn't fooling anyone. "Are those the same builders who work for Howie's company?"

Suspicion came into Robbie's eyes. Before he could ask Peggy any more questions, I intervened and said, "Peggy, let's go. We don't want to bother Erin and Robbie a moment longer."

From somewhere against Robbie's chest, Erin said, "Thanks for coming around so quickly, Karis. I'll phone you later."

I gave her a quick hug and then said goodbye.

Peggy and I retrieved the cans of paint from Robbie's car and put them in mine. I quickly locked Robbie's car, ran into their house and placed the keys on the table. I don't think the hugging couple even noticed me.

Then Peggy and I headed over to the café.

I said to Peggy on the way, "We're going to deliver the paint and then take some photos. That's all."

Peggy nodded. "That's all. Once we've done that, we'll have a quick chat with the builders about Howie. Leave the talking to me."

Chapter 14

I parked outside the café and headed for the boot of my car.

Peggy came over to me and said, "Leave the paint there. We'll get one of the workers to lift them out."

"They're not that heavy. I can manage."

"I know you can, but I need an excuse to strike up a conversation. Wait here."

She went inside the café and I saw her talking to a large man in denim overalls. He didn't look happy about being interrupted, and glowered at Peggy. She waved her arm in my direction. The man glowered some more and headed towards the door.

He came outside and grunted, "Paint?"

"Yes, thank you," I replied. "It's here in the boot." I pointed unnecessarily to it.

He grunted again and reached for the paint. He picked up two cans in each hand.

Peggy came rushing over to him. "Thank you so much, young man. Isn't it a shame about Howie McGarry? You must still be in shock about him."

"Not really," the man replied. He moved towards the door.

"Oh? Why do you say that?" Peggy asked.

The man shrugged, grunted and tried to move past Peggy.

Peggy didn't move. "How long have you worked for Howie? Was he a good boss?"

The man shrugged again, grunted twice this time and walked around Peggy. We watched him enter the café, pile the paint against the wall and then return to his work.

Peggy put her hands on her hips. "Well! He was about as much use as a chocolate teapot. What were those noises he was making? Isn't he capable of polite speech? Let me have another go at him." She marched back into the café.

I closed the boot, locked the car and went after her. Once inside, I heard Peggy attempting to make conversation with the man again. He stared at her unblinking until she'd finished talking. Then, unsurprisingly, he shrugged, grunted and turned away from her.

Peggy walked back to me and said, "I'd have a better conversation with a brick wall." She stopped talking and her eyes widened. "Karis! Look at this place. It's enormous. How are you going to fill it? Have you got enough furniture?" She performed a slow turn. "Look at the extended area. It's huge. How are you going to organise it all?"

"Let me give you the grand tour. Follow me."

I showed Peggy around the extended café. I explained our plans for it. She took photos with her phone as we went along.

I stopped at Robbie's plans which were still on the wall and pointed out the different areas to Peggy. I said, "This will be the area where we'll hold most of our craft evenings. And this will be the storage section."

"There's loads of storage there. I'd better get more supplies. This is amazing. Robbie's done a great job. I hope he hurries up and gets it completed soon. I'm itching to get started. Can I take some photos of his plans?"

"I don't see why not. I'll phone him later and make sure it's okay with him." I glanced towards the stairs. "I haven't shown you upstairs yet."

"There's an upstairs too? For us?"

"Yes. There's going to be a staffroom up there, along with more tables and chairs. I thought it would be perfect for customers who want to work on their laptops. A lot of people work online nowadays."

Peggy nodded. "That's very true, as I well know. I know full well the pressures of running an online blog. I might need to reserve a table for myself upstairs. Can we have a look up there now?"

"Yes. I haven't been upstairs since Robbie got his hands on it."

We headed up the stairs and I told Peggy more about our plans. She was as excited as me about our new venture.

We both came to a sudden stop near the top step.

Peggy grabbed my elbow and whispered, "Did you hear that?"

I nodded.

The words came out again: "Who would benefit from his death?"

Peggy gasped. "It's the ghost of Howie McGarry! He's come back to haunt us."

We heard footsteps moving about the room.

I said to Peggy, "Ghost or not, we can't stay here. Come on." I ascended the last step and walked into the room. Just like the downstairs area, it was bright and open.

Peggy scuttled after me and put her hand on my elbow again.

A man had his back to us. Thankfully, he looked solid and not at all ghostlike. He held his arm out and announced, "Who would benefit from his death?" He lowered his arm and nodded to himself.

Peggy and I walked over to him.

I said, "Hello. Sorry to disturb you."

The man leapt to the side and clutched his chest. "Sweet Molly Malone! You scared me half to death. Where did you two spring up from?"

"Downstairs," Peggy informed him. "Who are you, and what are you doing on our premises?"

"Your premises? And you are?"

"If you must know, I'm Peggy Marshall. This is my good friend and business associate, Karis Booth." Peggy thought for a moment. "She's my next door neighbour too."

"Pleased to meet you both," the man replied cheerfully. "I'm Nick, Nick Scott. I'm working here on the renovation. It's a great place. It's going to look fantastic." His smile fell. "Have you heard about my boss, Howie McGarry? He died suddenly. It's a pity, a great pity."

Peggy's eyes lit up. "Yes, it is a pity. Did you know him well? What was he like to work with? Did he have any enemies?"

Nick looked taken aback at the onslaught of questions. He said, "I liked Howie. He was always fair to us. A good boss. Decent chap. Even when times were rough for his business, he kept me employed. It was a relief when we got this café contract, I can tell you."

I recalled Vanessa's earlier words and said, "I thought Howie's business was booming."

"Who told you that?" Nick asked.

"It's just a rumour I heard."

"Well, it's not true. Howie had some financial difficulties over the last few years. But things have started to pick up." He scratched his chin. "Poor Howie. He's not going to see this project completed now."

I said, "We heard you reciting words from the play Howie was in."

"Did you? What did you think? Was I loud enough? Convincing? Engaging?" He gave us eager looks.

Peggy answered, "You were loud and clear. I thought Howie had come back to haunt us for a second or two. Why were you saying those words?"

"I'm taking over his role in the play. I'm his understudy." He lifted his chin proudly. "Howie was an inspiration to me. I was proud to be his understudy. I helped him with his lines. I know his part well."

"But why are you reciting those lines now?" I asked.

"For the play. I'll be going on tonight. Do you want to hear some more? I could do with an audience."

"Will the play be on tonight?" I continued. "Even after Howie died onstage? That seems a bit disrespectful."

Nick nodded. "That's what I thought too. The director phoned me about an hour ago and said the show must go on. He said Howie would have wanted it to." Nick moved a bit closer. "The director also said because of Howie's death, the play was getting a lot of publicity. Apparently, the local news might be there tonight. The director has contacted a couple of agents too. He thinks they might make his daughter an offer on the play. She wrote it."

Peggy tutted. "Some people have no shame. No respect for the dearly departed."

Nick nodded again. "I know what you mean. But if I don't perform, then the director will get someone else. I'm doing this as a mark of respect for Howie."

I said to Nick, "Those lines that you were saying, can you repeat them? And the next few lines too."

"Course I can." He cleared his throat and began to recite the lines of the play. He got to the part where he drank the tea. He coughed violently and fell to the ground.

I frowned at him as he lay on the floor. "What about those other lines? The ones about Lord Gresham's daughter not being his own, and that his wife had been lying to him for years."

"Eh?" Nick said. He stood up. "There aren't any lines like that in the play."

"Are you sure?" I persisted.

"I'm certain. I know that play inside out. Do you want some tickets for the play? I've got some spare ones. These are like gold dust now. It's going to be packed to the rafters tonight. What's that expression? There's no such thing as bad publicity."

Peggy retorted, "There's such a thing as common decency and respect for the dead. I'm not getting at you, Nick. This isn't your doing. We will have those tickets, thank you." She peered at him. "Good luck tonight. Don't drink the tea."

With those words, we left Nick and headed out of the café.

When we were in the car, I said to Peggy, "There's something weird going on with that director. Why would he let the play run tonight? Is it really respect for Howie or does he just want the publicity for his daughter? Either way, Toby Dawson is benefiting from Howie's death."

"Indeed. It makes you wonder if Toby Dawson planned this. He could have been the one who murdered Howie."

Chapter 15

I yawned as I drove us back home.

Peggy gave me a concerned look and said, "You've been doing too much. You need to catch up on your sleep."

"I know, but I don't have time. Shall we do some digging on Toby Dawson? Or should we let Seb know what we've found out?"

I pulled up outside our joined houses and switched the engine off.

Peggy mused, "If we tell Seb, he'll only berate us for getting involved. But there again, this information could be useful to him."

"He probably already knows about the play going ahead," I pointed out. "I'm sure Toby would have had to clear it with the police before proceeding with another performance."

"That's true. Let's not bother Seb for now. Do you want to come into my house? I was going to make a fish pie later with that smoked cod I'm defrosting. Do you want to stay for dinner? There's plenty. I much prefer cooking for two than one."

She gave me such a hopeful look that I didn't have the heart to say no. I was hoping I could sneak in a quick nap before dinner, but Peggy was more important to me than sleep.

"I would love to. Why don't I make it?" I suggested. "You can post those photos of the café online and reply to any comments about your blog post."

"That's a good idea. I'm sure some of my regulars would have written to me by now. I'm getting to know some of them quite well."

We left the car and went into Peggy's house. Once in the kitchen, we put the radio on and I got to work on the fish pie. Peggy tapped away on her computer and shared some of her readers' comments with me now and again.

I made us a cup of tea, yawning as I did so. I made mine extra strong. I was almost tempted to use two tea bags in my cup.

Peggy leaned back in her chair. "There we are. I'm up to date with my readers. I've put those photos on too. And I've done a Facebook post. This online stuff never ends does it? Thanks for the tea."

"Can I borrow your computer? I want to have a look for Toby Dawson."

Peggy's eyes glittered with mischief. "Go ahead. I'll watch. I love how you can spy on people online. Let's hope we find some dirt on him. Check on his daughter too."

At the word "daughter", we both froze.

Peggy stared at me. She said, "We are a couple of prize idiots."

"We certainly are," I agreed. "Why haven't we made the connection between Toby Dawson, his daughter and Howie's last words?"

Peggy groaned. "Because we're prize idiots. Numpties. Pudding-heads. That's what we are. Do you know what else we've missed?"

I nodded. "Toby's wife and that conversation she had with her manager at the bank. She didn't need to do any more overtime because she didn't need the money any longer. Are you thinking what I'm thinking?"

"That Amber Dawson isn't Toby's real daughter? And that somehow, Howie found out about this?"

I continued, "And he was blackmailing Gaynor Dawson? She had to work overtime to pay him. But after Howie died, she no longer needed the overtime."

Peggy concluded, "And those extra lines Howie spoke on his last night were aimed at Gaynor. She could have been in the audience. Maybe he was putting more pressure on her. He could have threatened to reveal all to Gaynor's husband if she didn't give him more money." She wrinkled her nose. "Are we being too dramatic? Have we been watching too many detective shows?"

"I don't think so. When Vanessa first came to the café, she boasted about how well Howie's business was going. She mentioned the holidays they'd been on. But Nick Scott told us Howie's business wasn't doing that well. So, either Vanessa was lying to me about Howie's business and the holidays, or Howie was getting money from elsewhere."

"He could have been getting the money from Gaynor Dawson." Peggy shook her head. "The despicable lengths some people go to never ceases to amaze me. Poor Gaynor. She's a lovely woman. We should let Seb know about this."

"We should." I paused. "Unless it's just our overactive imaginations getting to us. Let's have a quick look online first."

I made some searches and came across photos of Toby Dawson and Amber.

Peggy peered at the screen. "Amber doesn't look like her father. Not one bit. Mind you, a lot of children don't look like their parents. Thank goodness your daughter doesn't look like her father. She gets her good looks from you. Is there anything about Howie and his wife online?"

Another search brought up images of Vanessa and Howie McGarry. There were many photos of them on sun-drenched beaches.

I noted, "Some of these were posted last month. They're certainly not short of money."

"I wonder if Howie was blackmailing anyone else? Or was it just Gaynor?" Peggy stared at the screen. "If our theory is correct, this means Gaynor could have killed Howie. As the director's wife, she could have been at the church hall many times and become almost invisible, like a piece of the scenery. It would have been easy for her to slip some poison into Howie's tea."

We both sighed at the same time.

"What a shame," Peggy said. "I like Gaynor. I've been going to that bank for years. She always had a smile for me."

"Yes, but she could be a killer. I'll phone Seb. I forgot to tell him earlier about Gaynor and that overtime comment. I'll find out what's happening with Vanessa too."

Peggy said brightly, "With any luck, he'll tell you it was Vanessa who did away with Howie. She looks the murdering type."

Chapter 16

I phoned Seb but he didn't answer. I left a message for him and asked him to contact me as soon as possible. I also phoned Erin to make sure she was okay. She was. She said Robbie was still at home with her.

Before she ended the call, Erin said, "Tell Peggy I've knitted six rows now. I've got more stitches than I started with, and there are a few holes in my work. But I think I'm getting the hang of it."

I relayed Erin's message to Peggy.

"Good. She'll soon become an expert," Peggy noted with confidence. "I know it's a bit early, but shall we put that fish pie in the oven now? Investigating this murder and running an online business is hungry work. I'm famished. I think I'll make us an apple crumble for dessert. How does that sound?"

"Delicious." I frowned and looked towards the window. "Did you hear that?"

"What?"

"Some children playing outside. I didn't think there was anyone with children living around here."

"Perhaps someone's got little visitors over. Has Seb phoned you back?"

"No."

"Has he left you any messages?"

I checked my phone. "No. He might be in the middle of an interrogation. He'll get in touch when he's ready."

"He'd better. Let's get that pie in the oven. I'm going to pass out from hunger soon."

The pie was put in the oven and then I helped Peggy to make an apple crumble. She made some custard to go with it. I expected her to use a packet, but she made it from scratch. The energy that woman had constantly astounded me.

The kitchen was soon full of appetising smells and my mouth watered.

As soon as the fish pie was out, the apple crumble went in.

We added a few vegetables to our meal and then sat at the kitchen table.

Peggy pointed to the glasses of water at the side of our plates and said, "We could have a glass of wine, but I want to keep a clear head in case anything needs our attention. We'll make do with water." She raised her glass to me. "Cheers."

The fish pie was delicious. It was one of Mum's recipes and it never turned out wrong when I made it. Peggy tucked into the pie with gusto and pronounced it to be one of the best fish pies she'd ever had.

I grimaced as I took a sip of the water. It had a funny taste. I used a water filter at home. It made such a difference to the water. Perhaps I should buy one for Peggy.

Even though I was full from the main meal, I couldn't resist a portion of the apple crumble drenched in custard. I managed to scoop up every last morsel.

When I'd finished, I leaned back in my chair and rested my hands on my stomach. "Peggy, that was delicious. No, it was scrumptious. Hang on, let me think of a better word." I groaned and rubbed my stomach. "I'm too full to think straight. My brain is falling asleep."

"So are you," Peggy pointed out. "I've seen you yawning when you thought I wasn't looking. Go and have a nap on my sofa."

"But the washing up?"

Peggy came over to me and hoisted me to my feet. "Come on, young lady. You need a nap."

She took me into the living room and settled me on the sofa. She put two soft cushions behind my head and told me to lie down. She produced a cover from somewhere behind the sofa and tucked it around me.

My eyes were already closing at this stage. I muttered, "Don't let me sleep for too long."

"I won't. I'll be in the kitchen." I felt a kiss on my forehead and then heard Peggy walking away.

I felt comfy, drowsy and warm. Just a short nap. That's all I needed.

I drifted off to sleep.

When I woke up, the room was dark. It took me a moment to work out where I was.

"Peggy?" I called out. "Are you there?"

There was no returning call, so I got off the sofa and switched the nearest lamp on. I glanced at the clock and saw it was early evening. I'd been asleep for hours.

Where was Peggy? I called out for her again as I closed the curtains. I switched another lamp on and went looking for her. When I went into the kitchen, I found a note from her:

'Karis, I didn't want to wake you as you looked so peaceful. I'm going to see the play again tonight. I'll use those tickets Nick Scott gave us. I'm not going to interfere or anything like that. I won't talk to Gaynor Dawson if she's there. I won't talk to Toby or Amber either. And I won't talk to anyone else about Howie and how people felt about him. I hope you don't mind, but I checked your phone to see if Seb had phoned you back. He hasn't. Rude man. He hasn't even sent you a text. Some people have no manners. See you later. Help yourself to more apple crumble. From Peggy.'

I read the note again. It was obvious Peggy was intending to talk to Gaynor Dawson and anyone else of interest. What if Gaynor was the killer? I couldn't have Peggy talking to her and putting herself in danger.

I decided I had to phone Seb and tell him about Peggy. I went back to the living room and looked for my phone. I couldn't find it. Where had Peggy put it? I began to search the house. Nothing. She might have taken it with her by accident. Or taken it on purpose to stop me phoning Seb and telling him where she'd gone. Would she be that devious?

I couldn't remember Seb's number, so I used the landline to phone the police station. I ended up in a queue. In annoyance, I said to the piped music, "Hurry up and put me through. What if this was an emergency? What if I was about to be murdered?"

"Madam? You're about to be murdered?" a female voice said.

I hadn't realised the music had stopped. "No, sorry. I was just talking to myself. I'd like to speak to DCI Parker, please."

"Hold on."

I held on.

After a few minutes, I was told Seb wasn't in. I left a message for him.

What was I supposed to do now? I couldn't leave Peggy in danger. I had to do something. And I had to do it now.

The living room around me began to fade. A buzzing noise sounded in my ears. I was getting a vision. And like the original one I had of Howie, it was going to be a strong one.

Chapter 17

The vision began.

I was standing on the stage at St Anne's Church hall.

Nick Scott was sitting in an armchair in front of me. He was dressed in the same suit which Howie had worn in his performance.

I could hear movement in the hall in front of me. I could sense the presence of people in the darkness.

Nick spoke loudly, "Who would benefit from his death?" He swallowed and I saw beads of perspiration on his forehead. His voice was less sure now. "What if his wife had been lying to him for years?" He took a drink from the cup he was holding. The liquid inside it was clear. "What if his daughter wasn't his?" Another drink.

Like a hideous replay of Howie's death, Nick began to cough. The cup fell to the floor. Nick's face turned red as his coughing increased. He slithered off his chair.

There were screams.

Many screams.

The curtains closed.

People rushed onto the stage.

Someone cried out, "Another death! We are cursed!"

My vision faded.

My legs were shaking. I sat on the sofa and took some deep breaths. Nick was going to be murdered tonight. There hadn't been tea in his cup. It was something else. I had an idea of what it could be.

I went into the kitchen and grabbed a glass. I filled it with water and took a sip. It was foul. I poured it away.

Nick was going to be poisoned by water.

I couldn't let that happen.

I checked the time. The play would be starting in ten minutes.

I considered phoning Robbie to warn him, but I didn't have time.

I raced out of the house and jumped into my car.

As the church hall came into view, I could see I was going to have problems. The roads were packed with cars. Large vans with TV company logos painted on them were parked there too.

I remembered what Nick had said about the publicity surrounding the play. It looked like the whole world and his wife had turned up.

There was nowhere to park.

The minutes were speeding past.

I didn't have time to park further away. I double-parked my car next to a van and rushed towards the hall. A crowd had gathered outside it. The path was full of waiting people. Some were also standing on the grass at the side, and some were perched on the walls surrounding the hall. Cameras were trained on the building. Why was there so much interest? What was wrong with these people?

I tried to move along the path.

"Excuse me. Can I come through?" I politely asked.

"Hey! No pushing in!" a thickset man shouted at me. "This is a queue. I've been standing here for ages. Get to the back!"

The woman in front of him turned around and snapped at me, "There's no point you queuing. You won't get in. There aren't many tickets left. We'll be lucky if we get in."

The thickset man said to her, "We'd better get in, Sal. I want to see where that fella died. See if anyone in front of you has got any tickets. Offer them double the price. Triple if you have to."

I tried again, "But my friend is inside. I have to get to her urgently. Please, let me get past."

The man folded his large arms. "You're not going anywhere. Unless you've got a ticket. Have you got one? I'll give you twenty quid for it."

I realised with a sinking heart that I didn't have a ticket. Nick Scott had given them to Peggy. I looked at the building in front of me. There could be another way in.

I quickly walked away from the queue and made a tour of the building. There was a back door, but it was locked. I knocked on it, but no one answered.

I heard cheering coming from inside. The play must be starting. I didn't have much time. My heart was thudding like crazy in my ears. I couldn't let Nick die.

Feeling more determined, I marched back to the queue and began to barge my way through. I loudly declared, "I have a ticket! Move!"

Maybe it was because I was so loud, or maybe it was because I was so rude, but people shifted out of my way.

I was making good progress until I made my way through the door and into the entrance of the hall.

Two huge men in black suits stood there. They looked like they should be standing outside the doors to a nightclub, not inside the local church hall.

"Ticket?" one of them addressed me. There was a hint of menace in his voice as if he were daring me to lie to him.

I waved my hand in the direction of the audience. "My friend has got my ticket! She's in there!"

"Oh, yeah? Is that right?" He shared a look with his colleague. "How many times have we heard that tonight?"

His colleague sneered. "About a hundred. Do you want to throw her out or shall I do it?"

I tried another tactic. "My friend is Peggy Marshall. She's waiting for me. She'll be furious if you don't let me in."

Dropping Peggy's name got the desired effect.

The first man blustered, "Peggy Marshall? The same Peggy who's friends with my gran?"

"Probably," I said.

"Hang on a minute." The man walked away. He opened the curtain in front of him which led to the audience, and went through.

His colleague started talking to someone else who had entered the hall.

I could hear the voice of Lord Gresham onstage as he took his final breaths. Nick Scott would be in the next scene. Panic filled me. I had to stop Nick drinking that water.

I quickly took in the layout of the hall. There was only one thing I could do.

I spun around and headed for the wooden stairs which led to the stage. Ignoring the astonished looks of cast members who were standing there, I raced up the steps and ran on to the stage.

The lights on the stage momentarily blinded me and I blinked rapidly. I heard the audience gasp at my sudden arrival.

Nick Scott was oblivious to my entry. He was sitting in the armchair. The teacup was raised to his mouth. He moved it closer.

"No!" I yelled. I threw myself forward and knocked the cup from his hand. Such was my momentum, that I landed heavily on Nick's lap. The armchair tipped backwards. The back of Nick's head hit the wooden floor with a sickening thud. His eyes fluttered and then closed.

Someone in the audience screamed, "She's killed him! She's killed the inspector!"

Chapter 18

I'd never been in a prison cell before. Well, it wasn't a prison cell; it was a holding cell. That's what the policewoman had told me when she'd brought me in.

To coin a phrase, all hell had broken loose after Nick's accident. I'd heard many people screaming at me. Someone shouted my name. I think it was Peggy. Hands pulled me off Nick's still body and dragged me off the stage. Flashes of light exploded all around me which I assumed were people taking photos.

I was locked in a small storeroom in the church hall while phone calls were made. I kept calling out and asking if Nick was okay. No one answered me.

Then the police arrived. I was taken out of the hall through a back door. I was placed in a dark car and driven to the police station.

And now, here I was, alone and scared to death in a small, cheerless room.

I sat on the hard bed and wrung my hands together. Had I killed Nick Scott in the process of trying to save his life?

At one point, a solemn-faced policeman brought me a cup of tea. I asked him about Nick, but he said he couldn't talk about it. I attempted to drink the tea, but my hands were shaking too much.

After what seemed like hours, someone came into the room. I'd never been so pleased to see anyone in my life.

Seb Parker gave me a long look as he stood at the entrance of the room. "Karis, what have you done this time?"

I jumped to my feet and went over to him. "Is he okay? Is he alive? Please tell me he's alive. I didn't mean to hurt him."

Seb took my elbow and led me back to the bed. I sat down and he sat at my side.

He said, "Nick is in hospital. He was knocked out for a few minutes, but he's been checked over and he's fine. There's no lasting damage."

I burst into tears and buried my head in my hands. "I thought I'd killed him."

Seb handed me a tissue. "You gave him a bad headache, that's all. Here, wipe your eyes. I can't talk to you if you're crying, and I've got something to tell you. Would you like a hot drink? How about something to eat?"

I shook my head and wiped my tears away. "Are you going to interrogate me now? Do we have to go into a small room with a two-way mirror? Will you chain me to the table?"

"No. Unless you'd like me to?" His eyes held the faintest of twinkles. "Karis, I know you must have had a vision concerning Nick Scott. Why else would you have thrown yourself at him like that? Tell me what you saw."

I told Seb about my vision and the poisoned water in the teacup.

Seb nodded. "I thought that might be the case. The contents of the cup have been analysed, and there are traces of poison in it. It's the same substance that killed Howie McGarry." He gave me a gentle smile. "You saved Nick's life. True, you almost killed him straight afterwards. But he's still alive."

I frowned. "I don't understand why Nick said those words about Lord Gresham's wife lying to him about his daughter. Peggy and I spoke to Nick earlier today, and I mentioned those words. Nick said they weren't part of the play. So why would he say them?"

"Ah, I can solve that mystery." He reached into his pocket and took out a plastic bag. There was a small note inside. For a moment, I thought Peggy had been sending threatening notes again.

Seb continued, "This was found inside the jacket that Nick was wearing onstage. He was told to say those words as a mark of respect for Howie. The note isn't signed, of course, as it's been printed out. I spoke to Nick, and he said he found this note in the dressing room. It had been addressed to him. Respect for Howie notwithstanding, I asked him why he would say those words if they weren't part of the play."

"I can guess his answer. Howie was an inspiration to Nick, and he wouldn't think twice about showing his respect this way."

Seb nodded and put the plastic bag back in his pocket. "That's more or less what Nick said. Someone wanted him to say those words onstage. I suspect you might know who the words were aimed at." There was a fractional pause. "Actually, you don't need to tell me. Peggy's been hounding me since the moment you were taken away. She's told me about your theory concerning Gaynor Dawson and the possible blackmail."

"Did she? Is Peggy okay? I must have given her a fright by running onto the stage like that."

Seb looked towards the door. "She's here at the station making a nuisance of herself. She's been marching up and down the reception area and shouting, "Free Karis Booth! Free the innocent one!" If I wasn't so scared of her, I'd arrest her for causing a disturbance. She's having a cup of tea now and watching the TV with one of my officers."

I smiled. "She's a loyal friend. What do you think about our theory concerning Gaynor Dawson?"

"It's not a theory. It's the truth. Howie McGarry was blackmailing her. He'd found out that Amber wasn't Toby Dawson's daughter. He's been blackmailing Gaynor for months. She ran out of money and told

Howie that. He said he didn't believe her, and if she didn't pay up, he'd tell Toby Dawson the truth in the middle of the play. In doing that, the whole audience would know too. His words about Lord Gresham's daughter were a veiled threat to Gaynor."

I shook my head. "I only met Howie once. I didn't know he was like that."

"Most criminals come across as normal people."

"Have you spoken to Gaynor Dawson?"

Seb nodded. "We have. She's admitted everything. She couldn't take any more threats from Howie. She used her life savings paying him off as she was desperate to keep her secret. Toby Dawson thinks of Amber as his own daughter. Gaynor couldn't let him find out the truth."

Gaynor's face came into my mind. I said, "But Toby knew, didn't he? He's always known Amber wasn't his."

Seb gave me an incredulous look. "How do you know that?"

I shrugged. "I had a feeling. Gaynor should have told Toby about Howie's threats immediately. She didn't have to kill Howie."

"I know. I do have sympathy for Gaynor, but murder is never justified."

I asked, "Did Gaynor try to kill Nick too? Don't tell me he was blackmailing her as well."

"Gaynor did poison Nick's water. She got a note a few hours before the play saying that the blackmail wasn't over, and that Nick would be saying those incriminating words. Unless she paid up, of course."

"Who sent that note?"

"We don't know." He let out a small sigh. "We'll never know because Gaynor burnt the note. Anyway, that's for us to deal with. I wanted to let you know what's happened so far. I'm sorry you've been kept here so long. You're free to go. Do you need a lift home? I can't take you, but I can arrange for someone else to do that."

"I'll sort something out. I'll share a taxi with Peggy. I've left my car at the church hall." I grimaced. "Oh, I double-parked it. It'll be in someone's way."

"That's been taken care of." He got to his feet and looked towards the open door. "I have to go now. I've got a lot to do. I'll phone you later to see how you're doing."

"You don't have to do that, Seb."

He looked at me and said in a serious tone, "I want to make sure you don't fling yourself on any other seated men. I don't want it to become a habit." He gave me a smile before leaving the room.

Peggy was waiting for me in the reception area. She flung her arms around me and declared, "You're free! At last! Freedom for Karis Booth." She released me and said, "Let's get out of here before they change their minds. You've been here all night, and that's long enough considering you're innocent. Come on; I've got a lot to tell you."

Chapter 19

I tried to concentrate on what Peggy was telling me as we got into the taxi, but I was too exhausted. I was aware of her voice as she talked about Gaynor Dawson, Nick Scott and someone else, but I could barely take it in. My eyelids felt like they were too heavy for my face and they kept closing.

Peggy must have noticed how tired I was because she abruptly stopped talking, patted my hand and said, "We'll talk about this later."

Once we reached our homes, Peggy helped me into my house and up the stairs. She guided me towards my bedroom and said, "You get yourself into bed. You look dead on your feet. I don't need to sleep as I had a couple of power naps at the police station. Do you want to have a shower first? You might want to wash the scent of injustice off you. I can't believe they locked you up like a common criminal. I've got a good mind to write to my MP about this. Not that he'll do much about it, the useless lump of lard. He still hasn't sorted out those loose paving slabs in the precinct that I told him about."

I fell onto my lovely soft bed and closed my eyes. I muttered, "Thanks for looking after me, Peggy. You're a good friend."

I felt Peggy tugging my shoes off and then covering me with a blanket. She said, "I'll let you sleep for a few hours. Any more than that and you won't sleep properly tonight. I'll be downstairs on my laptop."

She closed the curtains and left the room.

My mind was too restless to let me sleep for long. I woke up after an hour and felt rested enough to get out of bed. I took myself into the shower and had an invigorating wash. I felt like I was washing away all the troubles from the last few days.

Peggy was sitting in the living room with the laptop on her knee. She said, "I heard you moving about so I've made you a cuppa. I won't be a moment. Nearly done with my blog."

I sat next to Peggy and picked my cup up. I took the smallest of sips. It tasted fine, so I took a bigger drink.

Peggy switched her laptop off, put it on the table in front of her and turned to face me. She said, "Where shall I begin? It's all been happening, hasn't it? You gave me such a shock when you ran onto the stage last night. As soon as you knocked that cup out of Nick's hands, I knew you'd had another vision. Am I right?"

I nodded.

"I thought as much. You really flung yourself at that poor man. He didn't stand a chance, not when you had all that fish pie and apple crumble in your stomach. I'm not surprised you knocked the chair backwards. You should have heard the crack his head made on the floor." She shivered.

"I did hear it. I thought I'd killed him."

"You're not the only one. Some idiot in front of me called you a killer. The twit. Then other idiots started taking photos of you."

I lowered my cup. "Did they? Are those photos all over the internet? I hope they aren't. That would be awful for our café."

Peggy said, "You don't need to worry about any of that. Seb took care of everything."

"Seb? What did he do?"

"He was a hero. A hero in a suit and tie. Don't tell him I said that. It'll only go to his head. When you were whipped away by the police, no one was allowed to leave the hall. Seb arrived and talked to a few people about what had happened. I tried to talk to him, but he pretended he didn't see me. He stood on the stage and told everyone they were in the middle of a police investigation. He went on and on about that. He recited some laws and whatnot. The upshot is that his officers checked everyone's phones and got them to delete photos of you."

"Did they?"

"They did. Seb made sure of it. Karis, I think he did that to protect you. When I followed him back to the police station, I saw him talking to an older fellow about you. The older fellow didn't look at all pleased and said something about you interfering. Seb went into an office with him. They closed the blinds, so I couldn't see what was going on." She gave me a look of disgust. "They must soundproof those offices too because I couldn't hear a thing when I stood right next to the door. Seb didn't look at all happy when he came out."

I looked down at my cup. "I hope he didn't get into trouble because of me."

"That's not all. He got a call about your car. It was about to be towed away. He was furious about that and said he'd take care of it. He got someone to go to the church and drive your car home."

I looked up from my cup. "Did he? I didn't even notice my car outside."

"You were half asleep when we came home. I'll say something for Seb Parker; he's gone out of his way to defend you. And he had to deal with Gaynor and that murder too. You should have seen her face when they brought her in. I almost didn't recognise her. She looked like she'd aged ten years. Her husband was due to come down to the station too, but we left before he got there."

"Do you know about the blackmail and Howie?"

Peggy nodded. "I do. I overheard Seb talking about that." She chuckled. "I followed him everywhere. I'm surprised he didn't arrest me. What did he tell you about Gaynor?"

I told Peggy everything that Seb had told me. I also informed her of the note Nick had found in his pocket before he went onstage.

Peggy frowned. "Who wrote that note?"

"I don't know. I'm still taking it all in." I tilted my head. "Those children are back again. They sound as if they're having a good time."

Peggy wasn't listening to me. There was a faraway look in her eye. She mumbled, "I wonder if…" She trailed off.

A phone rang. I recognised it as mine. Peggy reached into her cardigan pocket and pulled it out. She gave it to me and said, "Sorry. I took this by mistake last night. Who's ringing you?"

I looked at the screen. "It's Robbie." I answered the phone.

Robbie began speaking, "Karis, you need to come to our house immediately. We've got a visitor who wants to talk to you." He ended the call.

I stared at my phone.

Peggy said, "What did he say?"

I told her.

She got to her feet. "We don't get a minute's peace, do we? Come on. Let's hit the road."

Chapter 20

Robbie's visitor was Vanessa McGarry. She was sitting at the kitchen table when Peggy and I arrived. Erin and Robbie were leaning against the work counter with their arms folded. They both wore the same look of distrust on their faces. They looked like a couple of bookends as they silently watched Vanessa.

Vanessa looked our way as we came in. Her face was devoid of make-up, and her hair lay in a straggly mess over her shoulders.

Peggy looked Vanessa over before joining Robbie and Erin at the work counter. She matched their stance and physical expressions.

Vanessa got to her feet and gave me a wobbly smile. Her voice was subdued as she said to me, "Karis, thank you for seeing me."

Peggy retorted, "We didn't know it was you waiting here. If we had, we wouldn't have come. You've got a nerve showing your face after what you've done."

Vanessa nodded. "I know. I have no excuse. I'm so very sorry. Erin, I didn't mean to scare you when I came around last time."

Erin looked away.

Vanessa continued, "I wasn't thinking straight. I can't even remember what I said to you. I was out of my mind with grief." Her voice caught in her throat.

I went over to her and said, "I understand. Sit down. Tell me why you want to talk to me."

She gave me the smallest of smiles and sat down. I sat opposite her and ignored the confused looks that were coming from Robbie and Peggy. Erin was still looking away.

"I'm so very sorry, Karis," Vanessa said. "About everything. I was so awful to you at high school. I don't expect you to forgive me. I was jealous of you."

"Jealous of me? Why?"

"You were so confident and sure of yourself. You defended your psychic abilities even when I was being a total cow to you. You knew who you were and never apologised for it. You had Seb Parker's friendship and support until I ruined it for you. I take no pleasure in my past. When people talk about their time at school, they say it was the best time of their lives. It wasn't for me. I'm full of shame over what I did to you."

Erin snapped, "So you should be! Karis might have been strong at school in front of everyone, but she was in tears as soon as she came home. It's all your fault!"

Robbie put his arm around Erin's shoulders. "Now then, my love, don't get upset. Let Vanessa get on with her apology."

"Thank you, Robbie," Vanessa said. "I know I'm taking up your precious time. I'm sorry. For everything. For the past. For how I was at the café. For how I pounded on your door." She stopped talking and tears ran down her cheeks. "I don't know how Howie put up with me and my temper over the years. I'm never going to find anyone else like him."

Erin gave her a sniff of disapproval and begrudgingly said, "Would you like a cup of tea?"

"No, thank you. I won't take up much more of your time. Karis, I need your help." She turned beseeching eyes on me. "I know I've got a nerve asking you for help."

"Go on," I said. I gave her a studied look. "Is it about Howie and the blackmailing?"

She nodded.

I continued, "You knew about it, didn't you?"

She nodded again. "I should have known something was up when he started coming home with envelopes full of money. He said he'd been paid in cash for jobs he'd done. But no one pays in cash anymore, do they? Not reputable companies anyway. I knew he wasn't getting as much building work as he used to, so I was suspicious of where the money was coming from. I did the only thing I could. I checked his phone. I saw the texts he'd sent to Gaynor." She stopped and frowned as if recalling those texts. "I couldn't believe it. My Howie doing something like that. It didn't make sense."

"Did you confront him?" I asked.

"I certainly did. I told him to stop it immediately. He laughed in my face. I'd never known him to act like that before. He said he wouldn't stop. It was easy money. He told me what he was going to say during the play to get Gaynor to pay more. I pleaded with him to stop the blackmail, but he wouldn't."

I said, "Is that why you were there on the night he died? You were seen waiting by the side of the stage."

"I was. Your words about the poisoned tea had been on my mind. I know I'd made fun of your vision in the café, but I couldn't get your words out of my mind. I was worried about Howie and wanted him off that stage. I kept waving at him from the side, but he ignored me." She began to cry. I reached out and put my hand on her arm.

Erin placed a cup of tea in front of Vanessa and said softly, "I know you said you didn't want one, but I've made you a drink anyway."

"Thank you." Vanessa put her hands around the cup.

"Why do you need my help?" I asked as I pulled my hand back.

"It's Nick Scott," Vanessa said. "He's in on the blackmail too. He was good friends with Howie. He must have seen how easily Howie was making extra money. He wanted to be part of it too. Nick came around to my house yesterday. It was a few hours before he went onstage. He said he was going to take over Howie's blackmailing business." She let out a short laugh. "He actually called it a business. As if it were all above board. He knew Howie had details about Gaynor Dawson hidden under a floorboard in the spare bedroom. There was a copy of Amber's birth certificate and other documents hidden there. Nick said he would take them. I begged him not to. I said whoever killed Howie would come after him. He said they wouldn't dare."

"Did he know it was Gaynor who killed Howie?"

"He did. But he didn't care. He thought he could frighten her into paying more. Knowing she'd killed Howie was more ammunition for him to use against her. Karis, I'm worried about Nick. He'll be out of the hospital soon. He won't be happy that Gaynor's been arrested. He was planning to blackmail her for months yet. He might blame me. Can you help?"

"What can I do?"

"Can you talk to Seb and tell him to arrest Nick for attempted blackmail? Nick took Amber's birth certificate with him. It'll be in his house somewhere."

Peggy called over, "Why can't you tell Seb?"

Vanessa shook her head. "He won't believe me. He'll think I had something to do with it. He'll believe Karis."

A list of names suddenly came into my head. I said to Vanessa, "Who's Vicky Sims?"

"Who?" Vanessa said.

"And who's Bill Kelly? And Faith Casey?"

Vanessa frowned. "I don't recognise any of these names."

I continued, "Carolyn Torres? Warren McDaniels? Sam Hart?"

Vanessa said, "I don't know who these people are. Why are you asking me about them?"

I replied, "They were blackmailed by Howie too. He's been doing this for years."

Vanessa's hands flew to her chest. "No! He can't have been. I would have known. Karis, you have to get in touch with Seb immediately. You have to give him these names."

Robbie said, "Karis doesn't need to contact Seb. I can make the relevant enquiries."

I looked at Robbie. "Can you contact Seb anyway, please?"

"Of course. But why?"

I looked back at Vanessa. "Because it's Vanessa who's behind the blackmailing. She forced Howie to do it. Nick Scott had nothing to do with any of it. She's been lying to us about everything."

There was a sudden silence.

Vanessa growled with rage. She grabbed the cup in front of her and flung the hot contents at me. I was prepared and moved to the side.

Robbie was at Vanessa's side in a second and he restrained her. Vanessa struggled and called me the most obscene words.

Robbie said to Vanessa, "I won't be having words like that said in my home, Mrs McGarry. Come with me." He forced her out of the chair and took her over to the door. He called over his shoulder, "Erin, I've got my hands full at the moment, so can you do me a favour and phone Seb? If he doesn't answer, phone Charlie or Reg. Tell them to get around here quickly. Thanks, love. And leave that mess on the wall to me." He took the snarling woman outside and closed the door behind him.

"Well I never!" Peggy exploded. "The absolute nerve of that woman. Karis, did you get a vision about her? Did you see her hounding her poor husband?"

I shook my head. "It was the look in Vanessa's eyes which made me think she was lying. There was no emotion there, not even when she was crying." I thought of an analogy. "You know when you go to the fish market and you see lines of fish staring up at nothing? Dead eyes? Vanessa's eyes were like that. I don't think Howie would have stood a chance when Vanessa forced him to help her."

Peggy shook her head sadly. "Poor Howie. And poor Gaynor. What a mess." She came over to me and gave me a hug. "It's all over now. Thanks to you."

"And you," I added.

Chapter 21

The next evening, I invited a guest around for dinner. He looked exhausted when he arrived.

"You look worn out," I said to Seb when I opened the door to him. "Come in. I've got dinner in the oven."

Seb gave me a tired smile. "Thanks for the invitation. I've barely eaten these last few days. It's been one thing after another at the station with Howie McGarry's case and the associated complications." He held up a bottle of wine. "This is for you."

"Thank you. I'll have a glass now. Would you like one?" I closed the front door behind him.

He gave me a wry smile. "I'd better not. One glass of that and I'll fall asleep. Could I have a cup of coffee, please? I could do with a boost of caffeine."

"Of course. Come into the kitchen."

Seb followed me and I put the kettle on. I opened the bottle of wine and poured a glass for myself.

Seb sniffed the air and said, "What is that delicious smell?"

"It's leftover fish pie. I made it yesterday for Peggy and me and there's plenty left." I gave him a smile. "I've got some of Peggy's apple crumble too."

A glazed look came into Seb's eyes. "Apple crumble. I haven't had that for years. Is there custard to go with it?"

"There certainly is. It's homemade and much better than a packet one. Sit down."

I quickly made Seb a coffee and brought it over to him. He said, "Thank you. This is just what I need. How are you doing? Robbie told me how nasty Vanessa was to you yesterday. Did she hurt you?"

"No. She made a mess on Erin's wall with that tea she flung my way, but we soon cleaned that up. I'll get the fish pie out now and we can chat while we eat."

I took the pie out of the oven and gave Seb a generous portion. I piled some vegetables onto the side of his plate. His face lit up when he saw his meal. I put a smaller portion on my plate.

Seb tucked into his dinner as if he hadn't eaten for years. He was soon ready for his apple crumble and custard. Once that was in front of him, he wolfed it down in minutes.

He leaned back in his chair. "That was delicious. The best meal I've had in years." He cast a hopeful glance at my half-eaten dessert. "Are you going to finish that?"

"I am struggling a bit with it." I pushed the bowl towards him. "You have it. Seb, Peggy told me what happened at the police station when she was there. She said you organised for my car to be taken home. Thank you for that."

He gave me a half-shrug. "It was no trouble. I didn't want your car to be towed away." He scraped his spoon around the inside of the bowl and got the last remnants of the dessert out.

I continued, "Peggy also told me an older man at the station spoke to you about me. I hope I haven't got you into bother."

Another half-shrug came from Seb. "That man is a senior officer. We had a chat. It's nothing for you to worry about."

"Have you told anyone at the station about how I help you? You know, with my psychic abilities and whatnot."

"I haven't, but I will if I need to. I'd be proud to tell people about you. You have an amazing gift, Karis, and I appreciate all the help you've given me. I hope you'll continue to help me." He gave me a long look.

I shifted in my chair and replied, "Of course I will. Can you tell me anything about Howie's case?" I looked away from him and quickly refilled my glass.

Seb sighed heavily. "This has been a challenging time. I interviewed Vanessa yesterday. She tried to lie to me at first, but then her anger got the better of her." He shook his head. "I've known some nasty, heartless people in my time, but Vanessa McGarry is one of the worst. Robbie checked those names you gave him. All of them had been blackmailed by Vanessa and Howie over the years. Some of them had become bankrupt because of it."

"How did Vanessa find out so much private information about those people?"

"Don't you know where she works?"

I shook my head.

"She works at the town hall. She's got access to confidential records. I'll be having a meeting with her managers next week about their security procedures." He looked down at the table. "While there's never any excuse for murder, I do have a degree of sympathy for Gaynor Dawson. She was pushed to her limits. The notes she got from Vanessa and Howie were incredibly vicious."

I leaned over and patted his hand. "I wish I could say I was surprised by Vanessa's actions, but I'm not." I frowned and looked towards the kitchen window. "It's late for them to be playing outside."

Seb looked up. "Who?"

"Those children. I can hear them outside. I hope they're okay." I got up and walked over to the window. I could hear children playing, but I couldn't see them. I opened the back door and looked out.

I saw something. Something that made me break into a laugh.

Seb came over to my side. "What are you looking at? I can't see any children."

I turned to face him and told him about the vision I'd just experienced.

He gave me a smile. "You should tell them. Immediately. Go now. I don't mind."

I glanced towards my nearly-empty wine glass. "I'll have to get a taxi. I've had two glasses of wine."

"Nonsense. I'll drive you. Come on."

Seb drove me over to Robbie and Erin's house. He said he'd sit in the car while I spoke to them.

"Don't be ridiculous," I told him. "I want you to see their faces when I tell them."

Seb pulled a face. "But Erin hates me. She's never going to forgive me for how I treated you at school."

"She's warming to you. Seb Parker, stop being such a wimp." I got out of the car, walked over to his side and opened the car door. "Come on. Get out."

Robbie and Erin were surprised to see us. Erin gave Seb a tepid look which was better than the sub-zero looks she normally gave him.

"I need to tell you both something," I informed them.

We went into the living room. Erin and Robbie sat next to each other on the sofa and held hands. Seb hovered behind the sofa until Erin ordered him to sit down.

I knelt on the carpet in front of Erin and Robbie. I began, "I've had a vision. A clear one with a lot of detail in it. It's about your children."

"Pardon?" Erin said.

"Children?" Robbie frowned. "As in more than one?"

I nodded. "I've been hearing children's voices for days now. About ten minutes ago, I had a vision while I was standing at the back door of my house. Well, it's still Mum's house, but you know what I mean."

"Get on with it," Erin urged.

I continued, "I saw a boy and girl in the garden. You were there, Robbie. You were making a Wendy house for the children. The little ones were trying to help you." My eyes filled with happy tears as I recalled the scene. "They were about three or four years old. They were wearing dungarees, and they had belts with plastic tools on them. They were twins."

Robbie's voice was hoarse as he said, "A boy and girl? Dungarees? A tool belt? How do you know they were our children?"

Tears escaped from my eyes. "Because they called you Daddy. I was there too, and they called me Auntie Karis." I grinned. "They're a noisy pair. They never stopped talking. And they were more of a hindrance than a help to you, Robbie."

Robbie burst into tears. Erin's eyes brimmed over and she gave me a wobbly smile.

I heard a sniff at my side and saw Seb dabbing his eyes with a tissue.

Erin said, "Tell me everything. Every last detail."

Seb got to his feet. "This is a private matter. I'll leave you in peace."

Erin shook her head. "You can stay. Put the kettle on. There's some cake in the kitchen. Help yourself."

Seb looked taken aback by her words. "Right. Yes. I will do. Thanks." He headed for the kitchen.

I told Erin and Robbie again about my vision. I gave them as much information as I could remember. We were all crying happy tears by the time Seb came in with a tray of drinks.

Seb and I stayed with the happy couple for another hour. I had to repeat my vision many times. I told Erin that she had to take things twice as easy now because she had two babies to care for.

"I will," she promised.

As the evening came to a close, Seb drove me home. We chatted about general things and it was lovely to have his company.

There was one part of my vision which I hadn't told anyone about.

The twins had called me Auntie Karis. Seb had been at my side in the vision. The twins talked to him and called him Uncle Seb.

So, Seb Parker was going to be in my life for the foreseeable future. And it looked like he was going to be part of the family.

That was interesting.

THE END

THE KNITTING PATTERN MYSTERY

Chapter 1

I checked my watch for the tenth time and said, "They'll be here any second. I'm so excited! Are you excited? I am." I clasped my hands together and looked at my sister, Erin.

She gave me a sideways look. "I'm not as excited as you. What's wrong with you tonight? You keep grinning to yourself and jigging from side to side. Have you been drinking?" She moved closer and sniffed me.

"No, I haven't been drinking." I glanced around the café which we co-owned. It was currently undergoing an extensive renovation. I continued, "But look at everything. The café is nearly finished. The tables and chairs are all here. And we're going to have our first-ever craft evening in our new café! I could burst with joy."

Erin shook her head at me. "Your voice is going all screechy. Calm down. Look at me; I'm the picture of serenity." She pointed at her face and gave me a serene smile.

I put my hand on my stomach and grinned some more. "I've got butterflies. They're dancing like crazy in my stomach."

Erin's eyes narrowed. "Hang on a minute. You've only become this excited in the last ten minutes. Has your giddy condition got something to do with your psychic abilities? Are your psychic senses tingling and having a funny effect on you? Is it something to do with our café?"

336

I frowned and looked around us. "I'm not sure. Now that you've said that, I can honestly say I'm not feeling giddy about the café or the work that's been done on it. It's been a bit of a pain to get everything finished."

"It still isn't finished. According to my ever-helpful husband, it'll be another week before we can open the café to customers. Karis, are you excited about the kitchen? I love it, but does the thought of those shiny new appliances get you hot under the collar?" She smiled. "This is a weird conversation."

I looked over to where the kitchen was. It had everything Erin needed to make those delicious cakes of hers. I said, "I'm not getting even a flicker of joy as I think about the kitchen. Sorry."

"What about the seating area with those new sofas and tables over in our relaxing area? Is that area making your temperature rise?"

"It is a lovely part of the café, but no, it's not doing a thing for me." I studied the elderly woman who was near the sofas. Peggy Marshall was in charge of tonight's craft event and she was making sure everything was ready for our clients. I thought about the event which would start soon, grinned and then turned to face Erin.

Erin was one step ahead of me and said, "You're thinking about tonight's event, aren't you? Something about Peggy's knitting class is getting you all hot and bothered."

"I wouldn't use those words. But you are right. There's something about this evening which is affecting me. I'm getting more excited by the minute. I can't control it."

Erin nodded. "You'll be getting one of your visions soon. I'm sure of it." She folded her arms and gave me a stern look. "I hope you don't have another one of your murder visions. I don't want a violent act occurring in our café. Karis, if someone's about to be murdered, can you make sure it happens outside? I don't want any blood on the new furnishings."

I shook my head at her. "I can't control my visions, certainly not the murder ones." I grimaced. "If there is going to be a murder, I hope it doesn't involve knitting needles. We've got a lot of those on the tables."

"Maybe we should move them," Erin suggested. "You should have a good look at the people who are coming here tonight. When they come through the door, have a thorough stare at them. Watch out for any suspicious-looking people. See if any of them smell weird."

"Potential murderers don't smell any different to normal people."

Erin gave me a wise look. "How do you know? Have you studied them? Have you smelled them all?"

"Who's talking about murderers?" Peggy said as she came over to us. She sighed heavily. "Karis, you haven't had one of your visions, have you? Is someone going to get bumped off tonight during my knitting class? Do you know what time it's going to happen?"

"I haven't had a vision," I began. "I'm just—"

Peggy interrupted me, "I hope it's at the end of my class. I've got a detailed schedule of what I'm going to do. Will the murder weapon be a knitting needle? Will it be a metal one or a wooden one? I've got both kinds on the tables. Blood can be wiped off a metal one, but it'll stain a wooden one. Where's the murder going to happen? I hope the sofas don't get damaged. They're brand new."

I put my hand on her arm to halt the flow of words. "Peggy, I haven't had a vision. I've been experiencing a high level of excitement, that's all. I'm excited about the evening, and I know it's going to go well. You've got everything under control."

Peggy's brow furrowed. "Are you sure you haven't had a murder vision?"

"A murder vision? Tonight?" Robbie, Erin's husband, appeared behind us. "I hope no one gets blood on my new walls. It took me forever to paint these walls, and those were the last pots they had at the DIY place. If those walls get ruined, I'll have to paint the whole café again."

All feelings of excitement had left me now. I was full of irritation instead. I proclaimed, "I haven't had a vision of someone being murdered! Okay? Have you all got that?"

Peggy rubbed her ear. "There's no need to shout." She turned to face Robbie. "Have you got the recording equipment ready? Is it all set to record the class? Did you look at my schedule? Have you memorised it? I'll be standing near the sofas, to begin with. I'll be sitting at other times, and then walking about. You need to keep up with me. The readers of my blog are waiting with bated breath for the video of this evening's event. I don't want you making a pig's ear of it, Robbie Terris."

Robbie gave her a broad smile. "I won't. I have memorised your schedule. I have triple checked my equipment. I've been practising my recording skills on my wife." He winked at Erin.

She blushed and looked away.

Peggy tapped Robbie roughly on the arm. "I hope you haven't been making any rude videos. I don't want you putting the wrong one on my blog by mistake. I'm not running that kind of internet business."

"There's no need to worry," Robbie advised. "There's been no funny business going on with Erin and me. I just wanted to capture her radiant beauty as she progresses through her pregnancy." His gaze softened as he looked at Erin. "I didn't think you could get any more beautiful, my love. But each day, you're becoming more breathtaking."

Erin blushed some more. "Stop it, you fool."

Peggy rapped Robbie on the arm again. "Get your attention off your wife and on to me. My readers are expecting great things from me. You need to capture my every move."

Robbie chuckled. "Being an internet sensation has gone to your head, Peggy Marshall. What time are your clients getting here?"

"Seven o'clock," Peggy replied. "We've got five minutes. I've got everything prepared. Erin, have you got the refreshments ready?"

"I have," Erin replied.

Peggy looked at Robbie. "Is your recording equipment fully charged?"

"It is," Robbie replied with an increasing smile. "I won't let you down."

"You'd better not," Peggy replied darkly. "Karis, you know what you're doing, don't you? Some of my clients are total beginners. They'll need a lot of help."

"I know what is expected of me," I replied.

"Good, good. Then we're ready to go." Peggy patted her hair. "Do I look okay? Do I look camera-ready?"

We all nodded at Peggy.

The door to the café opened.

Peggy gasped. "They're here! Action stations, everyone." She gave me a stern look. "Karis, don't let anyone get murdered tonight."

"I'll try my best."

Peggy rushed over to the café door with a huge smile of welcome on her face. Robbie and Erin were right behind her.

And that's when I got a psychic vision.

Chapter 2

My surroundings faded.

I was sitting on a sofa in a warm room. Something was on my lap. My stomach leapt with excitement as I looked at it.

It was a knitting pattern.

I felt immense relief at having it in my possession. I'd been waiting ages for it to arrive.

I picked it up and studied it. The pattern was for a stylish twin set. The model was wearing the jumper and cardigan with elegance. A string of pearls adorned her neck. She was staring happily at something in the distance.

My attention went to the wool at my side. It was light blue. I picked a ball up and placed it next to my cheek. It was soft. I smiled. How would he feel when he saw me in this colour? Would he say I looked like a Hollywood star? I hoped he would.

Warm feelings of joy and happiness rushed through me. He was going to love seeing me in this twin set. He'd say I looked just like—

My thoughts abruptly stopped as I felt a sharp nudge at my side. I jumped when I saw Erin glowering at me.

Erin hissed, "Karis, what are you doing? Why are you stroking your cheek like that? Did you have a vision?"

I nodded and quickly looked around the café. "I'll have to tell you about it later. Peggy is giving me a dark look. I'd better go over to her."

Erin grabbed my arm and whispered, "Was it about a murder? Is there going to be one tonight? Tell me."

"It wasn't about a murder. It was about a knitting pattern." I smiled at the memory and how eager I'd felt about that pattern.

"A knitting pattern?" Erin's eyebrows rose. "You've been going all soppy over a knitting pattern? You need to get out more."

Before I could defend myself or explain the vision more, Erin walked away and headed for the kitchen.

I went over to Peggy who was standing near the sofas. The people who had entered a few minutes ago were sitting on the sofas. They were taking their coats off while keeping their wide-eyed looks on Peggy. They were looking at her as if she was a superstar. I suppose she was to them. She'd become quite a celebrity with her blog. Peggy had lived next to Mum for years. Erin and I had grown up with her in our lives. She was like a second mum to us.

Peggy saw me approaching and announced, "This is Karis Booth. She co-owns this business with her sister, Erin. I told you about Karis on my blog."

Some of the seated people gave me knowing looks and I wondered what Peggy had written about me. She wrote her blog posts every day, but I didn't always have time to read them.

"Hello," I said to them.

Peggy continued, "Karis will be on hand to help anyone if they need it. She's an accomplished knitter."

"Thanks to you," I said. I addressed the seated clients. "Peggy taught me to knit when I was young. She's an excellent teacher. She's very patient and explains everything clearly."

An older man nodded to himself and gave Peggy an admiring look.

"That's enough about me," Peggy said. A pink tinge came to her cheeks. "Let's get on. We'll start with the basic stitch for those who are new to knitting. I hope you more experienced knitters will be patient with me while I do that. I've got a wide variety of knitting patterns and wool if any of you want to make a start on your own projects. They're laid out on the tables over there. Help yourselves."

At the mention of the knitting patterns, my heart missed a beat. I had to find that pattern for the twin set. I looked at the patterns which were arranged on the nearby tables. Urgency rushed through me. I had to look at those patterns right now. I made a move forwards.

I felt a hand on my arm. Peggy said quietly, "Where are you going? I need help with the beginners."

I didn't know at this stage whether my vision was important, so I decided not to tell Peggy about it yet. It could wait. I said, "Where do you want me?"

"Follow me."

Robbie appeared on the scene. He had a smudge of chocolate around his lips. He said to Peggy, "I'm here. Ready to record."

Peggy's eyes narrowed. "Robbie, have you been eating cake that's supposed to be for my clients? No, don't answer that. I already know the answer. Come with me. I'm going to start with the beginners. Get your recording equipment ready."

Robbie shot a grin at me. "I'm always in trouble with Peggy. I'll have to be on my best behaviour."

"Me too," I added.

Some of the clients were now standing by the table of patterns and looking through them. My palms suddenly felt itchy. I wanted to be over there with them. I wanted to be looking through those patterns. What if someone found my pattern before I did? I couldn't have that.

Peggy's loud voice brought my attention back to her. "Karis, come over here and let me introduce you to everyone. This is Tom. He's a beginner." She smiled at the older man who'd been nodding at my words earlier. Peggy said to him, "Thank you for all your comments on my blog, Tom. You are too kind."

Tom gave her a huge smile which was almost manic. He gushed, "I meant every word. Your blog inspires me every day. I read each entry more than once. Just like you, I want to fulfil my creative side. It's been lying dormant inside me for years. You've woken it up, Peggy. I can feel my creative juices flowing as we speak."

"That's nice," Peggy said politely. "Karis, you sit next to Tom. Show him the basic knitting stitch." She swiftly moved away. I heard a small chuckle coming from Robbie as he filmed the exchange.

I took a seat next to Tom. It was obvious he didn't want me to be the one teaching him. Despite his indifference to me, I remained patient and polite as I taught him the basic stitches using a pair of large needles and chunky wool.

Tom barely paid me any attention. His eyes were on Peggy as she chatted to other people. He asked me various questions about Peggy, such as how long I'd known her, and what her favourite TV programmes were. I answered swiftly and tried to get Tom's attention back on his work. I stopped answering his questions completely when he asked if Peggy was single.

I gave Tom a stern look. "This isn't a dating evening. You're here to learn how to knit. Am I wasting my time? Do you want to learn or not?"

Peggy picked that moment to return. "Karis, please don't talk to Tom like that. You're scaring him." She gave him a kind smile. "Would you like me to take over from Karis?"

Tom's face lit up with joy. "Yes! I would! Yes!"

I quickly stood up and handed the knitting needles to Peggy before she changed her mind. I was in her bad books for sure now, but I didn't care. I had to find that pattern.

I headed towards the table. I didn't get very far.

Erin came towards me with two plates piled high with sandwiches. "Karis, give me a hand with these. I think I've made too much, as always." She shoved the plates at me.

I didn't have a choice as to whether I wanted to hold them or not. I took them and said, "But I wanted to look at the knitting patterns."

"Not the knitting pattern talk again! Put those plates on that table over there. Then come into the kitchen and get the cakes. Once those are out, you can get on with the tea and coffee."

I gave her a scowl. "Stop being so bossy."

She rested a hand on her stomach. "I'm taking it easy. That's what you've been telling me for weeks. You know full well I've got twins in here. I need to rest as much as possible."

I sighed. "I know. Sorry. I don't know what's wrong with me."

Erin was looking at the clients around the café and counting silently. "Didn't Peggy say there would be twelve here tonight? I can only see eleven."

"She did say twelve. Perhaps someone is running late. I'll take this over to the table now and get those cakes in a minute."

Erin nodded and walked back to the kitchen.

I placed the plates on a table which was a short distance from the knitting area. Peggy had insisted on food being away from her supplies. She said she didn't want crumbs and half-eaten sandwiches mixed amongst her precious wool.

I turned towards the kitchen but stopped moving when the café door opened. A young woman dressed in black came hurrying in. Her long hair was black and she had a variety of facial piercings. Plastic bags dangled from her hands.

Peggy stood up and called out to her, "Jade! There you are. I thought you weren't going to make it. Come over here. Let me introduce you to everyone."

Jade gave Peggy a bashful smile and moved closer. "Hello, Peggy. I'm sorry I'm late. I missed my bus."

"Don't worry about being late; you're here now. Come here. Let me get a good look at you," Peggy said. "Isn't it lovely to finally meet in the flesh? I feel as if I've known you and everyone else for years."

Tom piped up, "I feel like I've been waiting for you all my life, Peggy."

Peggy ignored Tom and said to Jade, "What have you got in those bags? Is it your food shopping? Do you need to put anything in the fridge? You can use the café ones."

Jade lifted the bags higher. "These are knitting patterns. Really old ones. I've been looking in charity shops recently. That's where I get most of my clothes from. When I saw these patterns, I thought you might like them."

Using Erin's previous expression, my psychic senses began to tingle. I moved towards Jade, took the bags from her and announced, "I'll look after these. Help yourself to food." I moved away from the curious stares that came my way and hurried towards the far side of the room.

I could barely contain my excitement as I knelt on the carpet and carefully tipped the contents out. Many knitting patterns slithered to the floor. Some were quite tatty-looking. Many had stains on them. I did wonder for a second if I should be wearing rubber gloves.

I pushed the patterns around the carpet to separate them. My heart was beating ten to the dozen as I scoured the images.

There! There it was! My pattern! The very one I'd seen in my vision.

I picked it up, held it to my chest and jumped to my feet. I cried out in joy and spun around on the spot.

There was a sudden silence. I stopped spinning and saw that everyone was staring at me.

I didn't care. This pattern was important to me. Really important. I could sense it deep down in my bones. Without any shred of doubt, I knew that whoever had owned this pattern desperately needed my help.

What that help was – I didn't know.

Who needed my help? Again, I didn't know.

But I would work it out. Somehow.

Chapter 3

The rest of the evening seemed to drag at an impossibly slow rate. As pleased as I was that we had customers for our craft evening, I was impatient for the event to end so I could go home and make a start on the knitting pattern.

Eagle-eyed Peggy noticed my agitation and took me to one side during a refreshment break.

She said to me, "What's got into you? You keep looking at the door as if you want to make a break for it. Have you got somewhere important to go?" Her glance went to the knitting pattern which I was holding to my chest. "Has it got something to do with that pattern which you're guarding with your life? Come on; spit it out. I know something is going on."

"I'm not sure it means anything," I began. I told her about my vision concerning the pattern. Peggy had always been supportive when it came to my visions.

When I'd finished telling her, she said, "I see. This pattern must be important for some reason. Let me look at it."

I handed it over.

Peggy examined it. "A twin set. You don't see many of these about nowadays. They were all the rage years ago. This pattern isn't too complicated. There's a bit of cable work, but you can manage that. Come over to my stash of wool and let's see if we can find you the right colour. You can make a start on this straight away." She gave me the pattern back.

"But I'm supposed to be helping you," I protested.

Peggy gave me a look. "No offence, but you haven't been much use to me since you found that pattern." She looked over her shoulder at the knitting group. "They're

348

doing really well. I can manage on my own with them."
She looked back at me. "You need to get on with this
pattern as soon as possible. With it being a jumper and a
cardigan, it's going to take you a while to get through it.
Come on. Let's find you some wool."

I knew I should have argued with her and insisted on
helping her with her knitting group, but there was a part
of me which knew I had to complete the twin set
quickly. Or at least make a start on it.

I followed Peggy over to the storage area and she
pulled out the bottom drawer. Balls of wool were lined
up neatly inside. I couldn't see the shade of blue that I
needed, so Peggy opened the next drawer.

She said, "I've got some more wool at home too. I've
been collecting it for weeks. Have a good rummage
about in this drawer. I think there's some blue wool at
the back."

I began to move balls of wool out of the way. My palm
felt itchy as I did so. I was getting closer to something.

"That's it!" I declared. "That's the exact shade I
need!"

Peggy gave me a concerned look. "Okay. Keep your
voice down. How many do you need?"

I checked the pattern and then gave Peggy the number.

She counted the balls of wool in front of her. Her
eyebrows rose. "That's the exact number that's here.
Talk about a coincidence. Let me pop these into a bag
for you." She handed a ball to me. "Take this one now.
Get yourself a pair of knitting needles and find
somewhere quiet to sit. And stop grinning to yourself
like that. You look as if you're a sandwich short of a
picnic."

I took the wool and went over to the table where the
knitting needles were. I was aware of people from the
knitting group giving me concerned looks, but that
didn't bother me. I was used to it. I'd been having

psychic visions all my life and I was often on the receiving end of many concerned looks.

I went over to an armchair at the side of the room and settled down into it. Robbie came over with a cup in his hand. He placed it on the table at my side. He said quietly, "Erin's told me about your latest premonition. Here's a cup of tea to keep you going. Do you want anything to eat? Erin's made a feast of treats."

"No, thanks." My attention was already on the pattern.

I felt Robbie looking at it too. He chuckled. "My gran used to knit things like that. She even had a set of pearls to go with her creations. Not real pearls, of course. Rightio, I'll leave you to it. Let me know if you need anything."

I shot him a swift smile. "Thanks, Robbie."

As soon as he'd walked away, I examined the pattern more closely. One of the sizes on the pattern had been ringed in pencil. The circle around the number didn't quite close. The same pencilled ring had been used throughout the pattern to indicate which size to use. Whoever had used this pattern was the same size as me. That was useful.

As I began casting on, the butterflies in my stomach did a happy dance again. The earlier feelings of excitement returned to me and an image of a smiling young man flittered into my mind. As soon as I concentrated on his face, the image faded.

I soon had the ribbed hem completed. My fingers felt light and energetic as I continued to knit. It was almost like the knitting needles were becoming part of me. Calmness and certainty descended on me as I completed row after row. I'd forgotten how relaxing it was to knit.

I'd almost completed the back segment of the jumper when I felt a tap on my shoulder. Peggy smiled down at me. "Karis, how are you doing?"

I lifted up the knitted piece for her inspection.

She smiled. "You've done a great job on that. Do you want to take it home with you? We're closing up now."

I blinked at her in surprise. "But the evening's only just started."

She waved her hand at the empty sofas. "It ended thirty minutes ago. Everyone's gone home."

"Have they? I didn't hear them."

"I'm not surprised. You've been in a trance for the last few hours. You've been quite a good advert for me."

"An advert? What do you mean?" I began to knit the next row.

"I was telling my group about how relaxing knitting was, and how it calms your mind. I pointed to you to prove my point. For the last few hours, you've had a peaceful look on your face as you completed line after line. It was like you were meditating or something. I didn't want to interrupt you now, but I have to get home. Erin and Robbie do too. They're in the kitchen."

"Are they cleaning up? Let me finish this row and I'll give them a hand. I can't believe I've been sitting here for hours and not helping anyone."

Peggy rested a hand on my shoulder. "You've got this work to do. Erin and Robbie know that, and so do I. I can get a taxi home if you want to stay here a bit longer. I've packed that wool up for you."

I finished the row and stuck the needles into the ball of wool. I said, "You're not getting a taxi. I'll drive you. You can tell me all about the evening on the way back. From what I saw, it was a great success." I paused. "I think you've got a secret admirer in Tom."

Peggy let out a small laugh. "He can admire me all he wants, but my Jeff is still in my heart. And he will be until the day I die and join him wherever he might be. I know he's waiting for me somewhere."

Erin and Robbie came out of the kitchen and headed towards us.

Robbie said, "Come on, Karis, clear off home and take this old lady with you. Erin and I want to go home and cuddle up together. It's taken all my willpower to keep my hands off her tonight. Look how beautiful she is."

Erin gave him a gentle push. "You are a ninny." She looked over at me. "Have you had any more visions yet? Any scenes of murder popped into your head? Any deceased bodies you want to tell us about?"

I shook my head. "Nothing like that, thank goodness. I'm sorry I haven't helped you much tonight."

Erin put her arm around Robbie's waist. "We've managed just fine. Off you go before I throw you out. I need some alone time with my wonderful husband."

I gathered my things together and then helped Peggy into the car with her belongings. It took several trips. At one point, I noticed her carrying bottles of gin and boxes of chocolate. I asked her where they'd come from.

A pink tinge came to her cheeks as she answered, "It's those lovely people in my knitting group. They've already paid a fee for the night; they didn't have to give me gifts too. But they insisted on it. They've been too kind. You'll have to share these chocolates with me. I won't be able to manage them all on my own. I'll be able to manage the gin, though."

As we drove home, Peggy told me how the class went. Everyone enjoyed it, and they promised to send her photos of their finished products.

Peggy said, "Robbie has already uploaded a video to our website, and there have been many comments. I'm going to read them when I get home." Her voice softened. "I never thought my life could change so much, and especially at my age. I'm so busy all the time. And I love it. It's all thanks to you. I'm glad you got a divorce and used your settlement money on the café. Perhaps that ex-husband of yours was actually useful in a roundabout sort of way." She gave a sniff of disapproval. "I must be tired if I'm thinking kindly about Gavin Booth. As soon as I've read those comments online, I'll be taking to my bed. I suggest you do the same. Don't stay up all night knitting."

"I won't," I replied.

We stopped outside the semi-detached houses where we lived. Mum owned the one on the left, and Peggy owned the one on the right. Mum was in a care home now and hadn't lived here for two years. Since getting divorced, I'd moved back to the family home. I loved being back here.

Despite Peggy's protests, I walked her to the door and waited until she was inside. She handed me a couple of boxes of chocolate before she said goodnight and closed the door. I collected my belongings from the car, made my way to Mum's house and let myself in.

I'd told Peggy I wouldn't stay up all night knitting, but I knew I would stay up at least half the night with my craftwork. I had to get this twin set completed. There was an urgency to it.

Erin had insisted that I bring some cake home. Once I'd put that in the fridge, I made myself a cup of coffee. Then I settled down in the living room with my knitting project.

I'd been knitting for a few hours when a soft knock sounded on the front door. I froze. Who was calling at this time of the night? If it was a burglar, it was a polite one.

Holding on to the only weapon I had, I moved cautiously towards the front door. I made sure the safety chain was on, and then I slowly opened it.

Chapter 4

DCI Sebastian Parker was standing on the doorstep. In a calm voice, he said, "Lower your weapon, Mrs Booth." He frowned. "Is that a knitting needle?"

I put the knitting needle behind my back and opened the door wider.

Seb Parker had been my childhood friend, but that had changed when we went to high school. I'd never shied away from my psychic abilities at high school, and that had been a mistake. My peers had made fun of me, even Seb. He bitterly regretted his behaviour now. I knew his remorse was sincere and we were back to being friends.

"Come in," I said to him. "What are you doing here at this time?"

He stepped into the house. "I've been working a late shift at the station. There's a mountain of paperwork to get through. I don't even think I've made a dent in it yet. I was on my way home when I saw your light on. Is everything okay? Why are you up so late?"

I quickly told him about my vision and the knitting pattern. I concluded, "I can't rest until I finish the twin set." I tucked the knitting needle under my arm and flexed my aching fingers. "I can keep going for a few more hours."

Seb said, "Would you like some company? I'm not tired enough to sleep yet."

I gave him a smile. "I would love some company, thanks. Would you put the kettle on, please? If you're hungry, there's some cake in the fridge. Erin made it for tonight's craft event."

"Oh, I forgot about that event. How did it go? I've been reading Peggy's blog. She's got many followers."

I moved over to the sofa and picked my knitting back up. "I'll tell you about it when you bring the tea in."

He laughed. "I get the hint. Won't be long." He headed towards the kitchen.

I'd completed three more rows by the time he returned. My fingers were aching a bit more now. When Seb handed me a cup, I wrapped my hands around it in the hope of giving my hands some reviving heat treatment.

Seb sat in the armchair near the fire and put his cup down. He had a plate in his other hand. He tipped it slightly my way. "Is it okay if I have this chocolate cake? I haven't eaten for hours."

"Help yourself. There's plenty. You know what Erin's like, she always makes too much."

Using a fork, Seb shovelled a big chunk of the cake into his mouth. With his cheeks full, he said, "How's Erin doing? How's her pregnancy progressing?"

"She's taking things a bit easier, at last." I smiled at Seb. "A bit too easy. She's even bossier now. She gives me orders from the minute we meet in the morning and doesn't stop all day. If I could go to the toilet for her, I'm sure she'd have me doing that too. But I shouldn't complain. I'm more concerned about her health than my feelings."

Another bit of cake went into Seb's mouth. He waved his fork at me. "Tell me about the craft evening. I read Peggy's post yesterday and she said she's going to put a video up following the event. I'll have to watch it later."

I cradled the cup some more. The heat was taking the pain away from my fingers. I told Seb about the rest of the evening, as much as I could remember before I'd taken myself away from all the action.

Seb finished his cake and put the plate down. He came over to the sofa and sat next to me. "Can I have a look at the pattern, please?"

"You can."

Seb picked it up and looked at the front cover. "This model looks like one of those film stars from the 1950s. Mum loves those old films. I don't mind them either." A faraway look came into his eyes. "Falling in love seemed so much easier in those days. There weren't as many complications. A man and a woman met, they fell in love, got married and lived happily ever after." He shook his head as if to clear his thoughts. "You don't get many films like that now. It's all zombies and the end of the world." He placed the pattern on my knee.

I cast him a smile. "I didn't know you were such a romantic, Sebastian Parker."

"I'm not. I'm a hard-hearted, tough-talking man of the law. I have steel in my eyes and titanium in my heart. Do you want a hand with that knitting? Or another cup of tea?"

"Can you knit?" I asked.

He lifted his chin. "I can. Don't sound so surprised. Knitting is not just for women." He dropped his chin. "I'm useless at crocheting, though. How far have you got with your pattern?"

I finished the tea and put my cup down. "I've done the back and front of the jumper. And one sleeve. I should have the other sleeve done soon, and then I'll sew them up."

"I can sew the completed pieces together. That'll save you a bit of time."

I gave him a surprised look. "Are you sure? Don't you want to go home and get some sleep?"

"Not yet. Pass me your completed pieces. Where's your darning needle?"

I handed everything to Seb and he got to work on sewing the pieces together. I returned to my knitting work on the sleeve.

We chatted amiably over the next hour as we worked. I told Seb how the building work was coming along at the café. He talked about his work at the police station. It was lovely to have company. Seb was easy to talk to.

I was so engrossed in my knitting that I didn't realise Seb had fallen asleep until I heard him snore. His head was resting on the back of the sofa and his hands were on the almost-finished jumper on his knee. I didn't have the heart to wake him.

I completed the casting-off row on the sleeve and put it down on the table in front of me. I carefully lifted Seb's hands and retrieved the jumper. I put that on the table too.

I shuffled down in the sofa and rested my head on the cushions. My eyes were stinging with tiredness. I decided to rest them for a while before I resumed knitting. My throbbing fingers needed a rest too.

It seemed like minutes later that Seb was calling my name. I opened my eyes and was surprised to find his arms wrapped around me.

He looked into my eyes, concern etched on his face. He said softly, "Karis, what did you see? You've been crying non-stop for the last ten minutes."

I blinked at him and tried to recall the vision which had invaded my dream. It came back to me and I mumbled, "He didn't turn up. I waited and waited. But he never showed."

"Who didn't?" Seb released me and handed me a tissue.

I took it and wiped my cheeks. I was surprised at how wet they were. I said, "I was standing in the high street. Opposite the supermarket. But it looked different. The cars looked different too. They were old-fashioned, but they looked new. I was waiting for someone." I looked towards the jumper on the table. "I was wearing my new twin set. I was excited. I knew he would like it." I frowned as I looked back at Seb. "But he didn't turn up. My heart felt like it was breaking."

"It sounds like you were stood up. Could you see the woman who was wearing the twin set?"

My frown increased. "No. This is weird. Normally, I experience visions as if I'm standing nearby and watching. I'm never part of the vision. This time, it was different. I felt as if I was reliving everything that went on. Every emotion and every thought. But why? I don't understand why I'm getting these visions."

"We can work that out," Seb said. "I don't have to be at work for hours. I'll nip home and get a shower. When I come back, we'll go to that area on the high street where you had this latest vision. You might pick up on anything there. You should take the completed jumper with you."

"I haven't finished sewing the other sleeve on yet."

Seb gave me a small grin. "I did that while you were asleep. I've made you a cup of tea too." He stood up. "I won't be long. I'll let myself out."

"Seb, you don't have to do this. I can go on my own."

"Nonsense. I'm coming with you. I like a good mystery. I want to see where this one is going. See you soon."

He walked out of the room and I heard the front door opening. I then heard an indignant voice aimed at Seb.

Seb replied, "I don't have time to chat, Peggy. Bye."

Peggy came rushing into the room. "Karis Booth! Have you been up to shenanigans with DCI Parker?"

I bristled. "I certainly have not."

"His car has been parked outside all night. What's going on?"

"Nothing's going on. Well, something's been going on, but not what you think. Sit down and I'll tell you everything."

Peggy sat next to me and I told her about my latest vision. I also told her how Seb had helped me with the jumper.

She nodded. "That's a good idea of Seb's to visit the scene. I wish I could come with you, but I've got my blog to catch up on. You should see how many comments I've got to reply to. The internet waits for no woman." She patted my knee and then stood up. "Let me know how you get on."

"Peggy, I'd like to know where this twin set pattern came from. I feel it's important. Would you be able to find out, please?"

"I'll try. I'll send a message to Jade and ask her where she got those patterns from. I know she mentioned charity shops, but I'll see if she can narrow it down." She gave me a long look. "Karis, if you're going to have men staying over every night, you should get them to park their cars down a side road so the neighbours don't know they're here."

"I wasn't planning on having men staying over," I argued.

"And you should get them to leave by the back door. Perhaps they should wear a disguise so no one recognises them. You know what people are like around here. They're always poking their noses into other people's business. Not like me. I keep myself to myself."

I said with a smile, "I know you do."

Peggy continued, "But if you are going to have more male visitors, keep your curtains tightly closed. You don't want any nosy nellies peeping through and seeing things they shouldn't."

I shook my head in exasperation. "I won't be having any more male visitors."

"Not even Seb Parker?"

"Well, yes, Seb might come back. But he's just a friend."

Peggy gave me a firm nod. "Make sure he stays that way. Seb's eyes twinkle far too much when he looks at you. I've noticed that. Don't let him bewitch you with his twinkles."

"I won't."

Peggy gave me another knowing look before leaving the house. I had a quick shower and a rushed breakfast before Seb returned.

As I opened the door to him a short while later, I did notice the twinkle in his eyes. It was a nice twinkle. A friendly twinkle. It couldn't be anything but a friendly twinkle, not between Seb and me. We were friends. That's all.

Chapter 5

My good friend, Seb, drove us the short distance to the high street. We parked up and walked down the street until we came to the area where I'd experienced my vision.

I stopped and looked at the supermarket across the road. It was the same well-known company that had been around for years.

Seb noticed me looking that way and said, "This supermarket has been here for as long as I can remember. That doesn't help us to narrow down the year your vision took place. Can you remember what the cars looked like in your vision? It could give us an indication of which time frame we're looking at."

I grimaced. "I'm not very good when it comes to recognising cars. I don't know whether they were from the 1950s or later."

"Hang on a mo." Seb took his phone out and tapped on it. He showed me the screen. "Do these look familiar?"

I shook my head.

He brought other images up and showed me them.

I tilted my head. "Sort of. But not exactly."

"Let me try another one. Here. Look at this image."

I peered at the screen. "Yes, they do look more like the cars I saw. What year was that photo taken?"

"1958. I think the style of that twin set could have come from around that era. Are you getting any visions now? Are you getting any tingly feelings? Do you need to close your eyes?"

I looked up and down the street. "Nothing's coming to me yet." I closed my eyes and brought to mind the image I'd experienced just before I woke up this morning.

Nothing.

I opened my eyes and looked at the building behind me. It was a bargain shop, and it had everything you need, and didn't need, for less than £2.

I said to Seb, "Do you know what was here before this shop?"

"It's been many things. I remember it being a charity shop, and then a clothes shop. I'm sure Peggy would know. So would my mum. I'll make some enquiries. Do you want to have a go at your vision again?"

"I'm not getting anything." I suddenly let out a sigh of exasperation. "I forgot to bring the pattern with me! And the jumper too! I meant to put them in my bag."

"It's okay. We can go back for them now." Seb's phone rang. He answered it and turned slightly away from me. He mumbled something to whoever was calling him.

He ended the call and put his phone away. "Sorry, Karis, I have to go to the station immediately. We can do this later. I'll give you a lift home."

"No, don't be silly. It's not far. I'll walk. I could do with the fresh air."

"Are you sure? I don't mind. I want to help you."

"You've already helped me. Off you go."

"I'll phone you later. Let me know if you have any other visions."

"I will."

He gave me a nod of farewell and swiftly walked away.

I stayed where I was. It was sometimes easier to have visions when I was on my own. I took a deep breath and softened my focus. I thought about the previous view of the supermarket I'd seen. I brought up the memory of the cars too.

New feelings washed over me.

My shoulders dropped. My heart. My aching heart. It was hurting so much.

The scenery around me didn't alter, but my feelings intensified. Then they changed.

The ache from my heart vanished. Sweat broke out on my forehead. My pulse quickened. I could sense danger. I swallowed and tried to control my breaths which were coming too quickly.

"Excuse me, love, are you alright?"

I jumped at the woman who was standing next to me.

"Are you having a funny turn, love?" she continued. "You've gone all white and still. Are you one of those human statutes? Those people who stand still for hours and then suddenly move. Are you one of them? Have you got a collection pot somewhere? I can give you a pound." She began to search her handbag.

I found my voice. "No, sorry. I'm not a statue. Sorry." I flashed her a smile before quickly walking away. The feelings of being in danger had passed, but I hadn't forgotten how intense they'd been.

I returned home and found Peggy sitting on the sofa in my front room. We had keys to each other's houses, so I wasn't surprised to see her there.

She took one look at my face and said, "Something's happened, hasn't it? Sit down and tell me everything. I hope you don't mind, but I've made a start on the cardigan part of your twin set." She pointed to the knitting at her side. "The sooner we get this done, the better."

"Thanks, Peggy." I sat next to her and told her about the feelings I'd experienced. I concluded, "Whoever was standing in the high street all those years ago is in danger." I thought about my words. "Or was in danger. I don't know if I'm getting feelings from the past or the future."

Peggy resumed her knitting. "We could be dealing with an unsolved murder. The woman who owned this pattern could have been brutally murdered years ago, and her murderer is walking around scot-free. Well, not for long they won't. Not with us on the case." She finished the row and switched the work to her other hand. "Excuse the pun, but on the other hand, we could be looking at a murder which is yet to occur."

"That's what I was thinking too." I watched Peggy's hands as they whizzed through the row she was working on. She wasn't even looking at it. I said, "I suspect I'll get another vision when this twin set is completed. I'll make a start on the sleeves."

I found another set of knitting needles and got to work. I was much slower than Peggy, but I kept going.

We put the TV on and watched a couple of detective shows while we clicked away on our needles. We stopped now and again for refreshments and the chance to stretch our fingers.

Thanks to the super speedy knitter at my side, the twin set was completed by late afternoon.

Peggy sewed it up and then handed it to me reverently.

I put the the jumper part of the twin set on first. It was a snug fit, but Peggy assured me that's how they were worn back in the day.

With trepidation, I put the cardigan on over the jumper. I smoothed it down and looked at Peggy.

She stood up and said, "You don't want me gawping at you while you concentrate. I'll leave you to it. I'll be in the kitchen if you need me."

"Thanks, Peggy." I could already hear a buzzing in my ears which indicated a vision was on its way. My scalp prickled with a mixture of fear and excitement. This was going to be a strong vision.

Chapter 6

The vision came to me.

I was standing opposite the supermarket again. Thanks to the images Seb had shown me, I could now identify the cars driving past me as being from the 1950s. A glance up and down the street showed people wearing clothes from that era.

I looked down at my own attire and smiled when I saw I was wearing the blue twin set. I touched my neck and felt the presence of a pearl necklace.

I jumped as I felt a hand on my arm. A rosy-cheeked young woman was standing at my side. She seemed familiar to the woman whose memories I was experiencing. The young woman looked me up and down and said, "Hi! You look cool in that outfit! How long have you been waiting here for him?"

I checked my watch. I felt a stirring of disappointment as I said, "Twenty minutes. I'm sure he'll be here soon."

The young woman made a face of disapproval. "It should be him waiting for you. He's lucky to have you. I'll tell him that the next time I see him. I'm meeting Bob inside. Do you want to wait with us in there?"

I shook my head and forced a smile on my face. "He won't be long. He'll be here soon. I know he will. He won't let me down." I tugged on the hem of my cardigan. "Do you really think I look okay in this? It's not too glamorous is it?"

The woman beamed. "You look like a star. If you change your mind, we'll be inside." She turned away and walked towards the building behind me.

I wanted to see what the building was, but my vision wouldn't allow it.

I waited and waited. With every minute that passed, my heart felt heavier. I was aware of couples walking past and giving me sympathetic looks. It was obvious I was waiting for someone. It was just as obvious that I'd been stood up.

My eyes prickled as I finally accepted the truth. He wasn't going to turn up. He didn't care about me. He'd been lying to me for months. He said he loved me. But he didn't. He wouldn't treat me like this if he loved me.

I felt tears rolling down my cheeks. The people walking by gave me a wide berth. I knew I should leave, but I couldn't. There was the smallest sliver of hope in my heart which kept my feet in place.

My tears dripped off my chin and landed on the beautiful blue twin set which I'd painstakingly created.

A soft voice called out, "Karis. Don't cry."

It was Peggy's voice. Her concerned tone brought me back to the present. I blinked and looked at Peggy's worried face. She was sitting at my side with a box of tissues on her lap.

She handed a tissue to me and said, "I didn't mean to interrupt, but I couldn't help it. Tears were streaming down your face. You looked so sad. I couldn't bear to see you like that for a moment longer. It made me too sad." Her eyes glistened. "I'm so sorry. Did I interrupt you at an important bit?"

I wiped my eyes and told Peggy what I'd seen. I said, "I thought I might get a different vision this time. But it was more of the same. The woman was waiting for someone. I tried to look at the building behind me, but I couldn't. Peggy, despite feeling so sad, I kept picking up on an element of danger. But I don't know why."

Peggy patted my hand. "It'll come to you. I've been thinking about that part of the high street and what used to be there. I don't know why I didn't think of this earlier. There used to be a cinema opposite the supermarket. It was there during the 50s and 60s. I used to go there with my Jeff." Her eyes crinkled up. "We used to canoodle on the back row. Lots of couples did."

I smiled at her cheeky expression. "That would explain why the woman I keep turning into is standing outside the building. She must have been on a date, but he didn't turn up. She felt so sad." I put my hand on my chest. "It felt like my heart was breaking in two."

Peggy frowned. "I don't understand why you're picking up feelings of danger. Did something happen to her after she left the high street? Did her date turn up later and attack her? I suppose we could look online for any suspicious deaths which occurred around that time. Or any missing people."

"We could do. Did you get a message to Jade about where she found the knitting pattern?"

"I did. She got back to me a few minutes ago. There are a few charity shops she visits regularly. She can't remember which one had the patterns, though. She said she'd go back to the shops and talk to the staff. She can't do it now because she's got university lectures for the rest of the day. I told her not to bother and said I'd go to the charity shops and make my own enquiries. I know a few people who do volunteer work at some of them." She let out a sigh. "There could be a problem."

"What sort of problem?" I asked.

"If someone brought the patterns in, a member of staff might remember who it was. But if the patterns came via a street collection, then they won't know who donated them. Karis, I'm not hopeful that I'll find any useful information, but I'll try. Do you want to come with me? You might have a funny feeling while we're in one of the shops."

"That's a good idea." I looked down at my twin set which was slightly damp with my tears. "I'll keep this on. It might help."

There was a knock at the door. Peggy went over to the door and opened it.

A moment later, Seb came into the room.

He gave me a worried look. "Karis, have you been crying?"

I flapped my hand in a dismissive manner. "It's nothing. I'm fine. Have you got some information for us?"

"I have. I've discovered the building on the high street used to be a cinema." He smiled proudly.

Peggy said, "I've already told Karis that. I used to go there with my Jeff."

Seb's smile died. "Oh, right. I shouldn't have bothered checking online. I should have asked you."

"Yes, you should. What else have you found out?" Peggy asked him.

Seb's chest puffed out ever so slightly. "The cinema was closed in the early 70s. The building is still there, of course. However, some of the cinema's fittings have been saved."

Hope bubbled up inside me. "Fittings? What kind of fittings?"

"Some of the seats and film reels. A local cinema enthusiast bought them. He converted his shed into a small cinema. I've been in touch with him. He said he can open the cinema for us." Seb looked uncertain. "Karis, would that help you if we went to the cinema? I don't want to assume anything."

I gave him an enthusiastic nod. "It would help! I know it would. I'm already getting excited about going there." I stood up. "Can we go now?"

Seb's gaze travelled up and down my twin set. He cleared his throat and said, "You finished it. You look very nice in it." He cleared his throat again. "Very glamorous."

Peggy tutted and said, "Put your eyes back in your sockets, Seb Parker. Don't look at Karis as if she's a piece of meat."

Seb blustered, "I'm not! I wasn't!"

Peggy chuckled. "I'm only kidding. You can't help yourself. You're just a man."

I suddenly remembered something. "Oh, Peggy, I said I'd go to the charity shops with you."

"That doesn't matter," she said. "I can go on my own. You go to the cinema with this eager young man." She turned to face Seb full on and wagged a finger at him. "You behave yourself. You're an officer of the law."

Seb replied, "Of course I'll behave myself. What do you think I'm going to do?"

A wistful look came into Peggy's eyes. She said wistfully, "I know what I'd do in that cinema if my Jeff was still alive."

Seb stared at her in shock and held his hand up. "I don't want the details."

Peggy chuckled. "Are you sure? I don't mind sharing my memories."

Seb looked at me. "Karis, are you ready to go now?"

I smiled at the pleading tone in his voice. "I'm ready."

Chapter 7

The cinema enthusiast was an elderly man called Charles. He must have been in his nineties. His voice was quiet as he welcomed us to his property. On unsteady legs, he took us to the large shed at the bottom of his garden.

When we reached the shed, Charles put a wrinkly hand on the door to steady himself. He wheezed while he got his breath back. He looked as if a stiff breeze could knock him to his knees. I noticed Seb's hands were raised at his sides to catch Charles if he suddenly keeled over.

Charles produced a key from a long chain around his neck and announced, "Good evening to you both. I will be showing a variety of films tonight for your pleasure." He stopped for breath again. A whistling sound came from his throat. He continued, "I will provide refreshments during the intervals. If you need to use the public conveniences, please ring the bell at the rear of the cinema and I will escort you to the nearest bathroom." He wheezed and whistled again. "Which is in my house."

He somehow managed to get the key into the lock. The door swung open and Charles went with it. Seb dashed forward and caught the old man before he collapsed to the floor.

Charles said, "I do apologise for the inconvenience that my advanced years are causing. My spirit is willing, but my body is refusing to cooperate." He gave Seb a smile. "Thank you for catching me, young sir. Please, make your way to the nearest available seats. The first film will begin shortly." He wobbled towards a curtained-off area at the back of the interior.

Seb whispered, "Do you think he's okay? I didn't realise he was so old when I spoke to him on the phone."

"We'll keep an eye on him." I looked around the shed. "Seb, look at this. Isn't it lovely? Look at all the fittings. They must be years old."

There were three rows of seats. Each row had four connecting chairs. The chairs were made of dark wood and had upholstered cushions made of red velvet. The colour on the lower cushions was a paler shade of red. I smiled as I thought about how many local shuffling bottoms had sat in these seats. A huge screen covered the front wall. There was something on a small table at the side of the screen.

I pointed it out to Seb and said, "You don't think he's going to play that, do you?"

Seb broke into a smile. "I think he just might." He crooked his elbow at me. "Shall we take a seat?"

We sat in the middle row, and in the middle seats. We heard some shuffling noises in the curtained-off area, along with some wheezing and whistling.

A few minutes later, we heard Charles shuffling down the aisle. He'd changed into a three-piece suit complete with bow tie. He waved a torch from side to side as he went even though he didn't need to. He settled himself on a stool in front of the item which I'd pointed out to Seb. He pushed his sleeves up and then began to play the small keyboard in front of him. A jaunty tune boomed out.

I gripped Seb's arm and whispered, "Isn't this wonderful? It's like we've gone back in time."

Seb winced. "I appreciate the musical effect, but he's not the most accomplished player, is he? I hope he doesn't go on too long."

Charles played for a few more minutes. Then he got to his feet and gave us an unsteady bow. I burst into applause. Seb clapped too, but not as enthusiastically as me.

Charles wobbled away from the keyboard and back up the aisle. He stopped to rest at the end of our row and put his hand on the nearest chair. He huffed, "The film will begin shortly."

"Do you need a hand?" Seb offered.

"No, thank you. I'll be okay in a second or two." He huffed a bit more and then wobbled away.

Seb said to me, "I feel guilty about asking him to do this for us now. Is being here having any effect on you?"

I nodded. "Something is happening to me. I can sense a vision coming my way. I usually get a buzzing in my ears first, and that's happening now. Seb, if you see me crying, don't stop me. I have to experience every emotion that comes to me."

He gave me an uncertain look. "Okay."

The lights dimmed and the screen lit up. The image of a film company's logo appeared on the screen. Music blared out. My stomach flipped in excitement.

The film began. It was a black and white one from the 1950s. I'd seen this one with Mum years ago. Just like Seb's mum, she loved watching old films.

As the film continued, the shed vanished from around me. I was now sitting in a large cinema and it was full of people. The same film was playing on the huge screen.

I was holding hands with someone at my side. I glanced that way and saw a young man with combed-back hair. My heart swelled with love for him. It was the same man who'd flittered into my mind when I'd first started knitting the twin set.

He looked my way, smiled and moved his head closer. He whispered, "Those Hollywood women are not a patch on you. You're much more beautiful." He planted a soft kiss on my cheek.

I felt my cheeks warming up and my heart filled with more love. I felt so safe in the presence of this young man. He was my world. My everything.

My attention briefly went to the screen and I noticed what the main character was wearing. I whispered to the young man, "Do you think a twin set like that would suit me?"

His eyes shone with love as he answered, "You would look even more beautiful. I'd love to see you in something like that."

I gave him a nod. "Then I'll knit myself one. I'll wear it when we next come here."

He squeezed my hand and turned his face back to the screen.

My head was full of thoughts about where I could get the pattern from. I could try the market but I doubted they'd have anything as glamorous as the twin set the film star was wearing. Could I send off for one? I'd have a look in Mum's magazines.

I was so lost in my thoughts that I didn't notice the scenery around me changing.

I jumped as an older man appeared in front of me and shouted, "You hurt him! You killed him! I know you did!" He lunged and put his hands around my throat. He snarled, "You'll pay for what you did!"

One of my hands clawed at the man as I tried to push him away. My other hand scrambled at my side until I located what I was searching for. I grabbed the metal item and thrust it towards the man. It connected with him and—

"Karis! Karis!" Seb was shaking me by the shoulders.

I focused on his face and realised I was back in the shed. My throat felt sore.

Seb still had his hands on my shoulders. He said, "I know you told me not to interfere, but I had to for your own safety. You had your hand around your neck. You were struggling to breathe."

I put a hand on my throat. "Was I?"

He nodded. "You were screaming and yelling. You were waving your other hand in the air. What happened? What did you see?"

I quickly told Seb about the young man in the cinema. I explained, "When that vision faded, I was in a room in a house. I didn't take it in much, so I can't describe it. The man who was shouting at me looked like an older version of the young man. I think it was him. He had the same eyes. He was going to kill me." I paused as I recalled the weapon which had been used on the older man. "The woman he was attacking stabbed him with a knitting needle. She thrust it into his neck." I abruptly stopped and began to tremble. "I could feel it going into him."

Seb pulled me into his arms and patted my back. "It's okay. It's all over now."

I looked up at him. "But it isn't over. I have to stop this happening. I could feel every emotion the woman was feeling. She didn't want to hurt that man. As soon as she did so, she was overcome with guilt. I can't let that happen to her."

Seb released me. "But didn't you say the older man accused her of killing someone?"

I nodded. "I don't think she did kill anyone. She was shocked when he said that. Really shocked." I lowered my head. "I have to find her somehow."

Seb put his hand over mine. "I'll help you."

Charles wheezed as he shuffled towards us. "Is everything alright? I heard the young lady screaming. Do you need some smelling salts? I've got some in the kitchen which belonged to Mother. It won't take me long to get them."

Seb stood up and said, "No, thank you. The young lady is okay. Thank you very much for your time. I'm afraid we have to go now."

Charles' face dropped. "That's a shame. I've got another film lined up."

I moved closer to Charles and said, "I know many people who would love to visit your wonderful cinema. Could I put your details online?"

"Online? You mean that internet thing? That one that goes all around the world?"

"Yes," I said. "My neighbour would love to come here too. She has plenty of friends who'd come along with her."

Charles wobbled on his feet. Seb put his hand out and steadied the elderly gent. Charles smiled. "That would be wonderful. Truly wonderful. You have my sincere thanks. Let me see you to the exit door. Watch your step as you go."

As soon as we got into Seb's car, I checked my phone. There was a message from Peggy. She needed to see me as soon as possible.

Chapter 8

Seb dropped me off outside Peggy's house. He said, "As much as I'd love to know what's so urgent, I have to get back to the station. Karis, will you keep me up to date with this knitting pattern mystery?"

I heard the concern in his voice. "Course I will. Why do you sound so worried?"

"It's the mention of murder. I don't want you putting yourself in danger." His brow furrowed. "When I get back to the station, I'll make some enquiries about knitting-related accidents or murders. If I find anything, I'll let you know."

"Thanks, Seb. And thanks for taking my visions so seriously."

"Thank you for letting me know about them." He gave me a soft smile. It abruptly left his face as someone rapped on my window. Seb lowered the window and Peggy pushed her head through.

She snapped, "Don't sit there chatting like you've got all the time in the world. Come inside. I've got something to tell you." Her eyes narrowed as she gave Seb the once over. "Did you keep your hands to yourself in that cinema shed?"

"I did," Seb told her solemnly.

Peggy opened the door and said to me, "Come on, Karis. Seb, are you coming in too?"

"No. I have to get back to the station."

"Fair enough," Peggy said.

As soon as I got out of the car, Peggy closed the door and waggled her fingers in goodbye at Seb. She took me by the elbow and marched me up the path. I looked over at Seb and managed to get a smile out before he drove away.

Peggy took me into the kitchen. I moved towards the chairs.

"Don't sit down," she ordered. "I want to take some photos of you."

"Me? What for?"

Peggy picked her phone up and squinted at the screen. "It's not so much you as the twin set you're wearing. I've got a plan." She looked back at me and raised the camera. "Stand up straight. Don't move." I heard the noise of a photo being taken. Peggy continued, "Turn to the side. Look straight ahead. You don't need to smile as I'm not including your face."

I turned to the side and grumbled, "I feel like you're taking police shots of me. Shouldn't there be a height chart behind me?"

Peggy chuckled. "Turn around. Let me get a back view now. I'll share my plan with you when I've done this."

She took a few more photos and then allowed me to sit down.

I took a seat and said, "How did you get on at the charity shops?"

She shook her head in disgust and took the seat opposite me. "Not very well. A lot of the staff I saw were young volunteers. Miserable as sin, they were. Why do volunteer work if you're going to stand there with a face like a slapped fish?" She tutted.

"A slapped fish?"

Peggy nodded. "When I do volunteer work, I'm happy as Larry. Whoever Larry is. I knew a Larry once. He was a misery guts. Never cracked a smile in all the years I'd known him. Mind you, if I looked like him, I never would have smiled too. He had this weird-looking nose and his eyes were—"

"Peggy," I interrupted her, "what did you find out at the charity shops?"

"I was just getting to that," Peggy said indignantly. "I went to all the shops that Jade visited and none of them knew anything about knitting patterns. To be honest, they didn't know much about anything. That's beside the point. The young fella in the last shop was slightly less useless than the other assistants. He thinks a bunch of patterns came into the shop last week. But he's not certain. His manager is in tomorrow and he said she might know more. So, we'll go there tomorrow."

"Okay." I looked at her phone. "Why were you taking photos of me?"

She lifted her chin and proclaimed, "Being an online entrepreneur has taught me many lessons. The main one is that people spend far too much time online. If you want to know an answer to a question, you should post your query online and see who crawls out of the woodwork to answer it."

"Woodwork? Peggy, you're full of sayings today. What question are you going to post online?"

"I'm getting to that. I'm only going to put it on my blog for my readers. I don't want just anyone looking at it." She raised her phone. "I'm going to put these photos on my blog along with a picture of the pattern. I'll ask if anyone knows where the pattern could have come from. Or if they have any relatives or friends who could have knitted this twin set in the 1950s. Whoever knitted it could still be alive. I'll mention the cinema and the year too. It's a long shot, but you never know. There are some very nosy people in this town." Her confident look wavered. "Is that the kind of information you need? Would it help to narrow down who could have used that pattern?"

I gave her a nod. "Considering her life is in danger, it would help a lot."

Peggy put her phone down. "In danger? What do you mean? Tell me everything."

I told her about my latest visions.

Peggy leaned back in her chair and surmised, "So, the mystery knitter could have killed someone in the past. And now the past has come back to haunt her in the shape of that older man. Is she going to kill again? Or has she already committed the dastardly deed?"

"I don't know."

"Is she the one you're supposed to help?"

"I don't know."

"Or are you supposed to help the victim before he gets impaled on a knitting needle?"

I shrugged. "I don't know that either."

Peggy nodded to herself. "This knitter of yours could be a serial killer. She could have been bumping off people for years. And now she's masquerading as a feeble old woman. That's a good disguise. No one would ever suspect an old woman of being up to no good."

I gave her a pointed look but didn't say anything.

Peggy was lost in her thoughts now. "I wonder where she puts the bodies? Do you think she kills them all with knitting needles? She'll have to use the thicker ones to do a proper job. There's no point using a thin one. It would only snap. Perhaps it was trial and error for her to begin with. Maybe she tried other weapons first. A crochet hook perhaps?"

"Peggy," I called out to her, "can we talk about something else? I don't want to think about our knitter as a killer. I didn't pick up on any murderous feelings in my visions."

Peggy gave me a wise look. "That's because she would have justified her actions. That's what criminal masterminds do. I read a book from the library about that. Put the kettle on and I'll post these photos online. I'm sure we'll have some replies soon. Whether those replies will be any use is another matter."

I stood up, moved over to the kettle and filled it up. Once I'd switched it on, I said to Peggy, "I'm going to change out of this twin set."

She gave me a knowing look. "Is it because you're picking up feelings of guilt about slaying so many people?"

I gave her a long look. "No, it isn't that at all. To be honest, I feel scared. Not just a bit scared, but thoroughly petrified. Something awful is going to happen to our mystery knitter soon."

Chapter 9

Despite my anxious feelings, I managed to get a decent night's sleep. When I woke up, I checked my phone for messages. There was one from Erin to say she was already at the café and she would meet me there soon. One from Peggy informed me she was working on some leads, but she didn't want to tell me what those were in a message. She added that she had some volunteer work to do at the local hospital and would meet me later.

I shook my head at Peggy's words. I didn't know where she got her energy from.

There weren't any messages from Seb, so I presumed that was a good thing.

After showering and having my breakfast, I headed over to the café. I found Erin and Robbie in the kitchen. The radio was on and they were dancing with each other. Erin looked radiant and my heart filled with love for her.

Even though Robbie had his back to me as he wiggled his ample hips, he said to Erin, "Don't look now, but I think we're being watched. I think it's one of those voyeur types. We should charge her if she's going to stare at us." He chuckled, looked over his shoulder at me and winked.

"I've only been standing here for a few moments," I defended myself. "You two make such a lovely couple."

"I know," Robbie said. He held his hand out to Erin. She took it and Robbie twirled her gently around and then wrapped his arms around her.

Erin laughed and freed herself. "That's enough messing about, Robbie. We're supposed to be getting the café ready." She picked something off the counter and came over to me. "Karis, the new menus have arrived. They look great. Have a look."

I took the menu and studied it. "I love the colours. The font is good too."

Erin tapped the top of the menu. "I'm still not happy about keeping the old name. I think we should incorporate both our names. You've put loads of money into this business. You should get the recognition."

I gave her the menu back. "It's been called Erin's Café for years. You've already built up a reputation. I'm not going to mess with that. Do we know when the café can reopen?" I sent Robbie an eager look.

Robbie cleared his throat and announced, "In my humble opinion, the café should be ready for opening next week."

Erin pulled the menu to her chest and her eyes shone with excitement. "Next week, Karis, next week! Can you believe it? There will have to be a grand reopening, of course. We'll put posts on our website. What about an opening day discount? Should we do that? We could have half-price cakes or something. We have to do something special. We have to celebrate the reopening." Her voice rose and the peaceful look on her face fled.

I put my hand on her arm. "I've already thought of that. I'll show you my plans later. Everything's under control. You don't have to worry. In fact, all you have to do is bake those wonderful cakes of yours."

Erin took a deep breath. "Thank you. I don't know what I'd do without you." She gave me a long look. "What's going on with you and that knitting pattern you were so excited about? Have you had any more visions?"

I gave her a half-shrug. "It's nothing important."

"Of course it's important. I want to know everything." Her eyes narrowed. "Have you witnessed a murder?"

Robbie called over, "If you're going to talk about murders, do it while you're sitting down. Erin, take Karis over to the table by the window. I'll bring you both a latte over. I'm going to have another go at that coffee machine. It's not going to get the better of me. It's man versus machine. And this man is going to be victorious." He gave us a nod to add conviction to his words.

Erin and I left the kitchen and took a seat at the table next to the window. The window was covered with paper as we didn't want anyone to see the inside of the café until it was finished. We took a moment to admire the table and chairs we'd taken so long to decide on buying.

I told Erin what I'd experienced in my visions so far. Her eyebrows rose at the mention of Seb's name. Thankfully, she didn't say anything.

When I'd finished, Erin said, "So, what are you going to do now?"

"I want to find out who the knitting pattern belonged to. If she's still alive, that is. Peggy's got some leads. I don't know what those are. I'll speak to her soon about that."

Robbie came over to the table. He had a defeated look on his face. He put two cups down and said forlornly, "It's tea. The coffee machine got the better of me. There are too many levers and buttons on it."

Erin said, "Don't give up. You can do this. Have another go."

He lifted his chin. "I will do. I'll sneak up on it when it's not looking. Do you want any cake?"

"Yes, please!" Peggy announced as she came through the door. She smiled at us. "I thought I'd find you lot here. Robbie, I'll have whatever Erin and Karis are having to drink. As long as it's not coffee. It's too early in the morning for coffee." She came over to us, pulled a chair out and sat down. She looked up at Robbie. "I'll have some cake if Erin's made it. If you've made it, I'll have a chocolate biscuit instead."

Robbie tipped his head at Peggy, gave Erin and me a smile, and ambled away.

Peggy began, "Erin, has Karis got you up to speed with her visions?"

"She has."

"Good. And how are you feeling today?"

"I feel great," Erin said.

"Good. Let's get down to business. Karis, I've had some comments about those photos I posted last night of you in that twin set." Her face twisted in disgust. "Some of the comments were quite inappropriate."

"In what way?" I asked.

"Certain people made remarks about your lovely figure. I won't go into details. I won't have comments like that on my blog. I gave those people a piece of my mind, and then I blocked them from making any future comments." She shook her head and added a tut of disgust. "Anyway, I did get the names of women who could have owned that pattern. Through one source and another, I've narrowed down who is of the right age, and if they lived in this area when that cinema was open. My readers have been extremely helpful, and I've managed to get the names and addresses of three potential knitters. I don't know whether these women can help us, but it's a start. We can call on them later."

I stared at Peggy in amazement. "That's great news. This must have taken you hours. When did you do this?"

"I was up early. You know I like to make an early start in the day." She smiled at us. "When you haven't got many days left in your life, you need to make the most of every minute."

Erin said, "Don't talk like that, Peggy. I want you to be around for at least the next forty years."

"Sorry, love," Peggy said. "I didn't mean to upset you. Old people like to talk about death. You should hear how some of my friends natter on about it. Back to the problem at hand. Look what I found." She reached into her big bag and pulled out a stack of knitting patterns. She put them on the table. "These are the patterns that Jade brought in the other night. Karis, there could be something here that could help you. Have a good look at them."

Robbie returned with a cup of tea and a slice of cake for Peggy. "Here you go, madam." He put them on the table.

Peggy said, "Where's the cake for your wife? And your sister-in-law? I don't think much of the service in here. I won't be leaving you a tip."

Robbie replied, "I've already got something nutritious cooking in the oven for my wife. And as for leaving me a tip, Peggy Marshall, I'll have you know—"

I interrupted his words. "Look! Look at this one." I held up a pattern for a man's jumper. "This has got the same pencilled ring as my twin set pattern. You can see how the circle doesn't line up. These must have belonged to the same woman." I continued to look through the patterns and soon found some more.

Peggy and Erin helped me. We located ten patterns for men's jumpers which had pencilled-rings on them.

Peggy said, "I can't find any more women's patterns with the pencil marks on them. Our mystery knitter must have given up making things for herself. You know what we have to do now, Karis."

I gave her a slow nod. "We have to knit these jumpers and see if I get another vision from them. It's going to take a while." I looked at Robbie. "I'm going to need that cake. Just bring the whole thing out."

Peggy shook her head. "We don't have time to do this. I'm going to call in the cavalry."

Chapter 10

Forty minutes later, three elderly women came into the café with determined looks on their faces and heavy bags hanging from their arms.

One of them looked at Peggy and said, "Where do you want us?"

"Over here, Celia. Thanks for coming here so quickly."

Celia nodded. "Anything for you, Peg. You said it was a knitting emergency?"

"It certainly is. I've got ten patterns for men's jumpers. They need knitting up as soon as possible. Keep to the size that's been circled on the pattern. I don't expect you to finish them all. I'll get on with some myself later."

Celia said, "We can do that. We've cancelled our social engagements for the day." She raised her bag. "We've brought supplies with us. Tea. Lemonade. Sandwiches. Medication. We can stay here all day."

"Thanks, Celia. I appreciate it."

Celia moved a bit closer and inclined her head in Peggy's direction. "Can you tell us what this is about? Or is it top secret?"

Peggy gave her a knowing look. "I'd rather not say at the moment, Celia. I hope you understand."

"Say no more, Peg, say no more. Mum's the word. Right, where should we set up camp?" She looked around the café. "I need somewhere comfy if I'm going to be sitting down all day. You know what my back's like. And I'll need to be near the toilets. My bladder's not as young as it used to be."

Erin, Robbie and I watched this exchange in stunned silence. It was like watching a well-organised army undertaking a military exercise. An army made up of pensioners in sensible clothes and comfy shoes.

Erin got to her feet and addressed the women. "There are some sofas on the other side of the café. You can sit there. The café isn't open yet, but Robbie and I would love to bring you refreshments. No charge, of course. I've made plenty of cakes, and we've got a new sandwich toaster that I'd like to try out."

Celia gave her a swift smile. "That'll be grand. But don't be on your feet too much, Erin. Not in your condition. Peg's told me about your pregnancy. Get this husband of yours to do the fetching and carrying." She looked at Robbie. "We'll have tea to begin with. We might need to move on to coffee later. How are you at making coffee? Can you make a decent one?"

"I've got a new coffee maker," Robbie told her, "but it's getting the better of me."

Celia quizzed him, "What model is it? What make is it? Does it have a frothing nozzle? What about a reheating section?"

Robbie looked dumbfounded. "I don't know."

Celia passed her bag to the woman behind her. "Jan, take this and get yourself settled in those sofas. I'd better sort this coffee situation out." She turned to Robbie and ordered, "Take me to the machine. Be quick about it. We don't have all day. Is it in the kitchen? Is it this way?" She marched towards the kitchen.

Peggy nudged Robbie and said, "I bet you thought I was a pain in the rear-end. Wait till you've spent a few hours with Celia. You'll soon realise what an angel I am."

Robbie gave her a weak smile and then rushed after Celia.

Peggy handed the patterns over to Jan. "Thanks again for doing this, Jan. I'll call back later."

Peggy and I left the café and got into my car. I said to her, "Where are we going now?"

"We'll call on the first possible knitter on our list. She's called Diana. She doesn't live far away."

I started the engine. "Are we going to just turn up? What are we going to say to her?"

"I've got that sorted out. I phoned each woman as soon as I worked out they could be a possible suspect. I told them we'd found a knitting pattern which could belong to them, and we'd like to return it. Of course, I didn't say anything about your visions and whatnot."

"But if they gave that pattern away to a charity, why would they want it back?"

Peggy's eyes glittered with mischief. "I told them there was something valuable inside the pattern. I didn't tell them what that was, but I hinted it could be money."

I shook my head at her and drove off.

Peggy said, "I had to think of something. We could be looking at a possible murder here."

"I know. I'm sorry. You've done so much to help me. What are we going to do when we get there? What will we say to them?"

"You leave the talking to me. All you have to do is concentrate on any emotions you pick up." She paused a fraction. "If one of them is a serial killer and they start having murderous thoughts about us, let me know."

"I will do. I hope it doesn't come to that."

We soon arrived at Diana's house. As I switched the engine off, I let out a small groan. "I haven't got the twin set pattern with me."

Peggy patted her bag. "I nipped into your house before going to the café. I've got it here."

"You think of everything," I said with a smile. "I don't know what I'd do without you."

Peggy released her seat belt. "Bear that in mind if Diana rushes towards me with a knitting needle and an evil glint in her eyes. Don't let her do away with me."

Diana was waiting at the door for us. She had grey hair and many wrinkles. Her back was stooped and her steps slow as she led us down the hallway of her bungalow. My heart lifted when I saw a knitting bag stuffed with wool at the side of her sofa. Perhaps Diana was our knitter and we would soon get to the bottom of this mystery.

"Do take a seat," Diana told us. She carefully lowered herself into an armchair, letting out a small moan as she did so.

Peggy and I sat on the sofa. Peggy took the twin set pattern out and showed it to Diana.

Peggy explained, "Thank you for seeing us at such short notice. This is the pattern I was telling you about. Do you recognise it?"

Diana squinted at the pattern through her spectacles. "I'm not sure. I had patterns like that when I was young. They were all the fashion at one stage. It was those Hollywood films, you see. We all wanted to look like those starlets." She turned the pattern over. "Ah, now then. This isn't one of mine. I never put a circle around the sizes." She looked as if she was going to say something else, but then she closed her mouth.

"Are you sure it's not one of yours?" Peggy persisted.

"I'm not absolutely certain," Diana said. "However, my sisters did borrow my knitting patterns. They could have put a circle around the numbers. It'd be something they would do. They could never keep their hands off my stuff. The cheeky blighters." She sighed heavily. "May they rest in peace." She gave the pattern back to Peggy. "Sorry, I'm not being very helpful. Would you like to stay for a tea? I haven't had any visitors for days. My son and daughter live far away, and I don't see them as much as I'd liked to. And I haven't been out to the shops for a week. Not with this cold spell in the air."

I could see the hope in Diana's eyes and said, "We can stay for a little while. Did you ever visit the cinema on the high street?"

Diana laughed. "I certainly did. I wasn't the only one. It was a magnet for couples in those days. I had my first date with my late husband there. Let me make you a cuppa and I'll tell you all about it." She let out a small moan of pain as she stood up.

Peggy got up and helped Diana to her feet. She offered, "I'll help you make the tea."

Diana gave her a smile before shuffling out of the room.

I whispered to Peggy, "She seems nice. I don't think she's the one we're looking for."

Peggy whispered back, "She could be lying through her teeth. Have a rummage about in her knitting bag. Touch her personal belongings. See if you can have a vision. Make it quick."

She went after Diana. I didn't relish the idea of touching Diana's property, but I knew it had to be done. I reluctantly made my way over to the knitting bag and put my hands on it.

Chapter 11

"Are you sure you didn't pick up on anything?" Peggy said as we drove away from Diana's house thirty minutes later.

"I'm sure. Diana isn't our suspect. She's just a kindly old lady."

Peggy's tone was suspicious. "Is it all an act? Has she got bodies buried in the garden? I'm not discounting her yet." Her tone brightened. "Although, she did make a super cup of tea. And I did like reminiscing about the past with her."

"Who are we seeing next?"

"A woman called Elaine. We'd better hurry up. I told her we'd be there before eleven. That Diana kept us chatting for too long."

"You did a lot of the chatting," I pointed out.

"I was gaining her trust. That's what investigators do. Turn left at this roundabout. Have you heard anything from Seb yet?"

"I haven't. I checked my phone just before we set off."

"We'll take that as good news. Take the second right."

We arrived at Elaine's house. She opened the door to us and a strong smell of perfume wafted over us. She was the total opposite of Diana. Despite being in her late years, Elaine looked radiant and full of health. She was wearing jeans and a silk shirt. A scarf was arranged elegantly around her neck. I could never get my scarves to look like that. Her face was perfectly made-up, and her hair was thick and shiny.

She gave us a warm smile of welcome and said, "I'd almost given up on you. Do come in. I'm afraid I haven't got long to talk to you. I'm going out on a date in ten minutes." She paused and her smile increased.

"It's a blind date. I met him online. Have you ever tried online dating? It's a marvel. My daughter told me all about it, and she showed me which sites to go on. I've had five dates so far this month. It's an absolute hoot! Come in."

I shared a look with Peggy and then followed Elaine into her living room. It was tastefully furnished and the furniture was expensive looking. I did notice a knitting bag half-hidden behind a chair.

Elaine perched on the end of her armchair and placed her hands on her knees. Her back was straight and her look direct. She said, "Peggy, you said on the phone you might have something which belonged to me."

"I did." Peggy handed her the pattern.

Elaine smiled when she looked at the image. "This does look like something I would have made. I do like the clean lines of this twin set." Her smile grew. "I have a set of pearls just like these. They're not real, but they're good imitation ones."

"Is that your pattern?" Peggy asked.

"It might be. It might not be. Mum bought a lot of patterns for me. She insisted on me taking up knitting. She said it was a skill that would stay with me for life." She lowered the pattern. "Between you and me, I think she wanted me to spend more time at home and less time out with my friends. I was a bit of a wild one in my youth. I had many boyfriends. I used to meet them at that old cinema in town."

I leaned forward. "Was there anyone special in your life at that time?"

Elaine let out a delicate laugh. "They were all special. Until the next one came along. I thought I was in love with all of them."

Peggy spoke, "Did any of them ever stand you up outside the cinema? That happened to a friend of mine and she never got over it."

A look of anger flashed into Elaine's eyes. She said, "They wouldn't have dared stand me up." She looked at the pattern again and shook her head. "I really can't say whether this belonged to me or not. It could have been one of Mum's. Didn't you say there was something valuable with the pattern?"

"I did. It was a five-pound-note," Peggy said. As if testing Elaine for her honesty, she added, "If you think there's a fair chance the pattern belongs to you, I can give you that money."

Elaine shook her head and handed the pattern back to Peggy. "That wouldn't be honest of me as I don't know for sure if it is mine. I hope you don't think I'm being rude, but I'll have to ask you to leave. I don't want to be late for my date. Actually, I've double-booked myself today. I'm meeting two men within a short time of each other, and in the same place. I didn't think they'd both say yes to me! One of them is an old flame. I haven't seen him for years, so I couldn't say no to him."

The hairs on the back of my neck prickled. "Oh? Where are you meeting these men?"

"It's that pub just down from the supermarket in town. My old flame hasn't been here for years and that's the only building he remembers." She stood up. "I'll see you out."

As soon as we got in the car, Peggy declared, "It's her! It has to be. Did you see how angry she looked when I mentioned being stood up? And now she's going to meet an old flame! It must be the young man you saw in the cinema. It all makes sense. He's come back on the scene, and for some reason, he's going to try and kill her. But she's going to kill him instead. She's got her knitting needles ready. Did you see them?"

"I did."

"We'll have to follow her, of course. We have to stop these murders before they get going."

"How are we going to do that?" I asked. "We can't march into that pub and tell Elaine about my visions."

Peggy considered the matter. "No, we can't do that. We'll have to spy on her from afar. We'll see what happens and take it from there. If Elaine is our suspect, I wonder who else she's killed? You said the older man in your later vision accused her of murder."

"I'm not sure the woman in my vision did kill someone. The man accused her, but he didn't give any information about it. What's the name of the third woman on your list?"

"It's Martha. Is there any point calling on her now? We should be getting ourselves ready for our covert surveillance of Elaine."

"Won't Martha be expecting us?"

Peggy sighed. "She will. She sounded nice on the phone. I suppose we should turn up. I don't want to let her down. We won't stay long."

Martha welcomed us into her home and insisted on making us a drink. Once in the living room, Peggy produced the knitting pattern and asked Martha about it.

Martha examined the pattern. "I don't recognise it. It looks too fancy for me. I don't think I would have had the patience to knit that cabled part. Sorry." She handed the pattern back to Peggy.

I said to her, "Do you still knit now?"

Martha shook her head. "Not with my arthritis. I find it too painful. I used to knit for my family when I had the time." A sadness came into her eyes. "I don't need to knit for anyone now. My daughter is grown up, and my husband passed away last year."

Peggy had lost her husband a few years ago and I saw her face soften at Martha's words. Peggy said, "I'm sorry to hear that. I know how you feel. What was your husband's name?"

394

"Leon. He was a good husband. He did everything for me. Took good care of me and the house. He did lots of DIY." She smiled at the memory. "He was useless most of the time, but he tried."

Peggy nodded in understanding. "My Jeff was just the same. He made a mess of our home many times with his handiwork. There's a set of shelves in the spare room which have never been straight. Jeff put them up. I can't put anything on them because they slide right off. But I can't bear to take them down."

Martha said, "It's the memories, isn't it? They keep you going on a lonely night."

"Aye, they do."

Even though Peggy was anxious to leave, we stayed with Martha for a while longer and the two of them talked about their late husbands.

Peggy's eyes were watery as we headed for my car. She said, "Poor Martha. Do you think I should invite her to one of our craft evenings? It would do her good to get out of the house."

"That's a good idea." I opened the car and we got in. "Where to now?"

"Let's go to that pub where Elaine is meeting her dates." Peggy wiped her eyes. "I'll just get myself into the right frame of mind for catching a murderer. Give me a minute or two."

I checked the traffic before driving away. Peggy was unnaturally quiet as we headed into town. I hoped her conversation with Martha hadn't upset her too much. In the silence, I thought about the recent visits we'd had to the elderly women. There was something bothering me, but for the life of me, I couldn't work out what it was.

Chapter 12

I did feel a sense of unease as Peggy and I walked into the pub where Elaine was meeting her dates. I didn't like the idea of spying on her and I voiced my concerns to Peggy.

She said, "We're here to stop a possible murder. Don't forget that." She looked around the pub. "Ah, there's Elaine over there. She's on her own. Let's get a table in the corner and watch her from there."

"Would you like a drink?" I checked my watch. "I hope they do tea and coffee. It's a bit early for something strong."

"It's never too early for a gin and tonic," Peggy said. She nodded to herself. "I should get that embroidered on a cushion. Let me give you some money for the drinks."

"No, I'll get them."

"No, I will," Peggy argued.

For the next minute, we did that ridiculous thing of both of us insisting on paying. I relented and took a ten-pound-note from Peggy. She headed off to find a table for us, and I went to the bar.

From my position at the bar, I could see Elaine. She had her back to me and I saw her looking at her watch. She was still on her own and waiting for her date. I got a gin and tonic for Peggy and a mint tea for myself. I was hoping the tea would calm my nerves. I was on edge as I cast cautious glances Elaine's way. What if she turned around and saw me staring at her? I didn't have an excuse ready as to why Peggy and I were here.

I took the drinks over to a corner table and handed the gin and tonic to Peggy. I gave her the change from her ten-pound-note.

Peggy picked her glass up and said, "I've been watching Elaine. She looks worried. Her date hasn't shown up yet. She keeps checking her phone." She took a long drink and smacked her lips together in appreciation. "That hits the spot. Karis, do you think you'll recognise the man from your vision if he turns up here?"

"I will. His face was very close to mine. I saw his features clearly."

We stopped talking as a man approached Elaine. He tapped her on the shoulder and she turned around. She looked at the man with uncertainty, to begin with, then she broke into a smile and held her hand out. The man took it and started to talk to her.

Peggy strained her neck as she looked at the couple. She muttered, "Turn around, mister. We can't see your face."

We watched in vain as Elaine and her date talked to each other. The mystery man still had his back to us.

Peggy said, "We can't see his face from here. We'll have to do something. Can you sneak over there and take a peek at his face? If you don't like the idea of doing that, I can walk past and casually take a photo of him. I can be discreet when needed."

I shook my head. "You don't need to do that. He's turned around now. It's not the man from my vision."

"Are you sure?" Peggy stood up and looked directly at the couple. Elaine and her date were now facing us as they stood at the bar.

"I'm sure."

Elaine suddenly looked Peggy's way and made direct eye contact with her. Her eyebrows rose in surprise. Then she smiled and gave Peggy a wave.

Peggy waved back and returned to her seating position. "Drat. We've been spotted. Our cover has been blown."

"It doesn't matter now. We've seen the mystery man, and he's not the one we're looking for."

"But what about the old flame? He'll be turning up soon. How are we going to take a covert look at him now that Elaine has seen us?" She shook her head. "I've let us down, Karis. I shouldn't have drawn attention to us."

I stiffened and hissed, "Elaine is coming this way."

"Act natural," Peggy hissed back. She picked her glass up, leaned back in her chair and took a big drink. She beamed as Elaine stopped at our table.

Elaine said, "Hello. I didn't think I'd see you two again, and so soon."

In a casual manner, Peggy lifted her glass and announced, "I'm having a gin and tonic. I have one every day. Sometimes two or three. I love them. When you mentioned going to the pub, I asked Karis if she would bring me here so that I could start on my favourite tipple." She laughed a bit too loudly. "It's never too early to have a gin and tonic! That's what I always say."

Elaine gave Peggy an uncertain look. "I suppose not."

I asked, "How's your date going? He looks like a friendly chap."

Elaine pulled a face. "He is friendly. Too friendly. He's already talking about us going on holiday together. He's barely let me say a word since we met. He's not my type. I'll have to make an excuse soon and leave."

Peggy offered, "Do you want me to get rid of him for you? I don't mind."

"No, thank you. I think it's best if I do it." Elaine smiled. "I've got rid of men before."

"Really?" Peggy said, "How? Did you use sharp implements on them?"

Elaine gave Peggy another uncertain look and took a step back. "Sharp implements?"

I quickly said, "Are you still going to meet your old flame?"

Elaine nodded. "I am. I can't wait to see him. But I'm not going to meet him here. He sent me a text to say he's running late. He's going to take me to a restaurant this evening instead. I don't know which one yet." She looked over at the bar. "I'd better get back to my date. I'll give him five more minutes before making my excuses." She said goodbye and walked away.

Peggy put her drink on the table and gave it a suspicious look. "How much gin is in there? It's gone straight to my head. I almost blurted out inappropriate questions to Elaine."

"You did blurt out an inappropriate question about using a sharp implement." I looked over at Elaine. She had a patient look on her face as she listened to her date. I said to Peggy, "We'll have to follow Elaine later when she goes to the restaurant."

"We will. We'll have to be more discreet next time. I suppose we'll have to hang around outside her house until she leaves." A noise came from her handbag. "Oh, that's my phone." She took her phone from her handbag and tapped on it. She said, "It's from Celia. A couple of the knitted jumpers are ready at the café."

"Already? That was quick."

"Celia doesn't mess about when it comes to knitting. We can't do anything else here. Let's go and have a look at those jumpers. With a bit of luck, you might have another vision." She stared at her half-full glass and then heaved a big sigh. "I'm not going to drink the rest of it. I need to keep a clear head. Come on, Karis, let's go before I change my mind and down this drink in one."

Peggy swiftly stood up and walked away. She waved to Elaine on the way out.

I looked Elaine's way and saw the discomfort on her face as the man in front of her chatted away. He was standing too close to her and seemed almost aggressive. I made a flash decision and headed over to her.

I announced loudly, "Elaine! I thought it was you." I pulled her into a hug and whispered, "Would you like some help?" I released her and saw the answer to my question in her eyes.

Keeping my voice loud, I said to her, "Elaine, I know I've got a nerve, but could you drive me over to my mum's? My car's just broken down, and there isn't a direct bus which can take me there. Mum's not well as you know."

Her date turned to me and gave me a dismissive look. He said, "Elaine is on a date. With me."

I said to him, "This is urgent. Very urgent. My mum was expecting me an hour ago."

"Then get a taxi," he snapped. "Elaine and I have a lot to discuss. We have holiday plans to talk about."

I faced Elaine and said, "I didn't realise I was interrupting. Don't worry about me. I can get a taxi. I hope it doesn't take too long. Mum will be so worried."

"There's no need to phone for a taxi," Elaine said. "I will drive you there immediately."

The man said to Elaine, "You can't leave me. I haven't finished talking to you yet. Tell this woman to clear off and get a taxi."

Elaine let out a gasp of outrage. "What a selfish thing to say! Kevin, you are not the kind of man I'm looking for. Goodbye!" She put her hand on my arm and led me out of the pub. Kevin muttered something, but we ignored him.

As soon as we got outside, Elaine started laughing. She said, "I couldn't get rid of him! He wouldn't stop talking. I couldn't get a word in. Thanks for your help."

"That's okay." I noticed Peggy waiting a bit further up the road. She was sending quizzical looks our way.

Elaine said, "I'll be off now before Kevin comes out. Thanks again. Perhaps we'll bump into each other again soon."

"Perhaps we will," I replied.

Elaine said goodbye and walked away. As soon as she'd gone, Peggy came over to me.

I said to Peggy, "I like Elaine. I hope we can do something to stop my vision coming true. I don't like the idea of some strange man hurting her."

Peggy gave my arm a reassuring pat. "We'll do all that we can."

Chapter 13

Two completed jumpers were waiting for us at the café.

Erin met us at the door with a huge smile on her face. She said, "You should hear how much Celia has been bossing Robbie around! She's been getting him to do all sorts of things for her. And my kind-hearted husband has agreed to everything she's asked for. I feel so sorry for him. But it is fun to watch."

"He's too kind-hearted by half," Peggy said. "Where is he?"

"Over here," Erin said.

We followed her over to the area where the sofas were. Peggy and I stopped in our tracks when we saw what Robbie was doing to Celia.

Celia was leaning back on one of the sofas with her arms stretched out in front of her. Robbie was kneeling at her feet and caressing her hands.

I hissed to Erin, "What's he doing?"

She hissed back, "Giving her a hand massage. She said her fingers were hurting from all that knitting. He couldn't say no to her."

"He could," Peggy said. "Let's put an end to this nonsense right now." She marched over to Celia and stood in front of her. "What's going on?"

Celia jumped at Peggy's stern expression. "This young man is massaging my aching fingers if you must know. He's doing a wonderful job."

Peggy pointed an accusing finger at Celia. "In all the years I've known you, you've never had aching fingers. You are taking advantage of Robbie, and you know it."

"He doesn't mind," Celia replied defensively.

Robbie said, "Well, I do have other things to—"

Celia interrupted him, "You've got a lovely touch, Robbie. You didn't mind giving me a back massage earlier on, did you? No, you didn't. And you don't mind giving my hands a massage now, do you?"

Robbie tried again, "Well, I—"

"No, you don't," Celia spoke for him. "You can give me a head massage next. You've got a magical touch. Keep going. I feel all warm and tingly."

Peggy exploded, "Celia! I did not ask you to come here so you could feel all warm and tingly! Behave yourself. Robbie, release her hands."

Robbie dropped Celia's hands and stood up.

Peggy stared at Celia. Celia stared back at her. There was a tense atmosphere in the room and it felt like everyone was holding their breaths.

Peggy and Celia suddenly burst into laughter.

Celia said, "Sorry, Peg. I couldn't resist the chance to have a young man's hands on me! It's been decades."

"I should have known better than to have put temptation in your way," Peggy said with a chuckle.

Robbie's head dropped and he muttered, "I feel used."

Erin went over to him and put her arm around his waist. "You should feel flattered. This just proves how irresistible you are to women. It's not just me who can see how wonderful you are."

He lifted his head. "I still feel used."

"Can I do something to make you feel better?" Erin asked with a small grin.

Robbie brightened up.

Before he could speak, I said, "Can we stop with all this talk about touching and feeling warm and tingly? It's making me feel very uncomfortable."

Peggy said, "Karis is right. This is a place for business, not a den of iniquity. Robbie, Erin, if you're going to get all mushy with each other, do it elsewhere. Celia, clear all thoughts of being warm and tingly from your mind and tell me where the completed jumpers are."

"They're right behind you on that table," Celia said.

I looked that way and noticed Celia's friends sitting on the opposite sofa. They were engrossed in their knitting and didn't look our way.

Celia continued, "We've only made a couple, but we'll have another one done soon."

"A couple might be enough," I said. I made a move towards them and then stopped. I cast a cautious glance at Celia.

Peggy picked up on what I was thinking and said to me, "It's okay. Celia knows about your psychic abilities." She looked at Celia. "This is why I wanted you to knit these jumpers. Karis is getting funny feelings about the knitting patterns."

Celia's eyes widened. "How exciting. I've never seen anyone being psychic before. Go on, Karis, pick the jumpers up and have a good feel. Get your psychic powers revved up."

Celia's friends stopped knitting and watched me as I picked up a jumper. I could feel all eyes on me now. I pulled the jumper closer and closed my eyes.

Nothing.

I put that jumper down and tried the other.

Still nothing.

I shook my head. "I'm not getting anything. Perhaps it should have been me who knitted them like I did with the twin set."

Peggy said, "Perhaps. Don't forget that you got a strong vision when you wore the twin set. I know that jumper is too big for you, but put it on anyway."

I did so. The jumper was huge on me and the sleeves dangled over my hands. I took some deep breaths. I was fully aware of being watched and I felt immense pressure to perform.

No visions came to me.

Peggy clicked her fingers. "I know what you have to do! Get a man to wear the jumpers. That might cause something to happen. Robbie, you'll do."

Robbie removed himself from Erin's embrace and said, "I am a person with feelings, you know. I don't appreciate being treated as an object." He came over to me and held his hand out. "Give me the jumper, Karis. Let's get this over with." Despite his act of martyrdom, I saw the sparkle of glee in his eyes.

I handed the jumper over and said, "You're enjoying every minute of this."

He smiled but didn't say anything as he took the jumper.

Celia said, "Hang on a minute. That jumper won't fit you, Robbie. I've been sizing you up and that one is far too small for you. The other one is too. Are there any other men around?" She looked around the café as if expecting a group of men to pop out from behind the tables.

My good friend, Seb Parker, chose that moment to come into the café. The smile on his face froze when he saw many pairs of interested eyes looking his way.

Celia stood up, faced Seb and said, "You'll do. Get over here. We need your body."

Seb didn't move. He looked at me and said, "Karis?" His eyes went to Robbie. "Robbie?"

Robbie cried out jovially, "Run for your life, Seb! It's too late for me, but you can save yourself! Run!"

Peggy dashed over to Seb at an amazing speed. She grabbed his arm and dragged him over to the sofas. He looked frightened to death.

Seb muttered, "I only came in to talk to Karis. I wish I'd phoned her now." He gave me a beseeching look. "What's going on?"

He jumped when he felt Celia's hands on him. She looked him up and down and proclaimed, "You'll do nicely. You're a perfect specimen. Yes, quite perfect. Do you work out? You must do. Flex your muscles. Have you got a six-pack? Lift your shirt and let's have a look."

"Celia!" Peggy snapped. "Back in your cage. Seb, sorry about Celia. Would you mind trying some jumpers on, please?"

"Why?" He took a step away from Celia who was still sizing him up.

I quickly explained about the other knitting patterns and how the completed jumpers might help me.

Seb smiled at me. "In that case, of course I'll try them on." He took his jacket off and pulled one of the jumpers over his head. He held his arms out and said, "What happens next? Do you need to touch me?"

Heat rushed to my cheeks and I looked away. I mumbled, "I think so."

Celia said, "Go on then, Karis. Get on with it. Have a good feel. We're all watching."

I looked at her and said, "I know. That's the problem. I need some privacy. I can't perform with an audience."

"Try," Celia said.

Robbie came to my rescue. "Celia, there's been enough touching in this café today. Karis needs some privacy, and that's what she's going to get. Haven't you got some knitting to do?"

"Party pooper," Celia muttered as she returned to the sofa.

"Karis," Robbie went on, "take Seb upstairs. The building work has been completed up there. Take your time. I know this is important. I won't let anyone disturb you. Seb, there's another jumper to try on too."

I gave him a grateful smile and then headed for the stairs. Seb took the other jumper and followed me.

Once upstairs, Seb smiled kindly and said, "Well, what do we do now?" He opened his arms wide. "Would you like a hug? You look as if you could use one." He waggled his eyebrows at me. "Come on, Karis, you know you want to."

I laughed. "I'm only hugging you because of my visions."

"Keep telling yourself that," Seb joked.

I moved closer to Seb and he put his arms around me. I rested my chin on his shoulder. The jumper felt soft under me. Seb's arms were warm.

The area around me began to fade, and a buzzing noise settled in my ears.

I prepared myself for a vision.

Chapter 14

The vision came and went in a few seconds. I stepped out of Seb's embrace and tried to make sense of what had just happened.

Seb said, "Did you see something?"

"No, but I felt something. I took on that woman's memories again as I hugged you. She must have had her eyes closed because I couldn't see anything. But I could sense her feelings. You're not the right man."

"Pardon? But you told me to put the jumper on."

"I don't mean it in that way. The woman was thinking this about the man she was with. He's not the right one. He's second-best. She felt sad about it but resigned to the fact. It was a hopeless cause, but one she had to put up with. I didn't love you. You'll never be the right one for me. Her, I mean."

Seb's lips pressed together, and I saw hurt in his eyes.

"Seb, you do know I'm not talking about you and me, don't you? I'm speaking from the perspective of the woman in my vision."

He smiled tightly. "I know. Shall I try the other jumper on?"

"Might as well. Thank you."

"It's okay. What are friends for?"

He quickly changed jumpers and we hugged again. Seb's hug didn't feel as warm this time. It was clear I'd upset him. I pushed that thought out of my mind and concentrated on my vision.

Another vision swiftly came to me, and just as quickly, it fled.

Seb whipped his arms away. "Well?" he asked. "Am I still second-best?"

"Seb," I began warily, "this isn't about you. But yes, the feelings were just the same."

There was a polite cough behind us. Peggy stood there with her eyes closed and her hand held out. She said, "I don't want to interrupt, but the next jumper is ready. Here."

"You can open your eyes," I said to her. I walked over and took the completed jumper.

Peggy opened her eyes. "Any news?" she asked. She stole a glance at Seb. "What's wrong with him? Why's he sulking?"

"I'll explain later. Thanks for this."

Peggy took another look at Seb before walking down the stairs.

I gave the jumper to Seb. He did have a sulky look on his face. I smiled and said, "Stop being such a twit. You know those feelings have nothing to do with us and our friendship."

He shrugged. "So, you don't feel that I'm second-best then?"

I moved my hand in a rocking motion. "You're okay. I can take you or leave you."

Seb broke into a laugh. "I deserved that. Sorry for being a twit. It's just that, you know, things have happened in the past to me which have made me feel second-best."

"Things have happened to all of us," I said kindly. "Put that jumper on, open your arms and wrap them around me. You're the one who needs a hug now."

Seb pulled the jumper on and we embraced again.

The vision that came to me was different now. I saw a man's face in front of me. He looked middle-aged. It wasn't the young man who I'd seen at the cinema.

The man smiled warmly at me, ran a hand down his jumper and said, "Thank you for making this new one for me. It's lovely. It'll keep me warm and snug on those cold days when I'm outside. I'll think of you when I'm wearing it."

I felt my heart fill with love at the tender look in his eyes. He really was a kind, thoughtful man. I was lucky to have him in my life. I moved forward and put my arms around him. My head rested on his chest. I felt safe and secure. Nothing could hurt me when he was around.

The vision faded, but I didn't move. I stayed right where I was and experienced the afterglow of those loving feelings. It was like being woken from a wonderful dream and I had to hang on to those lovely feelings as long as possible.

I let out a sigh of contentment.

Seb said, "Karis? Have you come back to me?"

"Shh," I mumbled. I rested my head on his chest. I could hear Seb's heart beating. I knew full well it was Seb I was hugging now. He was nice to hug. So solid and dependable.

"Karis?"

"Quiet. I'm revelling in the wake of joy and love."

Seb moved me to arm's-length and looked down at me. His eyes widened as he took in my expression. He said softly, "Karis, what happened? You're glowing. Your eyes are," he swallowed, "full of love."

"I'm not surprised." I took a step back. I explained what I'd experienced.

Seb nodded. "So, the woman in the vision now loves this man?"

"Very much so. He's not the man who was at the cinema with her. But that particular man comes into her life in later years and threatens her." I shook my head. "I can't make sense of it."

Seb considered the matter. "This woman was originally stood up by that young man at the cinema. Perhaps she ended up marrying someone else whom she considered second-best. But over the years, she learned to love him. She must have felt some affection for him if she kept knitting jumpers for him."

"That's true. But why does the original man come back and accuse her of murder? And why does he attack her?"

"That is a mystery. Do you know where the knitting patterns came from yet?"

Like a genie in a bottle, Peggy suddenly appeared at the top of the steps. She announced, "We have a suspect!"

"How long have you been standing there?" Seb asked. "Have you been listening to everything we said? Have you been watching our every move?"

Peggy retorted, "That's neither here nor there, Seb Parker. The point is, we have a suspect. Her name is Elaine and we know where she lives. She's meeting an old flame tonight in a restaurant. He could be the mystery man who attacks her."

"How do you know all of this?" Seb asked. "On second thoughts, I don't want to know."

Peggy continued, "We don't know which restaurant she's going to meet this man in. But we need to know what he looks like. Can you find out? Can you drive past her house and aim a listening machine at it? Something that will pick up her conversations? We could find out what time they're meeting and where."

"No," Seb replied.

"How about tapping into her phone and her messages?" Peggy persisted.

"No."

"What about running a police check on her and finding out if she's got any skeletons in the wardrobe. Or hidden in her cellar?"

"Peggy, I'm not going to do any of that." Seb looked at me. "Do you think Elaine is in danger?"

"She could be," I said. "But I'm not sure. I'd need to see what this old boyfriend of hers looks like."

Seb nodded. "And she's going to meet him tonight?"

"She is," I confirmed.

Peggy tutted. "I just told you that."

Seb ignored her. "In that case, I could keep a surveillance of her house and see when she leaves. I could let you know the name of the restaurant she goes to, and then you can have a look at her companion."

"That would really help," I said. "Thank you."

"What are friends for?" he said. He looked at me for slightly too long. "Once I know the name of the restaurant, I'll pick you up and we'll have a look at this old boyfriend together."

Peggy prodded him. "What about me? I want to look at him too."

Seb gave Peggy a patient smile. "I'll pick you up too. I'll be in touch later." He pulled the jumper off and gave it to me. "If anything happens in the meantime, get in touch with me. Don't put yourself in danger."

"We won't," Peggy said.

Seb shared a smile with me before walking away.

Peggy said, "What's going on with you and Seb?"

"Nothing. We're just friends."

"Really? Friends don't look at each other like that. You watch yourself around Seb. You've only just got a divorce. You don't want to get involved with another man yet."

"He's just a friend," I insisted.

Peggy gave me a look but didn't say anything.

I went on, "He's a very helpful friend. Thanks to him, we'll be able to go to this restaurant tonight and look at that old boyfriend of Elaine's. We'll stop any murders taking place."

"I suppose Seb does have his uses," Peggy relented. Her eyes narrowed. "Why do you look so worried?"

"I don't know. I've had a niggling feeling for the last few hours, and I can't work out what's wrong." I gave her a small smile. "It'll come to me."

Chapter 15

Peggy and I went downstairs. We were met by the curious looks of Celia and her knitting friends as they stared at us from the sofas.

"Well?" Celia asked. "What happened? Did you see something? Smell something? How does it work? Can you tell fortunes? Do you know the lottery numbers for next week?"

Peggy said, "Stop badgering her, Celia. It takes a lot out of Karis when she has these visions. Some of them can be quite upsetting."

I said to Peggy, "I don't mind talking about my visions. It might help to make sense of them if I talk about what I saw."

Celia shuffled along the sofa and patted the empty space at her side. "Sit next to me. Tell me everything."

I settled myself next to Celia and explained what I'd witnessed. I also told her what Seb's opinion of the situation was. Her friends paused in their knitting and listened attentively.

At some point, Robbie appeared with a cup of coffee for me and slid it onto the table before quickly moving away. I think he was nervous about being so close to Celia.

Once I'd told Celia and her friends about my recent visions, I filled them in on my previous ones.

When I'd finished, Celia concluded, "I agree with your handsome friend, Seb. It sounds like our mystery knitter didn't want to be with the man she was knitting for, at first. But as the years went on, she fell in love with him. I'm intrigued by this young man in the cinema. Why does he come back to attack the mystery knitter in the present day?"

I said, "I don't know the answer to that. And I'm not entirely convinced our mystery knitter is Elaine, but Peggy and I are going to check on her companion tonight at the restaurant." I paused and looked at the knitting patterns on the table. "I keep thinking I'm missing something, though." I looked over at Peggy who was perched on the end of the sofa. "I think we should go to that charity shop where Jade possibly bought the patterns. There could be something important there. Perhaps there will be other belongings which came with the patterns."

Peggy nodded. "Good thinking. We'll do that now."

"Peg, do you still want us to carry on with these jumpers?" Celia asked. "We've done five now. I don't mind staying here and carrying on. I like it here. And I like the company." She cast a glance at Robbie who had just come out of the kitchen. He saw Celia grinning at him, spun around and scuttled back into the kitchen.

Peggy raised her eyebrows in my direction. "What do you think? Do you still need the jumpers?"

I picked the nearest pattern up. A flash of a man's face came into my mind. The image vanished quickly and I couldn't work out who he was. I said to Celia, "Yes, it would really help me if you could finish these. If you don't mind?"

"I don't mind at all," Celia confirmed. "You and Peg get yourselves off to the charity shop. Leave the patterns to us. Let us know how you get on." She picked her knitting needles up and added, "If this week's lottery numbers come to you while you're out and about, let me know what they are."

I quickly drank the coffee before heading to the kitchen. I told Erin and Robbie about my latest visions and advised them where I was going next.

Robbie cast a wary look towards the café area. He said, "How long do you think Celia will be here?"

Erin patted his arm. "Don't you worry about Celia and her roving hands. I'll be the one who takes food and drinks out to our guests." She looked my way. "Take care, Karis. Even though you're not saying it, I can tell how worried you are."

I was going to say I wasn't worried at all, but there was no point lying to Erin. She knew me too well.

Peggy and I headed over to the charity shop.

As we went through the door, Peggy said, "Ah, the manager is in today. It's Irene. I used to work with her a while back. She's a good sort, but she can talk till the cows come home. Let me talk to her first."

"I will do." I was happy to do that as my mind was already elsewhere. As soon as we'd entered the shop, my scalp had begun to prickle with apprehension. There was something important in here. I scanned the packed shelves and my heart sank. There were hundreds of items in here. How was I going to narrow down what the important object was?

I followed Peggy over to the counter. A woman a bit younger than Peggy was standing behind it. She was wearing many colours in a variety of styles. Three beaded necklaces around her neck clicked together as she sorted out a tray of bracelets in front of her. As Peggy and I approached, she looked up and broke into a smile.

"Hello, Irene," Peggy said.

"Peggy! How are you? I haven't seen you for a few months. Are you still doing volunteer work at the hospital? I keep meaning to pop down there and do some myself, but you know me and hospitals. I'm worried that if I go in, I won't come out again." She laughed loudly and her necklaces jangled together.

"I do still volunteer," Peggy said. "Irene, we're here about—"

"I heard you were doing stuff online," Irene interrupted her. "I don't know how you do it. I can't make head nor tails of that world web thing. Our Steve keeps telling me it's easy, but it's not easy for me. I tried to order a book online the other day. I ended up getting a pair of walking boots delivered. I don't know how that happened."

"Irene," Peggy tried again.

"And you've been doing classes at Erin's Café, so I've heard. How you find the time and energy, I don't know. I can barely find the energy to come here every day. You know what I'm like with my troubles, Peggy. I've been to the doctors this morning about them, and he's put me on different medication. I hope it does the trick."

Peggy's voice was a tad louder this time as she said, "Irene, we want to talk to you about some knitting patterns we've got. They might have come from this shop. I've got one in my bag." She reached into her bag and pulled out the twin set pattern. She gave it to Irene.

Irene looked at it and then lowered it. "You'd be amazed at the things we get in here. A surprising number of false legs, for some reason. Do people keep spares and then no longer need them? We get false teeth too. Would you believe it! False teeth."

"The knitting pattern?" Peggy said with a hint of annoyance in her voice. "Does it look familiar?"

Irene put her attention back on the pattern. "Oh, yes. I remember this. A bunch of patterns came in a few weeks ago. I didn't think anyone would want them with the styles being so old-fashioned. But one of our regulars bought them. A young woman who always wears black. I thought she was going to a funeral when I first met her months ago, but no, she just likes to wear black for some reason. Aren't people strange? There was a man last week who—"

I thought I saw steam coming from Peggy's ears, so I swiftly interrupted Irene and said, "Sorry to be brusque, but we're in a rush. Do you know who donated the patterns?"

"Yes," Irene replied.

"And who was it?" Peggy asked.

"It was a woman. I would guess she was in her early fifties. Maybe late fifties. It's hard to tell these days with all that age-defying cream that everyone buys. She brought a whole stack of stuff in. She said they belonged to her dad who passed away a while back. Her mum refused to get rid of his belongings and they'd been cluttering up the house. But the daughter had insisted on getting rid of her dad's stuff and brought them here." She gave the pattern back to Peggy. "This was definitely with the items she brought in."

Peggy leaned closer to Irene and said, "Where are those belongings now?"

"I've sold them all. They went really quickly."

"You sold all of them?" There was disappointment in Peggy's voice.

I asked, "What items did that woman bring in? Besides the knitting patterns."

Irene replied, "There were some men's shoes and slippers, and some trousers and jackets. Oh, and some knitted jumpers too. They were in good condition and I sold them in a day."

Peggy's shoulders dropped. "I don't suppose you know the name of the woman who brought the items in?"

Irene shook her head. "I don't. She was in a rush. All the belongings were in a suitcase and she just left it next to this counter."

My heart missed a beat. "A suitcase? Do you still have it?"

Irene frowned. "I do. Tatty old thing, it is. I can't sell it, not in that condition."

"Where is it now?" I asked, half-fearing the answer.

"It's in the back. I was going to take it to the tip later."

"Can I have a look at it? Please?" I heard the pleading tone in my voice, but I couldn't help it.

Irene's eyes narrowed. "Why would you want to look at it? It's a scruffy-looking thing. It's no good to anyone."

Peggy said, "People say that about me, but I'm still useful. We'll pay you for it, Irene."

Irene shook her head at us and then walked away from the counter.

Peggy said to me, "Is the suitcase important?"

I nodded. "I had a funny feeling about something the minute we came in here. When Irene mentioned the suitcase, I knew it must be that."

Irene returned with an old-fashioned suitcase. It was of a medium size and was brown in colour. The bottom edges were scuffed, and there were a couple of tears in the top corner. I already had a ten-pound-note ready and I handed it to Irene.

Irene swapped the suitcase for the money and said, "This is too much money. Let me get you some change."

"No, keep it all," I said. I was eager to get out of the shop and to have some alone time with the suitcase.

"If you're sure? Thank you." Irene moved over to the till and opened it. With her eyes on the till, she said, "Peggy, I haven't told you about our Steve and his latest divorce. You won't believe what's happened now."

Peggy grabbed my arm and announced, "No time to talk, Irene! Bye for now." She propelled me out of the charity shop and on to the path outside in record time.

Once we were a safe distance from the shop, we looked at the tatty suitcase in my hand.

Peggy gave me an expectant look. "Well?"

APRIL FERNSBY

Chapter 16

"Well?" Seb asked me later that evening. We were sitting in his car outside a restaurant. "Was there something inside the suitcase? Some valuable clue hidden inside the lining?"

"No," I replied.

He continued, "Did you get a vision? A feeling?"

"No." I paused and tried to find the right words. "But something will come to me soon about it. That suitcase is important for some reason. Do you know that feeling you get when something is on its way to you? Like a parcel or something? You have this feeling of anticipation. You know it will arrive, but you don't know when."

Seb nodded.

I put my hands on my stomach. "This is what I'm feeling now. I can't rush the vision, but I know it's going to arrive at some point."

Peggy popped her head forward from the back seat. "I had to wait in all day once for a new fridge. They said it would be there between eight a.m. and six p.m., but they couldn't give me a specific time. I was on tenterhooks all day as I waited for that fridge. I didn't even go to the toilet in case I missed the delivery." She sighed at the memory. "That was not a good day. Seb, are you sure this is the right restaurant? Did you see Elaine go inside?"

"For the third time, yes." Seb turned in his seat so he could look at Peggy better. "Are you sure you don't want to sit in the front? You'll get a better view of the restaurant from here. I don't mind sitting in the back while we wait."

"No, thanks. I've got my knitting things on the back seat now. And my snacks." She frowned at the building in front of us. "You can't see a thing through those frosted windows. Are you sure she's in there?"

Seb pointed to a red car parked a short distance away. "That's her car. She's still inside."

"What about her date?" Peggy persisted. "Has he arrived? Where is he now?"

Seb said, "I don't know the answer to either question. As soon as Elaine came here, I drove away and collected you and Karis."

Peggy gave him a sniff of disapproval. "Some police stakeout this is. You're not even doing it right."

Keeping his tone patient, Seb explained, "This isn't a stakeout. This isn't official police business. I'm doing this for a friend." He smiled at me.

Peggy coughed.

Seb corrected himself, "I'm doing this for two dear friends."

"But we need to see Elaine's date," Peggy argued. "We can't sit here for hours on the off chance that we get a look at him. Go inside, Seb. Have a good nosy. Can't you use your police powers or something?"

"As I've just explained, this isn't a police matter. However, there is something I can do." He put his hand on the door handle. "I'm going inside. Peggy, do not follow me. Is that clear?"

She looked away from his glance. "What if I need to use the ladies?"

"You've just been," Seb pointed out. "I made sure of that before we left. I'm leaving the car now. Do not follow me." He gave Peggy another look before exiting the car.

Peggy chuckled as we watched Seb walking towards the restaurant. She said, "He's a bossy one, isn't he? I've a good mind to follow him just to annoy him. But I won't. I know he's doing us a big favour with this stakeout business."

"He is," I said. "I hope he doesn't get into trouble because of it."

"Me too. I'd better get back to my knitting. I've already completed the back of the last jumper. We'll have ten completed jumpers soon. It was good of Celia and her gang to do those other jumpers for us. I'll send them a thank-you gift." She shuffled back on her seat and I soon heard the clicking of knitting needles.

I said, "I'll send them something too." I kept my eyes on Seb as he entered the restaurant. He came back out a few minutes later and got back into the car.

He handed his phone to me and said, "Look at the photo. It's the man who's sitting with Elaine. This is the best I could do while being discreet. Does he look familiar?"

I squinted at the image and then enlarged it. "It's hard to say. I can only see half of his face. He looks to be of the right age. Did you get any other photos of him?"

"No. Sorry." Seb took his phone back.

From the back seat, Peggy said, "How did you take that secret photo without him seeing you?"

Seb replied loftily, "I am a highly trained officer of the law who has specialized knowledge in the art of covert surveillance. I can't reveal my methods to a member of the public."

A snort came from the back seat followed by the clicking of needles. Peggy said, "Did you go to the toilet and then sneak a photo on the way back out? That's what I would have done."

Seb's mouth twitched. "Perhaps I did. Perhaps I didn't."

I said to him, "Did you get a good look at his face? The man in my vision had brown eyes."

He shook his head. "He was sitting opposite Elaine and had his back to me. Elaine seemed happy in his company. They were chatting a lot and smiling. She doesn't look as if she's in any danger."

"Yet," Peggy added darkly from behind us.

A funny noise came from Seb. He grimaced. "Sorry. That's my stomach rumbling. I haven't had anything to eat for hours. And the food inside the restaurant smells delicious."

We both jumped as something appeared between our seats.

"Pork pie?" Peggy waggled the item in Seb's direction. "I've got sausage rolls and sandwiches too. I've also got a flask of tea. I thought we might be here a while."

Seb took the pork pie and ate it with relish. He then accepted two sausage rolls, a ham sandwich and a packet of crisps. I was too nervous to eat, so I only had a cup of tea.

I'd just finished the drink when the door to the restaurant opened and Elaine came out.

Peggy declared, "Battle stations! Eyes at the ready, Karis. Seb, switch the engine on. Be prepared to tail the suspect."

Seb said, "We won't be tailing anyone, Peggy." But he reached for his keys anyway.

I looked closer at the man who was talking to Elaine. I said, "It's not him."

Peggy said, "Are you sure? Take another look."

"I'm certain. His face is the wrong shape. And his hair is different at the front. It's not the man I saw in my vision." I pressed my lips together. I didn't know whether to be pleased or not.

Seb put his hand on my arm and said softly, "Don't sound so disappointed. At least we know Elaine isn't in any danger now."

"But who is in danger?" I said. "I'm missing something obvious, and I don't know what it is."

"What can I do to help?" Seb asked.

Hopelessness washed over me. "I don't know." Tears came to my eyes. "I have to do something, but I don't know what. Why am I getting these visions if they don't make any sense?"

Peggy put a comforting hand on my shoulder. "It'll come to you, Karis. Don't force it. I'll finish this jumper by tomorrow and then we'll see if it's of any use."

Seb added, "I'm sure you'll pick up on something else soon."

"I hope you're right." I looked out of the window and saw Elaine embracing her date. She waved goodbye to him and then got into her car. Her date watched her drive away before he left.

Chapter 17

I couldn't sleep at all that night. Every time I closed my eyes, all my previous visions flashed into my mind. It was like a film stuck in a continuous loop. Why were they in my mind? What was I missing?

I gave up on sleep in the early hours and got up. I made myself a cup of tea and then decided to write down my visions. Perhaps writing the details down would trigger something in my brain.

It didn't. I was none the wiser.

I thought back to the incidents which had led to my visions, starting from the knitting event at the café. I wrote as much as I could remember. The sun was coming up by now and I quickly made myself another tea.

As I wrote about visiting the three knitters in their homes, I got a buzzing sound in my ears. Something was coming to me. I continued writing and put as much information as I could remember about each woman we'd been to see. They had all mentioned a daughter. Irene at the charity shop had told us someone's daughter had brought the knitting patterns in. So, the daughter aspect didn't help me. I closed my eyes and tried to recall every tiny detail of our visits to those homes and what had been said.

Then it hit me.

The thing which had been niggling me.

That image which I'd discounted as not being important.

I remembered it clearly now.

When Peggy and I had driven away from the last woman's house, Martha, I'd spotted a car parked on the opposite side of the road. The driver's window had been down, and I'd got a look at the man inside as he stared in the direction of Martha's house. He was wearing sunglasses, but the jut of his chin was familiar.

It was the older man from my vision. I knew that for certain now. The woman who he was going to attack was Martha. Or had he already attacked her?

I jumped to my feet, grabbed my handbag and raced for the door. I rushed around to Peggy's house but stopped when I noticed her bedroom curtains were closed. She always opened them within minutes of getting up. I checked my watch. It was only seven a.m. Peggy could have been up most of the night knitting that last jumper. I didn't want to disturb her sleep. I left a text message for her and then got into my car.

Before I set off, I phoned Seb. He didn't answer, so I left him a message and gave him Martha's address. I told him I'd meet him there.

My heart was pounding in my chest and I had to wipe my sweaty palms on my jeans as I drove along. Was I going to be too late? Had the incident already occurred? Had Martha attacked that man in self-defence? Was he dead?

When I reached Martha's house, I spotted the car which had been parked there previously. It was empty. Where was the driver? I knew I wouldn't be able to wait for Seb. I had to make sure Martha was okay.

I jumped out of my car and ran down the driveway. I came to a sudden stop when I saw the back door was ajar. I could hear raised voices coming from inside.

Martha's pleading tone came to me, "I don't know what you're talking about. I haven't seen him in years."

A man's voice replied, "Stop lying to me! I know you killed him."

I pushed the door open and went inside. I followed the sound of the voices to the living room.

Just like my vision, the man was inches away from Martha. Fury twisted his features. His hands were moving towards Martha's neck. She looked petrified. I saw her hand scrambling for something at her side. There was a knitting bag next to her chair which hadn't been there yesterday. Martha's hand alighted on a knitting needle.

"No!" I screamed. I moved forward and grabbed the man by his shoulders. I yanked him backwards and we fell onto the carpet together.

He roared with rage and tried to get to his feet. He hissed at me, "She killed my brother! She won't get away with it!"

A shadow covered his face as Martha loomed behind him. She plunged a knitting needle into his neck.

The man's mouth opened in shock. His eyes fluttered and then closed. He slithered to the floor.

Martha screamed and dropped the needle. Her hands flew to her face.

Blood gushed from the man's neck at an impossibly fast rate. I put my hands over the wound and called out, "Phone an ambulance! Quick!"

Martha lowered her hands and mumbled, "I didn't mean to do it. I didn't."

"An ambulance! Now!" I ordered. My hands weren't doing a good job of stemming the flow of blood. I could almost feel the life slipping away from the man.

I shouted at Martha again, and she finally moved. I looked down at the pale man and said, "Don't die. Hold on."

Chapter 18

I was still shaking thirty minutes later. I was at the hospital and sitting on a plastic chair in a corridor. Despite washing my hands many times, I could still see blood under my nails. My sleeves were covered in it.

Seb came over to me and handed me a hot drink. He sat down and said, "How are you doing?"

I lifted the cup and took a small sip. The tea was weak but at least it was hot. "I'm fine. I think. How's Martha?"

"She's okay. She's being treated for shock. She hasn't suffered any physical injuries."

I took another drink of the tea. "What about that man? Is he okay? He lost a lot of blood." I tried to smile. "Most of it is on me."

"His name is Morgan Booker, and he's okay. He did lose a lot of blood, but he'll survive, thanks to you."

"Have you spoken to him yet? Have you found out why he was at Martha's house?"

"Not yet. He keeps drifting in and out of sleep. I'll speak to him soon. He's not going anywhere."

I hesitated before asking my next question. "What about this brother of his? Have you found out anything about him? He said Martha murdered him."

Seb gave me a slow nod. "I've made some enquiries. He did have a younger brother called Finley who went missing years ago. Karis, he went missing in 1958."

My hands shook. Seb swiftly took the cup from my hands before I spilled tea all over myself. "1958?" I repeated.

Seb put the cup on a table at his side. "Yes. I've made a few checks and discovered Finley Booker was registered as a missing person by his brother in that year." He took a deep breath before continuing, "Finley was last seen heading for the cinema in town. He was going on a date."

"With Martha?"

He nodded. "With Martha. He never turned up. He didn't return home, and his family became concerned. His brother never gave up looking for him, according to the police reports."

"Did the police question Martha about Finley's disappearance?"

"They did. I've managed to have a look at her statement. She claimed she'd been dating Finley for a few months, and it was serious between them. She was due to meet him that night outside the cinema, but he never showed up. He never contacted her again." He reached into his pocket. "I've got a picture of Finley Booker. It was in Morgan's wallet. Do you feel up to looking at it?"

I nodded and held my palm out. Seb put the small black and white photo in my hand. I looked at the smiling young man. I said, "It's him. It's the man I saw inside the cinema."

We were silent for a while.

I spoke first. "Does this mean Martha killed Finley?"

"I don't know yet," Seb answered quietly. "Once the doctor has finished with her, I'll take her down to the station and question her there. I wish you could sit in on the interview, but that isn't possible."

I shook my head in disbelief. "I can't believe Martha is a killer. Why would she kill Finley if she loved him so much?"

"We don't know that she did yet. But I do know she lied to you."

"About what?"

"About the twin set," Seb explained. "You told me she'd denied knitting it when Peggy showed her the pattern."

"She did. She said the pattern was too complicated for her. How do you know she lied to me?"

"It was in the police report she gave in 1958," Seb said. "She went into great detail about how excited she was for her date with Finley Booker. She explained how she'd knitted a special twin set in a light blue colour. It was going to be a surprise for Finley. She even mentioned the film which had inspired her to make it. It was the film we saw together in Charles' cinema."

My shoulders dropped. "I can't believe she lied. She seemed so sincere."

"Killers often do." He squeezed my hand. "You saved Morgan's life. If you hadn't been there, he would have bled to death. I'm going to drive you home now. Try and get some sleep. Although, I'm not sure that'll be possible with that nosy neighbour of yours. Peggy's already left me ten messages about your whereabouts."

"She's probably left some for me too. I haven't checked my phone for a while." Weariness settled on my shoulders like a heavy blanket. "Why would Martha kill him? She loved him."

Seb pulled me to my feet. "Don't you worry about that. I'll speak to Martha later and get to the bottom of this."

"Will you let me know what she says? Are you allowed to do that?"

"It depends what she says. I'll phone you later after I've spoken to her. Come on; let's get you home."

Chapter 19

Peggy was waiting for me in my living room. She gasped when I walked in and cried out, "Is that blood on you? Is it yours? Who's dead?"

"Nobody, thank goodness." I walked over to the sofa and was about to collapse into it, but Peggy grabbed my arm and said, "Don't sit down, you'll get blood everywhere. It's a nuisance to get out."

"It's dry. Mainly," I looked at the stains on my clothes and grimaced. "I didn't realise there was so much of it."

Peggy pulled me towards the door. "Go and have a shower. Leave these clothes outside the bathroom, and I'll deal with them."

"But don't you want to know what happened? Don't you want to know whose blood this is?"

"As long as it's not yours, that's all I care about. I'm presuming from your earlier message that Martha is our mystery knitter. You can tell me everything once you're clean. I can't listen to you while you look like something from a horror movie." She pushed me towards the stairs.

I had a shower and changed into fresh clothes. I went downstairs and found Peggy sitting at the kitchen table. Two cups of tea were on the table along with a plate of toast.

Peggy pushed the plate towards me and said, "Eat something."

"I don't know if I can." I sat down and picked up the cup.

"You can, and you will," Peggy said. "And once you've told me what's been going on, you can take yourself off to bed and get some sleep. Did you manage any sleep last night?"

I shook my head and then had a quick drink of tea. It was much better than the hospital one. Under Peggy's watchful eye, I had a slice of toast. After I'd eaten it, I told her about Martha and her visit from Morgan Booker. Peggy's eyes widened when I got to the part about Seb meeting me at the hospital and what Seb had told me.

Peggy shook her head in disbelief. "Martha lied to us. I feel so betrayed. I connected with her over our late husbands. She lied about being a knitter too. All that nonsense about not being able to knit because of her arthritis. She took us for fools. When she stabbed Morgan in the neck, did she have a manic look in her eyes? Did she look as if she was enjoying it? As if she'd done it before?"

"I don't know. It all happened so quickly. She seemed remorseful afterwards and covered her face with her hands."

Peggy said sagely, "Probably to cover the glee on her face. I wonder how she killed Finley? And where his body is now. I suppose Seb will let us know in due course. Have another slice of toast."

I dutifully did as I was told.

Peggy leaned back in her chair and said, "I finished that other jumper this morning. It's in your living room. I don't suppose you need it now. I can take it to the charity shop later. I'll take those that Celia made too. I hope Irene doesn't go on too much when I pop in. It's a wonder she doesn't give herself jaw ache. On second thoughts, I'll go when Irene isn't there."

As Peggy talked about what shifts Irene might be working, I felt my eyes starting to close. I put my cup down, opened my eyes wide and tried to focus on Peggy's words. My eyes had other ideas and began to close again. My eyelids felt like they were made of lead.

Peggy abruptly got to her feet and announced, "Off to bed you go, young lady. Where are those bloodstained clothes?"

"I've left them in a bag in the bathroom," I said. With some effort, I got to my feet.

"Sling the bag down the stairs, and I'll stick them in the washing machine for you."

"I can do that," I argued half-heartedly.

"I'm here. I'll do it. Just do as I say, Karis." Peggy put her hand on my arm and led me over to the stairs. "You don't have to be so independent all the time. If I was splattered in blood, wouldn't you take care of me? Yes, you would."

I thought Peggy was going to take me upstairs and tuck me into bed, but she didn't. She did watch me as I dragged myself upstairs. She was still there when I came to the top of the stairs with the bag of soiled clothes.

She held her arms out. "Chuck it down. I'll come back in a few hours and check on you."

I flung the bag at her and headed for my bed. I was asleep within minutes.

I woke up a few hours later and felt refreshed. A weird feeling ran through me. I sat up in bed and tried to pinpoint what it was.

Then it came to me.

It was time.

I got out of bed and went downstairs. I called out for Peggy in case she had returned, but she hadn't.

Good. It was better that I did this on my own.

I spotted the jumper which Peggy had knitted. I picked it up. It could be useful. I located the suitcase which I'd bought from the charity shop and took it over to the sofa. I sat down.

With the jumper on my lap and my hand on the suitcase, I closed my eyes.

The visions came to me one after the other in gruesome detail. Just as I'd had the last one, there was a knock at the door.

It was Seb. I took him into the kitchen and made us a drink. I definitely needed one after what I'd just seen.

I gave Seb his coffee and then sat opposite him. I said, "Has Martha confessed?"

"No, she hasn't. She said she doesn't know anything about Finley being murdered." He frowned. "I don't know why, but I believe her."

"Tell me everything she said."

"I began by asking her about the last time she'd seen Finley Booker alive. She last saw him one week before he went missing. She mentioned the dates she'd been on with him, mainly to the cinema, and said things were getting serious between them. She told me about the twin set she'd knitted, and admitted she'd lied to you and Peggy when you showed her the pattern."

"Did she say why she'd lied?"

"She panicked. It was the shock of seeing her pattern after all these years. It was the last item she'd ever made for herself. She couldn't bring herself to make anything after Finley went missing. Although, later on, she did knit jumpers for her husband, Leon." He gave me a smile. "She almost repeated the same words as you when she told me how she felt about Leon. The big love of her life was Finley, but when he disappeared, she started dating Leon. He'd known her for years and was constantly asking her out. When he proposed, she said yes even though she knew he was second-best. Over the years, she grew to love him."

I nodded. "The knitting patterns make sense now. She only knitted for her husband and daughter and not for herself. But she kept that twin set pattern. Part of her must have still been in love with Finley."

"You're right about that. Martha admitted it. When she answered the door to Morgan Booker earlier, she thought it was Finley. She let him into her house without a second thought. She soon knew she'd made a mistake when Morgan started asking her about his brother."

"Why did he turn up to her door like that after all these years?"

Seb gave me a wry smile. "Facebook. It's been a year since Leon died, and Martha's daughter posted lots of photos on her Facebook page in his memory. She put some information online about how Martha and Leon used to go to the cinema back in the day. She mentioned Martha's ex-boyfriend and said his name had been banned in their house by her dad. Morgan Booker had set up alerts for any mention of his brother's name. And, you can guess the rest. It didn't take Morgan long to find Martha. He'd been watching her house for a couple of days, and finally plucked up the courage to confront her early this morning." He picked his cup up and took a big drink.

As soon as he put it down, I said, "It was the leather jacket."

Seb gave me a look of surprise. "I was just about to tell you why Morgan thought it was Martha who killed Finley. Yes, it does have something to do with a leather jacket. What do you know about it?"

"I'll tell you that in a minute. You tell me what you know about the jacket."

"Okay. Finley had a distinctive leather jacket. It had been imported from the USA. It was Morgan who bought it for him as a birthday present. Finley first wore it on his date with Martha. It was on the night he went missing. Martha never saw the jacket."

"But Leon did. Was Leon wearing it in one of the photos his daughter put on Facebook?"

Seb gave me a nod.

"And that's what Morgan saw, isn't it? He knew that jacket belonged to Finley."

Seb gave me another nod. "How do you know that?"

I looked down at the table. "I've had a series of visions. From Leon's perspective." I looked back at Seb. "I felt his love for Martha. He'd loved her for years. He was riddled with jealousy when he saw how close she was getting to Finley. Martha confided in Leon and said she wanted to marry Finley. The rage I felt in Leon was—" I stopped and closed my eyes.

"You don't have to continue," Seb said softly.

I opened my eyes. "I have to. I saw Leon meeting Finley on the way to the cinema. Finley was wearing his new leather jacket. I saw—" I stopped again and gathered my courage. "I saw Leon kill Finley. I saw every horrific detail. Leon took Finley's jacket. He put Finley in a suitcase. He laughed as he did that." I inclined my head towards the living room. "The suitcase is in there. After seeing the murder, I got a snapshot of Leon's life with Martha. I could feel how satisfied he was when he saw genuine love in her eyes. He felt no remorse over what he'd done. Seb, after the investigation into Finley's disappearance died down, Leon wore that leather jacket with pride. He lied and said he'd bought it from America." Tears trickled down my cheeks.

Seb handed me a tissue. "That must have been awful for you to witness. I hate to ask this, but do you know where Finley's body is now?"

I wiped my tears away. "I know exactly where it is."

Chapter 20

"Under the shed," I said. I looked at Erin, Robbie and Peggy's surprised faces. After going back to Martha's house with Seb and making the gruesome discovery, Seb had dropped me off at Erin's Café. We were sitting on the sofas in the quiet area.

"Under the shed?" Peggy repeated. "The shed in Martha's garden?"

I nodded. "It was in the bottom corner of the garden."

Erin asked, "How did you know it was there?"

"I saw Leon putting it there," I explained. "He didn't put the body there straight away because he didn't own the house when he murdered Finley." I swallowed and my throat felt too dry as the image of what Leon had done came back to me.

Robbie stood up. "You need a coffee. I'll make you one. I'll make us all one. I have defeated the coffee machine and it is now under my command." He gave me a kind smile before heading to the kitchen.

Erin was sitting at my side. She put her hand over mine and said, "You don't have to talk about it."

"I want to. I have to get it out. After Leon killed Finley, he put his body in that suitcase and took him into the woods. He took Finley's body out of the suitcase, wrapped him a blanket and buried him there. But when he bought the house with Martha, he decided to put Finley underneath the shed foundations."

Peggy shook her head in disbelief. "Why would he do that? Why didn't he leave Finley in the woods?"

"Maybe he was worried about Finley's body being discovered," I answered. I paused. "Actually, that's not the reason. When I was having my visions, I could feel Leon's emotions. He moved Finley's body out of pure spite. He wanted Finley to be near Martha and him as they started their married life together. He got a lot of satisfaction from knowing Finley was under that shed."

Erin muttered, "The evil so-and-so."

I continued, "I'm surprised the shed was still standing. Peggy, do you remember what Martha said about Leon being useless at DIY?"

Peggy nodded.

"When Seb and I went to the shed, it was leaning to one side. The foundations weren't level. A few more years and it would have collapsed on its own."

Peggy's eyes narrowed. "Perhaps Finley was trying to rise from the dead. What's going to happen now?"

I said, "Seb's going to get all the evidence together. I've given him the suitcase. He thinks there'll be evidence on it." My voice caught in my throat. "I can't stop thinking about what Leon did. I didn't know people could be so evil."

Erin put her arm around my shoulders and hugged me. "You poor thing. I don't know how you cope with these visions. I couldn't deal with them."

Robbie came over to us with a tray of drinks. He put them on the table.

Peggy looked at them and said, "Why are there five cups? Are you expecting company?"

"I am," Robbie replied. "And he's here now."

The café door opened and Seb came in. There was a grey tinge to his skin and he looked like he was carrying the weight of the world on his shoulders.

Robbie said to him, "You look like death warmed up. Come over here, take a seat and tell us what's happened. I've made you a coffee."

Seb sat next to Peggy and ran a hand over his forehead. He gave me a small smile and said, "How are you doing?"

I shrugged. "I'm okay. I wish I could wash Leon's memories away."

"They'll fade in time," Seb said. "Or you'll cope with them. You're strong enough to do that." He smiled at me again.

Peggy nudged him. "Stop flirting with Karis and tell us why you look so defeated."

Seb's shoulders sagged. "I've been talking to Martha. I had to explain to her what Leon had done." He looked down at his knees. "She was distraught, understandably so. Once the shock had worn off, she cried and cried. We had to get medical help for her. She's never going to be the same." He looked back up and I could see his eyes glistening.

In a soft voice, Peggy said, "It had to be done, lad. Someone had to tell her. I'm glad it was you. That poor woman." She shook her head. "To find out something like that must have broken her. Her whole marriage was a lie. Her devious husband slaughtered her one love and then heartlessly stuck him under the shed to rot away."

Robbie said, "There's no need to go into so much detail, Peggy. Seb, drink your coffee. How's Morgan Booker doing? Does he know about his brother yet?"

Seb picked his cup up and stared at it silently for a few seconds. He said, "No, he doesn't know. I'm going to the hospital soon to tell him. I'm not looking forward to that conversation."

Peggy patted him on the arm. "You'll manage. You've got the strength of character to do this. Have your coffee first."

Seb looked at Peggy. "Are you being nice to me? In front of everyone? Am I dreaming?"

Peggy chuckled. "Less of your cheek. I am capable of being nice, even to you. I'll tell you something else too. When you've finished at the station, you're invited to my house for dinner. I'll make you sausages with mashed potatoes and lots of gravy. Your mum said that's one of your favourite meals."

Seb's eyes grew wide. "It is. Are you being genuine? This isn't a cruel joke, is it? You shouldn't joke about sausages and mash."

"I'm not joking," Peggy retorted. "There's going to be dessert too. Karis, would you like to come over for dinner too? I don't want you being on your own tonight."

"I will. Thank you. I'm not sure how much I'll eat, but I'd love to be there."

A tiny twinkle came into Seb's eyes. He looked my way and said, "Give your leftovers to me. I'll take care of them."

Robbie looked into the distance and said dreamily, "Sausage and mash. With gravy."

Erin added in a matching tone, "And dessert too. Aren't Seb and Karis lucky?"

Peggy laughed. "Okay. You two lovebirds can come around too. I've got plenty."

"Are you sure it's not too much work for you?" I asked.

Peggy smiled. "It's no work at all. I love having company, and I love cooking for so many people. It'll be a bit of a squeeze in my house, but we'll manage."

Seb quickly drained his coffee and put his cup down. "Peggy, you've given me the boost I need to talk to Morgan Booker now. I will see you later at your house. I'll make sure I bring my appetite with me." He stood up. "Karis, can I have a word with you?"

"Of course." I followed him over to the café door and turned my back on the three pairs of eyes who were watching me.

Seb said quietly, "I can't imagine how horrific the images in your mind are, but I wanted to say thank you for all you've done. You saved Morgan Booker's life.

And you found his brother. I know Martha's life is never going to be the same, but that's not your fault."

"I know." I sighed. "I can't stop my visions, but these last ones have been so difficult."

He put his hand on my arm. "You're not on your own with this. You've got me."

"And us!" Peggy called out. "Speak up, Seb. I can't hear everything you're saying."

Seb grinned at me and whispered, "I'll see you later." He waved at the group on the sofas before leaving the café.

When I returned to the sofas, I noticed an unusual silence. I looked at Erin and said, "What's going on now?"

"Nothing," Erin replied in a tone which confirmed something was going on.

Robbie said, "We were just saying how close you and Seb are getting."

"We're just friends," I said.

"Of course," Erin, Robbie and Peggy announced in one voice.

Peggy shuffled to the end of the sofa and said, "Let's talk about Karis' love life another time. And I don't want to talk about Martha anymore, it's too upsetting. I might call on her in a week or so and see how she's doing. Right, how are the plans for the café coming along? Are we going to open it next week?"

Robbie nodded. "We are."

"Great news," Peggy said. She looked at me. "Karis, try not to have any more murder visions before then. We don't have time for them." Her wrinkly face creased up in a smile.

I smiled back at her and said, "I'll try my best."

THE END

About the author

I live in a county called Yorkshire, England with my family. This area is known for its paranormal activity and haunted dwellings. I love all things supernatural and think there is more to this life than can be seen with our eyes.

I hope you enjoyed these stories. If you did, I'd love it if you could post a small review. Reviews really help authors to sell more books. Thank you!

These stories has been checked for errors by myself and my team. If you spot anything we've missed, you can let us know by emailing us at: april@aprilfernsby.com

You can visit my website at: www.aprilfernsby.com

Sign up to my newsletter and I'll let you know how to get a free copy of my new books as I publish them.

Many thanks to Paula Proofreader

Warm wishes
April Fernsby

Also by April Fernsby:

The Brimstone Witch Mysteries

Book 1 - Murder Of A Werewolf

Book 2 - As Dead As A Vampire

Book 3 - The Centaur's Last Breath

Book 4 - The Sleeping Goblin

Book 5 - The Silent Banshee

Book 6 - The Murdered Mermaid

Book 7 - The End Of The Yeti

Book 8 - Death Of A Rainbow Nymph

Book 9 - The Witch Is Dead

Book 10 - A Deal With The Grim Reaper

Sign up to my newsletter and I'll let you know how to get my new releases for free:
www.aprilfernsby.com

Psychic Café Mysteries

Box Set 1

By
April Fernsby

www.aprilfernsby.com

Printed in Great Britain
by Amazon